# THE TINNERS WAY

# THE TINNERS HUT

## GIL JACKSON

PROFESSIONAL BOOK PRODUCTION

The Tinners Hut
ISBN: 978-1-8382326-8-9

Author's address: **gilvjackson@hotmail.co.uk**

Historical events and names aside, The Tinners Hut is a work of
fiction and the product of the author's imagination. All names
(excepting two), are coincidental to any person either living or dead.

Cover design, Epaper make-up, and formatting by:
**www.hirambgood.co.uk**
E-pub2 formatting to industry standards.
HTML and CSS Validated.

DEDICATED
Bradley, who found water on
Dartmoor when it was
most needed

OTHER WORK

FICTION:
The Seventh Gift
The Tinners Hut

NON-FICTION:
Hiram B. Good's
Multi-Drop Training Manual
The London Apprentice

# CONTENTS

INTERPENETRATING DIMENSION DOME
BODNIM ASSIZE, CORNWALL 1716

YELVERTON–PRINCETOWN, DARTMOOR 2008

## SIX 69

DARTMOOR, DEVON 2008

AVON AND SOMERSET CONSTABULARY,
PORTISHEAD, BRISTOL 2008

OFFICES OF CRASKE–FORBES, BRISTOL 2008

## SEVEN 77

PLYMOUTH HOSPITAL, DEVON 2008

DARTMOOR, DEVON 2008

DEPT. OF ANATOMICAL PATHOLOGY,
MEDICAL SCIENCE PARK, PLYMOUTH 2008

## EIGHT 87

AVON AND SOMERSET CONSTABULARY,
PORTISHEAD, BRISTOL 2008

## NINE 99

PLYMOUTH HOSPITAL, DEVON 2008

DEVON & CORNWALL CONSTABULARY,
(PLYMOUTH CENTRAL SECTOR),
PLYMOUTH 2008

DAVY MASONIC HALL, PLYMOUTH 2008

DEVON & CORNWALL CONSTABULARY,
(PLYMOUTH CENTRAL SECTOR), PLYMOUTH 2008

## TEN 117

PLYMOUTH HOSPITAL, DEVON 2008

DEVON AND CORNWALL INCIDENT MOBILE,
YELVERTON–PRINCETOWN, DARTMOOR 2008

## SIXTEEN                                    187

INTERPENETRATING DIMENSION DOME
BODNIM ASSIZE, CORNWALL 1716

## SEVENTEEN                                  197

TINNERS HUT, NR. CROCKERN TOR,
DARTMOOR 2008

THE JURATE ARMS, NR. CROCKERN,
DARTMOOR 1716

WHITEWORKS, PRINCETOWN, DARTMOOR 1716

## EIGHTEEN                                   209

OFFICES OF ELLICK & WAITE,
PLYMOUTH 1716

## NINETEEN                                   213

INTERPENETRATING DIMENSION DOME
BODNIM ASSIZE, CORNWALL 1716

INTERPENETRATING DIMENSION DOME
BODMIN ASSIZE, CORNWALL 1716

BODNIM ASSIZE, CORNWALL 1716

INTERPENETRATING DIMENSION DOME
EXXETER 1716

## TWENTY                                     235

TRURO POLICE STATION, CORNWALL 2008

NANCEKUKE, CORNWALL 2008

DEVON & CORNWALL CONSTABULARY,

(PLYMOUTH CENTRAL SECTOR),
PLYMOUTH 2008

TRURO POLICE STATION, CORNWALL 2008

## TWENTY-ONE                                    251

DEVON & CORNWALL CONSTABULARY,
(PLYMOUTH CENTRAL SECTOR),
PLYMOUTH 2008

HOME OFFICE, MARSHAM STREET,
LONDON 2008

AVON AND SOMERSET CONSTABULARY
MOBILE UNITS, BRISTOL 2008

DEPT. ANATOMICAL PATHOLOGY,
PLYMOUTH HOSPITAL 2008

## TWENTY-TWO                                    259

DEVON & CORNWALL CONSTABULARY,
(PLYMOUTH CENTRAL SECTOR),
PLYMOUTH 2008

HOME OFFICE, MARSHAM STREET,
LONDON 2008

TORPOINT FERRY, DEVON 2008

GREYSTONE BRIDGE, CORNWALL–DEVON 2008

OKEHAMPTON, DEVON 2008

OKEHAMPTON, DEVON 1716

OKEHAMPTON, DEVON 2008

## TWENTY-THREE                                  273

AVON AND SOMERSET CONSTABULARY,
PORTISHEAD, BRISTOL 2008

STANNERS' AND HABERDASHERS' SCHOOL,
BRISTOL 2008

## TWENTY-EIGHT                                325

STANNERS' AND HABERDASHERS' SCHOOL,
BRISTOL 2008

CLARENCE HOUSE, LONDON 2008

AVON AND SOMERSET CONSTABULARY
MOBILE UNITS, BRISTOL 2008

STANNERS' AND HABERDASHERS' SCHOOL,
BRISTOL 2008

AVON AND SOMERSET CONSTABULARY
MOBILE UNITS,
BRISTOL 2008

STANNERS' AND HABERDASHERS' SCHOOL,
BRISTOL 2008

FORBES' APARTMENT,
ROYAL COURT CRESCENT,
BRISTOL 2008

OFFICES OF ELLICK & WAITE,
LINCOLN'S INN FIELDS, LONDON 2008

OFFICES OF CRASKE-FORBES,
BRISTOL 2008

## TWENTY-NINE                                 351

AVON AND SOMERSET CONSTABULARY
OPS. UNITS,
BRISTOL 2008

CROWLAS, NR. PENZANCE, CORNWALL 2008

AVON AND SOMERSET CONSTABULARY,
PORTISHEAD, BRISTOL 2008

# PROLOGUE
## Prison of Logroño, Spain 2002

'SMITH! HAS BRITISH INTELLIGENCE run out of imaginative names that they give you such a nom de plume to access me?'

Ford opened a pack of Fortuna, took one out placing the remainder on the table between them.

Charmolue pulled a cigarette out between two broken fingers, at the same time holding the pack down with his other hand. A hand looking as if it had been stamped on – several times. He put the cigarette carefully between his black and blue swollen lips and waited. Ford leaned across, flicked his lighter and put it to his cigarette. Then leaning back lighted his own. Both men simultaneously dragging, inhaling, then exhaling.

Ford looking at the state of Charmolue asked, 'Was there a need for your own people to have been so enthusiastic with you?'

'MI5 should ask such a question. How did you expect them to treat someone working undercover? I've a reputation. After all, it was your British government that approached the Director Générale de la Sécurité seeking my help. When I agreed, it was they that set out the agenda. Working undercover with ETA, you can't walk away. They would have put a bullet in my head. A beating by the home team was the preferred option. Your agenda.'

Ford nodded.

'No one likes infiltrators, especially ones aligned with the Basque Separatist movement. Out of curiosity, are there any more French working undercover that you know of?'

Charmolue smiled, taking a drag on his cigarette said, 'You expect me to answer that? Can't leave other countries' politics be, can you, you British—'

'As you say, Philippe . . . anyway, professional curiosity; but you do come highly recommended by your controllers, that's why we're offering you this change in employment status. Almost a holiday you might say. The General Commisariat of Intelligence, or rather its anti-terrorism lot consider you're overdue; discovered even—'

'I believe the phrase is, *shopped* not *discovered*. ETA wants a done deal with the legitimate Spanish Government in exchange for a cease in hostilities. To coin a phrase, I would be in the firing line in such negotiations. Names and suspicions get banded around, not least local regional politicians, if I should come under sustained torture; whether they have substance or not, no one cares, another body here or there,' he shrugged, 'well . . . an insignificant corpse, among many.'

'Exactly!' Ford affirmed. 'That's why I'm offering a quieter life; and being French from the Breton region, you should blend in well with the Cornish. Or to put it more succinctly, a particular brand of Cornishness; not a million miles away from Basque ideology of which you are familiar. You will need to do some homework first though. Shouldn't be a problem should it? They tell me you were an historian in another life.'

# ONE

## Okehampton, Devon 1716

*THE LETTERS GI* embossed in gold lettering on the brown leather dispatch case John Goode carried demanded a price he was not expecting. A ball from a musket went over his head with inches to spare. It was so close he heard it scream. So close he was convinced he had been struck by it. Cowering low, fearing a second, he put his fingers to his head feeling for the wetness that was now running down his cheeks. Looking at his fingertips he was relieved to find it was sweat. He was in shock. Immobile. He was going to have to move. He would not survive another salvo from wherever and whomever it came that clearly had his range and position if he did not. With his instinct for survival overcoming torpidity he ran for the protection of a barn that would afford him breathing space while he re-assessed his options. For whoever was out to get him were clearly professionals who would not give him a second chance should he show himself.

Another shot. This time coming from something heavier than a musket. A small cannonball came in hitting the iron stanchion holding up what remained of the barn's rotted wooden roof he had hoped would afford him some degree of shelter. The shell came in through a half-open grain service entrance taking the door off its hinges. Not stopping at that it continued out through another part of the roof bringing down what remained. Lowering his head, he covered his eyes. A debris of dust, rust, thatch, bird droppings, cobwebs, and mummified rodents came down on top of him.

Coughing and spluttering he rubbed his eyes clear. Gathering his senses, he pulled away the remains of the door and stared upward towards the top of a high street. Making out a butchers shop and an apothecary as well as a seed merchants it was clear to him that people that would normally be doing business at these establishments were short on the ground, an indication that a daytime curfew was in place. Even the inn, that would see farmers and labourers sitting outside in the sun smoking and drinking were conspicuous by their absence. But there were people. Soldiers. For some reason, these same soldiers had a determination to stop him getting onto the moor.

When he had asked the agent of the government station if he handled many dispatches from king's court the man shrugged his shoulders dismissing Goode as a lone courier that may have had some hidden resource at his disposal: that a one-man army carrying such an item might have some sort of invincibility that gave him the strength of ten men better able to defend himself from those anxious to relieve him of such a valuable piece of merchandise. There was no such accompaniment he could see. In his eyes, seeing the gold lettering blazoning as it did like a beacon would surely be of value to someone.

'Not to someone without an armed escort I haven't,' the agent answered. 'Only to our own people; part of the government's messaging service out of the Bristol station. Men that are known, that can handle themselves from outlaws and footpads on the highways and turnpikes.' He stared at Goode knowing full well the answer to the question he was to put to him before asking it.

'Have you, perhaps such a force of men at your disposal that can help me in my quest?' Goode asked.

Such an armed escort that this man was suggesting getting him clear of Okehampton; with riders and horses crossing the moor as opposed to the roads around its outskirts was a luxury the agent was not prepared to provide for him. Even with them, they would likely become bogged down and drown in one or other of the many rivers and quagmires that the moor was infamous. It was a crossing that this man was going to have to travel alone.

The agent had answered an emphatic, 'I have not Sir.'

Goode reconciled himself with the thought that he was at least the Stannary Officer for Devon responsible for the overseeing of tin mining in that region for the benefit of the House of Hanover. Many men that he might encounter would know of him if not by sight, then by name, giving him assistance should he need it.

He moved his head back inside at the sound of another explosion. The smoke from the cannon coming with next to no interval of time hit the barn once more. Whoever they were they were not seeking his surrender.

This time it was the dry-stone wall that took the brunt. The building was piece by piece yielding from the salvoes dismantling what a good thunderstorm would eventually get around to. It was only a matter of time before he was exposed. A lone figure standing amidst a ruin with nowhere to hide or run. Assuming he survived that long. More likely the shrapnel from the shells would cut his flesh from his body, bloody chunk at a time, before whoever they were came down to finish off anything still living. Sitting in the corner he buried his head in his arms as the bombardment continued. Contemplating his fate, he saw blood, bones and rubble being all that remained as raw material for any owner's rebuild.

### The Brat Arms, Sourton 1716
The Dartmoor mist clung cold with morning's first light when:

Three horsemen came at-a-pace along the well-used lane better suited for carriages than riders. Its water-filled rutted track, the consequence of run-off rainwater from the field at its one side and the flooded stream to its other undermined the ground slowing the horses to a trot. The overhanging trees laden with water from the persistent rain dripped over men and beasts, while the hedgerow, built up with blown leaves bordering the lane gave off the smell of late autumn rot. The coming into view of the inn signified the first half of a return journey at an end for the men. Their horses sweating and breathing heavy from their exertions were snorting steam from their nostrils as the horsemen now walked their mounts between two stone pillar uprights covered in orange lichen. The wooden gates they had once held upright broken away, were carelessly left to one side: a statement to better times past, were over-grown and covered with a layer of black rot and fungus.

The difference from mud to cobbled stone gave the horses a problem the result of their iron shoes adjusting to their new surface caused them to stumble before regaining their footing.

The man known as Sabine, Lifton prison's general bailiff for violence, shouted out across the inn's courtyard. His words echoing off the walls of the building and the outhouses surrounding it.

'Stable!' shouted. Then, 'Maclean! *Ostler!* Am I to be kept waiting?' he shouted once more. His voice had a threatening resonance that demanded a response. But he was out of his precinct, none was immediately forthcoming.

The rest of the riders began tethering their mounts when a boy, no more than ten or eleven came running out from one of a line of four stalls. He had a red face with light tousled hair. His shirt unfastened; his breeches too short, had a long smearing of horse dung down one side of them from where he might have slipped over while mucking-out. It was still wet. His boots, too big for him, a likely contributing factor for such an accident, Sabine thought.

The boy wiped his nose on the back of his hand and looked up at the man that demanded service.

'I'm the groom's son. I'll see to your horses, my lord.'

He threw down the two-pronged hay fork he had in his hands to one side, then reached up and grabbed the rein. His fist tightly closed, the horse dragged the boy's arm into the air in an effort too free itself and get to the water trough it could smell. The risk of stomach stitch from over-drinking was dangerous to a horse in this condition. The boy knew enough about that to know they needed rationing, and Sabine could see it in him. He pressed a half penny into the boy's hand.

'Rub them down well and feed them then. We ride again within the hour.'

The boy pulled his forelock then said, 'Good as done, my lord,' then spit on the coin unsure of the status of the man.

Sabine stepped up to the oak door of the inn and began hammering.

'*Maclean! Maclean!* Are you there? Answer me, *damn you!*'

Maclean had suffered a bad night's sleep when the row outside his window came to his ears. As if the wounds from shot and blade were not bad enough, the visiting night-time bedbugs aggravating them had done nothing to improve his temper. He might have known when he had first collapsed for a night's sleep, having had his fill of food and drink the evening before, that the odour of rotting raspberries coming from the bed meant an infestation. But it was a bed, in a room, with a roof that was dry; a welcome relief from sheltering under the barns and hedgerows he had become accustomed during this bloody uprising.

He looked at the tiny blood spots over his chest and down his arms and legs before he saw the cockroaches crawling out from under his body. The bedbugs having had their fill of his blood, it was the turn of their predators to dispose of their bloated bodies.

Maclean threw his blanket off in disgust and got up from the bed. Standing on the floor he brushed the remaining insects from his damp body not realising the scabs of dried blood formed on his arms were their result. Scratching them he cursed.

Taking up his sword and scabbard, hurriedly fastening them around his waist and over his undergarments he went to the window Pressing his face hard against the leaded pane he stared out to see who was using his name.

A boy was holding the reins of two horses drinking at a trough. A saddle laid across a blanket on one had an edging of Royal blue cotton ribbon. That was either a king's man or someone having stolen one of his horses he thought. The bearing of the man, his hands on his hips, inclined him to the latter.

Behind them, the door belonging to the inn's storeroom opened. Maclean recognised him from the previous evening as the landlord. He emerged with a barrel of beer wedged under one arm, his other, swinging a ring of keys. A great oaf a man with arms as thick as tree boughs wearing a leather apron buckled at the front over a woman's woollen skirt. He turned his attention to the man who was shouting giving him a cursory glance before turning his attention to the job in hand. Selecting a large iron key from between his fingers he inserted it into the lock and opened the door then turning to the man hammering on his oak door said:

'Something I can do for you, captain?' the landlord asked purposely putting the barrel down to catch Sabine's toe. He adjusted his skirt before apologising for any injury he might have caused.

'You got a Maclean staying here, woman?' Sabine replied sarcastically, closing his lips tightly against the pain to his gouty foot. 'Only if you have, I'd be obliged if you'd send for him, be quick . . . for this is king's business and I haven't the time to waste breath on the likes of you.'

If the landlord was worried by this early morning intrusion and insult, then he didn't show it. Instead he concentrated on finishing off adjustments to his skirt before working his foot back into one of his sandals that had come loose. He was in no hurry.

Sabine was fast losing his patience.

'Did you not hear me? I said—'

The landlord spat on the ground. Then glaring at him replied:

'I heard you. Along with the rest of the county. King's business is it; you say? What's it to you and your king who's staying in my hostelry? Come back when I'm open.'

A casement window above the men opened sending a shower of leaves and rotted window frame cascading down the sloping roof out, and over the horsemen. Leaning through the opening, the occupant shouted down.

'I'm Maclean! And what'd you want that you wake me at this un-Godly hour?' Sabine looked up. His first words of the name having been lost to an easterly breeze that was fast turning into a south westerly squall, he repeated himself.

'You, *Maclean?*'

'God's teeth, didn't I say so. And its Colonel John Maclean to you. I said, "What'd you want?"'

'I've come from Boscawen. You are to return immediately with me to Tavistock. He's unfinished business that for some reason, believes only you can deliver.'

God's-breath, Maclean muttered to himself. 'Well, you'd better show me more than your big mouth for identity,' he said. 'Because if you're not who you say you are, it'll be more than the content of my piss-pot over your head for raising me at this hour of the night, you'll feel the flat of my sword.'

Sabine, his face scarlet from being spoken to in such a manner, first by the landlord, then this jumped-up colonel from the High

9

lands, reached inside his tunic and produced a roll of cloth. Unfurling it, he held it up for Maclean to see.

'That good enough?' Sabine shouted back up to the window. 'Boscawen said you'd know I had his author-ity by this emblem.'

Flag of Scotland, Maclean muttered to himself. He shouted down to the man wearing the skirt, 'Landlord!' The man looked up at the window. 'Tell that idiot he'll wait at my pleasure. I'll be eating breakfast and cleaning up this pox I've inherited from your bed before I ride anywhere this morn.'

The landlord acknowledged him, then turning to Sabine said, 'You hear that, captain?'

## Staging Post, Tavistock 1716

Hugh Boscawen, as well as being steward of the duchy of Cornwall and Lord Warden of the Stannaries was also King George the First's representative in Cornwall; and with these positions and those of a minor nature, he wielded considerable influence in the county. But it was as his former title, the one that he had raised an army to put down the Jacobite rebellion in the Southwest of England that he was currently employed. In that role, he had enlisted the battle-hardened Scottish mercenary, Colonel Maclean as his Second-in-Command.

Now with Jacobite resistance in the Southwest all but put down Boscawen had now moved on to other matters of State. He had been entrusted by the King's advisors with a personal matter that if successful would achieve for him a political ambition he had yearned, that of Viscount of Falmouth. With information in his possession, that were it to become public knowledge, bringing on the collapse of the Hanoverian stewardship of England, he might yet obtain such an elevation. And with the leaking of such information being enough for him to be tried for treason, Boscawen needed a confederate tongue. Aware he was playing political games on a slippery slope where history had brought better men than himself to prostrate themselves before the block, he recalled the man, if ever there was one that could be trusted, the Scottish mercenary, Maclean.

It had not been an easy ride into Tavistock and Maclean had a mouth like the bottom of a horse's feed bag. Sabine had ridden him and his men hard and Maclean's irritability had not improved with the exercise. Seeing Boscawen holding back a curtain indicating to him where he was, Maclean seated himself opposite Boscawen while at the same time pointing to Sabine to obtain him service at the counter.

Intent on manhandling six pewter and leather tankards jammed together between his fingers in the crowded tavern the pot-man delivering service tipped the best part of three tankards of the liquor over him and Boscawen. At the same time, and doing his best to regain his balance, with the throng of tin miners celebrating having been paid seeing the man's dilemma and thinking it a good gibe to help him further on his way toward the floor, pushed him through the partly closed curtain pulling the threadbare cloth down from its retaining wires across the table draping all three of them.

Maclean pulled the curtain from his head and stood up. The tin miners laughed and jeered. Then, seeing this soldier's face alter from ugly to rage ceased, their expressions along with their humour faded. They began backing away. Maclean, dressed in a clean white silk shirt, now soaked in English porter, waded into them knocking some down before turning his attention to the instigator.

The pot-man wedged between the floor and the upturned table managed to get himself up. Seeing the soldier and his weaponry, he decided not to antagonise the man further by making excuses. A fastened chain belt with a suspended scabbard and sword that drawn in a flash was one thing. But more worrying for the pot-man was the man's knife, the like of which he shivered at the sight of. A weapon that was neither ornate nor pretty. Held in a half sheath, a full length of steel with a vicious looking blade on one edge, jagged on the other, its blood channel exposed showed rust from the use it had been designed. It was a plain and simple instrument for serious injury and death. Without the benefit of a background in the military, the pot-man looked at the soldier and considered an enemy fancying his chances against such a man being well advised to consider his first thought of flight from a fight in favour of living another day.

To Maclean's annoyance this was an unwanted assault; especially after he had gone out of his way to annoy an impatient Sabine by bathing in the horse trough and dressing in a clean shirt before their leaving. And while his dirty battle-scarred brown leather jerkin and black trousers had been beyond improvement for some time, his added effort to make himself more presentable had now been in vain. On top of that, he saw Sabine out of the corner of his eye. The man was standing at the counter in raucous laughter with others at his misfortune. Maclean wiped his mouth with what was left of a dry patch on his shirt cuff and turned his attention to the pot-man.

'You cretinous oaf,' he shouted in the man's face. He then dragged the unfortunate fellow by the collar, across the floor, then out the door into the inn's courtyard where he commenced to pummel the luckless soul's head against the damp green-white lime-washed wall securing his horse, until the pot-man's eyes rolled, and his legs gave way from under him. Lying on the ground up against the wall with fresh steaming horse dung sticking to the side of his bare arms the pot-man could do no more than wince with pain.

Maclean patted the horse's rump to settle the beast. Breathing heavily, he stood back and brushed himself down, satisfied that the man was not going to make any more mistakes. But in case, using them as a cleaning cloth, he pulled the man's trousers off and wiped the horse shit that he'd stepped in from the bottom of his own boots. Then throwing them over the pot-man's face he wiped the palms of his hands down his trousers before looking up. A movement caught his eye. The inn's sign. In need of a fresh coat of paint the words: *The Hanged Highlander* written above the depiction of a Scottish clansman roped by the neck from a gibbet held his attention. The sign swinging and creaking from its rusting hinges, in a breeze that came off the moor, sent a chill of foreboding down his spine.

Jasper Hook, landlord of the staging post stood on a barrel he had manoeuvred into position hitched back the curtain and its wiring into place. Then getting down, he apologised for the inconvenience caused.

The pot-man returned into the inn limping and doubled up, his face bruised and bleeding, with features barely recognisable. Seeing him, Hook, with no wish to go through a similar ordeal re-assumed his role of subservient host. These were dangerous times and he guessed that the person that attacked his pot-man was not a regular soldier. His appearance gave that of a mercenary – that fought for the highest bidder. As for his dagger, that could so easily have been pulled and stuck into anyone, he had shown a restraint that only a professional soldier sick to the stomach from fighting and killing could exercise. Hook placed two trenchermen of cold mutton, cheese and bread onto the table between the two men. Then, going back behind the bar after they had ordered fresh beers, brought up from the back of his throat a substantial ball of phlegm coughing it up into their pitchers of ale. Smearing the mucous with his fingers to break it down when he found it wouldn't sink, he added more ale foam to disguise it. Bringing the tankards over on a tray with a full pitcher of ale he placed them on the table between the two men slopping off part of Maclean's beer. Still unsure of the soldier's temper, he addressed the both of them politely with a semblance of grace that, all was well with him, them, and their continuing welcome in his establishment.

'Food and ale's on the house, gentlemen,' he said cheerily, sweating. He was conscious that he might yet be caught out by what he'd done, nervously adding, 'Anything else I can get you?'

Boscawen dismissed him with a wave of his hand as if it were of no consequence and proceeded to top up Maclean's tankard.

Hook acknowledged him with a smile then, with a trace of fear, pulled the curtain closed behind him. Breathing a sigh of relief, he returned to his duties.

For himself Boscawen was a man of dress without elegance. He had learned earlier in life that it was not good politics to appear better attired than a king was. He wore a flared embroidered coat with huge cuffs that kept dragging across spilled ale on the table. The colours of his coat, shot with silver thread, open to reveal a red waistcoat and white ruffled shirt under, were also less than lately laundered. A three-cornered hat hanging from a nail behind him, threatening at any moment to come away from the loose plaster holding it he guessed was his.

Boscawen paused and peered through a slit in the curtain. What he had to say was not for stray ears; having earlier satisfied himself that he was not recognised. As Lord Warden, a tavern full of tinners he may not be popular. Not that any would have recognised him, for it was not his like that would get their hands dirty out on the moors or down the mines. He pulled the curtain closed tight.

'You've carried the protestant cause well, Maclean,' Boscawen said. 'The King is pleased with your loyalty. Your help in securing Bristol, Exeter and Plymouth, though . . . it may be as well you do not draw attention to that fact here, Colonel. That temper of yours needs to be reined in,' he said removing something from his lips after taking a swig of ale from his tankard. Looking at it he rubbed it between his fingers before wiping it down his shirt front. Opening and diving into his leather satchel he produced a document. Checking he had the right one he handed it to Maclean.

Maclean looked at him suspiciously, then began to read for a full quarter hour.

What had this to do with him, for it was a Jacobite cause he was here, none other. This was England's politics, nothing to do with him. He let it fall to the table.

Boscawen picked it up and set a candle to it. The dryness of the parchment burst it into flames.

Maclean watched it burn out then got to his feet.

'I have no intention of involving myself in a plot that will see me on the end of a rope at Tyburn, Boscawen.'

Boscawen had clearly misjudged Maclean in the manner of his reaction. The man had fought for an English cause that had spread from Scotland; surely, he would take another. He had shown his trust by allowing him to read a damning document. Now with this rejection by him it presented him with a problem two-fold. He had never considered a replacement if Maclean declined. And for that he could not allow Maclean to leave Devon with the knowledge he now had. As it were, rumours that he was a possible informer for the Jacobite's during the rebellion had come to him from more than one source. His murder would not come as any surprise. He would need to act. He drew his dagger and put it to Maclean's throat.

Maclean did not flicker an eyelid. Not for the first time had he come across similar situations. His management to extradite himself, with his still being alive, was testament to that ability. Boscawen had the point of his knife into him, and with his chair up against the wall, there appeared no room to manouvre free.

'I'm disappointed in you, Colonel,' Boscawen said. 'We've always suspected you were an informer favouring the Stuarts. We let you carry on your double dealing because you were more use to us in spite of it. You now know too much.'

He had been neither spy for Stuart nor Jacobite. He was a mercenary plain and simple. He fought the side that rewarded the most. Politics never came into it. He had his own. No, Boscawen was wrong. It was not the thinking that the King of England was about to renege over an Act of Parliament that troubled him. It was the document for the passing of an Act of Parliament replacing another without the parties concerned being made aware of those changes, its treachery against innocent people was not something he was particularly up for. He had done worse in his time. But not this time. The revolution was over, and his life was too precious. But just in case. He slowly raising his foot onto the rail of the table that his legs were under he placed it hard against its tipping point maintaining the pressure.

'You don't need me for your politics, that man that brought me here is more than up for that I shouldn't wonder. Use him.'

Maclean was ready to spring, but conscious that Boscawen was not alone in this place. He had Sabine and his men with him. The crashing sound from a chair going over would be enough for them to come to his aid. A sword fight at close quarter, with so many others not directly involved; that would take a shot at stabbing him in the back for a shilling, the incentive to injure or kill for such an opportunity would be too much for most.

He decided to listen to what Boscawen had to say. If he had to, he would fight his way out of Tavistock using Boscawen as hostage after. Only in that way might he manage to get away without risking his life to an opportunist.

'Withdraw your weapon. We'll talk further.'

Boscawen smiled, replaced his dagger into its sheath, and then moved closer to Maclean.

'Listen then . . .' He poured them both more ale. Then reaching into his haversack produced two leather pouches. Heavy with coins, he threw both onto the table in front of Maclean, then, holding his tankard to Maclean said with a smile, 'Your reward, authorised by my King.'

Maclean looked at them, then picking them up, weighed them in his hands. Slowly pulling the strings loose he looked inside. Gold sovereigns.

'A hundred. Listen close then, for they're yours. Time is of the essence. It has to be the night after next. John Goode, Stannary Officer for Devonshire has left Okehampton. He's on his way to Crockern to meet another as we speak.'

'Out of curiosity, how *was* this document to be presented to Sir Richard Vyvyan?'

'If it was not to be intercepted?'

Maclean nodded.

'Through the other man. Joshua Timmins is his counterpart from the Cornish Parliament in league with Sir Vyvyan. He was to take it from him the day after on the first tide out of Plymouth to Falmouth, where he would then remove it to Helston by horse. That must not happen, and where you come in. The remainder of the facts are that the parchment Goode is carrying, is an Act that includes a pardon to Sir Richard, giving him governorship of an independent Cornwall along with the dissolution of the duchy. In return, Sir Richard is to disassociate himself and his heirs from Rome, along with any future of his Jacobite aspirations, which he has to date shown sympathies.'

'So, what's changed?' Maclean asked.

Boscawen picked up a piece of bread and meat from his plate with his fingers, dipping them together in his ale; he sucked at the morsel then chewed at it slowly. His teeth were giving him trouble.

'As a German, he is not . . . how can I put this . . . ? *Au fait*, when it comes to English practices, none of which has been helped by an argument between himself and his son, the Prince of Wales, Georg August. What king's take, borrow, or given, are seldom returned. Ill-informed advice by the King's court to placate a Jacobite cause, returning taxes to Cornwall, was never going to be on the cards. If for no other reason, the English would have an increased tax burden placed upon them in the event of war. Once it had been explained to the King that he would have a revolution on his hands with increasing taxation for the English for Cornwall's advantage to spite his son, seeing the folly of his ill-conceived idea deciding to leave things as they were. Much better an insignificant county far removed from London bear the cost for the Princes of Wales expenses than England.'

One hundred English sovereign was a tidy sum Maclean thought to himself.

Boscawen picked up his haversack from the floor and removed a brown leather dispatch case. On its closure flap was the embossed gold lettering, GI.

'Get the one from Goode and replace it with this. Show it to any Stannary Officers present. Tell them they have been made fools of; that no such arrangements are to be made for any dissolution of the duchy from England. Put simply, it will read in so many words that Devon distrusts Cornwall and its Stannary Parliament to continue selling its tin to England, favouring instead the French markets, and of the Roman Catholic King Louis XIVs support for a James the Third on the English throne. They will conclude that Goode, Timmins, along with Sir Richard had an arrangement with the King for rewards that can only be guessed. All lies of course, but wonderful politics, you must agree.'

'But surely, I don't have authority over Stannary officers.'

'That's where Sabine comes in. As bailiff of Lydford prison, he will direct matters for the two men's arrest. He will ride with you to Crockern where this business will be finalised. From that point on, your job is finished. You can return to Scotland a wealthy man from a grateful King George.'

'Why Crockern? Surely you could have apprehended the man at Okehampton, saving the King a deal of money?'

Boscawen went over in his mind what had happened. A botched attempt to retrieve the dispatch case had gone badly wrong. It was true that arrangements had been in hand to apprehend Goode and the dispatch as he was leaving the government's mail office.

'According to the officer commanding the King's special force, he escaped, after being helped by an unknown rider being pulled onto the back of his large grey, . . .

Rearing up on its back legs as the last cannon ball came crashing into what remained of the building, both horse and rider held their nerve, while Goode, making good his escape from what should have been certain death, took his rescuer's wrist with one hand holding the saddle with the other. Half running, sometime swinging, until jumping, he made it astride the back of the horse.

His paladin rode them up the hill, passing barren cannon and musket as they sped; excepting only a second shot from a sniper's rifle – the first suspended in mid-air, brought a derisory remark from his commanding officer as to the man's lack of powder – whistled harmlessly over their heads they escaped.

Such was the special force commander's surprise that such a bold move could have been attempted right under his nose, shouting all manner of orders and abuses for his men to stop them; after having been remiss in reloading their weapons so certain sure they had their man. Standing in disarray, with mouth's open wide, the rider, dressed in black gown and wig was at the top of the hill where he stopped.

Silhouetted against dark storm clouds filled with rain; the sky, lightning, the horse reared up onto its back legs, then turning headed out across the moor.

'. . . and he would have if he hadn't got away. As events have turned out, it's probably as well – the significance of Crockern being near Princetown, the meeting place of the Devon Stannary Parliament added a dimension I first overlooked.'

'How do I know I can trust you? For all I know those men of yours might be under orders to murder and bury me along with your plot. And one hundred sovereigns would be a great incentive to do that.'

'Half those men are tinners. The rest my people. The tinner's will be indebted to you for your assistance in bringing this treachery to their notice. There is no love lost between them and the Stannary Parliament that has Lydford behind them. Once all has been revealed, they will see John Goode and Joshua Timmins as the treacherous power that would exclude first Devon their rights of ownership of their resources; and Cornwall its right to self-determination. They will look on you as doing them a service when they see the document in Goode's possession; and is not one they signed up to. As to your murder, the State has no wish to see bodies cluttering up the moor that would cause confusion. Especially one that of a Scottish soldier.' He smiled.

Maclean had other concerns.

'Why do you need my help? Surely Sabine is capable of completing all of such a simple task?'

'While Sabine is useful with a sword, he's not a soldier that can handle himself should things go wrong. I cannot afford another mistake McClean. Should Goode manage to pass that dispatch to Timmins, making it to Helston, all hell's going to break out. Heads will roll – mine not being the least of them.' Boscawen placed his hand on the man's arm. 'I recognise your concerns and I am not without influence and friends. Remember, I am the King's representative for Cornwall, having a number of Whigs, as well as Tories I can count on; all owing me favours of one sort or another. Rest assured you will be allowed free access to pass from the county unchallenged. Will you then yet ride with Sabine?'

Maclean stared at the man that had the resource to offer bounty sovereigns of the quantity he had. He pulled open one of the purses and tipped a handful of the coins into the palm of his hand. Then replacing the coins, he said, 'Thirty pieces of silver for betrayal, eh?' Then looking into Boscawen's face, he nodded. He then kicked the chair out from under him picking up the money. Pulling open the curtain, he stepped into the bar of the inn and calling across to Sabine shouted to him.

'*Bailiff!* Your men, we ride to Princetown forthwith.'

'And return the King's horse with its all four legs,' Boscawen hollered at the door to him from the floor, the cuffs of his shirt soaked in ale to the pits of his arms now. He shouted once more, '*Landlord! Landlord!* Ready my coach and four. For Plymouth's eve'ng tide awaits neither king nor man.'

# TWO

## Helston, Cornwall 1716

*AS DESCENDANT OF THE LAWYER* Thomas Flamank, one of the leaders instrumental for inciting the Cornish into an armed revolt against Henry the Seventh during the rebellion of 1497, Joshua Timmins had pedigree. His family had risen by hard work, becoming respected members of Helston in the hope that one day, one of them would come along seeking justice for the family for what their ancestor had suffered in the rebellion. He himself had been matriculated at Trinity College at law to the Middle Temple. Called to the bar, he had not answered. While most would have looked on Thomas Flamank as a black sheep; having been hanged, drawn and quartered along with the blacksmith Michael Joseph at Tyburn for the treasonable act of undermining God's rightful heir to the throne of England, the family did not. Instead, the Flamank's through the maternal Timmins line, had taken it personally, looking to furthering an ambition to establish Cornwall as a country by fair means or foul. Such unjustified treatment for their ancestor gave him a hatred for monarchy as a carbuncle festering. Whether Protestant or Roman Catholic, the Timmins's family hatred for monarchy passed down his blood line. With the thought that the kings and queens of England were no more than thieves and murderers clinging onto power with every means at their disposal, even to the detriment of their own relatives should they get in the way, showed a total disregard for the peoples of the country they were supposed to be serving. Such was their curse that justice for their subjects was pitifully lacking.

*Treason! Bloody treason! Take them to the Tower. Rack them. Burn their flesh. Thumb their eyes as grapes bursting them. Hang them and quarter them while they yet still breathe. Watch them squirm as if they were a worm underfoot. Their suffering an example to others———.*

*Subjugate them———. Oppress them———.*

He held his breath and looked around him conscious that he had temporarily lost control of his mouth with these thoughts. As Stannator he was responsible for shipments of tin to London from Helston; more importantly, his one role that brought him into contact with mine owners the like of Sir Richard Vyvyan, that had vested interest in that most precious of metals. As Stannator he was also assessor of tin coinage for the duchy of Cornwall in the name of the future King of England the Prince of Wales. And now with his association with Sir Richard he could be on the edge of depriving the monarchy of their Cornish wealth bringing justice and revenge for Thomas Flamank.

One of the oldest families in Cornwall, Sir Richard, the man Joshua Timmins saw would exercise strength and leadership in taking Cornwall forward as a country, was a baronet and Member of Parliament. If he could not achieve the governship of Cornish autonomy, then nobody could. Sir Richard's support for James Francis Edward Stuart, the man who would be known as James the Third, declared King on the death of his father, was foiled. The Stuart line had come to nothing since the 1701 Act of Settlement declared Sophia Elector of Hanover and her Protestant heir's successors to the English throne that would never again see a Catholic prince. But Cornwall, that could be a different matter with independence. For a declaration of Sir Richard as Catholic Protector would leave a door open for successive Stuarts. An appeasement to the Jacobite causes the Elector had overlooked.

If it were not for Sir Richard's promise to quieten Jacobite opposition to that German, Timmins had told his closest family members, the opportunity for a Cornish Protectorate may be set back hundreds of years. As it was, Timmins toyed with the idea that his own fate, given other circumstances might not turn out much different from his ancestor Thomas. Rumours that the King may yet have a change of heart had been muted by many a Cornish nationalist. Even Sir Richard mentioned to him when he brought the subject of these rumours up:

'Of course, there is always that possibility, but given continuous unrest by the Jacobite's to return a Stuart to the English throne, I think it now very unlikely.' Sir Richard went onto say that, 'Given that, it was important the terms be brought to me as speedily as possible.'

Timmins saw no problem in his part of the arrangement. He was to liaise with John Goode at Crockern, the Parliament of the Devon Stannary on Dartmoor. From there it would be a routine matter of bringing the dispatch to Helston and Sir Richard. His thoughts were that although the Devon Stannary did not have as much to gain with this document as the Cornish, they would nevertheless enjoy the financial benefits with this cessation of the duchy of Cornwall. The taxation on tin being appropriated to the Stannaries' on behalf of the Prince of Wales was the same for Devon, albeit only half that of Cornwall under the authority of its duchy.

Wearing the loose overcoat uniform of his office, the emblem of the chough crow bird embroidered in silver thread on its red background gave all he was about his duty as Stannator, for he had no wish to be taken for a spy should trouble arise. With that and the additional protection of a pistol hidden under his fur and leather tunic, along with a dagger and sword he set off for Falmouth.

Standing on the quay at Falmouth, his wiry stature standing him out, he watched as the ship that would take him to Plymouth come closer into harbour. The Packet known as, The King of Prussia regularly plied its trade between Falmouth, Plymouth and the Port of London, and its officers, crew, as well as most of its passengers were known to him. Dock workers stood by the bollards readied themselves to take up the ship's berthing ropes. On deck, he could see regular passengers alongside a group of men and horses that because of their raiment he could not tell whether they were soldiers or marines. Initially giving the impression of a small army of militia with their Captain, as the ship came close, it appeared that this 'Captain' was not the military man he first thought he was. A man in his later years, fifty or so, he would no longer be suitable for soldiering, even though he wore a sword and dagger. Weapons that he thought were a combination of arms worn by someone not very far from danger. Timmins watched one of his men throw him his coat which he hurriedly put on over his white shirt and red waistcoat. Then taking up a tri-cornered hat the man had tied to the saddle of his horse he adjusted it on his head and readied himself to disembark the ship.

Waiting by the lowered gangway to the ship to allow what should have been an orderly disembarkation, Timmins was forced to one side by the men and their horses that came crashing down the gangway that did not appear to have time on their side. Their Captain ignoring those waiting to board on the quayside, pushed and shoved his way through them to make way. Timmins took the rein from one of the horses pulling it to one side to prevent a woman from being knocked to the ground.

Its rider immediately responded, 'Remove your hands from my beast.' He drew his sword at Timmins's reluctance to do so. 'You'll move now if you know what's good for you.'

Timmins held his grip on the rein drawing his own sword, not out of any sense of a fight, more, that the man expected him to stand aside knowing not whether he was his equal or otherwise.

'I advise you to reconsider your situation,' the rider said seeing him brandishing his weapon, 'for if you haven't noticed you are short of majority here. *Now step aside fool for we are on the King's business!*'

Timmins not wishing to involve himself in anything that would jeopardise his own mission considered returning his sword to its scabbard, nevertheless further stood his ground until he was ready to do so.

'Let it go, Samuel,' the Captain said stepping onto the hard. 'He'll have his day soon enough.'

'What do you mean by that, Sir?' Timmins questioned this Captain. 'Should I know you Sir? Or am I already considering my actions when next we meet?'

Hugh Boscawen smiled. A smile that implied that such a meeting may well be imminent.

Timmins considering the importance of his own mission of more importance than argument and made the decision to return his sword to its scabbard. He stepped to one side and with a flourish of his hand and a look toward Boscawen indicated that the man could have his own way – this once. Boscawen saluted him with a nod of his head, then ordered his remaining men and horses to disembark as quickly as possible.

Timmins standing to one side close to the low sea wall watched as the horses struggled to get safely down the ship's gangway, but a sudden sea swell from a passing ship caused them to stumble further toward him. He was now clinging onto the ship's side ropes to prevent falling into the sea between the vessel and the dock wall. He was about to topple into the water between the ship and quay when one of Boscawen's men held him up. In this action, the man's oilskin opened enough at the front for Timmins to make out the man's uniform under. He did not at first immediately recall where he had seen it before, but nevertheless nodded his gratitude to the man for his help.

It was only after he had boarded the ship, and having departed Falmouth, did it occur to him that the man was wearing the uniform of an officer from the Tower of London. If they were all the same, they were men, the like of which had not been seen so far west since the Cornish insurrection of 1648 following the English Civil War. And the one that had saved him from being crushed between the harbour wall and the ship bore the insignia of a Tudor Officer Guard. As to the Captain, who they were clearly under his orders, he was not able to ascertain as he wore neither uniform of militia nor army. The useful information he gathered from the duty officer of the Packet was that Jacobite sympathisers were being rounded up in Cornwall and were to be removed to the Tower of London for incarceration before trial. With the recent execution of the Jacobite Sir James Radcliffe, the 3rd Earl of Derwentwater at the Tower, Timmins suddenly feared for the safety of Sir Richard Vyvyan and his mission, with no way of warning him.

# THREE
## Trelowarren, Helston, Cornwall 1716

*IT WAS THE EIGHTH DAY* of October in the Year of his Lord 1716, when Sir Richard was hastily burning papers in the large ornate fire grate. Over it, the family crest of a lion dancing on water, enhanced by flames from the fire, had the legend: *Vive Ut Vivas* written under. These were documents that he recognised would be held as incriminating evidence against him; that could as easily have elevated his status within England had the Jacobite's won the day putting a Stuart on the throne.

Any circumstances for a reversal in the Vyvyan fortunes on that score necessitated a damage limitation in spite of the King's verbal pardon. Word had reached Sir Richard that George had rescinded that pardon and that his men were at Helston to impose others on him.

The besieging of Trelowarren was at hand. Its iron studded oak door pushed open in anger, despite the servant's endeavour to announce them in a manner befitting. On his knees at the fire grate, Sir Richard looked up at the sound of the intrusion and shrugged his shoulders. The game was up.

Five men entered, their hands on their sword handles ready for the worse. They had no need to worry. Sir Richard went to the large oak table and taking his sword and scabbard from it threw them to the ground. Recognising the coats-of-arms on their uniforms, his worst fears were realised. A yeoman guard with three officers from

London accompanied by another, one he knew personally, stood before him.

Hugh Boscawen of Tregothnan, Comptroller of His Majesty George the First's household; representative of that man's same government in Cornwall, came as no surprise to Sir Richard for he was a man of ambition.

Boscawen faced Sir Richard.

'Thank you, Sir. You know me well enough.'

'Well enough indeed, Sir. Like I should have trusted a Protestant, less one a German,' Sir Richard said. 'You'll take food after your journey I suppose?'

Sir Richard turned to his servant to fetch sustenance from his table for his guests. The man did as he was bid, then pouring wine into a glass he passed it to Boscawen. Before he could take it, one of the guards took it from his hand and sniffed at it before dipping his finger into it putting the wetness to his lips. Not wishing to give the idea that he might think his own cousin would poison him, Boscawen called for the man to pass him the wine without resorting to such measures. 'No need for that, man. Give it to me here.'

Taking the wine, he helped himself to a piece of bread from the table dipping it in his wine before proceeding to suck at it. Then putting it down he took the roll of parchment handed him by a yeoman guard. He made to speak.

'I have . . . a warrant . . .'

He broke the seal, and then began to choke on the bread he was trying to swallow. It became protracted and Sir Richard shook his head in disgust that such a man was short of manners. He lost patience with him.

'Give it to me, Boscawen. Don't stand on ceremony. Go choke on your family disloyalty in the corner. Over there.'

Snatching the parchment from his hands, Sir Richard broke the seal, unrolled it across his table, and began to read.

Word preceded Boscawen's arrival that the king's verbal pardon in the matter of Sir Richard's continued freedom would not be worth the parchment written on. They were referring to a spoken version full of political double-talk. He hastily read. The official document confirmed that this one was. The doubters had been right, though it had not come as a complete surprise to Sir Richard the grounds for his treason were not what he had expected.

'What's this? Am I not to be taken for a Jacobite?'

Boscawen had stopped choking.

'Do your duty Yeoman.'

The Yeoman-Sergeant stepped forward. He would speak the words his office demanded:

'Sir Richard Vyvyan, 3rd Baronet and . . .'

Hugh Boscawen became agitated interrupting him.

'Get on with it man, I'm not paying you by the word.'

The man ceased, then stared at Boscawen, his duty clear, the man had no authority over him in the matter. He would acquit himself to the letter. He then continued unabated, and to Boscawen's annoyance began to read aloud Sir Richard's full title, rank and position, as well as his home, before continuing with the charge proper in clear and concise tones.

'. . . that you are to be considered under the lawful arrest of our true sovereign, His Majesty George the First, after the legal Act of Settlement of 1701. You will accompany me and my yeoman officers to a hold in Exeter, thence to London and the Tower where a formal decision as to your future fate will be considered . . .'

The words went on with Sir Richard hardly hearing. Most of it being of a personal nature as to who he would be allowed to inform, those servants he would need, what books he was to be allowed.

Boscawen hearing the Yeoman-Sergeant's mention of the Bible

interrupted saying, 'For comfort in your cold cell, we'll allow you the King James's version.'

With the interruption, Sir Richard had not heard the reference the Yeoman-Guard made: that his wife was to accompany him; that she was a co-conspirator. When the man had finished speaking, Sir Richard turned to Boscawen.

'On what charge, Sir . . . I repeat, what indictment do you hold against me that I am to be arrested, when no other than that of treason – for which, I am most assuredly innocent – what Sir? For I cannot be guilty of treason, not for a mere Jacobite; a believer that James Stuart should be the natural successor to the throne of England. A political belief held by many; argued by government historians and academics alike. Pray, how is that treason, for—?'

'No Sir,' Boscawen replied angrily. 'Not for a Jacobite, Sir. You are being arrested on the charge of insurrection and high treason against any monarch and his heirs God's placement to England bequeaths – our liege lord, George the First is coincidental in this matter . . .'

'But not the Duke of Cornwall, I suppose.'

'Yeoman-Sergeant take him out. Find and bring his wife along with him.'

'*My wife!* What has she to do with any of this? You cannot take her, she's with child.'

## Dartmoor, Devon 1716

Goode was shy by ten minutes the Lord's hour of two after midnight when he approached the tin workings at Princetown, his non-communicative host ghost-rider having evaporated – with five miles to his destined rendezvous – into thin air he took to be mist, after asking to relieve his bladder. He was to meet the Mine Captain who would afford him shelter while awaiting the arrival of his Cornish brother. As an officer of the Devon Stannary Parliament, Goode had certain privileges not always appreciated by tinners; and certainly, distrusted by the Mine Captain. One of which was his standing and background, which were constantly the subject of whisper and rumour. For his family had land in this neck of the woods; with parents that were not constantly struggling in a county that was poor for farmers; and where hunger and deprivation was common. Goode knowing of these rumours guessed they were born out of envy, constantly going out of his way and striving to underplay his rank that was privileged, more so as the King's courier in this important matter of State, that most could see no profit, to the point he had been easily persuaded by people with other political agendas that he would be well advised to keep his own counsel.

Seeing the man, wearing a tinner's jacket of brown rough-cut cloth that had seen better days, only confirmed as to whom he was when the embroidered badge of office sewn on his vest showed when he opened his jacket to identify himself. Only then did the Mine Captain confidently approach Goode, and the thought, was he doing the right thing, brought doubt to his mind. But his political persuaders saying it was right for all concerned, that, and the gold coins they had pressed into his palms alleviated his fears. He put his hand into his long-coat pocket taking hold of its content to confirm they were still there.

'*Benjamin,*' Goode said by way of greeting, turning his back on the man without fully looking into his face, he unfastened his saddle harness from the horse's girth.

The wrong man, taking his opportunity, fetched Goode a blow to the back of his head with a cudgel of lead wrapped in leather, rendering him temporarily out of this world.

\*　　\*　　\*

## Devonport, Plymouth 1716

Timmins's arrival in Plymouth required a change of plan.

Berthing and departing the Packet, he sent the waiting coach away. He reasoned that if trouble were brewing, he would be better served defending himself from the back of a horse rather than the inside of a thoroughbrace and four. Although the agent advised him against travelling in the damp night air of the moors where many footpads roamed, he insisted on his right to make alternative arrangements, dismissing the man with a wave of his hand.

Removing additional clothing from his pack, he wrapped himself in a long cloak. He then tied a black silk scarf around his neck adjusting it below his eyes. He then put on his cavalier hat to hide whatever identity remained of himself and his office. Pulling the lower portion of his cloak inside his sword's sheath and pommel for an ease of draw, he then bared his right fighting arm, further removing from his pack a chain-mail sleeve pulling it tight over this arm. Satisfied that he was ready for any trouble he might encounter he rode swiftly the road to Princetown for business with John Goode, praying all was well, but knowing they were not.

## Dartmoor, Devon 1716

Maclean and Sabine pulled their horses up. Which way? Maclean shouted. Both riders were on the edge of a tor high above a valley. It was dark, but its slope, covered in bracken, disguised granite obstacles that would easily upset a horse, sending its rider and beast to injury and death from broken necks, were plain to see in the moonlight, Down there! Sabine answered laughing.

Maclean, for the first time that night, hesitated, while Sabine determined to make sport of the other man's trepidation said:

'Afraid are we, Colonel?'

'Only for the King's horse. Lead on down bailiff, for you know these woods better than I that you would trust to take such a risk. But make haste man, for I've a thirst for brandy for breakfast.'

The two men passed around the edge of the village of Princetown to the mining grounds, Maclean relieved they had safely traversed the streams and bogs and were now on steadier ground, their horses having cautiously picked their way over wet granite boulders without injury, seeming more capable in this exercise than Maclean gave them credit.

Sabine pointed out the tin workings in the dawn light. There were dozens of huts, with small pack horses grazing between. Amongst them, shafts driven deep into the ground, had groups of men smelting tin into granite moulds to be taken for assaying to one of the four Stannary towns they serviced.

'That is where the document is to be passed over,' Sabine said. 'And there's enough witnesses from the Stannary to see these two men sell them out once we've made the switch. We shouldn't have any trouble.'

A man wearing a bowler hat with the stub of a candle melted onto the front of its rim approached the two riders.

'That's our man,' Sabine said turning to Maclean. 'He's in our pocket. Has Goode arrived yet?' he shouted after him.

'He's asleep as we speak. We're waiting for his Cornish brother. A messenger brought news of a Packet's docking in Plymouth two hours since. A coach should have him here before the cock crows.'

He threw down the leather pouch.

'Exchange this while he sleeps, then bring it to me. See that no one sees you. Where's your watchmen?'


Hiding out behind rocks and bracken, Sabine's hired hands from Lifton were armed and waiting.

'Time to earn your pay, mercenary,' Sabine said pulling a musket from his saddle-pack, 'we'll wait on the other side of the highway.'

Maclean followed Sabine to a clump of boulders. Sabine removed a cartridge from his belt box, while Maclean took several swigs of brandy from his flask at the same time taking in as much of the road as was possible with his brass and leather telescope.

Tearing the paper tail off the cartridge with his teeth Sabine spat it out, then holding the cartridge in his hand, pulled the musket's hammer to half-cock and poured a little of the powder from the cartridge into the priming pan, the rest he dropped down the barrel followed by a ball and paper, then rammed the ingredients down with a rod. Bringing the musket level, he positioned himself and rested the barrel on a rock of granite flicking a large black slug away from him that looked as if it had settled down for the night.

Maclean smiled. This man was no soldier. An attack by an opposing force was for musketeers, not for a single coach with a whip-man and guard. It was important that they capture their man alive. With the fire-power Sabine had with his trigger-happy gaolers that was not likely to happen and he told him so. He himself had a large flintlock pistol and sword when he saw the rider approach on the distant road. He nudged Sabine on the arm, 'What's that, for it's not a coach?'

'*Mine Captain!*' Sabine shouted. The man came running. 'Did not your sources say that Timmins would be coming in a coach?' The Mine Captain looked at him and shrugged. 'Well who in hell's name is that rider?'

He shook his head. 'No one I know Sir.'

'Well you'd better find out and quick. Get your men and see to whoever that is on the road and take him out. For there are to be no witnesses to what is taking place this night. Now man! *Now!* For he's

36

a full quarter mile nearer than he was at the dawn of this conversation, and he's closing on us.'

Timmins had seen what looked to be an ambush having prepared himself mentally for such an eventuality, the three riders coming upon him at a pace were not in greeting, he was sure of that. An arrangement for a signal torch was to be his invitation from Goode. There was none from these riders, but surprises.

The lead rider, a left-hander coming in fast on his near-side flank had his advantage of length of sword and position. The other on his offside, was swinging a net as he rode towards him. Such a weapon or restraint before a kill was a Roman soldier aid against gladiators, commonly used to capture miscreants on the run from the law. The net he feared more than any wrong-footed sword arm. They clearly wanted him alive. Leaning back in the saddle, he pulled on his horse's reins viciously bringing the beast to a painful standstill, and then kicked with the back of his boot mercilessly into its rump. The horse, its head turned to face him, its eyes blazing yellow from this mistreatment, reared up, then pirouetted on its rear legs forcing it in the opposite direction positioning the left-handed swordsman on his offside. Bringing his sword down, backwards and across, he took the rider in the throat. The rider overtook him, his head now hanging like a rag toy upside down on the top of the back of his shoulders before toppling from the saddle. His one foot still in the stirrup he was dragged two score yards before the horse, not willing to run further into marsh by the side of a rivulet came to a standstill.

Timmins turned, too late, the net was on him. Tangled in his chain-mail arm protector. Unable to remove it, the third rider came upon him and hit him with a pick-axe handle as he went by knocking him, enmeshed in the net, off his horse unconscious onto the side of the road.

Dawn had broken when Timmins regained consciousness finding himself tied to another. He guessed from his clothes that it was John Goode. Looking through partly closed eyes, he had no wish to allow his assailants to see he was conscious he made out five men and six horses. A man – he heard a caller shout for Sabine – removed the contents of his dispatch case onto the ground. He then put the removed document into his saddle bag and closed it. Close by, the man he had partially decapitated lay out. His companions came over and lifted him up, taking him to the stream they took his arms and legs together,

'Ready? One, two, three. *Uhgg!*'

With the river in full flood from the rain, his body was quickly lost to view.

Timmins felt the man he had been tied to move. Whether it was the man he was supposed to liaise with he had no way of knowing as he had never met John Goode in the flesh to be sure. Whoever he was they were both thankfully still alive. Whether that was going to be a permanent state, again he had no way of knowing.

A lone horseman came into his view and he shouted out to him for water. He laughed, then shouted, 'Could we arrange a boundary for these two over there?'

*Boundary!* Timmins thought. What was that all about?

His bindings tightened as he felt his companion begin to come around.

If he had any suspicions that Timmins was part of this treachery, then they had just been allayed. He turned to look at the man he was tied up to, 'You Joshua Timmins?'

'John Goode?' he asked not needing an answer. 'Pleased to make your acquaintance. Well this is a fine Devon reception I must say. What's this boundary?'

As a Cornish Stannary Officer Timmins no more qualified for

Lydford justice than himself; he was clearly not involved treachery being elsewhere. The question, who that might have been came to his mind. Someone had had a change of politics, and that much was clear to him now; the question was, why could they have not made their intention clear before blasting the ground out from under him back in Okehampton.

With two traditional punishments for errant tinners, Goode prayed that with the mentioning of a boundary, although bad enough, it would not be the other. The second method did not bear dwelling on; and certain to bring a painful death. If all they wanted was the document, then they had got it from him. Whatever else they had in mind, that should be the end of it. If it wasn't, then he could do with his rescuer that had ridden him out of Okehampton once again. He never did establish who he was for the man spoke not a word. Setting him down when he asked to stop for a piss, only to ride off when he's back was turned. He struggled with his bindings, but the blow to his head had left him weak. Being Stannary Officer, he could try appealing to their better nature to be freed. With nothing left but his voice, he demanded from them an explanation as to what they thought they were doing. He pleaded who he was and what he was doing at Crockern; and that his business was good for all. They ignored him. The thought then came to him that they were not tinners, or, if any of them were, then they were not to give any succour, having been paid for their trouble. He resigned himself to his fate. Timmins was still waiting for an answer. He would not give it.

'*By God!*' Goode shouted out. 'Someone will pay for this day's work. Did you not here me. We are both Stannary Officers here.'

The relief at being cut free did not last for they were both dragged to a boundary post that had been driven into the ground. Pushed hard up against the post, his Cornish counterpart alongside of him unable to stand, they were both bound to each other to the post each with an arm free.

'This is none of my doing,' Goode said struggling to break away.

No sooner than the words were out of his mouth than the dark shadow of two men was upon them. Each had a lump of granite and a broken knife blade.

'Grit your teeth and think of Jesus,' Good cried out to his brother.

Both let out a scream that echoed across the moor as the blades went in.

Reverberating off granite Tors, rippling the still pools of brown metal-stained water, ceasing only for new breath, before beginning again, both men's cries, such was their tortured pain. Blades driven hard with a piece of stone, as a chisel into granite, went into the back of the two men's hands pinning them to the boundary board one on the other.

'Lydford punishment, Maclean. None come back for more of this,' Sabine said as one of his men held Timmins's head back. His Adam's apple flickering uncontrollably, fully conscious, having seen with his eyes what cruel fate awaited him. With his mouth forced open with a gag, molten liquid from a crucible fire-fanned with bellows for an intense heat to separate rock from the cassiterite contained within, was spooned towards it.

John Goode turned away in horror. The scream from Timmins, hardly a scream at all, instantly died in a choke. Was this to be his end? He looked up and screamed out, as a branding iron seared his forearm.

'Noooooooooo!'

Had any human ears with compassion that would hear the screaming from John Goode that early morning out on the moor, then they would know it to be an errant tinner being subjected to Lydford law. They would turn their backs for fear that those carrying out such punishment might see their witness.

Bailiff Sabine, his business complete, rode away with his fellow officers leaving Maclean.

Colonel Maclean stood before the two men, the air seemed to have hazed between them and himself. Time ticked up and down the centuries seeking a placement until it found its slot. His head fallen forward onto his chest, Maclean lifted it by the hair and looked into Timmins's face.

Turning his attention to the other man he asked, 'Are you John Goode, Stannary Officer for Devon. Speak plain man, if you can, for your life will depend upon it.'

Goode opened his eyes. Full of pain from his hand having been impaled, with the added weight of his body pulling down on the blade of knife that had cut veins and tendons, scoring and chipping bones on its way into the wooden board matched injury for injury the hand of Timmins's below. Sweat was pouring down his forehead. He nodded.

'Is that a yes?' Maclean shouted this time, for it was imperative he had the right man. 'John Goode, from Lovaton?'

Goode, not knowing why the man would want to know after such punishment. Didn't they know before they did this to me who I am? Why had they had gone to the trouble to brand his forearm with the sign of the Old Man of Crockern. A whisper was all he could manage his throat damaged from screaming.

'Yes, I'm Goode. Why have you done this to us?'

Maclean satisfied pulled the knife free. Both men collapsed to the ground. 'Leave this place,' Maclean said to him adding, 'whatever you've done, I didn't agree to any of this. Had I had known . . . well.'

Maclean hearing a whimper thought at first it was coming from Goode. But Goode was too far away now, stumbling, out of his mind he shouldn't wonder, wanting to get as far away from this place as he could. The sound was coming from Timmins.

Looking down at him, his body was in a tremor. At first, he thought his nerves and muscles were contracting as a headless chicken might after having had its head cut off where it would continue running around until death came. But this was not nerving. The man was yet alive, his body lying across a bush of bracken, as if trying to hide, or escape. To escape life. That was what he wanted for he was pointing at him. Molten lead being poured into a man's throat was torture too far without an accompaniment of death. Maclean drew his dagger and kneeling beside of him, using its jagged edge stabbed then cut deep into the man's throat until it would go no further, only stopping when a piece of the knife broke embedding itself where it stopped.

Timmins let out a final scream then died.

Goode hearing the cry from Timmins, turned around to witness this act of mercy to put the man out of his misery. A bolt of lightning. A rare phenomenon, but not unknown, came without warning striking the Mine Captain's hut reducing it to rubble, before the excess of its force went along the ground hitting the crucible of lead at Timmins's feet. The handle touching his leg, passed its energy through his body, turning him translucent. The pain from Goode's own hand left him and he saw the glowing body of Timmins rise up, to be dissipated into the air. Goode closed his eyes tight, then opened them. He was expecting to see Timmins where he lay; that what he had seen was no more than imagination, but he was gone. Goode left.

Maclean became aware his heart was beating irregularly. In no hurry to leave this place, sure Boscawen would have men waiting for him for what he knew. He would take the opportunity to rest. Sitting on a stone by the river, he put his head in his hands and watched the water passing before him. In this position he became aware he was not alone. Someone was standing by the side of him. Sabine and his men had returned to finish him off, he thought. His emotions still running high, he hurriedly stood up to one side, pulling his dagger ready to defend himself. Then he hesitated. His head to one side, a quizzical look on his face, he stared at the person stood before him. A man wearing clothes different from any he had ever seen before was speaking to him without any apparent movement of his lips.

Maclean's dagger arm relaxed at who was before him, for what he was staring at was a spectre he would be unable to dispatch.

'One thousand nine hundred and eighty-eight,' he said. 'Have you seen a boy?' He was a holding a strange picture in front of him. '*This boy!*'

*A boy* , he whispered to himself fearful that might have been the one he had stabbed in the throat. For if it had been the spectre would have surely seen. Laying him to rest after his act of mercy as best he could by the side of the river. For what was he apart from a soldier but a man.

In 1689, when he was fifteen or so, he first fought Jacobite's for the government army under General Hugh Mackay of Scourie at Killicrankie. A man who had taught him respect for battle dead, that they were no longer enemies. And now he had been instrumental in the slaughter of a man by the most barbaric of methods for one hundred sovereigns. A man who was not any enemy of his. All for a king's ransom, that now weighed heavily on his conscience. With a mix of self-pity and anger, he threw the two purses into the marshland alongside the river. He looked away, then returned to the spectre's blank gaze that held so many questions, but he was gone. God had robbed him of answers, putting him into a deep depression.

Wringing his hands dry after washing them clean of the bounty that had tainted him, he became aware of the wetness of his blood. He had severed wrists. His dagger on the bank at his side, its jagged blade wet. Mesmerised he put his arm out over the water and watched his life flow drip into it, making a mark as oil on water, before being carried away downstream one with the river. Dartmoor had him. The spirit of life that would no more recognise his breath from that of the trees was bringing him home to rest. Day by day into a future, washing emotion and hardness from his soul. Death's cloak drew warm around him. Life among many others gone before. The eternity of death no longer an end. He would be born again, and he knew it. A warrior soldier of fortune baptised clean would see a future day.

# FOUR

## Offices of Craske-Forbes, Bristol 2008

*CLUFF READ:* CRASKE–FORBES MEDIA CONSULTANTS lettered in silver over a hint of green shadowing on the company's glass security door. This was the advertising agency his girl-friend-cum-fiancée ran with her business partner Cyril Craske.

Electronically operated from within he approached the door. Signalling to the staff behind the reception desk that he was there it opened, then closed before he had the chance to squeeze through the gap.

Inside, at the desk, two of its employees, Mary and Christiana watched him. Then with the aid of the door entry switch they played with him moving and closing the door in a sequence that even though he moved quick was never going to allow him through. He smiled silently mouthing to them very funny. Seeing Jackie, he tried for her attention.

Out of the corner of her eye, she shook her head in despair at the way he had come dressed. Was this the man that was spoken of so highly in legal circles. A barrister that had silk in his view banging on her office door, that in any other circumstances would not have even been allowed into the ground-floor of the building had he not been known by security. Begging for her to let him in, sporting combat trousers with an old anorak over his shoulder that might have been worn by Scott of the Antarctic, was her fiancé. A white and blue striped shirt that she knew would have been the same he had worn in court that day. A collarless arrangement, its stud still attached. A fashion statement by him that if ever there was one failed miserably. She cringed. For some reason she had let herself be coerced to go on a foolish journey across Dartmoor with this man dressed as Rumpole of the Old Bailey. In a general discussion they were all having one evening in the bar at the Llandoger Trow about how people were generally becoming soft these days, and after Cluff had jokingly suggested to Christiana that he couldn't see a time when Jackie would ever get into a pair of hike boots she rose to the bait.

'Right ... Mr. Barrister, you're on. I'll show *you* who's soft, *name the day!*'

And he did.

Not being able to stand the sound of the door sliding backwards and forwards any longer, Jackie called to Christiana, 'Oh! let the idiot in.'

Christiana, twenty-seven going on fifteen, skipped like a schoolgirl towards the desk. Leaning over it she reached out for the door release exposing more than she intended. As the door opened, she caught him in what she could only describe as leering at her. She adjusted her skirt down to where it should have been, then hurriedly skipped back to join Mary, her hand in a half-rolled fist behind her back shaking it in his direction in a masturbatory gesture.

'You said ten, you're early,' Jackie announced to him. 'I've still one or two things to clear up first.' In her hand she had an empty bottle of whisky displaying a mock-up label for a new promotion. Showing him, she said, '*Stuarts Old Pretender*, do you like it?'

'Better full. How long you going to be? *Morning Mr. Craske.* Only we've a train to catch,' Cluff said at the same time acknowledging the CEO as he came from the executive bathroom.

Craske turned to Jackie, 'Have a great weekend. Don't do anything I wouldn't. Got an appointment with the accountants. See you later, Phil.'

'In three days.'

'*Coffee?*' Mary asked Cluff taking a stack of paper cups from Christiana who was bending over once more, this time rifling through a store cupboard looking for latte milk.

'Americano,' he answered aware that Jackie was still in reception with them catching him out. 'Two sugars and white.'

'Bring mine into the office while I finish off will you, Mary?' Jackie said.

Mary smiled and nodded at her as Cluff sat himself down, his booted feet on a low glass-top table on top of an old edition of *Campaign*, the advertising agencies' bible for what's going on.

'So, you've persuaded her then,' Christiana said bringing over two cups. 'You'll be marrying soon I'm thinking. As you seem to have persuaded her to swap her stilettos for Berghaus I'm thinking wedding bells.'

Mary came out of Jackie's office overhearing Christiana burst into a refrain of, ♫ – *Don't – Marry – Her, – Marry – Me* – ♫

'I'm not marrying anyone,' Cluff replied. 'Not until I get silk.'

'They all say that. Ver I come from vith cows to be milked and cabbages to be cut—'

'And vampires' molls to be staked – mind how you step out nights, Christi, especially in a skirt cut that low, your head must be permanently looking backwards.'

'Vhat, cheek! Anyvay, I'm from Slovenia not Transylvania, and if you haven't noticed I've a cross. I'm as Christian as you are.'

Cluff looked at Mary and winked.

'My life. Christian or not, still she looks like a girl waiting for a full moon.'

Coming up behind him she snatched out the magazine from under his boots and swiped him hard across the back of the head with it. She then looked around to make sure Jackie was still in her office;

but loud enough for Mary to hear, whispered, 'Didn't stop you sleeping with me last week when we left the Trow, did it?'

'*Aww!* You didn't,' Mary said snatching the gossip from thin air.

'In your dreams.' Cluff said his face reddening.

Christiana turned to Mary. 'Vell, he keep looking up my skirt.'

'Can't help that if you keep parading it front of me. Keeps getting in my line of fire.'

Christiana pulled down the neck of her blouse revealing a brown bruise. 'Eye line, my *derriere*. Look what he did to my neck, and *he* accuses me a vampire's moll. What's that make him? *Humph*.'

'All right, all right. I give in. Give it a rest before Jackie hears and thinks I have been playing away. It's taken me an age to persuade her to come on this trip, I was hoping . . .'

'You'd have your wicked way with her under canvas?'

Mary went to the reception desk to answer a ringing phone.

'It's not words in your mouth you're after. You naughty, *naughty* advocate, you. Anyway ... Yes, Jackie. OK, I'll tell him.' She replaced the receiver. 'Said she'll see you downstairs the taxis here.'

'Temple Meads,' Cluff said to the driver, before turning to Jackie. 'See you've a well packed sack.'

'Daddy did it for me – from your list. Why do I need toilet tissues, have they run out on Dartmoor?'

Not too keen to have to go into details at this juncture Cluff changed the subject.

'One of the last wildernesses in this great country of ours. I'm surprised you haven't heard of it.'

'If it's as barren as you say why should I? Anyway Exeter. They've a hotel there. I take it you did book a room?'

'Only tonight. Tomorrow, we take a taxi from there to Okehampton. Two days to Princetown, taxi to Plymouth station; then it's back to Bristol the day after. How's that sound?'

'Aside from two days walking, l-o-v-e-l-y. Remind me again why you want to do this.'

He went over his reason. How he had always wanted to experience what his father had done, perhaps get to the bottom of what might have happened to him back in 1988 when he disappeared on the moor. He should have done it when he was younger, but what with getting his law degree, then a placement at Ellick & Waite's; the same firm his father had worked as a barrister before him; he never seemed to have got around to it. Despite her initial reluctance Jackie did seem to understand his need cross Dartmoor. It was her, 'Why now?' question that he could not or would not answer.

Six months past when acting as defence counsel in the Rex v Mildenthorpe case that concerned the banker accused with others of inflating and deflating the London Interbank Offered Rate; a case as financial fraud goes turned out more complex than many first thought. As for the man himself, Cluff's defence hinged on him being a scapegoat for many that should have been in the dock instead of him. During a particularly crucial and mind-bending analysis of the bank's rate submissions his mind had wandered temporarily causing him to lose his thread. What he thought he saw, was his own dead father – bewigged and gowned – standing between the middle rows of jurors. Along with them, all remonstrating in unison, of a miscarriage of justice that had caused the deaths of so many children that had been held hostage.

In his mind the jurors returned to normal but not before he had been temporarily thrown into silence. Then taking a rebuke from Mr. Judge Gordon Molyneaux, eagerly awaiting 'our learned friend' to pull himself together and get on with his submission.

'Today would be most appropriate Mr. Cluff,' he had added before looking around No. 3 court of the Bailey, priming his audience with stares as if he were master of ceremonies at a music hall for the inevitable mirth that would follow his comment, 'Or, are we awaiting the return of St. Hilary?'

## Dartmoor, Devon 2008

The sun was hazy now even though it was still early afternoon and hot for the end of June the moor was sodden. It had been raining for weeks and the sphagnum moss acting like a sponge hid the water below preventing any evaporation caused the ground to move underfoot. At first, they walked with caution aware that they both might step through into a hidden bog below that would swallow them whole. Cluff had been open to that idea as a possibility for his father going missing. Alone and with no help it would have been all too easy to drown and disappear in such circumstances.

Having walked for a couple of hours only stopping to make a brew of tea they were both surprised how experienced they had become recognising what could be safely stepped on and what could not. Even Forbes to Cluff's way of thinking had taken to the ordeal with apparent ease, stepping confidently across puddings of grass, granite scrag, endless rivulets of water (that seemed to come out of the ground before their eyes), with the ease of a hardened explorer, all this while carrying an eighteen kilo rucksack. She had a smile on her face that was glowing from her exertion. He was quietly impressed. This trip was going to do the both of them a world of good.

Arriving at Ockerton an army lorry full of soldiers came down the track. Younger than themselves they were on exercise. Dirty and with camouflage paint streaked down their faces they looked all in. They waved at them as they drove by. It gave them a sense that although they were in a wilderness they were not alone.

The rain was coming in heavy when they came onto Cranmere Pool. A muddy hole the size of half a football pitch, Forbes was not impressed. The short distance they had covered getting here had taken it out of her. She slid her rucksack off her back dumping it unceremoniously on the ground. Taking the top off her water bottle she took a drink from it before attacking the wrapper of an energy biscuit.

'God, I'm all in,' she said. 'How long before we call it a day?'

Cluff stood on the rim of the pool drinking from his own water bottle looking at the sun. Half covered in mist that had come out of nowhere it gave it a dirty orange hue. The air around them was damp. He looked at his GPS clicking the Ordnance Survey number. 'According to this Hangingstone is east. That way,' he said pointing.

'It's those humps that are killing me.'

'Peat hags,' he answered.

'Whatever. I don't know about you but the way this weather is it might be a good idea we make for higher ground, get the tent up, and forget Hangingstone.'

'Agreed.'

Higher ground was easier said than done and she was behind him when she screamed out.

'*WHAT THE FRICKIN' HELL IS THAT?*

'*Ahhhh!* Get it away me. It's a frickin' snake. *Oh, my God!*

'*G-E-T-I-T-A-W-A-Y!*

'*Ohhhh!* This is not Australia. This is England; and that's a serpent. *GET IT AWAY!*'

He turned to see Jackie rigid with fear. An adult adder three feet long slithered away from where she was standing.

'Stand still it won't hurt you. See it's moving away.'

'Is it *bollocks* it is, it's going for the rest of its family. How many more are there? *GET ME OUT OF HERE!*'

She turned to make a move away, but the weight of her rucksack not helped by the high-water blisters of moorland grass pulled her sideways. Trying to stop herself from falling over she stepped into a bog up to her knees and began to sink. Her face said it all. She was helpless and going down.

Cluff removed his rucksack dumping it down then dropping to his knees grabbed her shoulder strap and held her. From this position he was going to have to drag her out but stopping her from sinking any further was one thing, breaking the suction on her body by the mud trying to claim her was quite another. All he could manage was to match the mud's pull, but he was fast losing his grip. With his body angled he searched with his boots for firmer ground. The bog was sucking and hissing when he finally did. Then straining against the efforts of nature for its victim's soul, it finally gave her up.

Spitting, swearing and covered in mud she came out like a cork from a bottle to land alongside of him on ground, although firm, was laid with two good inches of water. Pulling her to firmer ground he waited her reaction. Her eyes closed she gently opened them and laughed. Then thinking about the snake her emotion turned to anger.

'Where's that frickin' thing gone now? I don't suppose you'd considered the consequences of being bitten by a snake, had you?'

He tried to make light of her anxiety by making the point that he had taken a first aid course with St. John Ambulance some time ago. Then seeing the look on her face, he wished he'd kept his mouth shut.

She got to her feet. '*Yeh! Right!* Come on let's get moving. A girl could die out here. Give me a hand to straighten this thing up,' she said her rucksack hanging precariously off her left shoulder.

When the peat hags gave way to more even ground, they found they were now having to contend with driving wind and rain coming down on them. Cluff became anxious, they were both getting cold, but setting up camp where they were with run-off water coming down from the hill that was not going to be possible.

'What's that there?' Forbes shouted at the same time pointing.

With the wind coming at him he had difficulty making out what she was trying to say. He stopped, turned around and lifted his head.

'*THERE!*'

A raised island of land. The remains of a hut circle presented itself to them. A river running each side of it that on reflection to Cluff might have been one split in two, if not ideal and dry was at least clear of water running over it. With the both of them not having the strength to go on for much longer it was going to have to be a possibility. Whether that possibility was going to be big enough to take their tent was another matter.

He nodded at her.

A small crossing point of large rocks over one of the river divides took them onto it.

'Can we get the tent up here?' Forbes asked.

He looked at the space. A slight hollow with a wall of stones at each end. He scanned the darkening horizon for anything better. Seeing none he thought he would make it fit.

'This'll do nicely.'

The wind had died down to a manageable force three when Cluff removed the kettle from the stove filling their mugs with boiled water. Passing her the Craske–Forbes logoed mug he said, '*Tea!*'

'Earl Grey?'

'What else?'

'Thanks,' she said taking a sip. 'Ooh, that's good. What's that you're cremating in the pan?'

'*Bloody cheek!* Sausages, if you don't mind. Want beans with yours?'

'Ooh! you know how to treat a girl on a night out don't you,' she said taking another sip of her tea. 'And two slices. By the way,' she asked with a smile. 'Where *are* the toilets?'

When they had finished supper, Jackie went inside the tent to make her sleeping arrangements leaving Phileas outside to clear away the cooking. He had changed out of his boots into his trainers and was settling down with a flask of whisky to look at the darkening sky when he thought he heard a voice.

He looked at his flask to see how much he'd drunk.

'Did you say something, Jackie?'

She didn't answer. He guessed she was already asleep. Putting the voice down to his tiredness and imagination he went inside the tent and climbed into his sleeping bag. It wasn't long before he had dropped off, but not before an echo in his head played out, *We've a brief for you barrister.*

Waking from what she thought was a quick nap, Jackie couldn't at first make out where she was. Something had awoken her. She had heard a strange sound outside of the tent and it had unsettled her. Flicking on her torch she looked at her watch. Two am.

'What is it?' Phileas asked turning over trying to lift his head and shoulders from the warmth and constraints of the sleeping bag.

'God, it's freezing in here,' she said. 'Are you cold? You can see your breath in here. I thought I heard something outside.'

'Probably nothing more than sheep trying to eat the guy lines.'

'Listen. Did you hear it? Sounds like someone weeping.'

'I'll take a look; I need a pee.'

He unzipped the flap of the tent. Sitting himself back down with his feet out through the entrance, he pulled on his trainers. Then peering out giving his eyes a chance to accustom themselves to the darkness, he stepped out onto the wet grass.

'Is it sheep?' Jackie called from inside.

It wasn't. He wished it had been. For what he saw he began to shudder.

Jackie was waiting for him to answer her. When he didn't, she muttered to herself, *If you want something doing. . . .*

She got herself up on all fours. 'Where's that *bloody* pullover? *Christ*, a cat being swung in this tent would be over the moon. *Phil! What is it?* Say something, damn you.' There's was no answer from him. 'I'm coming out.'

Emerging through the flap of the tent relieved to see him standing there she stood up alongside him. With more room outside she pulled the remainder of her jersey over her head.

'Thought you were having a pee. What the *fuck . . . !*'

He had wanted a piss, but his interest had waned, for sitting on the stones they were earlier using for cooking was a man dressed in clothes that bore an uncanny resemblance to those from the English Civil War.

Jackie's head now clear from the turtleneck of her jersey and after straightening her hair tidy from the struggle, saw Cluff's Laughing Cavalier.

Phileas was transfixed. She nudged him hard for his reaction to do something.

'*Who is it?*' she whispered.

'Escaped from Dartmoor prison, I don't know?' Phileas whispered back trying to reassure her with some jocularity.

She looked at him as if he were mad.

'What in those clothes. I don't think so. I suppose you're going to say he's Magwitch's brother next.'

'You're the fashion aficionado. Year-wise, what? Eighteenth-century?' His voice trailed off. He didn't know. Neither did she. All he did know according to the GPS was that they were six miles from the nearest road. Not a distance a person could easily wander across in this weather *pissed* after a party that much was obvious. Apart from that, the poor sod was hardly wearing clothes suitable for the moors. Woollen top and rough trousers – and nothing on his feet, hardly conducive to walking on Dartmoor at any time of day, less so at night, when you can't see where you're going, he thought.

Jackie shook her head trying to make sense of someone from the eighteenth-century standing before her, because if she was right, he was a ghost first, from a dead man second. She tried to rationalise the situation by suggesting that Phil had pulled this as a stunt; that any second, Christiana and Mary, along with Cyril would turn up with cans of beers and boxes of fried chicken having come across the moor on quad bikes. After a second or two of that as a thought, with that not materialising, she feared for their well-being.

*'THEY'VE DONE FOR ME!'*

When it came his voice boomed. Cluff likened it to that of an announcement through a public address system at a football match. It hit him with terror.

Forbes's mental state fared no better. This man could be a killer. A murderer. How long he been sitting outside the tent while they slept, she could only speculate. As for Cluff his thoughts did not diminish as to what this creature might have done to them as they slept. His understanding of the mind of a psychopathic killer, from his training for law, only made matters worse. He knew the psychology that drove them. He was not expecting to confront one on Dartmoor. Going down fighting was not the point here, for if he did, then it was sure that Jackie would be his second victim. His promise to Jackie's father that he would take care of her screamed in the back of his mind. Slain on the moors at the hands of a maniac, was not a good headline to be the subject of. He recalled the film, *Blair Witch*, in which victims with their backs to their slayer, unable to raise a finger to defend themselves such was the fear that they had within them came to his mind with a dread, and like them, he feared intoxication from that mental malady.

Jackie, with more presence of mind than he would have given her credit had now moved closer to this homicidal maniac. She had worked out, with him sitting the way he was, that as he had not made a move to attack them, he might well be, *Safe!* Is that what I'm thinking, she asked herself?

'Who's, "Done for you" Who are you?' she asked.

With this as her opening gambit, Phileas came out of his torpor grabbing the first weapon that came to hand. A frying pan of water left out to soak overnight to remove the 'cremated' sausages. He stepped between them and threatened him with it.

'What do you think you're doing? He's clearly got murder on his mind and all you can do is ask him who he is. *Get away!* Or I'll land you with this,' Cluff said, pushing her aside, swiping at the man's head. When no connection came, he tried again thinking that he had missed first time. When there was no second connection, he dropped the frying pan, his mouth opens wide.

'Listen to him, he's trying to tell us something,' Jackie said.

'What'd you mean, listen. He's dead for *fuck's sake!*' Cluff screamed in horror. 'How can he tell us *anything*?'

'No, listen.'

The man turned his attention to him, repeating in that same voice, a boom from the bowels of the earth.

'*ARE YOU THE LAWYER FROM ELLICK & WAITE?*'

'*WHAT?*' Cluff shouted back.

Was this some kind of a wind-up? It had to be. Over two hundred miles from London, and a complete stranger – a dead one even – knows he is a barrister. Not only that, but one working for a particular practice. How would he know that unless someone had told him, setting him up? Jackie and her friends. On reflection, more her friends than her he would have thought.

'How does he know I'm a lawyer working for Ellick & Waite if it wasn't you that told him?' he said turning on her.

She hit him with her clenched fist on his shoulder. Then after verbally abusing him said, 'Is that your idea of a joke, accusing me of having anything to do with this? If you think I'd organise a stunt of these proportions for your amusement, you can *fucking* well think again .'

Seeing the seriousness in her face he knew he had stepped out of line.

'Okay, okay, I'm wrong. But put yourself in my position—'

'No, you put yourself in mine.'

With that she went up to the man, figuring, if he is being here knew so much about Phileas, then it was time to put him straight.

'If you're lost, need money or food then help yourself. On the other hand, if you really do need a lawyer then take Rumpole here with my blessing,' she said pointing to Cluff.

'Move away, Jackie,' Phileas shouted to her. 'Look at his hand, he's been in a knife fight, it's covered in blood.'

She turned back to Phileas and with no concern for the man she was now within touching distance of said, 'Why? We can't run, anywhere can we?' She turned back to the stranger and said, 'And who's "Done for you", that you feel free to wake up total strangers in the twilight hours, in the middle of nowhere to enlist a lawyer?'

'"Done for you". Enlisting the hounds of hell, more like. This doesn't make good sense, Jackie. Not a good place at all, it's got form. Now come away from him. Oh, shit! he's coming towards us . . .

'He's walking right through you . . .'

Jackie collapsed from the transmogrification in front of him.

# FIVE

## Yelverton–Princetown, Dartmoor 2008

*IT WAS THE MORNING* of August the seventeenth when Sergeant Bill Turnbull with his co-driver, Constable Dave Rawlins was driving the main Princetown to Yelverton road. Seeing a woman stepping off the moor too late, Turnbull, with hardly time to take in the predictive result of moving metal against the softness of the human body, attempted to pull the steering-wheel of the navy-blue Land Rover violently to the right. Missing a foal that had strayed onto the road in search of food he encountered her. Although he didn't hear what should have been the sickening contact, he brought his vehicle under control.

Rawlins made no mention at the later inquiry that his first thoughts were that Turnbull had momentarily lost control due to lack attentiveness, putting to the back of his mind that he might have played it differently, gave him the benefit of the doubt.

Jackie had never felt such pain in her life. All of her body seemed to have gone into what she could only imagine was a computer shut down. All her memories copied, re-pasted, and then deleted as a program no longer needed. Switch me off, and switch me back on again, she said to herself. Was she dying? Was this how it was all to end?

As to how she had been struck when the driver seemed to have had all the time in the world to avoid her was a mystery. And if that was a mystery to then be slammed face first onto a tarmac road was an even greater one for there didn't seem be a mark on her.

They were supposed to be the police. They didn't even bother to stop to see if she was all right. Had she imagined what had happened. Looking up the road she spotted tyre marks. The kind that are made by a vehicle making an emergency stop. If that was the case then where was it. Seeing a hollow on the side of the road she wandered over expecting to see the underside of a Land Rover smoking and hissing its two occupants trying to get out. But there was nothing.

She thought back to how she came to be here. Who *was* that man they had seen? More to the point where was he now. Had Phil confronted the man to protect her only to get himself murdered in the process. It would be just like him. Now alone on a moorland road and needing help she was in trouble. Whatever was happening now was strange to say the least. Something she had no control over. And now she feared she was no longer alive. Someone dead. A ghost forever walking the moors confronting hikers in the middle of the night as their visitor had.

She began to shake uncontrollably. Breaking down into floods of tears, she said, 'What in God's name is going on with me?'

## INTERPENETRATING DIMENSION DOME
### Bodmin Assize, Cornwall 1716

Standing in the middle of a throng of people that looked as if they were the cast of Les Misérable, Jackie was both bewildered and terrified. There were hundreds of them, all looking in one direction. All screaming. For some reason she wondered if they were screaming out for Phil. And if they were after his desertion by him, she would likely join them.

She did cling to the idea that she had stumbled onto a film set and these people were extras. It certainly had all the hallmarks for it being so except for one small detail. Would an historical film production make the mistake of spelling the town set wrong? The town's two words, BODNIM ASSIZE had been carved in relief on a granite arch over the building's large wooden doors. Surely a mason worth his salt would not make that mistake. *BODNIM.* She said the word out loud as if doing so would correct it. It didn't. And apart from anything else there was no sign of a film crew with their general paraphernalia that would be associated for such a production. Whatever this was it was for real.

She had to find out who the unfortunate soul was that these people seemed so keen to see retribution against and to do that she was going to have to get closer to the front. That was not as easy as it seemed for making her way forward people were turning on her commenting on what she was wearing suggesting to each other that she was a spy. One even suggested that she might be a leper threatening to cast her out. How they could think that of her with her long dark brown hair shining with a cleanliness that was not exactly prevalent among any here was a mystery. For it appeared these were the poor, the original great unwashed, their bodies odorous with the smell of body putrefaction. She could perhaps understand her general demeanour as being one taken for a spy. With her woman's wholesomeness, scarce enough among the aristocratic wealthy in, she guessed to be an eighteenth-century representation, it would be apparent she was not one of theirs. But *a leper!* – come on. One woman came close into her face. A face pock-marked she guessed the result of smallpox when a child, inquisitively looked at her skin. For a fleeting moment of time Jackie sensed she was searching a common sisterhood from down the centuries. She felt it herself and would have liked to have spoken with her, but the moment was passed, and they were being separated by the crowd before having a chance. She reached feeling a need to touch her, but she was gone. For all she knew she might have been a figment of the woman's imagination. A ghost. One that didn't scare, that reacted to flesh and blood that she could not recognise as being dead. *Dead!* Was that where she was.

She found herself standing below a scaffold. Their manifestation, his arms and ankles bound, stood below a rope noose. She shuddered. This was no film set. The realisation came to her that this was real time. And being in a different century from her own was now apparent to her.

An official in a tricorn hat with a brown overcoat to his ankles was making a speech using scroll:

'In the Year of Our Creator 1716 the condemned soul known as John Goode the Stannary Officer of Devon having been found guilty of the murder of his brother officer, John Timmins of Cornwall, has this day been duly sentenced. His execution set. Lord Save King James the Third.'

She showed a look of incredulity. For even though she never was one for English history when it came to naming kings and queens, she knew something was wrong when she heard this one. James the Third was definitely a no-no.

As for the man on the scaffold she felt both pity and at the same time relief that it wasn't Phil. It was the man that first confronted them setting off a chain of events that had brought them all to this place. And if her understanding of the process of execution was anything to go by then this was not going to be pretty. Drawing and quartering swiftly followed by emasculation would still have been a punishment in 1716? She shuddered, but it wasn't the cold of the day that caused it.

The mob were jeering and shouting insults at the man at the gallows. Trying with all his might and main to avoid what was to occur, he was no match for the soldiers restraining him. In front of him, a priest recited from a Bible. Except she did not recognise the words he spoke from what should have been the Christian King James version, sounding instead as if they were being read from some fantasy sci-fi novel version of an alternative faith. Displayed on his jacket, an emblem she had not noticed the night before, was of an old man. Above it, in gold thread, she made out the title, Devon Stannary. She needed to somehow question him if she were to find Phil, but then hesitated. Was she doing the right thing? She put her hand to her mouth, My God! The thought hit her like a thunderbolt. He must have murdered us, and we didn't know it.

If that had been the case, she surely would have had some sense of recollection. After all, to lose one's life at the hand of another no matter how quickly, the deed was likely to be indelibly imprinted on one's soul. Death, unlike birth, remembered at the time. For all of that she would speak with this man. He might have murdered them and have a need to seek redemption in order to save his soul.

She climbed the steps of the scaffold with a determination that feared no consequence for her action. A strange feeling came over her. Was she trespassing into another world?

The crowd seeing her, thinking her the man's relative started to chant bringing her antic to the attention of the soldiers who grabbed her and dragged her off. Struggling, she found herself alongside the condemned man. The executioner, wearing his mask of office to protect his identity was in the process of pulling the man's nightcap over his head before securing the rope around his neck. Pulling herself free from the restraints of the soldiers she turned on them:

'Get your hands off of me,' she shouted at them. Then quickly turning her attention to the condemned man she asked, 'Who are you? The man you took with you was my husband. Where is he?'

She saw little point arguing the difference between a husband and a boyfriend. If this is 1716 the union of marriage would have a sway no other would.

Whether it was out of a sense of pity, she could not say, for the executioner loosed the rope from around his client's neck lifting the nightcap to reveal his face. A face that was white with terror. His lips were purple, and he trembled with an anticipation of the act of strangulation.

For the moment time stood still for her. The executioner was allowing her an opportunity to have her say. The mob was of the opinion that the hanged man might like a last chance to cleanse his soul of any further sin before he met his Maker and went quiet. Someone heard the word wife and assumed it was his.

'You know me, right?' she said to him in a quiet voice.

The man looked at her and shook his head. A look of horror was in his eyes. His body's portal to the outside world showed an expression that his soul was about to vacate it. With some effort he strained to recall her. But he saw nothing, and much as he yearned to cling to this woman that offered him slim hope as an alternative to his fate for the trade of the answer to a question – he had none to offer.

The prison governor seeing no reason to stay business further signalled the soldiers to remove her. He had lunch waiting and she was keeping him from it.

The nightcap was pulled back down over the condemned man's face, followed by the noose, to be tightened for a second time. Then with a roar from the crowd the box that he was standing was pulled away by the attached ropes used for such purpose by the hangman's young assistants. Holding the hand of her brother; dropping her dolly that was under her arm, the hangman's daughter took the lead and walked off the scaffold allowing the condemned man to swing.

An instant of silence fell after the initial hoorar from the mob. For the time it took for those with a heart to hear, the sound of a bird could be heard singing from a tree alongside the prison wall to be followed by an answering call from its potential mate. Suspended by his neck under the weight of his body that tightened the rope causing his eyes to distend beneath the nightcap she turned away.

For the condemned man, his chest muscles fighting to work for air was useless. The shutting off of his airways preventing his heart from pumping the blood that nourished his brain was futile giving way to coma before death.

The roar from the crowd dropped to a whisper at what came next, for the kingspar, that held the weight of the hangman's rope and his victim cracked. A weakness in its timbers brought with it a rent in its grain. The split wood opened up bending enough to drop the condemned man an inch or two then held him. The creaking of rope and hanging man seemed to be in time to the shaking and dancing of the victim's legs. The crowd looked up anticipating the gallows collapsing completely sending man and woodwork down among them. But the kingspar of old dried oak, formerly the main prop of a post-mill originally used for the grinding of grain was of English oak, made of sterner stuff and not given to failure.

The hangman's daughter came back onto the scaffold to collect her dolly. Placing it back under her left arm she skipped back off the failing scaffold leaving John Goode, Stannary officer for the county of Devon to swing; her final connection to the man being his shadow crossing her as she did so.

A man bearing an uncanny resemblance to John Goode; residing in the village of Heavitree near Exeter, collapsed in the street outside of an apothecary. He, clutching at his throat, the precise moment John Goode was hanged at the end of a rope in the interpenetrating dimension that was Bodnim was hovering between verses. The coroner gave a verdict of death by mystery after an examination of his neck revealed bruising and rope burns reminiscent of being hanged, with no apparent apparatus to hand.

Yelverton-Princetown, Dartmoor 2008

'Did that just happen?' Turnbull asked agitatedly of Rawlins. 'Or did I imagine it?'

'You didn't, and I have your imagination,' Constable Rawlins said reaching for the door handle of the Land Rover to let himself out. He looked under the vehicle's wheels. 'Nothing,' he said relieved that the tangled mess of body parts jammed beneath the vehicle's chassis had not materialised.

Both men went back up the road. The tyre marks were plain to see. The fronts especially where Turnbull had pulled the wheel to the right to avoid colliding with the woman. For here was a wide band of rubber where it had broadsided up onto the grass bank alongside.

'Anything?' Turnbull shouted after Rawlins who was looking down the road. Distant heat haze was coming off the tarmac and Rawlins wondered if he could have mistaken the woman for an optical illusion.

'No but . . .' Rawlins said in answer to him, 'we're hardly likely to both imagine a woman in the road at the same time. *Are we?*'

Turnbull shook his head.

'Come on then we'll walk back and check out that water channel running under the road. She might be lying under there injured,' Turnbull said.

The culvert running under the road took a minor stream from one side of the moor to the other. Rawlins got down on his knees and looked in. He could see daylight from the other side but nothing like an obstruction suggesting that a woman might have crawled in there. He got back onto the road and shook his head towards Turnbull.

'Well it's a mystery to me, that's for sure.'

'Rudyard's never going to believe this,' Turnbull said lighting a cigarette.

'Do we need to mention it?' Rawlins asked mindful of the

reaction the both of them had got from their boss over a previous report: that of a sighting by them of an unidentified flying object.

'Don't think we've a choice. After all it might have something to do with that missing Forbes woman and her barrister boyfriend that were hiking out here and are overdue by a week.'

'But there are two of us to back each other up over what we saw. We'll have to say we saw what we thought was a woman, but she did a runner before we could detain her,' Rawlins said.

'We definitely saw her, didn't we?' Turnbull asked again.

'Well, to be honest, with it all happening so quickly it does leave a question mark as to our reliability, but yes, I definitely saw something. Whether that something was a woman or a man, I wouldn't swear for sure other than it was person.'

Turnbull nodded, satisfied.

Both officers turned and walked back to the Land Rover. Parked on the side of the road with its doors open and its blue hazard light flashing on its roof. Then Rawlins stopped. His jaw dropped open. He pointed hesitantly.

'*Look . . . there!* Lying on the road. She's back. Where the *hell* did she just spring from?'

They ran up the road toward her anxious to get there before she disappeared once more. Although she had scrape marks on her legs and arms, she did not appear too badly injured. Certainly not to the extent she would have been had she been struck by a vehicle weighing in at two-ton cruising across the moor at forty.

Jackie tried to raise herself from the road. She was confused as to where she had been and what had happened but knew the present well enough.

'Please help me. My name is Jackie Forbes. My fiancé and I were abducted. He's still out there somewhere.'

She was on all fours, her hair bedraggled sweeping the road in a breeze that had come from nowhere, she managed to raise her arm to point out onto the moor before passing out.

They both looked out to see a rambler about a hundred yards away heading in their direction.

'That must be him,' Rawlins said to Turnbull.

Turnbull chased across the moor to confront the man. When he resisted, he wrestled him to the ground putting handcuffs on him.

'What are you doing?' the man shouted. 'I'm Joe Treadway from the local paper. I saw what happened. I'm here to help. *Get off me!*'

Forbes coming around and seeing the arrested man screamed out, 'No officer, not him. Someone else. From another world where King James the Third is on the throne,' she said passing out once again smacking the side of her head on the road.

## SIX

## Dartmoor, Devon 2008

*THE PILOT* circled yet another tinners hut. He'd been up here for hours searching for an elusive green tent pitched on one. *Green!* What kind of colour's that up against this landscape, he thought to himself? Like searching for an orange baked bean with the name of Heinz in a tin of beans all named Arnold. One more pass and he'd have to call it a day. He was going snow blind from looking at green. And those orange beans were now compensating his eyes from staring at too much green.

With three hundred and sixty-odd miles of moorland below him he knew this was not going to be easy.

Then, banking the 'copter round a there came a break in the mist and there it was. With luck over judgement the remains of an abandoned tent appeared out from nowhere. But that was going to be enough. He radioed the co-ordinates to the ground search party. Then banking hard to starboard, stuck his hand out of the window to give a passing wave to anyone watching below before making his way back to Plymouth airport.

## Avon and Somerset Constabulary, Portishead, Bristol 2008

'Coincidence have a habit of hampering police work. Know what I mean, chief inspector? I'm sending photographs of the inside of the tent, email – new technology – it's sound, I say, sound. Something to get your teeth into with family or friends,' Rudyard said.

'That's cool,' Goode replied, not sure he should have used that turn of phrase to a superior officer.

'Cool, you say. Umm – quite so, capital. Sound. We'll speak again. Thank you!'

Goode put his mobile back into his pocket.

'Well, this case won't take any solving. Devon and Cornwall's got sound people in that man, Hymer. Sound, I say.'

'Presumably, that'll be as in, Plymouth, Sir?'

'Thank you, Hymer. The chief superintendent's irony, intended or otherwise, hasn't quite gone over my head with age.'

### Offices of Craske-Forbes, Bristol 2008

The young woman showed the chief inspector and his sergeant into Cyril Craske's office.

'Bring us some coffees, please, Chris. *Gentlemen*,' Craske said holding his hand out as an invitation to the two policemen to make themselves comfortable while at the same time closing the door.

'Thank you, Sir,' Goode said sitting down in the proffered chair, while Hymer, dragging another chair from across the other side of the office put Goode's teeth on edge with its high-pitched scrapping noise on the parquet flooring. 'In your own time, Hymer.' Hymer nodded at his boss and sat down unembarrassed.

There was a dull sound of a bump on the door then the handle moved. Backing in with a tray of coffees, using her rear end as a door stop, Christiana put the tray down on the edge of the desk.

'Will that be all, Mr. Craske?'

'That's fine, Christi.'

She smiled at the two policemen then left.

Wearing a short white skirt, with a white ruffled blouse, Hymer coughed gently from an ignoble thought that had entered his head.

Concentrating hard he took up his notebook and pencil. His apparent unease had not escaped Goode who gave him one of his stares.

'Gentlemen,' Cyril Craske said, 'I'm sure this is something of nothing . . .'

His words were lost in mid-sentence as Goode watched Hymer help himself to coffee.

'Please, inspector,' Craske interrupted trying to be polite to the senior man, 'help yourself.'

'Thank you, Sir. You are, Cyril Craske—?'

'Spinster of this parish and senior executive of Craske Forbes, alongside Jackie Forbes my business partner, yes,' he interrupted partially distracted, as he watched Hymer.

The sergeant was putting cubes of sugar into his cup before firmly taking hold of it. Then collapsing in on itself the plastic cup spilled steaming coffee over the table missing the tray.

Goode gave Hymer another stare.

'Excuse us, we don't run to china. I do that all the time,' Craske said in an effort to excuse Hymer his clumsiness.

'Afraid my sergeant is a bit on the heavy-handed side.'

'Sorry Sir.'

'You reported an overdue absence of your partner,' Goode said looking down at his own notebook. 'Along with her boyfriend, a barrister, name of *Phileas Cluff?*'

'Yes. They've—'

'We've tried to get in touch with relatives of Mr. Cluff. He doesn't appear to have any.'

'Far as I know both his parents are dead.' Craske replied uncertainly.

'We've managed to get in touch with Miss Forbes's family though and according to her father she and Cluff had gone hiking on Dartmoor. Is that right?'

'To the best of my knowledge they had. We were getting anxious. As we haven't heard from them for a week, Dartmoor being . . .'

'Quite so. We're not sure, but information from Devon & Cornwall police suggests they have found an abandoned tent out on the moor. We are waiting confirmation as to who it might belong to. In the meantime, we have photographs of some articles found in the tent. It would be helpful if you could identify them.'

Goode flicked his thumb and second fingers together in Hymer's direction.

'Sorry Sir,' Hymer said moving his coffee cup from one hand to the other before taking an envelope from his briefcase and passing it to Goode.

Craske took the photographs from him and scanned through them. A collection of personal possessions, make-up mainly, L'Oreal Colour something, Estee Lauder spray, hairbrush, packet of Durex Dream, driving licence, car keys.

'Ah. That's Jackie's watch, I think. And yes, that's her soft handbag. She said she was going to use that when she went for an evening out in Plymouth. But I think she had her tongue in her cheek when she said that. Oh, I think that's . . .' he laughed, 'yes, hair black and brush. That'll be Mr. Cluff's.'

'Hair black?' Goode inquired. 'Is that significant?'

'Well, yes. Barrister Cluff has been going grey since he was a young man – he touches up his moustache to match the hair on his head which is black and grey, you see, while his moustache is all grey.'

'You mentioned that Miss Forbes might have been talking tongue-in-cheek about going out in Plymouth.' Hymer said. 'Did they go out much, clubbing for instance?

'Well, yes. She dresses immaculately when she does. Especially if it has anything to do with Mr. Cluff's legal friends and she wants to impress. More causal for clubbing. Of course, she wouldn't have had any of her clothes with her in the bottom of a rucksack. I think she was making a token gesture with that particular handbag.'

'I see, Sir. And has she ever stayed away before – after a long weekend I mean. That was what it was supposed to be, wasn't' it?'

'Two days. Yes. Well, she has. Three or four days. Not a week though. She did stay away once without letting me know. We had an important meeting to attend. I suspected she was with Phileas. I paraphrase the woman when I mistakenly asked where she had been, "None of your damned business Cyril". Having said that though she did have a hint of a smile on her face. I never poked my nose into her personal life again. Until now that is. Now I am worried, and I welcome her asking me not to poke my nose into her love life.'

'These keys. Are they hers?' Goode asked showing him the photograph. 'That's a Mercedes emblem isn't it?'

'Where's her car now Sir?' Hymer interrupted.

'Yes, it is. It's in the underground car park. I've a spare set if you need to take a look. She leaves them hanging up in the office. I'll get them for you.'

He disappeared, returning a few moment later.

'Here they are,' he said dropping them into Goode's hand.

'Thanks,' Goode said. 'Do we need a pass code to get into the car park if you have—?'

He shook his head, no. 'The bays on the right are all marked with the company names.'

'How long has she known Cluff?' Hymer asked.

'Couple of years I suppose. We had some dealings with his law firm in London, Ellick and something—'

'Waite,' Goode added.

'What? Oh, yes. Ellick and Waite. You've obviously had dealings with them in the past, inspector?' Goode shrugged. 'He's obviously well-educated, being a barrister and all that. But I can't say I know him too well, but his credentials do speak for themselves. What more can I say?' Craske said.

'Were you jealous of his relationship with Miss Forbes?' Goode asked.

'It wouldn't have worked. I would be deceiving myself if I thought otherwise. I am Iranian. I will return to my country one day. I couldn't expect her to uproot her life.'

Goode nodded. 'Very noble of you Sir.'

Craske's face showed disdain at Goode's remark that he might be being considered a martyr.

'Apart from anything else it would be unusual,' Hymer interrupted.

'What'd you mean by that?'

'Well. Bit of a come down wouldn't you say, shacking up with someone in the advertising industry? Cluff being a barrister and all,' Hymer said.

Craske stared at him in disbelief.

'Is that what you think of the advertising industry, sergeant? We're not placing small ads in your local paper here. Craske–Forbes is among the top reputable blue-chip companies in the world. And like a lot of agencies of our standing, has people from all sorts of backgrounds, including the legal profession, to say nothing of politician's. Not many policemen, though. Now that I come to think of it. No. Can't understand why that should be. Still, might only be a matter of time, sergeant. Miracles do happen,' Craske said as if he was putting a heckler in his place.

Goode looked back from Hymer sighing. 'Yes, well, no one is suggesting that Mr. Cluff shouldn't be liaising with someone from the advertising profession, Mr. Craske. I'm sure my sergeant could have phrased his question better. However, getting back to what he was trying to establish. How would you describe Phileas Cluff? What you've told us so far leads me to believe he would hardly abduct his own girlfriend. Any reasons that you can think of that you might think otherwise – money perhaps. Her father is wealthy.'

'Wouldn't have thought a barrister of his standing, plying his trade in Lincoln's Inn; making regular guest appearances at the Old Bailey had money worries would you inspector?' Craske said put out by the change in tone of the questioning.

'Well if there's nothing more you can add Mr. Craske we'll leave it at that for the moment. And thank you.' Getting to his feet Goode gave him his card. 'Anything you think might help us in the meantime please do not hesitate to call me. Sergeant, when you've finished what remains of your coffee.'

'There was something else while I think of it inspector. Something Phil said to us concerning his own father's demise. How he had gone missing doing the same . . .'

Hymer scrunching up his empty cardboard cup placing its remains on the tray interrupted saying, 'Dartmoor. Missing sometime in the 1980s. His body never found. Lost, presumed dead. According to the Coroner that is. Yes, we are aware of that.'

Goode nodded.

'Thank you Mr. Craske. We'll be in touch if we should hear anything. In the meantime, if they call you first you will let us know. We'll hang onto her keys for the moment sergeant.'

'Of course.'

Cyril Craske got up to show the two men out.

Passing through the reception the girl in the mini skirt called after them that she would open the door.

'Excuse me miss, you are?'

She stopped and turned. So did Hymer.

'My friends call me Christi. My name is Christiana Bencek and I'm from Slovenia and I'm graphic artist. She saw my work while I

75

was at art school in Slovenia. She gave me job. I hope she okay. She very good to me.'

Walking to the car Goode mentioned to Hymer that he ought to brush up on his bedside manner.

'What'd you mean by that Sir?'

'"Shacking up with someone from the advertising industry" . . .'

'Yes Sir. Never did give advertising its proper credit. Not until I saw a real live graphic artist that is,' Hymer said smiling.

'Right. Well here's Miss Forbes's keys. Go check out her car. Then when you're done you can take them back to Slovenia and don't be all day about it.'

*DS ABLE WAVERLEY STOPPED* on the steps outside the hospital. Patients and visitors that had come out for a smoke surrounded him. For himself, he needed to make a call on his mobile and was having trouble getting a signal. Close by a sign that read, THIS IS A NO-SMOKING AREA, a woman dressed in a NHS regulation gown using an equally regulated NHS wheelchair. By her side, a trolley holding a drip tube inserted somewhere in her upper arm was supported by a chrome metal tube. No bars went to three from his regular T-Mobile provider to Orange. He nodded at the woman. She smiled back at him. He guessed the chrome metal upright on her trolley was the reason for the newly found signal. DCI Steven Cocksworth answered.

'Sir. I'm at Plymouth hospital. She's not in a good way. Doc reckons cataleptic shock.'

'Not surprised the way Turnbull drives around the county. Have you had a chance to interview her?'

'No. Too delirious, mumbling, none of it making much sense. Except for . . .'

'What?'

She mentioned a hanging. That it wasn't her, but herself from another time,' Waverley replied.

'Interesting. Apparently Cocksworth took a call from Avon and Somerset. Their chief inspector questioned Forbes's business partner as to the possibility that Cluff might have abducted Miss Forbes himself. The man said that given Cluff's status and financial position that he thought that was unlikely. But he did say he had heard that Cluff's own father went missing out on the moor sometime in the 1980s, which of course we already knew about. And we know what Rudyard thinks about coincidences.'

'Something on the lines of a person being born unlucky enough to be running into accidents began by someone else.'

'Um, close enough. The hanging's interesting though. Did the Forbes woman mention that Cluff himself might have been the victim, only if he had had hanged himself—?'

'That would be Wistman's Wood Sir,' Waverley said adding, 'If somebody was hell bent on topping himself, then Wistman's was as good as any other. We could start there.'

'A hanging in Wistman's Wood might well kill two birds with one stone,' Cocksworth said.

'How so Sir?'

'Find Cluff junior swinging over the grave of Cluff senior as a plumb bob, and it's job done.'

Waverley removed the phone from his ear. He could hardly hear Cocksworth speaking. Three or four guys from the press had turned up in two taxis. He watched them run into the main entrance of the hospital, and to the consternation of patients and visitors alike, they were pushing into the front of a queue at the reception desk demanding to know what ward Jackie Forbes was on. One of them seeing him and recognising who he was came back out and began to bombard him with questions.

'*Ghosts!*' Waverley answered the gentleman from the press. 'Are you mad. There are no ghosts on the Dartmoor. Sorry about that Sir.'

'What's happening, Waverley?' Cocksworth asked hearing the commotion.

'Sorry Sir. All hell breaking out here. The press picked up that we found Jackie Forbes.'

'Where do these people get their information?' Cocksworth asked.

'Well you know what the press are like Sir. Someone must have told them.'

'It was a rhetorical question, Sergeant; I know perfectly well that someone's told them. Perhaps you could put them straight on my behalf,' Cocksworth replied angrily. 'and then move them on Waverley.'

## Dartmoor, Devon 2008

Seven am the following morning and Rudyard had cut himself shaving. With a slip of tissue still stuck to his face his driver took him to the closest road accessing the site of the tent.

The ground search organised by Cocksworth was underway. Not that Dartmoor Rescue and Royal Marines would take any organising, he thought. They knew the moors like the backs of their hands both outfits capable of surviving in its environment with what they stood up in. His chief superintendent had declared Ordnance Survey map OL 28 600750, 600780 to 620750, 620780 a crime scene to all barring authorised personnel. Anyone coming off the moors from those co-ordinates was to be detained for questioning with their DNA being taken.

Cocksworth handed over the briefing arrangements to Rudyard who – megaphone in hand – climbed up onto the bonnet of a Royal Marine Provost Land Rover put at his disposal and addressed the multitude as if they were the Biblical Hungry 5000.

Standing as close as they could to Cocksworth – in anticipation of any slip of the tongue whispered between the two men – hungry, the press, BBC Spotlight, and ITV News crews with as much cable and technical gear as they could muster – hung on their words listening for the magical G-word.

This was not how Rudyard liked his exercises to be conducted preferring instead searches to be carried out with as little fuss to police and rescue procedure as possible. Clearly this one with talk of ghosts was not to be.

Having been pre-warned that the press had heard rumours that an Old Bailey barrister from London, having hanged himself, rumoured over the grave of his father, was witnessed by a woman from 1716, not to mention three bodies having since been discovered at the luckless couples camp site would be too much for them, likely sending newspaper sales and television reportage through the roof. Rudyard was going to have to make the best of a situation he had no control over.

Sometimes I despair, he muttered to himself.

'Ladies and gentlemen. Thank you for your interest. I am looking to be reassured that your professional approach in this matter, hopefully, with your help, conclude in the finding of Mr. Cluff, and will not hinder the police. As to the missing barrister, those of you that don't know is 34 years-of-age, six-foot-tall of average build. He has grey and black hair with a grey moustache; and to the best of our knowledge is wearing a faded brownish anorak. He is also wearing a blue pin-striped shirt – the type that has a detachable collar.' He removed the megaphone and whispered to Cocksworth. 'Better consider your Waverley's suggestion and treat his search of Wistman's Wood as a matter of urgency.' Re-addressing the press he said, 'We will be concentrating our search around the Crockern Tor area and for the moment that area is restricted to all but the police. A crime scene. I'll take a couple of questions. Yes?

'Crockern? Isn't that the old meeting place of the Stannary Parliament? And how did you find the tent so quickly?'

'Yes, it is, though that's not relevant to our inquiry. We put a police helicopter up to aid our search as a time saver. We didn't know if anyone was injured and needing help. Excuse me. *You are?*'

'Tony Noyon, Mr. Rudyard. The Sun newspaper. Any chance I can have permission to accompany a team of your people searching the area?'

'DCI Cocksworth is in charge of the search; you'll need to ask him. What happened to your face?'

'Had an accident outside the hospital yesterday,' he answered not wishing to further his fracas with a detective sergeant.'

Rudyard gave Waverley a wry smile before looking toward Cocksworth for an answer.

'Health and safety Sir. Might not be advisable at this stage.'

'Health and safety of course. Sorry Mr. Noyon. Some other time perhaps.'

Rudyard spoke into the megaphone once more.

'Thank you everyone. One more thing. We don't want any accidents, where possible keep in pairs. And I know it's raining, and the moors are bleak. You're all professionals. Keep it thorough. Wet is going to be the order of the day, nobody is to return dry,' he smiled. 'especially my people – Sound. Good luck!'

A journalist pushed a newspaper under Cocksworth's nose. A morning edition of the Western Morning News. Rudyard took it from him before he had the chance to read the headline reading it for himself. He shook his head in disbelief returning it to Cocksworth. He then took him to one side.

'Where do they get their information?'

'Nobody's going to take any notice of that Sir. There have been stories of strange occurrences out on Dartmoor since time dot.'

'A woman seeing a man hanged. Likely her partner. God, the woman's in hospital the consequence of one of our cars on routine. Half in and half out of a coma muttering all manner of tripe. Has someone been passing on information, that's what I'd like to know,

Steven? At the very least, we'll entertain no talk of ghosts and apparitions.'

'I think we've moved on a tad for ghosts and the supernatural to be taken seriously anymore Sir. Can't see any journalists asking us questions of that nature, can you?'

Rudyard gave him an old-fashioned look.

'I can as it happens. And I'm as open-minded on all matters concerning the supernatural as the next. But if ever the day dawns when Admiral Nelson should ever take me into his confidence, tap me on the shoulder asking me to keep an eye on George Romney and Emma Hamilton while the big man's at sea, I should not be a bit surprised, taking it as suspicion entrusted to me alone by God that the supernatural is real. As the great bard said, There are more things in heaven and earth, Horatio, than are dreamt of in your philosophy; and until that day dawns, my sound line will always be one of open-mindedness Steven.'

## Dept. of Anatomical Pathology, Medical Science Park, Plymouth 2008

Forensic pathologist Mary Poltair with her assistant Hugh McColl were finishing up their initial investigation of the three bodies found alongside the East Dart when Cocksworth entered.

'Morning, Chief Inspector. Did you have a nice day yesterday? Saw you meandering around the moors in all that rain. Luuvly hat.'

'A fruitless exercise Doctor. Should have come over for a cup of tea seeing you were dry under your forensic tarp. Find anything interesting?'

McColl unzipped the three body bags.

'Haven't finalised the post-mortem,' Poltair said. 'Skin samples have gone off for carbon dating, be a couple of days yet; but I would say that one has been in the ground since the eighteenth century. All remarkably preserved. One. How does 1980 grab you?'

'Very much indeed. Is that a whiff of aftershave coming from him?'

'That's my assistant,' Poltair said giving the man a look of disapproval. 'But look at the condition of the bodies. The skin for instance is like parchment. This one that was found under a granite boulder is spongy and corrupted. He looks as if he was attacked by something long and bladed.'

'While this one guy here,' McColl interrupted enthusiastically before Cocksworth had time to make a proper study of the first, 'is wearing the military uniform of Scotland, or at least part of it. I would say he was a high-ranking soldier. Suicide. Look at the cut marks on his wrist.'

'We can't be sure of that Hugh,' Poltair said trying to curb her assistant's enthusiasm. 'However, the wound to the neck of the third man indicates his throat was cut.'

Noticing a sheath with a knife on the instrument table next to a sword Cocksworth asked, 'Are they the culprits?'

McColl passed Cocksworth a pair of latex gloves to put on while Poltair handed him the sheathed knife. Cocksworth pulled it out and studied it. The handle was of ivory inlaid with bands of silver. The blade with its ugly cutting edge reminded him of a tin of beans that had been badly opened with a Boy Scout utility knife.

'That was around the man's waist,' Poltair said.

Cocksworth stood between McColl and Poltair sniffed the air.

'While this,' McColl said moving swiftly to the other body, 'was an official of some kind. Possibly a king's courier.'

Cocksworth was becoming agitated with Poltair's apprentice.

'And how would you know that?' Cocksworth asked.

Poltair went to the body and lifted the man's arm, then pointed out his finger.

'History Steven. This ring is a royal authority – a passport if you will. While this,' she said picking up a washed-out leather satchel, 'bears all the hallmarks of being the royal insignia of George the First. The man owning it has a Stannary parliament insignia on his jacket. And being found close to Crockern Tor, the site of the ancient Stannary parliament of Devon, and might have been of some importance. And look here, what looks like a burn to the inside of his arm is still visible. Showing black on the bone the way it does kind of indicates to me that he subjected to a vicious branding.'

Cocksworth studied the burn, 'What is shape?'

'Not sure. Although I did look out a book on matters Stannary and came across a sketch called *The Old man of Crockern*. Does that look like it could be a tattoo of an old man bent double?'

Cocksworth studied the ring before turning his attention to the satchel.

'May I?' he asked Poltair. She affirmed. Turning it over in his hands, he opened it and peered inside. The leather was soaked with black from the wet and the peat.

'Did you find anything inside?'

'Yes. A badly deteriorated parchment of vellum. I've had it sent to Plymouth University for deciphering.'

Cocksworth nodded. He moved closer to the body of the Crockern man. 'This is interesting. Did you make anything of the discolouration around the neck?'

McColl interrupted with enthusiasm, 'It has all the hallmarks of a man having been garroted. With a cord!'

'Assuming he didn't first die from the shock of the burn,' Poltair interjected. 'Hugh's right. The pain from such torture would have sent his brain into free-fall. And it wasn't a straight branding either. The branding iron had been bound to his arm making it impossible for him to remove it. I've only ever seen that done to one other human before. When I worked in London. Rough criminal gang justice. A man was found restrained with a Morphy Richards iron strapped to his bare stomach along a timer. It doesn't bear thinking about.

'No, it doesn't.' Cocksworth said trying not to imagine the terror the man would have gone through wondering what time the iron would switch itself on. This man would have suffered the same agony, he considered. 'Well, these particular crimes have nothing to do with any of what we're investigating at this moment in time.'

'Well this one is going to be,' Poltair said unzipping the body bag of a third person. 'Is this the man you're looking for?'

Cocksworth moved closer. The black and grey hair on this man's head along with his grey moustache matched that of the description given to the police for being Phileas Cluff.

'Have you his clothes?'

She emptied a black bin bag out onto a table. The shirt that Rudyard had described, blue pin stripe without a collar, the stud still in place, was bloodied down the front. Reaching into the bag she pulled out a brown anorak, a pair of brown cords with trainers. Cocksworth nodded. This had to be Cluff. When he looked at Poltair his face lit up.

Poltair read his mind. She knew him from old.

'No, you don't.'

'I was only going to ask . . .'

'Well, you can ask when I know more. I'm not saying anything until forensics have returned with the evidence,' she said adding, 'You're going to have to be patient on this one, Steven. Sorry.'

# EIGHT

## Avon and Somerset Constabulary, Portishead, Bristol 2008

*DESK SERGEANT IAN DUFFY* was trying to explain to his civilian assistant the intricacies of filling out a lost property form. He used the voice that had the most effect for grabbing a person's attention, that of Sir Winston Churchill, the prime minister that led Britain to victory during the second world war.

Fast losing patience; trying to control his emotions in spite of the much practiced method of, How was it for you, when you were first trying to learn? school of political correctness he had picked up on one of those police courses so popularly arranged by their bosses, he told him that dealing with the public from the other side of a police station desk came with experience. Furrowed brows accompanied by the shaking of head disagreed. How it should be done, did no more than inflame experienced recruits enjoying a 'day's jolly', being forced to endure by their newly dubbed chief superintendent, Sir James Kirkby – himself a product of an Oxbridge education who, being fast-tracked from point duty to inspector so rapidly he could have safely crossed the road at Cabot's Corner with his eyes shut.

To be fair to Duffy's new civilian recruit this was his student's ninth mind numbing form in two days, and it was a wonder to him that anyone could sustain the memory stamina to cope with one of those without making mistakes. Nevertheless, it would be as well if he completed the form himself if they were ever going to get home tonight.

When he answered his phone, he was momentarily off the pace understanding what was being said to him. It sounded like one of those obscure calls from a hoaxer that had got bored, deciding it would be a laugh to make a call to the police and wind them up. Coupled with the first possibility that they were wasting police time Duffy made the decision not to drag out an armed response unit on the pretext of a hostage siege. The disguised voice clearly having watched too many films – the caller attempted to muffle it with a handkerchief – went onto explain how they had taken over a school and were threatening the lives of the children attending. Another instance, he thought, where the academic achievements of a university recruit would not have the experience to disseminate a hoax call from the genuine and relay it with confidence that in his opinion it was for real. Further, that if the receiver of the call had thought otherwise, the desk sergeant would not have brought it to his attention – acting on it without question. Such a call required a rare insight, with today being the day for such a test, Duffy decided that he must act. Straining to hear the voice on the other end staying his assistant's wrist he tried to get an answer to a routine question.

'Who is this?'

Hymer had no doubt that it was for his inspector to make the call. But with no other superior to hand, it was down to him, and he would have to suffer the consequence should Duffy have fucked up misinterpreting such a call. He had no other choice but to telephone Sir James. A call he was not relishing.

He waited, his heart pounding for the recipient to pick up the phone, his lips pulled back over his teeth.

Sir James was in his garden potting shed at his home in Cleveland when he heard his mobile's rendition of the Moonlight Sonata. The vibration toppled the phone off the edge of a wooden rack that held pots dumping it gently into a bag of opened compost below. Cursing to himself, he got down on his knees and reaching down into the bag retrieved it, brushing the peat mixture from it before saying, *Kirkby*.

'Sir James?' the voice at the other end queried.

'Yes, yes, who is this?'

'DS Hymer, Sir.'

Sir James wondered what they would do when the day for his eventual retirement came. Two days into his holiday and someone wanted him already.

'Isn't there anyone there that can deal with whatever it is, Hymer?' he answered annoyed.

'I am well aware you're on your holiday,' Hymer answered conscious of the two men's status. An attack on the freedoms of people overruled sensitivities of rank. 'I'm afraid you'll have to listen to me, Sir James . . .'

He wondered if Sergeant Hymer had given any thought to calling him. 'Where in hell is your senior officer—?'

Lady Kirkby looked up at her husband, gardening gloves in one hand, a pair of secateurs with the pruned stem of a geranium in the other. His face had gone from a shade of red to ashen grey.

'What is it, dear?' she asked.

Despite his attempt to admonish the man, Hymer's words of, He's not here, shut up and listen, had forced him to obey. Then slowly, he removed the phone from his ear.

'What is it, dear?' Lady Kirkby asked once more fearing he was about to have a stroke seeing his face contort the way it had.

Sir James put his hand over the mouthpiece of the phone and whispered, 'We've terrorists in Bristol.'

Sir James tried to imagine the scenario involving schoolchildren. His memory recalled an incident in Russia, and he went cold with fear and apprehension. He had no reason to doubt what Hymer had told him as being anything other than what it was, and he felt foolish for talking to the man the way he had. The responsibility for the lives of a school full of children had dropped onto his patch; his reputation as a one-time good cop was to be put on the line. This was what his whole life's work had come down to. Everything he had learned. All his experiences of running the force from the top down would count for nothing if he got this wrong. He was the man in charge that would oversee the police operation. The chance that no one would be injured or killed was a tall order with no shortage of people washing their hands if he got it wrong – passing blame – his knighthood a sham. He would have to meet this challenge head on.

His brain kicked into gear.

'I'll be in straightaway, Hymer. Thank you for calling me. You did the right thing – And Sergeant. Put a call out for the Acting Chief Constable while you're looking for Grantley.'

Not having had the chance to change out of his garden leave clothes, Sir James hurried through the hastily set-up operations room at police headquarters. Wearing a dirty old pair of dark brown corduroy trousers, a navy-blue seaman's cap and an old blue collarless shirt, he trod garden mud into the carpet. Still holding the dead pot plant given him by Lady Kirkby to dump on the compost heap in his hands, he tried passing it to one of the WPCs. No takers were forthcoming.

'Goode! Goode, where are you? Isn't he back yet?' Sir James asked impatiently turning to Hymer.

He was.

Hymer had called Goode's dentist getting him dragged out of the chair having root canal work, telling the dental receptionist that he was to return to the station as a matter of urgency.

Spitting amalgam and pieces of cotton wool bud the dentist had not had the chance to remove from his mouth, Goode had not wasted a second getting a preliminary assessment from Hymer. He had managed to get some witness statements. But they were scant. Calls from officials were coming in thick and fast in the last hour from the Deputy Chief Constable of the United Kingdom, the home secretary, and a person with the name of Gerald Ford from the British intelligence counter terrorism branch; all asking the same questions:

*What was going on? Who was in charge? What was the cost to the taxpayer? Contain and do nothing until experts have had the chance to assess the situation properly.*

That last one – by way of an order – came from the Home Secretary; was to Goode, a typical reaction from a government of the day:

*Do nothing that will make the situation worse.*

Presumably, Goode thought until they'd had the chance to organise a committee with the prime minister under the auspices of Cabinet Office Briefing Room A. In the meantime, if anything did go wrong an endless queue of politicians and media would be asking why the police hadn't done something when they knew the possible outcome of doing nothing. Goode could hear the words in his head:

When we said do nothing, we didn't mean, literally!

This was going to be a no-win situation with people's lives on the line. More especially that it was a school that had come under siege and children were involved. What sickened Goode more than anything else was that not one person from government had had the decency to inquire if any children had been injured or killed while the terrorists were making themselves comfortable. It was only a matter of time, he thought, before calls started coming in from anxious and frightened parents. As things stood, he had nothing to say to alleviate their fears. For Stanners' & Haberdashers', not in the same educational league as Merchant Taylors' or Haberdashers' Aske's in London; but nonetheless as elitist, with children coming from well-to-do families that were doing rather well financially and wanting an education outside of London for their 'little darlings'. Like all hostage sieges it would be a waiting game until the leader whoever he was made demands. What they might be, at this stage with nothing else to go on, he couldn't imagine?

'Over here, Sir James.' Goode said when he saw the Chief Superintendent.

Goode had initiated the nuts and bolts of the operation in readiness for his certain replacement by re-commandeering the large Perspex planning screen from the lecture room; tearing off the Blu-Tacked lecture notes on Diversity Within The Force; replacing it with a single map of Bristol city and its surrounding suburbs, he marked out the school perimeter with a solid red line.

'This is a right mess, Goode,' Sir James said greeting him.

'I've had the area in and around the school sealed off Sir. All emergency services have been told to stand by.' He had taken the decision to call in an early response team with a firearm unit, as a matter of procedure.

'Good work. Do we know who they are and what they're doing? Because if we don't, careers could be in jeopardy. And, not yet is an answer you'd like to reconsider, Goode.'

The direct verbal response to the man that had begun to organise a team of police officers like a military operation in the time it would have taken most to wonder what colour marker pen they should be using for the white board might have been a bit over the top. Sir James wished he'd phrased the question with a little more tact.

'I'd be lying to you if I gave consideration to that Sir James.'

'All right, Goode. As you are. Ah, Merriweather,' Sir James said turning to greet the acting chief superintendent with a shake of the hand. Merriweather walked into the operations room back from a secondment. 'How was Manchester?'

'Well enough, Sir James. How are you, Grant?' Merriweather said turning to Goode.

Goode wasn't a particular fan of Merriweather. To him, he was the epitome of all career policemen that always thought they knew best in whatever situation they encountered. Textbook policing. A copper that had the knack of being able to pass blame when he screwed up, making it stick elsewhere without it sliding down the wall. An overused word, he thought, but Teflon coated was a good phrase for the hypothetical cloaks they sported about their shoulders.

Even though Goode had done all preliminary work in readiness, he knew his rank would get him no further in this incident than that of an assistant. Protocol demanded a senior officer, at least to the standing of chief super; and that he, a chief inspector would have to stand in someone else's shadow. An acting officer sprang to mind. Not that Merriweather was necessarily unsuitable, he was more than qualified; but that was not the point. Sir James's appointee, as far as he guessed, likely a member of the same lodge, would make sure that Merriweather would not remain 'acting' too long after a successful outcome in an operation of this magnitude. An operation that would not depend on his expertise as much as that of professionals on the ground that would be made available to him as and when. It would not have been the first time, but he thought that the higher ranks relished a major incident or two. Always good for careers.

He ignored Merriweather's hand, smiling and nodding at him instead.

Both felt the same for each other.

'Well enough, Sir. As you can see the board's empty. Not much to report yet, but that'll soon change, likely sooner than later.'

Sir James smiled mindful of both men's career rivalries. He was determined with both working together that they might gain a better understanding of each other.

'I'm placing Merriweather in charge with you as his number two. Andy has been working alongside an old colleague of mine in Manchester,' Sir James said to Goode. 'Thought it would do him good to get away from Bristol for a while.'

Merriweather did not take to this platitude directed at him, taking it that perhaps he was not up to the job of acting chief superintendent; and that he had needed to gain some extra experience in areas that were more demanding than Bristol. As if Avon and Somerset did not have its own problems. As for Manchester and their like, he never did see them as being particularly beneficial to his career.

'Equally Goode,' he said adding. 'You can learn a lot from Andy I'm sure.'

'I'm sure Sir James,' Goode replied muttering to himself. How to play golf and slope shoulders.

'I believe you've had some experience of sieges before, Goode?'

Merriweather took notice of what Goode would say without showing a particular interest. Instead he looked around the operations room at what was going on thinking to himself how he would have better organised it.

'Only the one, Sir James,' he said watching Merriweather. 'Certainly not on this scale. In London. During the riots in 1999. Anti-capitalists decided to take over the Corn Exchange. Wasn't in the same league, although we did have to call in the SAS when they threatened to kill some hostages. They tend toward the messy Sir.'

Sir James impressed by Goode's modesty, but not his use of the word, 'messy'. He changed the subject. 'Right. Job in hand. You've had calls Grantley?'

'The deputy chief constable, and the home secretary. All asking to speak with you as a matter of urgency. Gave them a brief of what I had. home secretary Blunt said he'd call back. Oh, yes, nearly forgot. MI5, as well.'

Goode hoped that Merriweather knew what professionals to bring in. He had upset more fellow officers than enough during his short career in the force since university. Sir James had made a mistake with this appointment of him he was sure, but he was going to have to live with it.

A WPC came in asking if the chief super was about.

'MI5? Great. Nice to know they're on the case.' He looked up. 'Yes here. What is it constable?'

'It's the home secretary on the phone for you Sir James. In your office,' she smiled and turned to leave.

'Tell him I'll be right with him. Hang on, before you go. W-P-Ceeee—?'

'Cooper Sir James.'

'Of course, Cooper. Have the builders finished re-tiling the showers yet, Geraldine?'

'Only the ladies Sir James,' impressed he remembered her name.

'That'll do. Can you spare me a minute constable? I need someone to collect my spare uniform from my office and bring it down to me. Feeling a bit Monty Don on a bad day . . . and somebody . . . please find a home for this damn pot,' he said placing it on a desk. 'Andy, take Blunt's call, you're in charge. Nothing like hitting the ground running, eh, Grantley?' he said turning to Goode.

DC Helen Moyle was closing her handbag when her phone rang. Hurriedly placing the bag on the floor, she picked it up then listened. Clamping her hand over the mouthpiece she called across to Sir James as he was leaving the operations room.

'BBC Sir James,' she called across to him.

Sir James came back and went to take the call, then thought better of it.

'Tell them there'll be a press conference later.'

She relayed his response then replacing the phone immediately picked it up for another call. Sir James waited.

'Guardian newspaper Sir James,' she whispered before returning to the caller, 'There'll be a press conference later today—'

Sir James butted in.

'I said, later. Not later today, Helen.' He noticed her hand. Not that he had noticed it before, he wasn't on the shop floor that much. A white scar, almost invisible showed enough for him to see.

She saw him looking at her.

"That Sir. My cross to bear. Caught it on the sharp end of a javelin taking it out of its cover.' He looked quizzically at her. 'I'm a sports coach in my spare time Sir.' He smiled and nodded.

'Okay Helen, let's go.' He left the operation room with Cooper, leaving Moyle to make the necessary excuses to the Guardian.

Hymer sat at his desk opposite Goode when his phone rang. He was in no mood to make a wrong decision while Sir James was in the vicinity and indicated to the caller that he would pass him over to his chief inspector.

Goode looked at him annoyed that he hadn't given him any option before taking the phone off of him. 'Who is it?' he whispered.

'DCI Cocksworth, Devon & Cornwall,' Hymer whispered back.

'God, what do they want? Haven't they heard? Better give it to me then.'

'Chief Inspector. Nice to hear from you. Haven't much time, bit of a panic on. What can I do for you?'

He listened intently. When he had finished, he passed the phone back to Hymer.

'Problem Sir?'

'Not sure,' he thought for a second before answering. 'You know this Jackie Forbes business, well, they've found her alive by all accounts. And this is the weird bit. Buried near where they were camping, three bodies, two in the river and the other below a granite ledge. Two of no real interest to us, having been carbon dated to the eighteenth century. The third ticks all the boxes for being our Cluff.'

'She murdered him, then?'

'Forensics having decided *how* he died, but it could be she-what-done-it.'

'Unless it's Cluff's father,' Hymer added as an afterthought.

'That's stretching a coincidence even by your standards Hymer. The point is with this body turning up after all this time . . . where they'd happened to pitch a tent for the night would be right for her being the murderer.'

'Planned that way?'

Helen Moyle took a call then looked hesitantly across at Goode. 'What?'

He reminded her what Sir James had said reference press statements given later.

'It's not that Sir. It's Devon and Cornwall again. They've got a package addressed to us, apparently sent to the BBC in Plymouth. Because of its damage they couldn't help reading it. It's a letter. An ultimatum to the Prince of Wales to relinquish the duchy of Cornwall. Thought you might like to know.'

'Are they the same consequences we have in Bristol now I wonder? Who sent it?' Goode asked sceptical of threatening packages and letters being anonymous.

'*The Democratic Republic for Cornwall.*'

# NINE
## Plymouth Hospital, Devon 2008

*ALTHOUGH HE WAS UNDER* implicit instructions not to mention that they had found Cluff's body, Waverley had been sent to speak with Forbes as a matter of urgency. There was a possibility that his murderer was still roaming the moor. Accompanying the nurse, she gently knocked on the door of the single room before opening it. She looked in making sure she was decent, then ushered him in when she saw she was. She was half asleep.

'The doctor said that you can have five minutes,' the nurse said to Waverley. 'First sign of stress, and you call me. Understand?' He nodded. 'She's had a shock and is muttering all manner of things. Most will be nonsense . . . well, I suppose you know what you're doing?' She leant over and whispered to her. 'Jackie, policeman here wants to ask you some questions, are you up to answering them?'

She opened her eyes immediately asking if they'd found Phil.

'Call me when you're done. I'm down the corridor.'

She left him and he pulled up a chair and sat down beside her bed.

'Hello, Miss Forbes. I'm Detective Sergeant Able Waverley. I've a few questions I'd like to ask you regarding Phileas.' She opened her eyes, but he couldn't be sure she had heard him. 'I've spoken with the police officers that found you. They mentioned that you spoke of a hanging. Can you explain?'

'What would I be doing in a place calling itself BODNIM? Wrong pronunciation for starters.'

Waverley was puzzled by her sudden outburst.

'Bodnim! Don't you mean, Bodmin? You saw your boyfriend being hanged at Bodnim; I mean Bodmin?'

She shook her head.

'No, you don't understand. He had wandered off with the man. King James the Third. When they read him out his crime, that of murdering Joshua Timmins, and they were about to hang him.'

Waverley thought. He might be wrong. But didn't history teach him another was on the throne in 1716. He couldn't be a hundred percent sure, but he didn't think there ever had been a King James the Third. He would have been a Stuart if there had been. To his knowledge, the last Stuart monarch was Anne. He mentioned surely it was the Hanoverian German, George the First on the throne then.

'Not where I've been, he wasn't,' she added fully conscious now with surety.

'And where might that have been, Jackie?' he asked trying not to sound too cynical.

'Well, I was back in time, but not the time that would have put a James the Third on the throne of England, I was in another,' she said.

Waverley hesitated. He was having trouble understanding what she was implying. Her eyes were closed now as if she was reliving the moment. She opened them and studied his face.

'Are you the policeman that found me?' He shook his head no. She continued, 'Phil went with him, you see. I think he must have been an official of some sort.'

'*An official.* What makes you say that?'

'He was waiting to be hanged; they let me speak with him. On his jacket he had an embroidered emblem.'

'An emblem. What sort of emblem?'

'On his jacket, it was leather with fur trimmings, he had the words Devon Stannary Parliament embroidered in gold thread over a red background of a bent-up man. I guessed he was someone of importance. They hanged him for the murder of a Stannary officer from another county.'

'Did any other conversation pass between you and the man they were hanging?'

'At first, I told the prison official that I was his wife, he must have thought I was referring to the condemned man. Then I asked him what had become of Phil.'

She was beginning to doze off.

'And what did he say to that?'

'He had a blank expression on his face like he didn't know what I was talking about. Then they pushed me off the scaffold.'

She broke down and started to cry. Waverley looked anxiously around in case the nurse heard her. This was important and he needed to know more before he called them back in. He sat closer to Jackie. She reached out and took a tissue from a box on the cabinet by her bedside. Wiping her eyes, she continued:

'A small boy and girl pulled a box he was standing on out from under him. He swung in the air, I heard him gag, watched him tremor, then that it was all over . . . *Hanged!*'

He tried another line of questioning.

'When you were on the moors; when your Phil went with this man, can you recall what direction they went? Was it further out onto the moors, if so what direction?'

'I couldn't say. Though what difference that makes—'

'Because it might help us. If he did go off with this mysterious stranger, we would be able to track him.'

She thought what had happened to her. For the first time since this nightmare had begun someone was talking to her.

'They headed toward Princetown. There's a television mast up there, isn't there?' He nodded that there was. 'With a light on top?'

He was at a point where he was going to have to be more direct with her. He laid his cards on the table.

'Jackie, I think that's not the whole of the story is it? Or at least the part where Phil went with this man. The man went on his own didn't he, leaving Phil with you.'

She was stunned. He had not listened to a word she had said.

'I believe you had an argument with Mr. Cluff then murdered him. I have to tell you that we found a body answering the description of Phileas Cluff at a tinner's hut you were camped on. Can you account for that, Jackie? Only as I see it, you were the only person there. He couldn't have walked off. You were the last person to see him alive, and by implication, you are his murderer.'

Waverley had to admit to himself that she had the look on her face of someone that was confused by what he had implied. She was not stupid. He had deliberately put the seed into her head that he thought it was she, and she clearly had the look of someone wondering if she, unbeknown to her sense of rationality, had committed his murder without realising. She laughed hysterically. The shaking of her head in disbelief mirrored hard with her lips that could utter no words. Her long dark brown hair passing back and forth across her face, revealing it in phases before she stopped and brushed it away from her eyes. Her forehead wet with perspiration.

'What you are saying is absolutely ridiculous,' she eventually replied. 'I'm a sane businesswoman. I can't account for what I saw. If I did murder Phil, then I think I would have remembered don't you? Then there's a motive, or lack of it in this case. We were lovers. We'd talked of marriage. Why would I have murdered him when we had so much going for each other?'

Tears were in her eyes. She reached to her bedside table and took another tissue from the box blowing her nose and wiping her eyes once again. He was not entirely convinced with her story. But that story of a hanging from the eighteenth century was intriguing. And with that as part evidence in a court of law, she would not have a cat in a hat's chance of an acquittal.

'If you found his body where you say you did, then it could only have been the stranger that killed him after he went with him. As to him being the same man I saw hanged, that part I cannot explain.'

This woman was either delusional or a good storyteller. To his mind she was covering up for what did happen. She and Cluff had had an argument and he had walked off, or worse, she had lost her temper and killed him burying his body in a bog thinking there would be little chance that he would ever be found. Then the realisation of what she had done. The trauma of it all, left in the dark on her own in the middle of Dartmoor – it was small wonder she was in the state she was. Though she was still sane enough to stick to her story of a ghost. Dartmoor had a reputation for spiriting up apparitions. Unless the stranger she spoke, was nobody in particular, stalking the moors looking to murder anyone that came his way. But why would Cluff walk away with a complete stranger. Fortunately, for him, whether she was a liar, or plain delusional would be for others to decide.

'In 1716. In a place called *Bodnim*, I don't think so. Jackie Forbes, I'm arresting you for the murder . . .'

## Devon & Cornwall Constabulary, (Plymouth Central Sector), Plymouth 2008

'We have procedures, Sergeant. Procedures you are fully aware of. One of those is going into a hospital ward of a sick person and arresting them. As if it wasn't hard enough getting permission to interview her in the first place. What were you thinking?'

'I was thinking nothing but how things were looking. Personally, I'm not convinced she murdered Cluff, but with the evidence the way it stood, what other choice did I have *but* to arrest her?' Waverley affirmed.

Cocksworth was only relieved he had come into the hospital ward in time to his sergeant carrying out her arrest. What the papers would have made of it didn't bear thinking about. To say nothing of Rudyard, who, not being an advocate of bedside interviews having witnessed people with serious injuries being dragged out of hospital in foreign climes, suffering beatings and torture, would have likely seen the pair of their arses for a sound kicking.

'The choice you had was to have called me first. All right, her explanations were clearly off the wall. But if anyone was a candidate for taking their own life, then that charge of murder might have just done it for her?'

'At least she would have been under supervision from one of our officers.'

'*What!* Prison custody. Get real Waverley. Half asleep security staff would take it as a chore looking in on her every three hours, let alone suicide watches every twenty minutes. Suicide watch, don't make me laugh!'

Waverley had his mouth open to protest, but Cocksworth was not finished yet.

'And there's something you're overlooking. Lack of evidence. You might think she's as guilty as sin, but we're unlikely to find any concrete evidence. Poltair told you that. She found nothing incriminating on her clothes. No blood spats, no saliva. not his or hers. Only semen.'

For all the inspector said, Waverley was still sure he had done the right thing by attempting to arrest her. She was only suffering from exhaustion for God's sake, not multiple wounds from being run down. But at the end of the day, Cocksworth was in charge, and he had to accept things as they stood.

## Davy Masonic Hall, Plymouth 2008

The following day Rudyard called a press conference set for 8.30 am. The recent search for the barrister Phileas Cluff, with the finding of a man hanging in Wistman's Wood had not turned out as expected. A body answering the description of Cluff had been found, not at the end of a rope, but in a bog. While that of the hanged man was of no consequence.

The conference room at Devon and Cornwall police headquarters was too small for the interest this case had now generated, he had hired a hall. Rudyard suggested that Cocksworth open proceedings.

Cocksworth stood up. What passed as a smile showed in his face, but not for long. He studied the audience for any that he recognised. One or two. Regional journalists from the newspapers and television he had had dealings over the years. To his left, on one of three trestle tables locked together in front of assembly, sat Rudyard. His cap of office strategically placed on display in front of him. Next to him, a female police support officer acting as secretary to take notes, a blank pad in front of her. A largish woman in her thirties with an identity tag around her neck. To Cocksworth's right, sat DS Waverley. Still convinced of Forbes's guilt. Next to him the Devon and Cornwall police lawyer. A middle aged, grey haired man sporting a bristling moustache with a pompous expression and an expensive hand tailored grey suit, that Cocksworth had to reluctantly admit to himself did go well with his tan. A constable was putting out jugs of water and glasses while Cocksworth wondered how many wedding breakfasts these trestles had seen.

'Good afternoon, ladies and gentlemen,' Cocksworth announced by way of invitation. 'Thank you for attending at such short notice. I know you've been waiting patiently for a statement.' He closed his eyes from the flash of cameras that blinded him temporarily. A movement of TV camera crews moving forward began recording. 'For those of you who don't know me, I'm Detective Chief Inspector Steven Cocksworth and I'm officer-in-charge. And for those of you who don't know this man,' he pointed to his right, 'my boss, Chief Superintendent Irvin Rudyard . . .'

Smiles as well as the odd mutter of acknowledgement went around members of the press. Most needed no introduction to the ex-Royal Naval officer turned policeman. His style, charisma and plain old-fashioned standards had turned the Devon and Cornwall constabulary from a run-of-the-mill one to something special. The man himself held in regard by (not all) those at the Home Office; was likely in line for a knighthood.

'. . . Yes, thank you . . . thank you, ladies and gentlemen, the chief inspector is aware of your commitment to honest journalism when it comes to relaying news items of interest to the public. Now, we will try and answer any questions that you may have regarding the recent discovery of what we believe to be the body of the barrister Phileas Cluff as well as those of the two bodies from the eighteenth-century close by, that are,' he smiled, 'and for the moment all coincidental to these inquiries. *Chief Superintendent.*'

Rudyard rose to his feet and thanked Cocksworth. He had barely begun when a voice from the back of the room shouted out once more:

'Are you going to call in, Jonathan Creek, Chief Superintendent?'

The assembly laughed. Their mood reflecting relaxed anticipation for some good entertainment. Rudyard was not impressed. He stared at them with an expectation that someone would own up. He was not surprised when they didn't. Nor was he going to comment or rise to any uncalled-for outburst.

'Thank you, whoever that gentlemen were, and no. Let's keep this meeting on a sound footing, shall we? In anticipation of any sympathetic questions as to the well-being of Miss Jackie Forbes that you might be champing at the bit to ask, I should like to pre-empt them and say the lady in question is making good progress after our officers found her out on the moors, and who, hopefully will be able to afford us some assistance over the discovery of one of the aforementioned bodies when she has fully recovered.'

There were murmurings of belated agreement that it was he that first mentioned the well-being of Jackie Forbes. Rudyard had with purpose deflated their egos that strangers lost out on the moors could die.

'As to the bodies my colleague mentioned, we are in the embarrassing position of having initially lost two, found four with three dead. The one suspected of being Mr. Cluff, we are waiting forensic and DNA confirmation. The other two are the remains from the eighteenth-century. Obviously, nothing to do with the later find. You will understand that for that reason I cannot comment or speculate as to the cause of the man in question's death. What I will say is that an inquiry into it is our number one priority.'

A reporter from BBC Spotlight in the Southwest asked the question:

'The police think he was murdered. Is that your considered personal opinion Sir?'

Rudyard was not going to be drawn on his own view.

He answered succinctly, 'We cannot rule out anything at this time. As I mentioned we are awaiting DNA results.'

'Only a man was supposed to have gone missing on the moors in the 1980s, he was also a barrister, rumoured the same name as your body of Cluff. Are they related?' the *Spotlight* journalist came straight back at him without drawing breath.

Rudyard looked toward Cocksworth. He needed assistance to answer that one.

'That is something we are aware of,' Cocksworth came in, 'but as to him being Cluff's father – I assume that is what you are driving at . . . *coincidence?* or *speculation?* We cannot say. Neither will we rule it out. If you have further information you think might be of use regarding any relationship, we'd very much like to hear from you.' She nodded that she couldn't. 'DNA,' Cocksworth continued, 'along with toxicology assessments may establish more. By the way, the reason I ask if the media have any information is because paper records from that time are incomplete due to a fire and a need to relocate.'

Another question, this time from Joe Treadway, of the Western Morning News. He had a bruise to the side of his cheek.

Rudyard immediately stood and apologised for his wrongful arrest. Roars of laughter from his peers as to it not being the first time; drunk and disorderly springing to minds.

'Goes with the territory,' Treadway said standing smiling. 'But thank you for mentioning it. I won't be pressing charges.'

Rudyard, although relieved, knew it might come with a future price tag. He smiled, 'Your question, Mr. Treadway.'

'How can you match DNA from one body without the existence of another for comparison?'

Cocksworth looked to Rudyard who nodded at him to answer the question before sitting down.

'You are talking of Cluff's DNA I assume?' Treadway nodded. 'Current practice within the legal profession is that DNA is held by their employers, as it is of the police and security forces in line with professional codes of practice. It is that DNA that will be used for comparison.'

'I'd heard Forbes mention to the police that she had been back in time. Can you treat anything she says seriously?' Treadway asked ignoring Cocksworth who was still standing.

An immediate commotion from laptops and mobile phone

activity came as their operators went into the world of hyperspace sending out voice and e-mails to their respective organisations at this revelation from the questioner and where he had sourced such information.

Rudyard with a furrowed brow looked at Cocksworth. He had an expression that asked, *What was all that about?*

Cocksworth, who agreed with his Sergeant's assessment of events by Forbes regarding her going back in time as the ramblings of a woman traumatised by her experience, had failed to mention such a revelation to his boss. He regretted his decision. Rudyard having that knowledge would have been able to dismiss such wild speculation as fanciful.

'You might have mentioned that earlier to me Steven,' Rudyard whispered to him.

A reporter from The Sun, not having his head buried in his laptop, an exponent in the art of lip-reading and hand-sign language to those such challenged watched the conversation. A man that had used this skill extensively when conferences between police and journalists – better still with politicians – was questionable. Tony Noyon was the mythical fly on the wall.

Rudyard shook his head after making his statement to Cocksworth, then, standing up, turned to back to Cocksworth saying in a voice for all to hear:

'And which one of them did you say was three sheets in the wind, Chief Inspector?'

To Cocksworth's relief the audience joined in Rudyard's witticism. They might have got away with not having to further the *Sun*'s man's opinion.

'Any more questions?' Cocksworth asked seeking out Treadway as the idiot in question, that clearly having been privy to a witness statement from a person suffering shock and exhaustion should have had the sense to disregard it. Seeing no one else, he called the conference at an end when the reporter from The Sun stood up introducing himself.

'You're a long way from home, Mr. Noyon?' Rudyard stated. Noyon nodded and smiled. 'None the less welcome I'll one last question Sir?'

'Thank you, Chief Superintendent. Following on from Mr. Treadway's question. Whether it is to the police's liking or not with regard to Jackie Forbes and Phileas Cluff seeing an apparition. Please forgive me if I appear to be in Mr. Treadway's camp, but did Forbes say these things or not?'

For the second time away went the laptops and phones. Rudyard gave Cocksworth a sidelong look and once again shook his head. Recovering composure, he said:

'Anyone else in from the Fortean Times? Only I was rather hoping for some sound and sensible questions at this conference. Alas, I am to be disappointed. I would have thought the discovery of bodies from the eighteen-century would have been enough for most of you, instead of which, the concerns of the shadowy world of the supernatural is of more importance. Can I get it into your heads that contrary to what any of you have heard, or think you have, wild speculation will serve the interests of no one? And whilst I know that Dartmoor in particular, and Devon in general, are not what some of you people from the big cities regard as civilised; and might like to think historically as places of legend,' he smiled. 'I'm as open-minded as the next man; but might I remind you that this is the twenty-first century and will enhance nobody's reputation as serious journalists following this path of nonsense. You are professionals after all. The westcountry is no longer the land of the piskie, the ghoulie or the ghostie. Headless horsemen are not galloping the lanes in search of virgins, and Old Clooty is not leading a pack of fire-breathing hounds across the moors on stormy nights. I wish he did. It would be welcome relief from the weekend night-time drug dealing, drinking and fighting in Union Street that we have to contend with regularity. Such stories that Mr. Treadway and Mr. Noyon might enjoy should be consigned to waste bins outside souvenir shops.' He sighed an expression of boredom on his face. 'If that's all.'

'Just an observation Sir,' the man from the *Sun* came back. 'Thank you for reminding us that we are all professionals. . . .'

Rudyard sighed and subconsciously read the headings his WPC had written on her notebook,

CLUFF DNA.

RELATED TO THE BODY FOUND. APPARITION.

LINKS

with accompanying notes in shorthand on her notepad.

' . . . But do you think there could be a connection between Forbes and Cluff with their coming from Bristol, and a siege that has broken there?'

A resonance of voices broke the silence in the room before dying away as Rudyard began answering.

'That's an interesting slant, Mr. Noyon,' Rudyard said adding, 'Not one we will be giving any special consideration. Obviously, the hostage situation in Bristol didn't kick off until yesterday. Of course, we will be looking into aspects of it if for no other reason than members of the public living in the westcountry may well have relatives at the school needing assistance. Does that answer your question, Mr. Noyon?'

'Only inasmuch as extending the siege further afield to whoever is behind it adding leverage to the hostage takers demands. It is not beyond the realms of possibility that Cluff and Forbes might well have some connection with that siege. Rumours are that the hostage takers are Cornish nationalists. Perhaps Cluff and company are terrorists in the westcountry; or if not, agents working on the government's behalf; working for them on behalf of the the duchy of Cornwall.

Questions came in thick and fast at these revelations. Anything news-wise that would rock the monarchy was always welcome in a media hungry world. More so where the Prince of Wales was concerned. Cocksworth tried to bring order to the situation well aware that such issues were sensitive wherever they emanated.

'Let's keep it simple shall we,' Rudyard announced angrily. 'They were hikers exposed to the vagaries of the Dartmoor weather when circumstances overcame them, that's all. Let's not go getting ahead of ourselves. That's all. I cannot comment on information we may or may not hold that might be relevant to what is happening in Bristol. Before I draw this meeting to a close; as Bristol's hostage siege has been mentioned, I understand that families in the westcountry will have children at that school and will be worried. I can assure them that our colleagues in Avon and Somerset are doing, along with the rest of the security forces of the United Kingdom, all they can to expedite that situation . . . however. Yes, Chief Inspector.'

Cocksworth whispered to him.

'Thank you, Steven. I have been reminded by my colleague to mention to you guys that we'd appreciate the telephone numbers of Avon and Somerset be put into your respective news outlets for the benefit of any parents that are involved. One of my constables is writing them up on the white board now. Thank you for your cooperation—'

The conference descended into chaos.

'God, you'd think people would have more concern for people's feelings than trying to turn this into a two-ring circus. When we get back, my office Steven – bring Waverley with you.'

'Very good Sir.'

Cocksworth's stood up collected his papers and noticed that his

WPC taker of minutes had added,

SIEGE, CHILDREN

PARENTS. TELEPHONE NOS.

## Devon & Cornwall Constabulary, (Plymouth Central Sector), Plymouth 2008

Rudyard opened the bottom drawer to his filing cabinet and placing his brief case in it slammed it shut with his foot. Sitting down behind his desk he indicated for Cocksworth to take a seat. 'We've got a problem here. Where's Waverley?'

Rudyard was furious. Thanks to a certain mode of questioning by the press that had he known was coming he would have nipped in the bud was way out of hand. The press had blown out of all proportion the Bristol hostage situation with the murder investigation clouding the issue. And talk of the supernatural was adding another unwelcome dimension. Any link between these issues was pure conjecture. Finding Cluff's killer after that questioner had brought in a tenuous link would only complicate Avon and Somerset's problems.

'Just to cover our backs I think we might want to consider some discrete and formal inquiries regarding connections between Forbes and Cluff with regards to Cornwall and that siege. There's nothing in it I'm sure, but its having been mentioned we would be remiss if it later turned out there was a link and we had ignored it,' Rudyard said.

'I don't think you need worry over anything that came up at the conference being taken seriously; and if it does make tomorrow's headlines, well they will be chip paper the day after. We have nothing here that can possibly link our happy campers with any unrest in Cornwall I'm sure,' Cocksworth replied.

'Someone's picked up on something they should not have. If

we've coppers in this station that have got big mouths, wanting to make a few quid on the side, spreading stories of faeries and the like, I want them brought to book Steven,' Rudyard said.

'You did say you were open-minded, Sir.'

Rudyard stared back at him.

'I'm not that bloody open-minded, Steven. If that Forbes woman saw a hanging, then as far as I'm concerned it was a stunt performed by a man of flesh and blood who has a fetish for dressing in clothes from the past. If it wasn't her that done it for Cluff then it was someone from this world. Has forensics come back to us yet?'

'Only on Forbes's clothes. Waverley had a call from Dr. Poltair saying the other was on its way. It should be with us shortly.'

What Rudyard could not understand was why a detective inspector from Avon and Somerset should have his name on a package first sent to BBC Plymouth instead of an officer of similar rank in Devon. The package, after being placed in a fire-bucket of water by a security officer thinking it an explosive device, before calling out bomb disposal unit from the Navy was correct procedure and commendable. But now there was nothing of any worth left to check for fingerprints. Rudyard opened his desk drawer and handed it to him.

'Right,' he said sheepishly. 'You'd better take a look at this. Probably what that journalist was intimating at as his source I shouldn't wonder. Came to me yesterday. Should have shown it to you before the conference I know.'

Cocksworth took the wet package and pealed apart its pages. It was a weighty copy of a document with the words for the attention of a DCI Goode barely readable.

'Obviously, someone was not keen for us to see it first,' Cocksworth said going straight to the last page.

Even though the document was running smeared with ink

Cocksworth managed to make out a name. William Timmins was its author on behalf of the *Democratic Republic for Cornwall*. Skimming it – it mostly contained writings of an historical nature citing dates, kings of England, Celtic culture and the annexation of Cornwall from England – he managed to glean the gist of the document, that the Prince of Wales's ownership of Cornwall as his own private and personal fiefdom for his own personal financial gains was illegal; and not in the spirit of the English Constitution.

Rudyard shook his head.

Cocksworth continued to read. He had personally been involved with various threats of bomb attacks over the years in the southwest, mostly aimed at celebrity restaurants and holiday homes in Cornwall all of which could have turned out nasty. Fortunately, the threats had petered out. Now it was looking as if those old threats were returning with a vengeance from whoever this man was that had been under their radar. What he couldn't understand was why Bristol.

'I've called Avon and Somerset informing them that we're in possession of the package,' Rudyard said. 'Fortunately, being damaged the way it is I've been able to put off sending it to them. But we can't afford to ignore its content. What that *Sun* man was suggesting was that our two people might be involved. And that someone had taken one of them out and was now threatening to do the same with causing him to have gone to ground.'

'In a bog.'

'Quite. Well I'm not necessarily buying it, just speaking out loud thoughts. Concentrate on matters as they are, Steven. Mindful of this fresh, I was going to say evidence, but perhaps information would be a better word. That way we can keep all this to ourselves. Have we anything on this Timmins fellow? Any Cornish action groups we should be aware of. Graffiti artists with a penchant for spraying up flags of St. Piran on important buildings; looking to spread their fame

– if there are, then we need to bring them in, and quick.'

There was knock on the door. Waverley entered breathlessly.

'Sorry to keep you waiting Sir. Took a call from a DS Hymer, Avon and Somerset. They have full record of Cluff's father going missing on the moors in 1980.'

'Sit down Waverley,' Rudyard said, 'we know. Avon and Somerset's records are in the same place as ours. When the powers that be decided on a central records office for the southwest at Western-super-Mare they sent all of them there. No doubt gathering dust still waiting to be collected out from under platform four at the railway station.'

'Well what we didn't know was that his father was a barrister with the same firm his son practices now,' Waverley said adding. 'Ellick & Waites of Lincoln Inn Fields in London happen to be lawyers for the duchy of Cornwall. And have been since the eighteenth-century.'

'We didn't know that,' Cocksworth announced.

'Something else Sir. The forensic report. Cluff's blood DNA matches that held in their company data bank. His trainers don't follow suit though. They're Adidas, manufactured in the eighties. The body we believe to be Phileas Cluff has been in the ground at least twenty years.'

'At the same camp site?' Cocksworth said.

'And Dr. Poltair hasn't ruled out as much as twenty-eight.' He paused. 'The number of years ago Cluff senior supposedly went missing.'

'Suggesting the body, we have is not that of Phileas Cluff at all, but his father,' Rudyard said.

'Then Cluff's gone to ground then, Sir.'

# TEN
## Plymouth Hospital, Devon 2008

*RIFLING THROUGH HIS POCKETS* Noyon came up with £1.60 in change. Arriving at the ticket machine he cursed. The machine demanded his car's registration number. Returning to his car, memorising the number, he returned to the machine once more, inserted his money, returning once again to the car, he stuck it on the windscreen. Leaving the hospital car park, he sighed and wondered how the elderly or disabled managed this chore before noticing the terms and conditions for parking. He needn't have bothered. No fee applied between 6 pm and 6 am. That exercise in wasting time had confirmed to him that at forty-eight he was getting older; and fast approaching the way of the elderly. Looking at his watch. It was 11 pm.

The idea of breaking into the hospital in order to spy on one of its patients was making him nervous. How he was going to walk through the main entrance, into the reception then find for a lift to take him to the ninth floor. All this without a challenge by its security staff. Doubt sprang to his mind the enormity of the task.

During daylight hours, none of that would be a problem for him. The volume of traffic going in and out of the hospital, sitting in the café, buying papers, flowers, fruit and the like for their relatives, left any unauthorised visitor to go unnoticed. He noticed a patient sitting at a table in what was the closed-for-the-night café area drinking a cup of something hot from the vending machine beside of him. Wearing a blue hospital gown, he figured that with one of those he could move around unchallenged. He out set to finding one. Fortunately, the League of Friends charity shop was still open. Attracting the attention of the woman volunteer through the window about to close and turn the lights off she opened the door for him.

'Cutting it fine aren't we,' she said, adding, 'come on in, but be quick, I've a bus to catch.'

He thanked her. Among the shelves of books was a clothes rail with donated gowns. He bought a book, then, giving the idea as an afterthought, took a gown down from a clothes rail saying, *Forgot to bring one in for the wife.*

He gave the woman a ten-pound note telling her to keep the change, and with the gown wrapped in a polythene carrier bag he found the gents' toilets where he put it on. He then found the lift that would take him to the ninth floor and Jackie Forbes, adding a limp to his gait for affect.

He knew there was a story here. Joe Treadway questioning a statement made by Jackie Forbes he had overheard; that she had gone back in time; with his own lip-reading abilities convinced him that not all was right with any of this. Tales of people coming and going from future to past, whether true or not, was not the issue here, though it would fill column inches with stories of the supernatural was always going to sell newspapers. No, in this case it was the sprinkling of bodies from the past being found that added credence that intrigued him.

Of course, he thought, it may all come down to an insurance fraud. That idea had come to him some time ago. And not for the first time has a missing presumed dead scam been carried out. But why concoct such a story with time-dimensional overtones? That would hardly expedite an insurance pay out. That part did not make sense and would certainly do nothing to enhance either of their future reputations if it turned out they were found to be later innocent of criminal intent – or got caught. As far as he knew, both Cluff and Forbes had careers that were financially sound. Or so it seemed. If they were complicit in criminal fraud, Cluff would have to disappear for the rest of his life and she would not be able to join him. Insurance companies' have long memories. As a barrister, Cluff would know that. Intelligent people as them would surely come up with something better.

Unless . . .

Would an insurance company want to investigate an insurance scam that had become cross-threaded with time-travel? Paying out on a claim that would do their company's reputation irrevocable harm with such a back story. Especially if they refused to pay up because one of the parties involved had lost it; and was not capable of bringing forward a reasonable explanation of how the other had gone missing other than the story than were sticking with.

The lift stopped and the door opened. Hesitantly stepping out the door slid closed behind him. He momentarily froze. The thought that he was standing in the corridor of a hospital late evening, a trespasser, sent a tingle through him.

Oh, well, he said to himself. Get on with it.

When he had earlier called on the phone to ascertain what ward Forbes was on, the receptionist had asked if he was a relative. He had said that he was her brother. She had told him that she was on Maple Ward, floor nine, room seven. He went down the corridor, muttering seven repeatedly, when he was confronted by two arrow indicators on the wall. Half of one had been damaged, its ward name removed. The other, to its left, read Cherrytree. He took a right turn, going straight to a closed ward door and looking through guessed he was here.

He could see the nurse's station. It didn't bode well that no one was manning it. She, or he, could be doing their rounds. Turning a corner in soft shoes – coming on him, and he, with no explanation of what he was up to with the question, *And what ward have you come from?*

He made the decision to wait in the visitor area, read a magazine, drink a can of coke from the vending machine; at least he would not look as if he were up to no good, merely a patient that could not sleep. From here he could keep an eye on who was coming and going, then when he thought the coast might be clear, slip into room seven and find this Forbes woman, hoping against hope she would not scream blue murder with his intrusion.

He had no sooner removed the ring-pull from his soft drink, spraying its contents across a table where magazines and papers were lying, when the door to maple ward was flung open. Two nurses, a man and a woman, she in her thirties and he, well, Tony thought to himself, like policemen came running out passing him into the lift area leaving a waft of one that smoked and one that used perfume in their wake. He wished he had not quit smoking, cigarette smoke seemed to be everywhere since. They'd hardly had time to notice him they were in that much of a hurry. The older nurse inserted a key hanging from a chain at her waist into the lock at the side of the lift. Within seconds, it had arrived, its doors opening they were inside. Closing now the indicator showed they were descending. He went over to read the notice above the lock. He was in luck. Effectively immobilising lift access to all but medical staff by activating an over-ride facility, in this case the two of them were part of a heart-crash team needing immediate access to another floor. He would not get a better chance. With two gone there was a good chance the ward was clear.

Going through the door the nurses had come through he moved fast, his head going from side to side making quick assessment of who might see him all the time trying to think of an excuse for his being here. He was in luck, there was no one here. Hurrying down the corridor checking names on doors, passing beds with patients in the open ward asleep, some snoring, some coughing. He continued down the corridor, *Christ where's seven!* Had he missed it. He remembered. A corridor in the opposite direction. He had come down the wrong one. Approaching this new nurse's station, one was standing alongside it reading notes. He had no choice but to continue walking, praying that she would not look up at him.

Once again, his luck held. She turned her back on him going to a drugs cabinet. She had not seen him. He hurried through the corridor. Three, five, seven . . . seven. He opened the door and stepped into the room breathless. His heart was racing. There was the woman in bed. Was this Jackie Forbes? He had never seen the woman before. He looked above her bed on the wall. The name of the consultant was there, but not hers. He was going to have to assume it was she.

Studying her, he startled, her eyes were open, and she was speaking to someone. Was there a doctor or nurse in the room with them that he was unable to see in the dim light. He pushed himself flat against an alcove to hide. Such movement, that should have been quick fast was nothing of the sort. Instead it was the action of someone trying to wade through treacle. Something was happening to his body and he felt nauseas. Unable to move now, he panicked, but with none of the actions that accompanied such an emotional state. He was as a statue. He could hear but had no other sense or movement. He was in another place.

Something was happening to him that was beyond his comprehension, seriously undermining his ability to reason. Had he stepped over a line into his own death? Had the shock to his heart been too much for him? The conversation he was now listening gave him cause for concern. He was in another time and could do nothing to interact with the persons in it. He could only think that the man between him and the woman in bed was the cause of his immobility.

How someone that had not acknowledged his being in the room with them could manage that he could not imagine. Noticing that the man had a vicious wound to the back of his hand and was dressed from another time. His standing over her gave the impression they were about to indulge in some sexual play act. Not that he was any great expert in such matters. Their conversation was not sexually explicit . Theirs was an altogether different conversation. He listened intently.

Then without warning his muscles relaxed as an uncoiling spring and he found he could move once again. His journalism kicked in. Moving forward better to listen to their conversation he instinctively put his hand out to touch the man. Whether it was to attract the man's attention or pure curiosity, he could not say. Whatever it was the result was the same. His hand felt no resistance from the form going instead right through him. His heart was racing now. The unexpectedness of putting his hand inside what should have been a solid body was nothing more than an illusion.

For an instant she opened her eyes. Looking at him she was showing signs of recognition as to who he was. Quickly removing his hand from the space his hand was occupying he felt concerned that she might think he had his hand out too touch her. Judging by the look of surprise on her face, for she had now slipped back into sleep, she seems to have seen him. With talk of bodies being found on the moor both present and past coupled with what was before him now, he feared his retaining of presence in this his own time.

Doesn't a person usually realise they have been dreaming? Jackie asked herself. For if they did then such dreams involving the same person would occasionally cease regeneration. The question in her own mind now was, was she an illusion of reality in his world or he in hers? If she were his, the scenario suggested Tweedledum and Tweedledee, alongside Alice Kingsleigh finding the Red king asleep in her Wonderland: dreaming of her before she disappeared in a puff of smoke. If this fey creature was still here, then the possibility that she was in a world of reality, as she lived and understood the concept of the word, would give part weight to the philosophical argument that everything was a figment of one's own imagination – made flesh by an unreliable brain with her version of truth suspect. Using that hypothesis alone, it would be a wise woman that accepted the truth from her sleeping mind: that her past had turned out to deceive her on more than one occasion; and never be trusted. From her point of view, her sleeping mind was messing with her reality. But which was real and what was causing the messing. Had she been back in time? Was it that? Did time travel begin with dreams, emerging into a reality, and given the right circumstance, a predetermined destination by that part of the mind we were not consciously aware. Mind-dust theory was perhaps going too far, she thought. She would make an inventory of her psyche when she awoke.

She was in hospital. That much she was sure of. One of two missing people picked up by the police in a state of exhaustion and desolation, getting herself run-down by them; and all the cause of the transparent illusion standing before her. *Bastard! Bastard! Bastard!* she said to herself without looking at him. As if ignoring him, insulting him, would make him go away. But he would not.

'Why did you bring me to this if you knew this was going to happen? Looking for a man whose genes had all the attributes of brains without common sense, passing them on to his son.' She studied him in the vain hope that he would have an answer for her. Was there any point in wasting breath on someone that was quite obviously a dream? 'Why don't you return from whence you came, and leave this world and me in peace?'

Her words of dismissal were not getting through to him. The mist of time in her throat was short on clarity. She appeared to be screaming at him but all he got was a muffled sound. He could get into her dreams, but not her reality, 'What do you want of me, John Goode? And where is my husband?' she asked of him. She had remembered his name. It was a start. But now he had to depart.

Typical, she said to herself exasperated. When you want an answer to a straight question, they up and leave you. Finding it safe now to return she awoke from her slumber.

Years later he could not say how many he returned to her bedside. No longer transparent.

His form, she took at first to be a hallucinatory flashback, made whole put the fear of God into her. She put her hand to her mouth. Out on the moors, a place of legendary power and magic, people and events were never what they appear to be. She had put out of her mind any actuality that he was anything other than the 'nutter' she had first taken him to be. He was now substance.

She screamed, '*Ahhhh!*'

When he spoke, his voice calmed her outburst. An altogether different voice from first she heard it. A cross somewhere between Old English and Shakespearean. Now, although still difficult to comprehend, if she listened intently, she could get the gist of what he was saying to her. He was well-spoken and well-educated from the period of history he came. He must have been persuasive, for whatever he had said to Phil had clearly swayed him in his decision to go with him. Throwing one of the rocks used for a windbreak for the stove at the back of his head she thought at the time might have helped show him the folly of his ways and leave them in peace. But she discovered earlier on that illusions are not solid matter capable of hurt. Not that that could be put to any test, for missing his head completely, her misdirection should have damaged his shoulder had it not gone straight through him, to land quietly with a dull phlopp on the wet moorland.

'Your husband . . . ah, I'm afraid we've lost him,' he said. 'But we shall find him, be not afeared in the matter,' he continued before she had the chance to interrupt him.

She found herself saying, *That's all right then. If he's lost, then he's safe. Right?* With no expectation of an answer she shook her head and tried to drag one from him.

He looked at her trying to understand the phraseology of her words. Talking to him in the way she was, was not the English he was familiar. Cluff spoke the same. He had struggled with his vernaculars.

'He walked away before we had the chance to explain,' he said.

'There's a surprise, innit,' she said angrily, 'and there's that "we" once more.'

'We were deceived co-conspirators in a plot not of our making. It went badly wrong. I'm lost in the wrong time, while your husband is in another trying to help the wrong me.'

'Well, you got the bit of it going badly wrong right. Not just for you, but us as well. Why were we dragged into your plot, that's what I'd like to know?'

She hesitated studying closer that she might get more of a clue as to what was going on and how she and Phil might have got involved in all of this, forming the conclusion that it was something to do with his father. That or some bizarre reality television show, staged for other's amusement. God, that would have been sick given the circumstances of the man being hanged in front of her own eyes, and that, for some reason did not recognise that it was her on the gallows when she sought an answer to her question as to what became of Phil. Returning from a choking death in 1700, wanting a resolution in 2008. He was on her playing field now, and she would call the shots.

'Were you responsible for the disappearance of Mr. Cluff's father as well?' she demanded of him. The thought having entered her head with no apparent reason. Was that any doing of yours? If you can cheat the hangman with your God-given power for resurrection, can you not restore the status quo and return my fiancé . . . my husband to me,' she reminded herself. 'And yourself to your own time?'

She waited for his answer. When it came, it came as a bombshell.

'That was not me,' he said. 'That was a different me hanged on the other side of the drape. The lawyer was no more able to obtain an acquittal for me than his father before him—'

'His father defended you. Then himself. What would have been the cost of that for lawyer's fees I ask myself?' John Goode smiled. So, laughter is seen up and down the centuries she thought to her. 'Then perhaps you didn't deserve one, died on this side of your drape. How do I know you're innocent? Did that veil of time have any more faith in your supposed innocence than the law that sent you to your Maker on the other?'

'I never did get as far as my Maker . . .'

'Sent you back, did He?' She remembered something. When she was in BODNIM. '*Who is the king?*'

'The king?'

'Yes. Out of curiosity, who is the king, damn you?' He stared at her. 'Or don't you recognise what a king is?'

'Don't insult my intelligence woman. I have blue blood of a queen coursing through my veins. But for my father's false accusations of my mother's supposed infidelity in this half world of madness history will acknowledge I have a king's too.'

He turned his back to her. Going to the ward window he rested his hands on the sill and looked out. His head bowed now; he shook slowly from side to side. She had painfully touched hurt him.

This might have been too much information, she thought.

'I'm sorry,' she said. 'Please continue. I think we've established you're educated enough to know what a king is, but you still haven't answered the question.'

'King James the Third,' he said turning away from the window to face her. 'I was sentenced and executed at the pleasure of a Stuart.' He continued. 'None of which has helped the situation – not in that world, nor this one, as you will soon come to realise. Is death on *your* horizon, madam . . . ?'

'Death! Whose?'

'I cannot say for any certainty, for I died in 1716; and from that time all future events ceased for me. I have no knowledge of your world. I work from a darkness. I believe evidence exists that will substantiate my innocence.'

'An ideology,' she replied. 'History is littered with what was, or what might have been. Who lived and who died? There's nothing new in that. And to coin a phrase, You cannot turn the clock back.' He was quiet. Facing her his expression said something different and she got it. 'You can, can't you—?'

'Joshua Timmins was an officer of the Cornish Stannary Parliament. A good man turned sour. Tortured and murdered by the king . . .'

'James the Third?' she stated cynically.

'No. George the First.'

'*George!* The Hanoverian? Make your mind up man. Was it a Catholic or a Protestant on the throne of England?'

'Joshua Timmins has returned to your world seeking what he sees as revenge. He is wrong to do that. He has mistaken justice for revenge. He should have died from his suffering, the opposite happened. He lived in another time, and one I am not guilty for his death in; neither can I exist in both forever. For this encroachment is the beginning. Your world is at the point of tipping chaos and although the clock cannot be turned back in this world, it has yet to be wound in another. He is me, mine, and your last hope. We desperately need a lawyer from your time and Phileas Cluff has the pedigree.'

Noyon was close to collapse when his brain took control of his mind preventing him from making an exhibition of himself by passing out on the floor in front of her.

He was totally confused as to know what to make of any of what he had heard. Cluff was alive, that much he had established. But where was he? According to Miss Forbes's visitor he was, Lost in time. With that weirdo following me, I'd want to be lost too, he thought. Neither of them appeared to have recognised he was in the room with them overhearing their conversation. How could that be? Or had they? Were they plotting? Was this all part of some insurance scam subterfuge for his benefit? If it was, they were good, very good. The parties concerned needing a witness for a story that was so far-fetched that no insurance company would want to contest for any longer than they had to; that as an alternative to what was a plain and simple missing person, an assumed dead claim they would have to pay out on. That was something he was going to have to consider. In the meantime, *Jesus*, he said to himself, *It's getting light*. He was going to have to get out before any nurses on a shift change wanted to know what he was doing and who he was. Back to the main entrance, get a coffee. The café would be open. Maybe some breakfast. He looked at Jackie one more time. She was asleep now. The Ghost of Christmas past now gone and seeing him standing over her instead she might well scream the place down. When she did it took him by surprise. He backed into the alcove once again and watched her take up a glass of water and sip it. Then replacing it on the bedside cabinet she laid her head back down on the pillar, striking the back rail of the bed. Tears were in her eyes. Whether it was the pain from the hit he could not say. She reached across to where she had placed her glass and took out a paper tissue from its box and began wiping her eyes. Then she saw him.

With a broad grin, he embarrassingly smiled at her.

'Who the hell are you and what are you doing in my room? *NURSE!'*

He stepped out of the alcove and opened the door.

'Sorry miss must 'ave taken a wrong turn. Looking for the wife.'

Closing it behind him he breathed a sigh of relief. All clear, he hurried back the way he had come what seemed like hours before and back to the lift. He took the hospital gown off and put it over his arm. With people coming into the wards he no longer saw the need to act the patient. The lift doors opened, and he stepped in pressing the down arrow button The doors closed immediately and the lift began its descent. Stepping out on the ground floor he hurried on down the corridor towards reception. The League of Friends shop was opening. He went in donating back the gown. An elderly gentlemen volunteer thanked him giving him a leaflet explaining how the League always needed help and donations. He smiled at him and put his hand in his pocket pulling out what he thought was a five-pound note. He gave it to him not at first realising it was a tenner. Oh well, he thought, I'd had paid a lot more than that for what I've heard.

The volunteer protested at being given such a large sum.

'That's all right Sir. You have a nice day.'

With a feeling of benevolence, he made his way out of the hospital to his car. Here the feeling melted away. He had been wheel-clamped. A plastic envelope with a yellow document inside gave details of his crime. Tearing it open the expected penalty notice for overstaying his welcome presented itself. It was dated the day before yesterday. *SIXTY QUID! What was that date again?*

Jackie dressed in the clothes she had been admitted did not intend staying another night. With bad dreams and strangers coming and going – well, she thought, so much for being safe and undisturbed after what the doctor described as a traumatic experience that only required rest and quiet for recovery. She would be better off back among friends and colleagues. She made the decision to return to Bristol without Phil. As far as she was concerned, the man got himself into this mess it was up to him to sort it. On his own.

Hurriedly washing she then cleaned her teeth. Then packing all she had with her into her black leather travel shoulder bag she put put into her rucksack. Opening the door to leave she was immediately confronted by the same man that had previously tried to arrest her. With him was her doctor.

'One-minute sergeant, I think you've caused enough trouble as it is with this woman. Must I remind you that as long as she is here, she is my patient, not your suspect.'

'I'm no longer your patient,' she announced. 'Nor am I his suspect,' she added recognising Waverley. 'I'm off. If anyone wants me, they can do it through my solicitor. My secretary will be delighted to give you his name.' She put her hand into the back pocket of her blue waterproof trousers and took out two business cards, giving one to each of them. 'Now, both of you, out of my way.'

Waverley read the name Craske Forbes Media Consultants, then she was gone. Into a waiting lift. Racing down the stairs he was just in time to see her walking toward a horde of waiting reporters and cameramen.

'What did the ghost look like miss?'

'Where is Mr. Cluff?'

'One for the album!'

FLASH

'Did he hang himself?'

'Did you kill him?'

FLASH

Waverley pushed them aside and took her by the shoulder hurrying her through them. She tried to resist his help not trusting his motive.

'I'm not here to arrest you,' Waverley said trying to reassure her. 'In fact, quite the opposite. I want to help.'

Noyon was on his mobile calling the security company responsible for immobilising his car. They asked him if he had any good reason for leaving his car two days. He was to say that he didn't understand how that could have happened but changed his mind. He thought it would sound pathetic as an excuse.

'Will you be paying cash or by debit card Sir?'

'*Cheque!*'

'That could take two days to clear, in the meantime . . . who pays by cheque these days?'

'*I do!* Do you want it or not?'

He did not intend to listen to the rest of this well-rehearsed homily intended to make people feel that they were inconsiderate in taking up a parking space that another person might require. He removed the phone from his ear until the man at the other end had finished. Replacing it, he told the guy he would be back later for his car, minus the Denver Boot, adding that he would be leaving his details with the hospital reception along with his cheque in an envelope adding, 'I'm from the *Sun*, son. And if you don't want the public to know how patients' and visitors' are being treated when it comes to parking on hospital grounds by hospital security, you'll sort it personally.'

Seeing Jackie Forbes being hustled out of the hospital by Waverley, he terminated the call. Waverley was trying to get her into a taxi. He hurried after them, but with reporters pressing in on her he could not get close enough to them. He needed to speak with her alone. Looking around he spotted a cab rank. He went over and got in the first one, then, kneeling on the floor, he leaned against the glass and passed the driver a twenty-pound note pointing back to the hospital entrance.

'Can you get in front of that cab. Pick that woman up?'

'It'll be my pleasure,' he replied putting the Guardian newspaper he was reading to one side. He started the engine.

U-turning the taxi on the proverbial sixpence he drove at the crowd temporarily scattering them. Taking his best opportunity, he opened the cab door, then hanging onto the door to prevent himself from falling out he called after her.

'Jackie? *Jackie Forbes?*'

She looked across at the person calling her name.

'Me,' he shouted at her. 'Tony Noyon, The Sun. I believe you. Get in.'

Deciding he would be a better option than a night in a police cell broke the hold Waverley had on her and got into the cab.

'Thank you,' she said breathlessly.

Waverley seeing her tried to stop the cab, banging on the window as it slowly pulled away. He managed to get the door open, while at the same time running alongside the moving vehicle.

'*Heh!* Miss Forbes. You're backing the wrong horse with that man.'

She pulled the door closed as the taxi started to speed up. Waverley continued running alongside shouting into the open window directing his remarks at Noyon.

'You people can't resist a story whether it's a pack of lies or not. Can you?'

'She's not under arrest, is she?' Noyon shouted back at him. 'Drive on, driver. Decent hotel if you please.'

# ELEVEN

## Avon and Somerset Constabulary, Portishead, Bristol 2008

*GOODE WAS IN THE PROCESS* of Blu-Tacking and felt-tip marking the Perspex operations board with drawings, maps, and images of the school with the surrounding area of the hostage scene when Hymer came in with cheeseburgers and coffees for the two of them. Running out of board space, Goode was having to use the wall behind that had only recently been re-plastered and re-painted after it had undergone previous abuse with drawing pins. The chief inspector was adding to the next layer of flaking. He relieved Hymer of a latte, removing its lid he began sipping at it leaving a tell-tale white foam under his nose.

'No wonder you're putting on weight Hymer. Can't you buy coffee without burgers,' he said biting into his.

This hostage siege at Haberdashers' would not have the luxury of a time span beyond three days, Goode thought to himself. That would be its critical turning point one way or another. That would be when the hostage takers cause was lost. When they would be at their most dangerous. Until then he would keep a cool head. He pulled a face and threw the remains of his burger in the bin when Ian Duffy knocked on the door. He had a foolscap brown envelope under his arm.

'Morning Sir. That package.'

Goode wiped his mouth on the back of his hand indicated to Duffy to throw it to him. Catching it he tore it open pulling out the still damp contents and read the top sheet:

For the Attention of Avon and Somerset Police

Democratic Republic of Cornwall

Then he read his name and a chill went through him.

*What the hell am I to do with any of this that they know me?* he said to himself.

'Will that be all, Chief Inspector?' Duffy asked.

'Thanks Ian.'

'Did you say something?' Hymer asked hearing him mutter.

Peeling the sheet so as not to tear it further, he read out loud the third paragraph:

That the continuation by Caradon, Carrick, Kerrier, North Cornwall, Penwith and Restormel to fly the flag of St. George, above and outside their offices; and after repeated requests to remove them by 27th June, 2008, the anniversary of the execution of Michael An Gof after his failed rebellion in 1497 against the English and its continual line of Princes of Wales, having not been done will result in direct action being taken against England and the English Prince of Wales.

There Will Be Blood.

Goode looked at his watch. 'They didn't waste any time. It's the twenty-ninth today.'

'1497. Still a constable then wasn't you Sir?'

'You up for promotion shortly sergeant?' He prised more pages apart. 'This wants drying out properly. Get it sent over to forensics, see if they can't do something with it. Hang on. Here it is. AN GOF. That is an AN isn't it Sergeant?'

Hymer looked closer adjusting his glasses and affirmed.

'An Gof. Who the hell are they? Look into them. In the meantime, send the rest of it to forensics,' Goode said.

'Devon and Cornwall might be our best bet Sir.'

'Agreed. See to it will you.'

Goode pulled out a red marker pen and wrote on the flaking plaster wall in capital letters, AN GOF.

Hymer was putting the pages together in a plastic wallet when another part of the document caught his attention. Opening it he began reading. It was the end of the letter. Another page that had got itself buried under the page in front.

'Oh my God! You'd better take a look at this Sir. You might want to let Merriweather and Sir James know asap.'

## 10 Downing Street, London 2008

Sir James was sullen faced. Cabinet Office Briefing Room A was a place heads rolled. His appointment of Merriweather as officer-in-charge of the Bristol siege was a commitment by his signature for his own death warrant should it all go wrong. He was not alone. Others with similar aspirations would also be feeling the weight of their status at this time. Members of the security services, the military, as well as the home secretary, all accompanied with a scattering of note-takers hanging on their words, ready to read them back when the inevitable inquiry seeking the person responsible at the first death was called for. When his phone rang Sir James immediately put it on speaker.

'Yes, Grantley.'

A minute later he rang off then looked at the prime minister.

Up until that point, the hastily called meeting of COBRA by the prime minister began well enough. With that one call the meeting took a twist. The prime minister suggested that the home secretary call the Prince's personal secretary immediately and speak with him.

Clarence House answered, and the prime minister passed him the phone. He smiled and looked around the table.

'This is not good,' the prime minister said passing the phone to the home secretary. 'I know its Clarence House but put it on speaker anyway. We don't want anyone to be under any misapprehension,' he said before excusing himself under the pretence of a call of nature after seeing his housekeeper in the garden with a tray covered with a starched white cloth. He knew what she was secreting from the rest of the party.

Outside in the garden of No. 10 Hetty Cheshire handed him the phone from underneath the cloth set on a tray with a coffee alongside. A subterfuge should he be needed urgently by telephone away from those who might think they were being excluded from affairs of State and that he could not be certain he would be able to devolve. Stepping from view of the cabinet office window, he lighted a cigarette and put the phone to his ear. The accent was Russian.

'Is this the prime minister of Great Britain? I have President Putin here for you. I will translate.'

The home secretary turning to Sir James said:

'Couldn't be bloody Islamic fundamentalists, could they?' When the telephone rang, he picked it up. 'Sir Bernard. Tony Blunt ... Yes, I'm well thank you. Something has cropped up. A question. For His Royal Highness. We've got a problem in Bristol ... Yes, we're not sure at the moment, but we do need some information from His Royal Highness as a matter of urgency ... Yes, I guessed he might be busy, but we're in a COBRA meeting and we need this information urgently. Has he reported any threats against either himself or the Duchess in the last day or two?' The silence seemed to last a lifetime before the home secretary continued. 'Well, of course, I guessed His Royal Highness had his fair share, but I was thinking on the lines that would be taken seriously enough for him to report directly to you ... Well, I don't know ...'

Sir James was beginning to get frustrated with all this diplomatic-speak. It was not helping that the home secretary was seemingly pussy footing around such a simple request as if the very question would lead to him losing his head.

When the office fax machine whirred into life, one of the note-takers got up from the table and went over taking the page out. She passed them to Blunt.

The home secretary, in answer to Sir Bernard, took Sir James by surprise. He read the fax as he spoke.

'Something on the lines in a tome of a letter we've received, asking the Prince of Wales, and I quote, "to get his dirty money grabbing hands out of Cornwall while he's got the chance". Yes, Sir ... Signed William Timmins on behalf of An Gof and the Democratic Republic . . .'

The home secretary alone with the prime minister asked how he got on with the call from Putin.

'Wasn't very useful. Reckons we ought to go in with tanks as he did in Ossetia.'

'The Beslan siege. Well he may have a point there prime minister.'

The prime minister gave him an old-fashioned look.

'Just thinking out aloud Sir.'

'If these people were career terrorists, we might have an awareness of their mindset. But they're not. At least, we think not. I just wish to the devil we knew who they were. MI5 have had trouble with similar organisations in Cornwall apparently. The Jamie Oliver's and the Rick Steins' of this world? But these people are a different kettle of fish. Cigarette?'

'Speaking of MI5 Sir. Are they going to be involved in the west country?'

'They already are.'

# TWELVE
## Offices of Ellick & Waite, Plymouth 1716

*SO, THIS IS PLYMOUTH,* Cluff thought to himself with no idea of how he had arrived where he was, then immediately dodged to one side to avoid being run down.

'*STAND ASIDE FOR A NAVAL OFFICER OF THE KING!*' the driver shouted down to him at the same time cracking his whip over the hind quarters of one of six horses pulling the coach at speed.

The passengers inside, lustily drunk and boisterous, looked on him with a disdain that only aristocracy from exalted positions can.

'Oh-hh—*boll*-oes,' Cluff cursed, as he stepped into a pile of fresh horse dung neatly deposited, packaged, black-brown and shining, by the side of what passed for a pavement leaving a perfect imprint from the tread of his right foot trainer impressed in it. Angrily he gave a one-fingered salute to the occupants. The coach continued on its journey at apace, laughter coming from inside and the name, Sir William, shouting out from within.

Standing against a horse trough at the side of the road he wiped his trainer against some wet moss built up along the bottom while at the same time thinking of those shoes Jackie threw away. I don't think I'm going to find a pair of Alexander Mcqueen's for her here. Satisfied with cleaning the mess off, he lifted his foot up, then passed his hand in front of his nose to fan the smell away from what remained.

He looked about him. He needed to find a street called the Crescent. Stopping a young lad, he asked him for directions.

With a difference in dialect, notwithstanding the boy having a cleft lip, he managed to get from him a direction of sorts. *To'ards the sea*, he said. Without thinking, Cluff put his hand into his pocket to give the boy a tip. A farthing coin, bearing the face of George the First shone. In his open palm he looked at it, the boy, without unfamiliarity, took the coin from him, bit into it, then walked off with it satisfied.

Away from the sea, but close enough for the wind and rain to make its presence felt, The Crescent was, as its name implied, a hemicycle of three storied offices of law practices. Pulling up the collar of his windproof he walked down its office frontages. When he came across a sign in red and gold with the typeface he was familiar he was relieved. For this was the same as the one modestly displayed over the double latticed window to his own offices in Lincoln Inn Fields. Advertising the name, Ellick & Waite, Solicitors at Law, Notaries and Commissioners for Oaths & Wills; new in this time, old in his own, he felt comfortably at ease. Even though he was suspicious of what was happening to him he would play the game. He went up two white steps and lifted the large black knocker to the door banging it down. He then repeated the exercise. He felt as Jacob Marley might have done, turning up to demonstrate to Ebenezer Scrooge the error of his ways while at the same time wondering if he was to be confronted by as many ghosts of doom as the miser himself. He did not have to wait too long to gain an entrance. The door was opened by a short man with long thin legs who bade him enter. He was then shown into a room. The man closed the door behind him leaving him to his own devices. He looked around. There were two desks separated by a large square wicker basket. Inside were freshly laundered and pressed court gowns. Partially covering them an assortment of white fronted ruffled shirts. On each desk was a wig. Made up from long hair, not ones tight curled to the skull that he was familiar, but more like ones worn by women solicitors – or a drag queen, he mused. An assortment of chairs, rigid and single sofa-types haphazardly furnished the rest of the room. On a wall behind the desks were legal diplomas in frames alongside a few odd pictures. He guessed local views. Lithographs if he was any judge. Plymouth dockyard. The waters, berths and wharfs full of warships, a testament to Britain's naval superiority. A further print, he guessed the town's harbour, had baskets of fish manhandled from boats by women on a shining wet cobbled stone hard. Other women and girls were awaiting the baskets gutting the fish at trestle tables, before being loaded onto carts to be carried away, he assumed to market. Further lithographs were of country scenes of pretty girls in long wide skirts of floral and ribbon, their legs enclosed in white stockinet, wearing pink court shoes pushed on swings by young men. Behind them, a large country house. A pair of fine horses attended by a well-dressed stable groom and his master. He went over to the window and looked out. He could see the town of Plymouth. A hill on the horizon gave it its extent. In the far distance, Dartmoor. He shuddered. On the opposite side of the room a pair of windows with open wooden shutters gave the view of a ship anchored in what he guessed was Plymouth Sound. If this was a set-up, then someone had gone to a great deal of trouble, he thought to himself. When someone coughed behind him, it took him by surprise.

He turned around to see a man sat at one of the desks. He closed his eyes, and then opening them again on the off chance he was mistaken, for he was sure he was not there when he first came in. Though, on reflection, with the pile of books, scrolls and other office paraphernalia on the desk, he could have been working behind and hidden, he might easily have missed him. Was this the one Goode had mentioned, that would further him an explanation? One of two lawyers. Was he Ellick or Waite? Whoever he was the man was gesturing him to take a chair. He hesitated, before doing so, for he gave all the appearance of a man with impatience and authority. As soon as he sat down the man got up and coming around to the front of the desk planted himself in an uncomfortable seating position on it and looked down him.

A man of medium height with a pockmarked face, he had long straggly grey hair. A weird feeling went through Cluff. It was not every day one had the chance to meet the founder of the law firm one worked for. In fact, considering the difference in years, everyday would have been an overestimation of one, two hundred years was not an interval of time two men could reach out to each other in the ordinary course of events. But these were not ordinary events.

'Our office tells me that you have the discernment to succeed as a barrister of worth, Mr. Cluff. If you don't mind my saying the standing of my position as senior partner within the law firm forbids me to show any recognition of that fact. Whether you are up to this brief . . . well, only time and the life or death of our client will be the judge. However, ah, here he is now.' He stood up at another's appearance, the palm of his hand spread, gesturing him that they had their visitor. 'Mr. Waite, Mr. Cluff.' Waite smiled.

Looking around in anticipation of who Ellick was speaking, he saw no one. Then a veil was lifting, the man this Ellick was addressing who Cluff would have sworn on oath was not there seconds before was sitting at the other desk peering out at him through half glasses balancing neatly on the end of his nose.

His face was unfamiliar despite his portrait hanging in the London office he worked. An oil painting in reception alongside that of Zac Ellick bore little resemblance to this Hilary Waite standing before him now.

'How do you do, Mr. Cluff,' Waite said in a voice a lot less authoritative than Ellick.

'I have seen a picture of a man the name of Hilary Waite. A painting. It does not look like you. Did they perhaps run out of oil?'

Waite had a look of hurt on his face.

'Is not my picture on that same wall as your own Mr. Ellick?' he said turning to Ellick. 'How is this? Was I discarded from company history as an old felt hat?'

'Look,' Cluff continued, 'your acting is great, I've no complaints on that score, but come on, either I'm going stark raving mad or this is a film set. Which is it to be?'

Ellick turned to Waite, a look of incredulity on his face.

'What did he say? A f-i-l-m—'

'Yes. F-i-l-m, film,' Cluff repeated. 'Come along the pair of you cut the comedy and tell me what game you think you're playing? Or. Wait a moment. Oh, I see it all now, it is a comedy, a period drama of sorts. What is it, Blackadder? Dr. Who?'

Waite leant across his desk and whispered in answer to Ellick's question as to Cluff's state of mind.

'Did he accuse us of being stark raving mad?'

'Oh-h-h,' Ellick replied moving his backside back into position at his desk. 'I see. A turn of phrase without true meaning is it. Mmm. 'Fraid we don't know any Dr. Black Adder. And as for drama, I cannot imagine why you should think that we were putting on a play act, although, there'll be scarce few actors and less of an audience for this performance, at least, not in the way the dramatist, William Wycherley, of "I weigh the man, not his title, 'tis not the king's stamp can make the metal better or heavier" fame, for this Sir is a dreadful business, and one we would as soon be done with as you yourself in time to come will see. In the meantime–'

Waite clapped. 'A singularly put observation, Mr. Ellick. Fine sentiments of Mr. Wycherley succinctly put. A second career awaits you,' he said with a smile in his old eyes.

Zac Ellick ignoring his remark continued. 'Did not John Goode explain why you'd been sent to us?'

Cluff's thoughts returned to the encounter the night he and Jackie separated by an apparition sat heavy on his mind. He could forget any ideas of reconciliation he might have on their getting back together after his leaving her. The apparition had been persuasive. The mentioning by him of his father's wish that he helps them thwart a hostage siege in a school. The large number of children being involved had a ring of truth to it. He had studied him intently for any sign that he was not what or who he said he was, and that it was all a wind-up. A time traveller or a ghost was his only conclusion for nothing solid in flesh and blood can fade and reappear as this man had. A ghost with tears. With children at risk of death, who wouldn't help? He was waking in dream chapters, with a story that kept going around and around. He did not seem to be in any one place for more than five minutes at a time. In a world that he no longer had any control over and that, he might never escape was his fear. Or would all this reveal itself as a mere nightmare culminating in him waking in his bed bathed in a pool of sweat. For the moment though, these pair of play actors were his best opportunity to get this over and done with and get the hell out of this world he did not belong.

'Only that he was an innocent. But then they all say that, don't they?'

Ellick and Waite looked at each other. Doubt ingrained into the two men's faces. Was this man right for the job after all, Hilary thought? Seeing Zac's face, his guess that his own face showed reservations similar to his own turned to a certainty. Could they be sure that what they were attempting would have a better chance of success than times before? His father hadn't survived that attempt, would the son fair better? For time was running out for all of them.

'Not after the event they do not, Ellick replied.'

'You are forgetful in your argument,' Waite commented. 'For it was not the death penalty that stood in the way – it was the guilty conviction that condemned Time to go unchallenged. 'Tis true, Goode might have escaped the rope, but he was still convicted of the murder of William Timmins, and most certainly exiled to the Antipodes never to return to Cornwall. The outcome was routine.'

Ellick nodded his acceptance of the argument by his partner.

'Why is there such importance of a man being hanged?' Cluff asked. 'And when was this supposed to have taken place?'

'Where we are,' Ellick asked of Waite. 'As opposed to where we were a month before—'

Waite hesitated. Time had played out this trick so many times – he tried to say, Before but it wasn't, it was, After before, then, After before that. The confusion was causing problems to not just himself but also to Ellick. And it was to him that he now turned to give an explanation to this twenty-first century barrister as to what they wanted from him.

'We are locked into a single year. The, *When is 1716*, and it is moving forward into another time,' Waite explained. 'The whys and where for, we do not know . . .'

Cluff's mind was wandering unable to take in explanations for understanding. He wanted them to go away and for himself to wake up and to find himself back in the tent in the driving rain with Jackie. He attempted the tried and tested act of pinching himself as children do, to convince himself that he was dreaming. Nothing changed, except he now had a red mark on the back of his hand.

'This 1716 you speak of, that moves into another time, do you mean another century?'

'Let me try and elucidate,' Ellick said. 'Understand this. It is still 1716 but in a different place.'

He looked towards Waite for acknowledgement of his facts.

'How can that be?' Cluff said getting annoyed. 'Explain to me your understanding of a different place?'

'Consider. George the First replaced by James the Third as king. Assuming one has not died, and that politics has not been involved in the removal of the other's head. That is the other place. A man was hanged because the Hanoverian George had been ill-advised,' Hilary Waite said to him affirmatively.

Jesus Christ! Cluff muttered to himself. 'Time shifting!'

'More, back or forward, it's all at the same time. And would you please, refrain from blasphemy.'

'My apologies for my offence, but in my world, you are speaking of the theory of a multi universe. And I cannot listen to any more of this.'

He excused himself, leaving the two ancient barristers open-mouthed. Back out in the corridor he caught sight of the servant that had shown him in. He appeared to making tea in a small kitchen area. 'Not for me, thanks,' he shouted down the corridor, and then opening the front door, he stepped out into the street. There was nothing to show that it was some candid camera stunt as he first thought, instead, people passing by in clothes he guessed were not of – his time. God, those two barristers had done a good job attempting to brainwash him into thinking he was in the eighteenth-century. Any minute he expected to see a film director, wearing his cap around the wrong way on his head, to come shouting down a megaphone: Cut. What's that idiot doing walking across my set, get rid of him?

For such an event, the better part of three hundred years past – assuming production went ahead from day one – for what took his attention for detail was impressive. A carriage came into the Crescent pulled by six horses. *Déjà vu*, he said to himself. He watched himself, only unlike before, when he avoided being run down, this time he was tumbling under its wheels. His body broken in the road, his head hideously contorted as the coach went on its way, leaving him with little doubt in his mind that his neck was broken. He put his hand to his mouth and cried out, *No!* But there was no one to hear him. He was dead. And now, his ghost, frightened enough to return and get answers from his ancestral employers turned and went back in.

Opening the door, he shouted down to the servant who was now pouring the remainder of a kettle into a large teapot. 'Better to make that four sugars for me, Eadhild.' Not waiting for an invitation to enter the office he had recently left he went in and sat himself down opposite the two men in the same chair for the second time that day. If day was the operative word in this crazy world, he thought, while at the same time trying his best to stop himself shaking from the shock that had come over him. It was then that he saw himself though the open door outside in the corridor. A small girl, holding a dolly behind herself and to one side of him walk was walking alongside of him. Falling forward across the desk scattering papers and a full well of ink among the two partners he was gone.

'Get the young Lawyer a stoup of water Hilary. Hurry for he's swooned right away likely to die—'

## Llandoger Trow Public House, Bristol 2008

An evening conversation with the staff of Jackie's company led to talk of holidays. Jackie and Cluff had been discussing the merits of crossing Dartmoor.

'Well, far as I'm concerned Mr. Barrister Ibiza has the edge. What'd you reckon? Wouldn't you prefer that as an option?' She turned the conversation to Christiana. 'What do you think Christy? Fancy spending some quality time in a nice hotel, lying in the sun, or walking across Dartmoor? Dance music, Pete Tong, or a tent in the rain, duh . . . ?'

Cluff was no longer in his company. The weather was bad. The rain was lashing down. The sky was black, and the wind was tearing the tent to shreds. Outside in the dark Cluff was trying to peg it back down, but he was losing the battle.

'A killer is on the loose,' he shouted into the wind. His words were lost. 'Doesn't anyone care?'

He heard himself say, *Father*. 'I'm coming for you.'

Jackie was trying to shake him from his nightmare, 'Phil . . . *Phil!* Wake up.'

Another voice overrided hers, 'You're next to our last one hope Lawyer Cluff—'

### Offices of Ellick & Waite, Plymouth 1716

Waite interrupted his thoughts, 'Your father—'

'My father. Gerald Cluff went missing back in a time closer to your madness than mine.'

'We know. We were with him when he died,' Ellick said. 'There was nothing he could do to help them. They were consumed in an explosion of fire.'

'With him, you say. And now you want to use me to make amends? You put him at risk of death, and you wish to do the same with me!'

'*NO!* At the hands of a man that should have known better had his other, truer self, not been tipped over into another time – the result of a cruelty inflicted. Not ours. As for your father, it was over for him before he had the chance to alter time. No one could have saved him. A sharp pain to his chest, and he was no more. A brave man.'

'Brave indeed,' Ellick added thoughtfully.

'A heart attack?'

'Is that what you call the malady in your time? And not even a funeral,' Ellick said.

Waite shook his head. 'We couldn't reach out to him.'

'And no closure for my mother and sister, let alone myself. Don't suppose you thought of that when you recruited him did you?'

Ellick looked at his partner.

'Had we known; we would have prevented him. But your father was adamant he wanted to help. He saw the situation and gave his life for it. He knew what was involved. We're sorry. Perhaps it's not too late. We assumed—'

'*What!* What did you assume? That I would follow in his footsteps to doom?'

'No, no. You have us wrong,' Waite said. 'If it's any consolation, we'd both as soon go back to being dead, or whatever state we were in before you came knocking on our door . . .'

'Excuse me, but I didn't knock on any door.'

'Mr. Cluff. You may not have intentionally called upon us. Neither did your father before you. We can only assume there is a relationship on your paternal side to that of either John Goode or Joshua Timmins. Do you know of any?' Waite continued.

'Of course not.'

'Well, the point is, there are children's lives that are in jeopardy and us all three have been drawn together by forces beyond our – your relationship notwithstanding – understanding of the matter for a second time.'

Cluff heard but did not completely understand. Had these two men reappeared on earth for some bizarre time twisted re-enactment? Was an unknown force capable of replaying history, locked into a natural time computer? Or was our existence copied onto another medium, twisted, surrounding us, uncoiling itself for a replay. The core of the earth perhaps upset by a natural occurrence within Dartmoor's granite that would allow men another chance to put right wrongs lost first time around. An historical conscience, a natural existence as natural as nature itself. He feared for such theory proven. If it was, then all manner of wrongs committed in history might be righted. Or wrongly depending on one's point of view. The problem with that, he mused, was where did that leave the divine intervention of His justice?

'And where are those children now?'

'Back in your time . . .' Ellick replied.

'At a school in Bristol,' Waited added.

Ellick opened a drawer to his desk and took out a newspaper unfolding it. It was a copy of the London edition of *The Guardian* newspaper, dated June 27, 2008 with its banner headline screaming at him:

## SACRIFICED! FOR A
## REPUBLICAN CAUSE!

Turning the page he saw that it mentioned a hostage siege situation in Bristol that had been going on for three days and that had culminated in the deaths of three hundred children. The perpetrator, a Cornishman by the name of Timmins; supporter for an English county to become its own country – *Cornwall!*

He shuddered, 'I know this school.'

The date was the same he and Jackie first set foot on Dartmoor. He shuddered. Why had he not heard the news before? He studied the newspaper further. Was it a photocopy? How could it be, he stupidly thought to himself. *The Guardian*, with an advertisement flagged next to its title extolling the virtues of some ointment for an unmentionable complaint. If he had any doubts as to the authenticity of the situation he found himself then this newspaper from the previous evening had confirmed the validity of the story. It was 1715.

'How can I help? For I am not in that time, I'm in yours mores the pity. And the sooner I can return the better. Though what exactly I can do back in my own time is frankly beyond me.'

'You can help by being here. John Goode was hanged for the murder of Joshua Timmins,' Waite said. 'And we need a barrister capable of modern day argument that can back it up with incontestable evidence that John Goode is innocent.'

Cluff shook his head. 'No such animal as incontestable. Not even with a well-paid prosecutor. You should know that. Anyway, if he's been hanged, there's not a lot I can do for him now.'

'Then, not now. Before, after before, and after before that,' Waite said with the hint of annoyance that he had explained this to him already.

'The case of Rex v John Goode was well under way when your father collapsed,' Ellick said.

'I understood you to say that he died of a heart attack.'

'Yes, he was in court. He was summing up for the defence when he collapsed,' Waite said.

'Why didn't the case continue?' Cluff said. 'All right it might have been my father, that for want of a better explanation, was incapable of continuing, but that's hardly reason for a case to be stopped when the defendant's life was on the line. Couldn't you have continued with the evidence that you had winding up the case and bring the man's acquittal to a successful conclusion?'

Ellick was at pains to point out that it was not that they were incapable as a law firm of continuing the defence of their client, but more a case of others having an interest in not seeing an acquittal, seeking a guilty verdict on the grounds that it must be an Act of God that his defence counsel was no longer able to continue, and that a guilty verdict must be His will.

'And who were these others, that you speak of, did you ever find out?' Cluff asked.

'That would have been an act of treason to suggest,' Waite answered.

'The king . . .'

Ellick shrugged.

'Well, your Act of Treason tells me so,' Cluff said. 'So who were these men? Goode and . . . Timmins did you say?' Cluff asked.

'They were tinners,' Waite said continuing, 'not ordinary miners, but men of substance. They represented the Parliaments for Cornwall and Devon Stannaries.'

'*Stannary Parliaments?*' Cluff queried.

'Stannary Parliaments of Devon and Cornwall. Overseers for mining tin, representatives of the Princes of Wales on behalf of the Crown. Joshua Timmins for Cornwall in Helston and Lostwithiel, John Goode for Tavistock, Ashburton, Chagford, and Plympton. Timmins was murdered at Crockern, the Stannary Parliament meeting place on Dartmoor—'

'Why was he murdered?' Cluff demanded.

'You know the place?' Waite asked.

Cluff nodded.

Ellick continued. 'As I understand events, John Goode and Joshua Timmins were carrying a document of pardon from the king to Sir Richard Vyvyan, a major player in the Jacobite Rising that was taking place in the southwest at the time. That pardon – and we'll give George the benefit of the doubt here – with his granted blessing had conditions. One was that Sir Richard was to organise both Stannaries into one for the mutual benefit of both Devon and Cornwall. There must have been some political influence brought to bear on the king for Sir Richard's pardon never reached him. Sir Richard was subsequently arrested by Hugh Boscawen and taken to London where he was incarcerated in the Tower.'

'Further to that,' Waite interrupted, 'there's little doubt that

Boscawen employed Timmins and Goode to carry that pardon in the first instance knowing that neither man would be allowed to achieve its objective. Tinners have little time for the Crown Mr. Cluff, the Cornish, especially—'

Ellick continued, 'Reason being Joshua Timmins was a descendant of the Cornish Flamank's, a family sworn to break the bond between Cornwall and the Duchy who they saw as an imposition bordering on theft of Cornwall's natural resources. With the rights of past and subsequent Princes' of Wales being able to take those resources for their own has been the subject of legal conjecture since the state of the duchy was first founded by Edward the Third in 1337. This provided an income for his son Edward the Black Prince and all Dukes of Cornwall since. Can we take it you are familiar with the duchy?'

'Not overly. Something to do with a monarch's first born son not being short of a bob or two and not wishing to tax the English for the pleasure. Established forty years after Magna Charta, its writing in Latin, while the indigenous population only spoke Cornish, was inspired,' Cluff said smiling.

'He's good isn't he?' Waite suggested to his partner.

Ellick nodded a smile. They appeared to have the right man.

'What Timmins had against all of this was that the Cornish Parliament were obliged to swear an allegiance to the monarch and not the unwritten constitution, that would impose English taxes from the country from that time forth . . .'

'Rendering,' Waite interrupted, 'Magna Charta's objective to prevent abuses by royalty, in respect of that tax to an unfortunate part of England always considered Britain invalid.'

Ellick further continued.

'And with it, the creation of a private estate. A country within a country.'

He leaned across to Cluff whispering, 'Someone let the cat from the sack that night giving the whereabouts of those two men and what they were doing crossing Dartmoor.' Leaning back in his chair he raised his voice. 'Joshua Timmins knowing the document was the pardon from King George to Sir Richard for any Jacobite involvement in exchange for Cornwall's right to determine its own future, would not have parted with it willingly. Once it was realised by the Devon tinners that they carried an arrest warrant for Sir Richard and not a tool for the amalgamation of the two Stannaries, the courier's fates was sealed.'

'So it was the king?'

Waite answered. 'Once it had been explained to him the error of his ways. You have to remember he was German, a Hanoverian; and not particularly *au fait* with the English monarchy and their ways until some devil whispered in his ear certain advantages he was about to give over. That whisperer sitting on the king's shoulder was Hugh Boscawen . . .'

'Who employed a mercenary soldier from the Highlands who had been engaged by the High Tories to help quell the Jacobite Uprising in the southwest now at an end. To speed a return to his homelands he was persuaded to help,' Ellick added.

'So who did murder Timmins if it wasn't Goode?'

'Colonel Maclean was the Highlander that brought the two men before tinners justice that saw the death of the one and the execution of the other. Whether it was him personally, or Lydford Law, the arbiters of Stannary justice, is open to conjecture.'

'So who Boscawen?' Cluff asked.

'Comptroller to His Majesty. Steward for the Duchy of Cornwall and one-time Lord of the Stannaries. In short – a man who knows the ins and outs for any political manipulation that might be required in the southwest,' Waite said.

'Here!' Ellick said getting up from his desk.

Going to a double-panelled oak cupboard he began sifting through scrolls of ribboned parchment while at the same time muttering to himself. Waite interrupted him by asking what he was seeking.

'Those king's papers.'

'Should we let them out into the public domain? There's treason here, and I for one do not wish a spell in the Tower alongside Sir Richard.'

'Hilary you are overlooking something. They are already in the public domain. In the twenty-first century.'

'Ah, here we are,' he said blowing dust off of the roll of parchment.

'Zac are you listening to me? It's the here and now we should be concerned with not then.'

Ellick turned to Cluff, 'Let him make the decision, see what he thinks. If they are useful, and they can be proved. Well.'

'Thin ice, Mr. Ellick. Thin ice. We are dealing with Skull remember.'

Zac Ellick hesitated.

'Ah yes. You are right there Mr. Waite.'

Cluff put his hand into his forehead, then looking up said to the two men, 'Who the hell is, *Skull*?'

'Ah, did we neglect to mention him?' Ellick noted.

'Nearly. Though you've still the chance for redemption,' Cluff retorted.

This would be the young barrister's *Sword of Justice*, as far as the law firm that was Ellick & Waites was concerned Zac Ellick told him. For if he were to take on Judge Skull in the defence of John Goode then pedigree along with hard argument and evidence was what it was going to take. For Skull was an enthusiastic advocate for the laws of Lydford that would see a man hang for his very presence in front of him guilty or otherwise. With that for a legal attitude it would be difficult to think how Cluff was going to get a fair trial from such a man.

'As Mr. Ellick has tried his best for you to understand Skull is a complex man who, though not in favour of England's monarchical rule of Cornwall, until something better comes along, will tolerate it. Skull was not a believer in the Cornwall Stannary Parliament, or any other parliaments for that matter; as for Jacobite's, the like of Sir Richard Vyvyan, neither was he of Catholics.'

Cluff was beginning to become exasperated the size of the document he was going to have to digest in this case if he agreed to take it on. Assuming (he had come around to that as a state of physics possibility writ real), that he would not wake having fallen asleep in the Pen and Quill at Lincoln's Inn as Zac Ellick spread the vellum roll out on his desk, enthusiastically brushing aside obstacles such as papers and quill pens, being careful to remove a decanter of sherry and two glasses by hand, putting them on a sideboard.

'Read on my young barrister, read on,' Ellick said.

Cluff sighed and leaned across the desk holding one end of the parchment to prevent it rolling back on itself and began to read:

*An Unknown . . . ,*

the words partially illuminated began the manuscript written in a scratchy hand with a quill that could have done with sharpening, he thought

*. . . and Believed to be the true Son of Count Königsmarck, with the king's estranged wife, Sophia Dorothea, after a consummate relationship with Count Königsmarck while still related in marriage to the King. The Count fearing for his life and that of his son had him taken into the care of Sophia*

*Dorothea's dresser until a better time sought. Alas that will no longer be the case. Count Königsmarck disappeared in 1694. Sophia Dorothea imprisoned at Ahlden Castle, forbidden to see what King George considered his true off-spring, later known as George the Second. The belief is that the Königsmarck boy child, the half-brother to George the Second, resides in Devonshire.*

'That dresser was Jessie Goode of Lovaton,' Hilary Waite said watching his eyes move down the scroll. 'The politics of this case open greatly from that point on. Königsmarck's removal from Europe, believed George the First's work, never proven but implicated. The Jacobite's smelling a rat, meddled that the king could no longer be sure of any of his children which was a rallying cry for supporters of the Stuarts and the Jacobite cause.'

Waite added, 'You see, why John Goode didn't have much of a chance avoiding the hangman's noose. He was likely the king's estranged wife's bastard son.'

'Now, as to your fee,' Ellick said opening his daybook while Waite taking down the tray with its decanter and glasses pouring them each one out. 'Your fee. Let me see.' He ran his fingers down a list of accounting figures, and then turning the page, continued on the other side. 'I don't suppose we can match your current earnings in London.' He looked up at the young barrister with a business-like expression upon his face. 'I should think a barrister like yourself could expect to receive, what, £8 a day, what eh Mr. Waite? We might manage to run to £3. 6s. 8d. a day. The Stannaries of Devon and Cornwall are subscribing to this, so keep it tight. Of course, finding the body of Joshua Timmins might attract an additional fee of, shall we say, a guinea.'

Cluff's mouth fell open. He was still trying to digest the parchment he had read.

'By-the-by. Do you know what parallel time is?' Waite said in a manner that suggested neither had heard of it either, except in passing.

'Only as far as we can ascertain it's where Joshua Timmins has disappeared to. Or that part of him you might know as his soul. Subjected to the pain of torture his body had no other choice than to move across into that other world. Unfortunately, the door didn't close. And he's caught betwixt . . .'

'As your father theorised to us before he . . . passed away. Timmins' soul in seeking justice is sucking everyone in. Goode, Judge Skull as well as us. We are all actors on this stage, Mr. Cluff,' Waite interrupted.

'Along with anyone else that wanders too close,' Ellick came back.

Cluff was getting annoyed.

'Right. Let me tell you. I've seen this magic door you speak of. I was run down by a carriage outside and killed . . .'

'Naval man with company, was he?' Waite asked.

He affirmed saying in an annoyed voice, 'As it happens. . . . Is he in the habit of running down members of the public, only if you've a time that he will return, perhaps I can go drag the officious scoundrel from his carriage and give him a good kicking 2008 style?'

'A figment of time. A figment. Nothing else. Unless you can get into his time, he's vapours,' Ellick said.

'Thought I heard the name William—'

'George the Third's sons. William Henry the future Fourth with his brother, the future George the Fourth with their other brother, Frederick Duke of York . . .' Ellick recounted.

'They've left the Citadel on their way to the Assembly Rooms at Stonehouse for a ball held in William's honour. Already a little worse for wear I vouch,' Waite continued.

'They were. Missed me first time around, got me the second. Did you say George the Third's sons?' Waite nodded a smile on his lips. 'What the 1738 to 1820 ones. I was under the impression that this was 1716,' Cluff queried.

'This is that year. Suffice to say;' Ellick came back, 'extraneous events are occurring all the time. You witnessed one from January 8, 1788. You have to separate them from your objectives in this matter. Rest assured they couldn't kill you. All you saw was an alternative version of events.'

'Sorry. I didn't know that I had landed in reality.'

Ellick went on to explain that they were told by his late father that they were in what was known as a theory of interpenetrating dimensions. He had apparently discovered a place on the ground close to Crockern on Dartmoor. The site of a tinners hut where a time portal exists that has brought into being this theory.

'Where we first encountered John Goode—'

'We believe Crockern is where these time mists come together,' Waite said.

'And I suppose you want me to conduct my case from out of these mists of time?'

'He is ahead of us isn't he Zac? Yes.'

So much for English monarchical history Cluff thought. These two had explained to him time. Future and past. With their knowledge of twenty-first century knowledge of physics, with their ability to move freely back and forth through time he wondered why they needed his help.

When they explained he was gob-smacked. The implication was that he and his father were descendants of Sir Richard Vyvyan and Sir Richard's cousin Hugh Boscawen. And while doubting the truthfulness of such elevated ancestry he enjoyed briefly that air of superiority over his would be past employers that caused him to momentarily raise his head at them and sniff the air saying, 'And is Judge Skull also a friend of my family?'

## Devon & Cornwall Constabulary, (Plymouth Central Sector), Plymouth 2008

Waverley, with a paper cup of coffee in each hand, fought with the office door for entry with his backside. Cocksworth hearing the commotion outside got up from reading his newspaper and opened the door the rest of the way for him. With a tightening of one hand, the lid of one of the cups popped off spilling hot liquid over his skin. In panic, Waverley made a quick entrance trying to maintain balance while at the same time looking desperately for somewhere to deposit the coffee cups while at the same time burning his fingers. He spied Cocksworth's *Telegraph*. Slopping coffee on it, he left two cup impressions across a picture of Chris Hoy showing off his three gold medals from the Beijing Olympics. Seeing his chief inspector's face, he quickly removed them.

'For God's sake, sort yourself out Waverley,' Cocksworth said picking up his newspaper from the desk tipping the spilt coffee from nine down and four across into the wastepaper basket before sitting back down to study the rest of the puzzle.

Waverley sat on the chair opposite sipping his coffee in an effort to reduce the over-filled cup.

'According to the doctor of forensics it would have been rough justice,' Waverley said wiping surplus coffee from his lips with the back of his hand.

Cocksworth looked up at his sergeant.

'That the other body, the one that wasn't in military uniform, the two hundred-year-old. Well, she found a strange mark on his hand.' He continued ignoring his boss's shake of his head.

'What strange mark?' Cocksworth asked annoyed at his fatuous statements for feeding him piece-meal.

'Well, Dr. Poltair didn't notice it at first, but it looks like a nail had been driven right through the palm of his hand crucifixion style.'

'Nasty,' Cocksworth said writing in the crossword's squares *Odessa* in answer to seven down, *Black Sea oil town in Texas?* 'I trust that Miss Forbes didn't get any further than the Travel Lodge to finish her expedition? And is that Noyon fellow still with her? You did explain that we hadn't finished questioning yet?'

'Yes, he is.'

Cocksworth continuing his studying of the crossword in between sips of coffee said.

'That could turn out to be an interesting exercise in intercourse for readers of *The Sun*.'

When the office door opened with barely a knock of announcement Waverley, seeing who it was, hurriedly stood up eager to make himself scarce saying, 'Okay Chief Inspector, I'll get on to that right away. Good morning Sir.

Rudyard caught him by the shoulder.

'Not so fast sergeant. It'll do you no harm hearing what I've got to say. At ease.'

Waverley did as he was told eager to hear what he had to say to Cocksworth.

'Just to mention that I've had a call from Chief Superintendent Kirby . . .'

'Avon and Somerset?' Cocksworth interrupted.

'Quite so. And he's not a happy man.'

Cocksworth put his pen down to listen.

'I don't know where that journalist got his information regarding Cluff's father previously working at the same law firm as his son, and then to go missing in similar circumstances, but he did.

It's not sound, not sound at all. There seem to be a few members of the press getting information that could only be from our people. I want a stop put to it,' Rudyard announced fervently.

'Well, it is primarily an Avon and Somerset case Sir. Perhaps he'd got it from them,' Cocksworth said astonished that his chief superintendent hadn't worked that one out.

'Well, CS Kirkby insists that they didn't get it from his people when I suggested that it could have been one of his team. And in any case, that's still not good enough, Cocksworth. And there are other matters I am not happy about. And this is between us. And just to underline matters, CS Kirby makes the point that this Forbes woman comes from their patch, and that they were hardly likely to jeopardize their case inquiry by passing out information to the press.'

'And what was your answer to that Sir?' Cocksworth asked knowing that Rudyard was not a person to be dictated to on matters of policing.

Rudyard hesitated. He had no wish to undermine a fellow officer from another area, but as he had started, he decided to continue.

'Again. Between these walls.'

Both Cocksworth and Waverley said that it went without saying. Rudyard looked at both men before continuing.

'I reminded him that if it was the case, Cluff lives close to Lincoln's Inn, which is City of London, and that they cannot conduct their inquiries from there anymore than Avon and Somerset can carry out full inquiries down here. Not that I've any time for City of London police. Too tall, too tall by half. The point is this is going to have to be a both forces investigation.'

'And what do you propose I do about the City of London should they wish to be kept in the picture?' Cocksworth asked.

'Just use your initiative, Steven. *Carry on gentlemen!*'

# THIRTEEN
## INTERPENETRATING
## DIMENSION DOME
### Bodmin Assize, Cornwall 1716

*THE CARVED STONE RELIEF* over the entrance gate to Bodmin Assize sometime displayed the royal crest of King James the Third, on other occasions, the crest of King George the First. No one noticed.

A file of men chained together was out in its courtyard. Filthy and in poor health the consequence of bad food and being held in small, cramped cells barely high enough for a man to stand had taken their toll. Manhandled up the steps to the court room by bailiffs, each man's hand on the shoulder of the one in front they shuffled. One chanced to speak to the man behind him asking, 'Who's presiding?'

A soldier with a truncheon hearing him struck him across the back of his head. Blood was drawn.

'Skull,' the man behind answered, holding his head.

Entering the court by way of the granite steps the voice of an clerk bellowed out that if any man had appeared before Judge Skull in the past then this would be the time to speak up as:

'Any felon here, guilty or otherwise, hoping the judge might not recognise him, would be deceiving himself.'

Skull's abilities of recall for a face that had been before him on a previous occasion was uncanny. They would be assured of transportation at best or hanging at worst for a similar second offence. Newcomers to appear before him could at least reckon on a lighter sentence. Branding or flogging being order of the day. Those that had the means to employ a barrister (scarce few), said that he was fair.

Taking their places in a line, the prisoners' with heads previously bowed, looked up at the man who was to administer their fates.

Judge Edmund Skull sat high on the bench overseeing all before him ready to dispense justice in his inimitable style few could match. With the court about to settle for the first case, his clerk, Quince, struggled below the judge with a young lad who had tried to escape. Restraining him with an arm lock around his neck, he released him after the boy sank his teeth into him. Then ducking down from under his arm attempted to make good an escape right into another's arms. A bailiff coming in from outside hauled the boy off his feet putting him down below the judge.

'What's all the fuss, Quince? He won't bite!' Judge Skull said as his clerk wiped blood from the wound with a kerchief.

Quince hurriedly read from the Christian Bible extolling the virtue of truth from those up before the bench. He then gestured for the boy to stand up straight. The charge of poaching read out Quince asked the boy how he pleaded. The boy muttering that he wasn't guilty then looked toward his mother sitting among the gallery of onlookers. She had tears in her eyes, and tears in her clothes that she was doing her best to cover with a large shawl.

'Give me, give me,' Judge Skull impatiently beckoned his clerk for the paperwork.

Quince rubbed his arm and passed them up.

Skull briefly scanned the notes before looking at the boy.

'Anything to say before I pass sentence? Never mind. Transportation to the Antipodes. Send him down. Next case, Quince, if you please.'

The boy was hauled away by two bailiffs. His mother screamed.

'Hold fast,' Skull interrupted. 'How old are you boy?'

'I think I'm ten Sir.'

'He's nine years and three months, Your Honour,' his mother called from the gallery.

'You'd better join him on his journey, don't want anyone to think I'm separating a boy from his mother. *NEXT CASE QUINCE!*'

Henry Bassett made his way up into the dock. He farted from his fear. Fellow prisoners closest to him waved their hands under their noses.

'Absconding from His Majesty's Ship, the *Azore* out of Falmouth, Your Honour,' Quince said behind his perfumed lace edged kerchief his words indecipherable.

'You are, Henry Bassett. Ship's carpenter?' Skull asked. 'How do you plead?'

'I am guilty with circumstances Sir,' Bassett answered his voice croaking with fear. He farted again.

Quince intervened addressing himself to the prisoner.

'Your Honour – *Bassett!* You will address the bench with propriety as befits a navy man. I am, *Your Honour!* Say it.'

'*Your Honour*, Sir,' Bassett echoed.

'Yes, yes, I haven't all day, Bassett. Get on with it. What are these circumstances you speak of?'

'My wife, Sir . . .'

'Yes, yes. What of her? What's she to do with His Majesty's warships?' the Judge looked up at the gallery, 'apart from providing you with conjugal comforts when you're home.'

Rare laughter broke out. Judge Skull was in an unusually beneficiary mood.

'She's with the consumption, Sir – *Your Honour* – there's no one to care for her.'

Skull addressed his clerk, 'How long has this man been in custody, Quince?'

'Three weeks Your Honour.'

There was silence as Skull read from the headed notepaper provided by naval prosecutors.

'Says here the navy hasn't anyone to conduct courts marshal and has asked that you be brought before the civil. Navy is of the opinion you are important to them. *Are you, Bassett?* Are you important to the navy?'

Bassett said nothing.

Judge Skull looked up from the case notes.

'I don't want anyone to think that I'm short on compassion.' Looking at Bassett he said, 'By your own admission you're guilty of dereliction of duty by absence. Navy man . . . used to the cat . . . ten lashes.' He turned to his clerk, 'After, Quince, see that this man is taken to his wife for a day before returning him to a hold in Falmouth to await another ship.' Turning back to Bassett, 'Carpenters are essential on fighting ships, examples have to be made. God willing your wife will remain from His keeping while about her malady. Next case, Quince.'

'Thank you, Your Honour,' Bassett said to Skull.

Judge Skull waved the man away, unusually taking little pleasure in the man's demise. He hardened himself for the next case.

'John Goode, Your Honour . . . of the Stannary Parliament for Devon.'

'Ah,' Skull said with a hint of pleasure reading out aloud the Lifton prison report. ' "Justice or injustice of this case is to be decided by a Cornish judge".'

# FOURTEEN
## Avon and Somerset Constabulary, Portishead, Bristol 2008

*ACTING CHIEF SUPERINTENDENT* Andy Merriweather was nervous but confident in his appointment by Sir James Kirkby as officer-in-charge of this siege. He was to work alongside Goode who had set the ball in motion.

'Our Cornishman in Somerset,' Kirkby had laughingly told him. 'But don't tell him I said that.'

Merriweather's acting status had been largely one of training and shadowing Sir James for the last year, and if enjoying his new role was too strong a phrase, he looked forward to it as a career opportunity that would afford him introductions to people of influence that could enhance his future career prospects within the force. He was ambitious. Gaining a first in politics at Oxford, as a graduate police officer, he was fast-tracked. It was this that brought him to the attention of Sir James. For this hostage siege was a unique opportunity that would either make him or destroy him. Sir James reminded him there would be a darker side in all of this, where mental flashbacks, the inevitability of things going badly wrong would haunt him in later life.

A good man, with an Oxbridge education was how Sir James had put his recommendations for him to his superiors. As a foreigner he was instilled with the same attributes that made him a Great Britain, the result of his father, a Canadian, working as a doctor in India, and his mother the daughter of a High Commissioner.

The mobile incident room set up for Goode, was to be the liaison base. A hundred metres or so from the school, out of view from anyone, it offered protection from any stray armaments they might be targeted by.

Packed with the latest technical innovations they would need; three additional incident cabins were installed. Delivered on a low-loader from the Defence Equipment & Support Procurements base at Abbey Wood, near Bristol, specialist teams quickly installed themselves and their equipment. One of these cabins contained the Specialist Firearms Unit. Most of the rest of the armed police had been positioned in office blocks and similar high buildings that afforded an overview of the school, armed, and what a local television anchor-woman from ITV Southwest added rather unhelpfully as, 'Could be a danger to the public below', until Merriweather reminded her that his people were professionals and not likely to engage in some crazy fire fight, threatening to ban ITV from any further press conferences should they persist in further negative remarks.

Other unhelpfuls in the name of a free press had been told by Goode that they could put their equipment and crews wherever they liked provided it was nowhere near them by at least three hundred metres. Both BBC and ITV asked why al Jazeera were given preferential treatment given it could be Islamist Fundamentals laying siege in Bristol.

'Like we need all this,' Goode said after he had sorted them all out by threatening to have them all moved to the other side of the Severn if they didn't toe the line and act like the professional journalists the public saw them on the other side of the screen.

When an operational member of the Special Firearms Unit came into the incident room, Merriweather and Goode were talking to each other. Pulling off her balaclava, she ran her hands through her red hair to straighten it.

'Hi Guys, I'm Acton-Vean, who's in charge here?' she asked of both men.

Merriweather turned to Goode and pulled a face of disbelief that they would send a woman to organise a probable final assault on these terrorists.

'I'm he,' Merriweather said holding his hand. She smiled and shook it. 'And this is DCI Grantley Goode, my right hand on the ground.'

She smiled at Goode.

'Chief Inspector . . .' She turned her attention to Merriweather, 'You look as if you're expecting someone else.'

'Well, frankly, yes. I wasn't anticipating someone of your rank to be in charge of a firearms unit that's all. I asked for a team with dedicated weapons experience.'

'And they sent you a woman with those attributes. Problem?'

They both looked at her.

'Let me answer that straight away, so we all understand each other. Two years in Baghdad keeping back insurgents using the most up-to-date weaponry around, while my engineers were erecting the Green Zone. Remind me what you were up to in 1998, Chief Superintendent? Oh, and I'm not insisting on the epithet Major.'

'*Right!*' Merriweather said.

'Have I a desk or an office?'

Goode pointed her in the direction, 'This is it. Over there.'

Acton-Vean sat down at the double desk inside the incident cabin opposite the two men. Strewn with maps of Bristol, along with drawings of the interior of the school, she picked up the plan of the school.

'This current? she asked. Merriweather nodded. 'From a war zone perspective there is a textbook for driving the enemy from positions such as these,' she said studying the playground area. 'These people certainly know how to pick their targets don't they? Nothing's ever straight forward. Do we know who they are?'

Goode retrieved the papers from the envelope that had been delivered to the BBC office in Plymouth.

'Far as we know the leader is a man calling himself, Wheal Brae. Real name William Timmins. Until recent a member of *Mebyon Kernow* until they kicked him out for his extreme views. More than that, we have nothing. MI5 and Special Branch are working on him. The man does not appear to be on anyone's radar,' Goode said.

Merriweather cut in, 'We've been asked to liaise with Devon and Cornwall Police and to keep them informed. They've parents of children in their region that are at the school. They are currently carrying out inquiries with the Stannary Parliaments of Devon and Cornwall, the Tinner Society, and the Cornish Druids. So far, they have drawn a blank regarding the organisation this man supposedly represents. The *Democratic Republic of Cornwall*, according to *Mebyon Kernow*, is the brainchild of Timmins.'

'And what are these Stannary Parliaments?' Acton-Vean asked.

'Don't know. You've got Cornish ancestry,' Merriweather said turning to Goode. 'Perhaps you can explain.'

'*EH!* Who told you that? Technically they no longer exist, more an historical title. Basically, they represented the tin mining interests for the Princes of Wales in Devon and Cornwall, or the duchy as it is better known, the Crown. In 1305 Edward the First established the Devon Stannaries, while in 1337 the third Edward established the duchy of Cornwall to provide an income for the Duke of Cornwall as the prince is also known.'

'And do they still mine tin?'

'Not a lot. The falling price of tin has seen to that. The point is, and this is an argument some Cornish have been having for a long time. Property and other interests outside of mining are still with the duchy of Cornwall, who enjoy tax advantages that another organisation does not. It does not go down too well with some, and from time to time trouble rears its ugly head.'

'What trouble? Riots.'

'Damage to businesses. Pubs and restaurants owed by the English. *English Heritage* labelling everything they control with its country of origin. Then there's the Crown imposing restrictions to keep them down and poor in the name of the Princes of Wales. They want Cornish autonomy with the right to self-rule; wanting nothing to do with the English or its Crown.'

'And this man Timmins, is he one of them?' Acton-Vean asked.

'Until some other intelligence comes up, the jury is out, but we do think, yes. Thames Valley has been sent into the region for the purposes of interviewing suspects, see if they can find anyone that's heard of him,' Goode said.

'Thames Valley, eh? Bet Devon and Cornwall are delighted with that. They've a reputation,' Acton-Vean said.

'We don't have a choice. The Home Office agreed. Chief Superintendent Rudyard being the man on the ground down there wasn't overly happy when they told him what they had in mind. He suspected they didn't trust Devon and Cornwall. That they might be too close to the grass, so to speak. Rudyard asked to speak to someone higher placed to get the situation reversed. In the meantime . . .' Merriweather said before being interrupted.

'The Home Office may have a point?' Goode said.

'In the meantime, you'd better make a courtesy call to CS Rudyard, Grant. Something on the lines of all having a need to cooperate on this one – the Home Office included,' Merriweather said.

'Oh, thanks.'

\*   \*   \*

## Polgarrow, Cornwall 2008

The local Spar shop, next to the medical centre, leading to the beach was where holidaymakers could buy beach balls, windbreaks, swimming gear, polystyrene surf boards, sweets, films, cigarettes, suntan cream. An assortment of medical supplies – for those never-ending emergencies – were displayed hanging out front along with the ice-cream freezer and a postcard display. Wearing shorts and close to nothing else, in flip-flop footwear, holidaymakers were an essential part of the business community for three months of the year.

Tregarrow Holiday Park accommodates three thousand families in its lodges, caravans, and ready erected tents. Being the largest site in that part of Cornwall, not quite Newquay, it inadvertently increased the surgery's workload. Mainly children with scraped knees, banged heads and sand in their eyes.

In winter, when they had gone and were planning their next year's break the town, save for builders and decorators making good repairs to holiday lets, caravan sites, pubs, clubs, cafes and restaurants all was quiet. But not now. Now, all eyes were on the helicopter directly above Polgarrow's Medical Centre.

On the ground, a Tactical Aid Group team descended on the surgery, an operation that should have been clandestine in its approach amidst holiday traffic jams, went down badly. Visitors seeing armed men in black suits with masks, not immediately recognising them as the police special armed unit, got out of their cars and ran for cover. Some were carrying children in their arms. Caravanettes, cars trailing boats, surf boards and camping equipment jammed the roads. The Kernow building and conservatories lorry was at the front of the traffic queue. It was trying to get past the local post van blocking the side of the road. A traffic warden suddenly finding himself thrust into a position of responsibility by armed officers to clear the street was overjoyed. Directing traffic into a field, the green and red daubed woolly occupants chewing grass looked up before running en masse down to the bottom corner of the field, where, but for a stream bounded by broken fencing and barbed wire, brought them to a halt. Here they baa-baaed for their lives. Forgetting for a moment their ailments, patients came running out from the surgery while the TAG team brushed past them. Then crouching, their semi-automatic carbine weaponry at the ready, they formed a half circle in front of the reception desk, who, according to one over enthusiastic witness, demanded the head of Dr. Treffry.

The receptionist, a woman with grey hair that had been tied in a bun said that he had a patient with him and, *Would you all please take a seat!*

Ignoring her polite request, part of the team went down the corridor seeking his name on a door. The senior officer finding it kicked it open and went in. Others followed.

Outside on the road, the doctor, his wrists tied with plastic tags, a black cotton bag over his head, was dragged out shouting. He was then unceremoniously bundled into the back of an unmarked blue van. His receptionist ran out after him. Going up to the driver seated the other side of the vehicle's armoured glass window, she demanded to know what the hell was going on. And if they were making a film it might have been polite if someone had told her. The police driver ignored her pleas putting the van into reverse gear before driving at speed back up the street where he screeched to a halt. Flicking the Siren switch on, he crashed first gear, dropped the clutch and made his way through the crowd that his buddies had cleared a path for him.

Within minutes the rest of the TAG team were moving out in an assortment of armed response vehicles and Land Rovers, leaving two vehicles, a specialist team of forensic people and detectives from Truro to bring out the surgery's computers and files. Locking the surgery door, POLICE DO NOT CROSS tape was put across the entrance walkway. Then leaving two officers to stand guard they too drove off.

Overhead the helicopter banked away to the east, leaving an echo of its engine to resonate down the valley to the sea before it too disappeared.

## Penzance

Thames Valley were making an uninvited call at the offices of the political party for Cornish home rule, *Mebyon Kernow*. With no one home to receive them the police removed computers and files. The offices were then secured with police DO NOT CROSS tape and two officers left guarding.

Detective Inspector Kent Knapp never saw England as a holiday destination, preferring instead vacating in Benidorm. So, to arrive in Newlyn to a heatwave every bit as hot as Spain came as a surprise to him. And bright. As an amateur photographer, he thought, he was going to have to give a notion to moving here when he retired. For the moment though, it looked as if it was going to fall to him to stop local fisherman Christ Wright from firing up an old Evinrude outboard motor on his rubber dinghy in an attempt to escape arrest the local police were intent on carrying out.

Wright was shouting from the water at police constable Trethewey, who was running alongside the edge of the harbour in his attempt to keep up with him as he floated away.

'The English doing a proper job for you, Trethewey. Make you proud does it? All this fuss over fishing quotas—'

The rest of his words were drowned out by the engine starting up. Knapp spotting a slack mooring rope on the water running from a trawler that was attached to a bollard on the quay picked it up. Pulling it taut he caught Wright in the chest causing him to lose balance sending him tumbling into the harbour.

Passing through Newlyn on his way to Truro, Knapp came on an art studio being raided by a police team from Bodmin. One of officers he recognised was struggling with a man and a woman. Both were attired in white robes doing their utmost to resist arrest. The officer had got them as close to the rear of the police van where they found the strength to resist his even further efforts. Knocking his helmet from his head and ripping the front of his tunic open. Recognising the officer from his Thames Valley days before the man relocated to Devon and Cornwall, Knapp not being able to resist the opportunity stopped the car, wound down the window and called out, 'Standard of dress, sergeant. This is not London! Your Rudders will have your guts for garters looking like that.'

Sergeant Flintlock wearing his helmet by the strap down over his neck, his face red from the fracas of two druids shouted after him, 'And you can *piss off*. I transferred for some peace and quiet. Seeing you down here, Kent, I can see why that's all changed now.'

Knapp returning a smile and a wave closed his window and drove to Truro police station where his investigating team from Thames Valley had begun their particular style for questioning.

## Devon & Cornwall Constabulary, (Plymouth Central Sector), Plymouth 2008

Rudyard was on the telephone to Sir Wellington Beaufort, the Deputy Chief Constable for the United Kingdom. Unfazed by the man's rank he was far from satisfied with a developing situation that was getting out of control in Cornwall.

'. . . it's slapdash and un-satis-fac-torily *sound!*'

He was red in the face and it reflected in his voice.

'On top of that, to get a call from an officer from Avon and Somerset, what was his name now . . . oh yes, a DCI Goode, an officer incidentally below my rank, speaking to me as if he were selling me life insurance was far from regular *procedure* – it is ditching *sound* police protocol. We have *sound* information on all organisations within the southwest, including *Mebyon Kernow*—'

To Beaufort's annoyance, trying to get Rudyard to understand the reasoning behind their decisions for the last five minutes was forced to interrupt him once more. Reluctantly – for he could see where Rudyard was coming from – he nevertheless felt he had to pull his own rank.

'Your conversation with an officer from another force is as maybe, but you still don't dictate my policy around a national emergency, Rudyard. Have you been out of the marines too long that you don't understand the gravity of a situation, and . . . ?'

Rudyard replaced the receiver slowly. The displeasure in Beaufort's command was ringing in his ear. He had lost his patience with the man. Regretting now that he should have put his case over better and not lost his temper. Quickly recovering his composure, he sighed and muttering to himself said, *A knight of the realm or no, that man would not have got away with that for an attitude in the marines.*


## Travel Lodge, Plymouth 2008

Jackie made her mind up. Having to come to terms with Phil having gone missing was all too much for her. She opted for denial. She would return to Bristol. Frighteningly, the circumstances were not dissimilar to those of his father. Except, unlike his father who no one had seen disappear, supposedly from on the moor (he might have been there), she at least had seen his son walk into oblivion with another. All of which, to her mind, he had brought on himself. Convinced now he had an ulterior motive for this trip he had not mentioned to her, she wondered why he had needed her with him when his father had gone it alone. He had never shown any sign to her that he was holding a belated mourning for his father that would last some thirty-odd years. Only that he must have experienced some last-minute psychological trauma walking out on her.

Noyon telling her his version of events from what he had supposedly overheard was one she would not confirm should he need proof or witness. Not everything in this world could be explained, nor was it ever likely to be so. And a man, stalking Dartmoor before being condemned for murder, hanged in front of her own eyes, she would put to the back of her mind the result of an overactive imagination made dream. She had pointed this out to the journalist seeking more, that his credibility would be shot along with the rest of his working life should he continue pursuing her and this story as she couldn't or wouldn't fill in the missing passages. She had gone on to say that her own credibility would be no better served. Her company about to go public, was not the time for a director to talk of time-travel. The corporate finance world rumouring one had lost their grip on reality would send potential investors running for cover. Media promotion might be creative when it came to the sanity of a director going off the wall in a wonderland that saw a man hanged in 1716, but it wasn't that imaginative that it could spin its way out of that one.

She needed caffeine.

'*Waiter!* Could I have another pot of coffee, please?'

'Certainly, miss, and will you be checking out this morning?'

She was not sure.

She tried to put events out of her mind looking instead at the pictures that were on the wall. Extolling the Dartmoor experience for residents spending a few days was not how she saw the place now. High Tors and wet valleys. Where what would pass for an easy crossing from a distance would be fraught with ravines, rivers, and bogs. Where peat hags could snap an ankle. The incessant passing before her eyes of bramble and granite could, she supposed, turn one blind, as snow might. Then there were the huge black soft slugs that seemed attracted to their cooking area in the half-light of evening (check the frying pan in the morning before you put the bacon in Phil had suggested to her) where the dryness of day turned to damp and dew. No mention there of stepping into a time–portal. Tinner's huts, along with poisonous serpents and spiders would all occupy her list of no-noes for the foreseeable future. She had no wish to return to such a God-*awful* place – ever.

'You told me you didn't murder your friend. What of Phil, who's killed him, can you answer me that?' Jackie asked of the phantom.

'He needs vital evidence,' it answered.

'Tell him to get it himself then. What's so special that you can only bring messages? You have the power of illusion, get it yourself.'

He held his finger to his lips, that she should keep this quiet.

'Long since. 'Tis the nature of time, that events should happen in one place, whilst in others, the same should not – 'twixt a void—'

'Like James the Third being on the throne of England,' she said sarcastically. 'I would like to know how you managed that?'

He continued.

'Wars that have gone different ways, that have taken a wrong turn into a bleakness of human suffering not always prosecuted with evil intent. A world forever upset where fate has gone awry – an endless task of entanglement going nowhere, reflecting back and forth across time divides like facing mirrors are an endless eternity. People giving no consideration to where they are and how they came to be there, what is happening to them, with the inability to question; and where the deaths of hundreds of children in your world are an inevitability. No madam believe me when I say it. I would not presume to have you believe that I have the wit or power to carry out such illusions, if illusions you believe them to be – I fear they're a reality for the briefest of time they exist; and where they are capable of inflicting damage that is irreversible, so should you. I am not special. I know not how I am part of this illusion of yours, and I cannot command the living to do any bidding that they are blind or otherwise, you are in disordered time as I am myself and I suspect you know it.'

She feared what this man was saying was true. It was no matter she didn't understand it. What she did comprehend was the reality of what he had spoken and how it had affected her. Was there no other way out for them?

'You speak of events going in different directions. Are those the children in Bristol you are referring?'

He was trying to recall, but time was spinning inside his own head and he couldn't halt it long enough to establish an answer. He wasn't dead. He was before his death; in a place he shouldn't be in; that broke natural laws of time. How could he answer her other than inside of her head?

James the Third, king. How could that be?

'No James—'

He was gone, but his words echoed on through her mind.

'But will be in your world. Three hundred souls. The need of a barrister. That can defend me – for an act that his father was unable to bring to fruition. The world of James the Third does exists and it is turning your world back for the briefest of time. An acquittal could reverse that trend. An outcome to what you witnessed of me hanging by the neck I could bear if I were guilty – I was not.'

*John Goode,* she said thoughtfully.

For the first time she had used his name, casting aside her previous thinking that the past could not engage with the present, though she knew that this man had existed – lived. His appearance in the twentieth century could well be normal, it's place and time not recognising that he might be construed as an illusion in the presence of others. By chance, the scientific world of CERN had achieved time travel and that he, John Goode, could be the first of many pilots on such a mission to affect a future that had gone badly wrong.

What happened to Phil's father could happen to his son. Could she alone prevent the picture that was in her mind now? A school full of children sitting cross-legged on a parquet floor screaming in terror. The fire taking hold from the bombs strapped to them.

She looked up at the waiter standing expecting a reply.

'No, I shall be staying a few days more.'

'Very good, miss. I'll bring your coffee. Caffè Americano isn't it?'

# FIFTEEN

## Avon and Somerset Constabulary Ops. Units, Bristol 2008

*MERRIWEATHER REMOVED* the binoculars from his eyes, adjusted their focus, then looking back through them, reappraised the situation. He panned along the school building concentrating on windows and doors before moving up to the name sculptured in the plaque over its ancient doorway. He read the lettering to himself:

---

**STANNERS' & HABERDASHERS'**
**SCHOOL FOR THE POOR.**
**Inaugurated by**
**Sophie Dorothea, 1727**

---

Standing next to him, Acton-Vean, was taking a call from a mobile handed to her by an engineer in blue coveralls. She listened then passed it to Merriweather.

'We're through.'

'And you are?' William Timmins asked.

'Andrew Merriweather, officer-in-charge of the situation you've instigated. My first request is that you give it up and release the children back into the arms of their families. I must warn you, Mr. Timmins, there has never been an instance of hostage taking in this country of children, that did not result in their release. I suggest you take notice of what I am saying to you and give it up while you've the chance.'

Timmins was sitting in the head teacher's office. Each side of him, a Cornish flag of St. Piran. Placed against the back wall behind, what should have been the arms of the Duke of Cornwall with its fifteen heraldic bezants, the claw of a Cornish chough on a crown; along with the words, onen hag all (one and all) scribed in Brittonic Celtic, had all but been removed and replaced with the words, *The Democratic Republic for Cornwall*. His only compromise to tradition being the artwork of a fisherman and a miner. Except they now had crossed automatic rifles over their heads.

He was wearing a black leather jacket, black T-shirt, combat trousers with long lace-up leather boots. The two men either side of him, excepting the wearing of balaclavas, were similarly attired. As things stood, he held all the cards and the officer-in-charge knew it. He also knew that three hundred children held captive would not involve any gung-ho approach by any tactical teams such as the SAS or the police. Also, unlike the Russian government of 2004 in Beslan, North Ossetia who inevitably killed one hundred and eighty-six children using tanks to break that siege. He would not be using them.

A video camera was recording him. The legend: Coming to you through You Tube would inevitably be seen by him. And if they didn't, below it was the website domain Cornwall for the Cornish, with a Facebook logo.

Listening intently for any sound of a reply, or any sound at all that might give him the edge, Merriweather did not at first notice what the engineer had brought up on the internet until he drew his attention to the Facebook page on the screen of his laptop. He put his hand over the phone.

'Can you get in any closer? On his beret perhaps?'

'Facebook!' the engineer signalled to him on another screen.

Merriweather re-directed his attention. Timmins was wearing

his beret at an angle that suggested to him that the man had modelled himself on the leader of the Ernesto "Che" Guevara. He then replaced the telephone to his ear.

'Congratulations, you'll be the first officer in charge that failed in a rescue bid. I'm afraid you are not in a position to make any demands of me, Merriweather. I take it you do have a rank. Might be as well if I know who I'm dealing with. Keep everything professional and respectable. I shall be making my demands in half an hour.'

'Acting chief superintendent.'

If Timmins heard his name, he didn't comment. He ended the call with no more formality than goodbye. Merriweather turned DC Helen Moyle who had entered the operations cabin.

'Ah, just the man,' he said to her. 'I need to know how many armed people he has with him. An exact number of children, with names and home addresses. Also, the school staff, and where everyone is in relation to his operational area. Here, a rough drawing of the school. Until I get an architects plan mark everything up on that.'

'Sir.'

Goode came in as she left.

'How are we doing with our inquiries in the southwest?' Merriweather asked.

'Ah, just the man. You'll have to speak with Rudyard from Devon and Cornwall yourself on that one. He won't talk to me. Afraid he's not a happy bunny.'

'Then he'll have to remain an unhappy bun—'

'I'm afraid you haven't a choice, Andy. And, as he's the assistant chief constable for the southwest, he insists on speaking to you personally. He felt that, what with you being closer to his rank than mine, you might place closer attention to what he has to say to thine over mine,' Goode replied with a smile.

'He said that?'

'No, I made that last bit up.'

'Idiot!'

## Devon and Cornwall Incident Mobile
## Yelverton–Princetown, Dartmoor 2008

'You sure she said that, Sergeant?'

Waverley was, but had been reluctant to say so. He bit into his ham sandwich and sipped the cup of coffee passed to him by Mudge. He was coaxing a second kettle of water to come to the boil on an upturned orange box procured for the role.

'Well, it was as I said Sir. There is no question in my mind. She said she thought she was in another world,' Waverley added.

'That's the Travel Lodge for you, full of strange people with strange ways,' Mudge said pouring the freshly boiled kettle of water into more cups.

'Yes, thank you constable,' Cocksworth said.

'And we had company. The newspaper guy was seated at an adjacent table behind her. He would have heard everything. She was talking to someone. Whoever he or it was, they were not visible to us.'

'Like I said, Travel Lodge.'

They both looked at Mudge. Cocksworth pointed his finger in a reprimanding fashion.

'What I don't understand,' Cocksworth added, 'was why would a woman of her obvious intellect . . . oh, we've had this conversation before.'

Mudge interrupted.

'Perhaps I could I run a check on this John Goode? You never know he might be a figure from history.' They both looked at him. 'Well, what do we have to lose by assuming she's telling the truth as she sees it?'

'Do it then constable,' Cocksworth said looking in Waverley's direction. The man clearly had something on his mind. 'What is it Waverley? Come on man, spit it out.'

'Well it's this past thing. This 1716 reference to the Stuart James the Third. I've been on the internet but can find nothing that says there was a James the Third of England at that time. There was a Scottish James the Third in 1460. But he was a Stewart, spelt as in the actor, James Stewart. There would have been had the Jacobite Revolution had its way turning over the 1701 Act of Settlement where James Stuart, of the Old Pretender fame would have made the line. George the First, on the other hand broke the Stuart succession of Queen Anne, and the Hanoverian line was established. The Forbes woman has been talking as if there was an alternative history here.'

'Without the knowledge for argument myself, I'm impressed Waverley. Though for the moment, and in keeping with the chief super's policy for open mindedness, we'll keep that hypothesis of yours under our hats for the moment sergeant.'

Waverley was looking surprised. Concealing a critical part of this investigation from Rudyard was not something they should be taking lightly, and he said as much.

'I know what you're suggesting Sergeant, nevertheless, for the moment we will keep this to ourselves. A reputational death will be a lot worse if this turns out to be no more than a crock of shit, follow?'

Mudge seemed happy with Cocksworth's decision, while mentioning to Waverley, that while present company might be relied upon to keep their mouth's closed, there was still the matter of another whose reputation might be enhanced should it get out that certain police officers in the southwest had tacitly taken seriously the meanderings of a delusional woman.

'Not that I'm suggesting for one minute that *The Sun* would indulge their readers in such nonsense,' Mudge added smiling at the two detectives while sipping at his tea. 'But as my old dad used to say, keep your powder dry son.'

# SIXTEEN

## INTERPENETRATING
## DIMENSION DOME
### Bodnim Assize, Cornwall 1716

*JOHN GOODE* stood in the dock staring at the judge. He sensed all was not well. The coat-of-arms on the wall behind the bench – like that outside the assize building – had settled on James the First. He was not aware of it changing.

Judge Edmund Skull was looking anxious, and returned Goode's stare, going so far as to acknowledge him. For even though he recognised John Goode had status, he was not sure what that status was and where it came. Pouring the remaining port from his decanter into his glass, he quickly emptied it down his throat. Then indicating to his clerk with a point of his finger and a nod of his head, the man refilled it.

'When you've returned with another decanter Quince you can read the indictment,' Skull said to his clerk. Quince returned after a minute placing a fresh one at his honour's elbow.

Skull poured another while Quince waited for the Judge to nod for him to continue. When he did, Quince read out the reason a man from the Devon Stannary was to be tried in a civil court instead of under the Stannary laws of Lydford appropriate to tinners. Interrupting him, Skull addressed the jury.

'Let me be clear. This court was obliged to undertake such a prosecution for Lydford after the handing over of the defendant indicted for the crime of murder. This was a case that Lydford needed to be sure of. *Though why they are bothering now when they've never before,*' he whispered to himself as an aside. 'Carry on, Quince.'

'For the murder and torture of Joshua Timmins, while in the service of King James the Third. How do you answer to the charge, John Goode?'

James the Third? Judge Skull thought. Doesn't sound right, I must have misheard. Oh well. Must've been the venison I had for last night's supper. Now I think to it, it did taste on the side of rank.

'Have I a defence barrister?' John Goode asked anxiously. He had not been given direction or preparation for this indictment against him.'

'No one would take his case father, I mean Your Honour,' another Skull interjected.

'Not needed as long as I'm on the bench, eh, ladies and gentlemen of the jury?' Skull said appreciating and enjoying the mirth of laughter from them. Turning to John Goode he said, 'No barrister. Did you hear that John Goode? Not very well thought of by your Stannary are you? You'll swing to English law the same. Tinner's taxes have some use eh Quince?'

'Who's for the prosecution Quince?'

'Your son, I mean, ah, Mr. Justice Ventonwyn, Your Honour.'

Ventonwyn Skull stood up and smiled. He nodded at the court then sat back down with an air of satisfaction.

In spite of his father's attempt in bringing his son the best of education, the words of the King's College Cambridge dean, Reverend Sir Morgan Stanley, that he might have more success investing his money educating one of his pigs had done nothing to prevent him thinking that his son might make something of himself in law. Another uphill struggle for the judge. But with persistence, and more money than sense being thrown into the affair, he had succeeded to the point that his wife's face broke out in a smile that she hadn't given birth to the idiot her husband said he was.

Ventonwyn Skull was blessed with a young face and an old nose. His physiognomy was in its twenties, while his protuberance approached eighty. Thin edged ears and thick lips that oozed bad breath to any person too close, a feature that did nothing to enhance his barristership. This would be his first appearance in court as a lawyer for the prosecution. His previous was of acting defence attorney, resulting in an ever-embarrassing number of people being sent to the gallows. Though some were clearly guilty, even this was too much for his father. Judge Skull convinced that his son would be hard pressed to make a mess of this case with him presiding gave him little comfort. For this indictment of murder of an officer of the crown coupled with the word that James the Third was showing an interest without giving him legal direction pointed him to the path he might wish to take. None the less, he still prayed. If John Goode was found innocent, notwithstanding his influences on the contrary, he might well end up finding himself the first judge in the land to be hanged for the mismanagement of the English legal system.

'Can I have the case for the prosecution.'

Judge Skull sat down.

Ventonwyn Skull stood up.

'The defendant. . . . The accursed . . . I mean the accused stands before you, father, sorry, Your Honour, on the heinous charge of the murder of Joshua Timmins, Stannary Officer for Cornwall. Murder! Murder of a messenger in the employ of Hugh Boscawen of Tregothnan and Falmouth after King James the Third, John . . .'

The counsel for the prosecution went on for a full half an hour, going into the history of tinners and the Stannary parliament. When he had finished Quince nudged his father who had fallen asleep from interest or lack of it between bouts of port. Waking with a loud snort of breath, Quince brought the judge up to date. Skull nodded his understanding, and despite there being no body of Timmins, summed up for the benefit of the jury the likelihood of his having been murdered and buried in one of the bogs out on the moor before addressing Goode as the culprit.

'We can take it from written evidence supplied by Lydford that you did carry out the murder of Joshua Timmins. As such it is my duty to pass sentence on you.' Placing a black cloth over his head given him by Quince he continued. 'The sentence of this court using guidelines offered by Lydford is that you be taken immediately to a place of execution where you will be hanged by the neck until you are dead. We have gallows to hand, Quince?' he asked.

His clerk nodded.

'Send him on his way.'


Two soldiers manhandled John Goode from the court to the place of execution. Twenty yards from its side door that, not half an hour before, he had entered with his fellow accused. A high scaffold affair with wooden steps leading to a rope suspended from a cross kingspar was an adequate, if not a well-constructed arrangement. An executioner waited, his eyes with a covering of a red mask under a brimmed leather hat, his hands, one crossed over the other showed his thumb caressing his first finger in anticipation for this was his first day as duty executioner. He turned to face his client.

John Goode pulling himself from the restraining arms of the soldiers climbed the steps unassisted. The executioner took him by the shoulder and helped him up onto a wheeled platform. Alongside of it was a small girl clutching a dolly underneath her arm. A smaller boy, Goode thought, for some reason might have been her brother, then dismissed the thought for a higher one. A rope was attached to the platform. The little girl preoccupied with her dolly in one hand was holding it taught with the other. Alongside them was a priest, a bible in his hand. Seeing the noose attached to the overhanging spar John Goode's legs momentarily gave way. Recovering his composure, he stood upright. Shaking his head, he attempted to convince someone of his innocence. Whether it was God, the prison governor, or the priest standing next to him, no one gave much thought to. What did occur to him was an unreality he guessed had gone through the minds of every man that was to suffer the fate of being put to death by strangulation from a rope noose in front of a crowd of well-wishers. For this audience, victualling themselves on half-penny lung pies, or crunching on roasted pig skins sold from a tray by the local butcher's daughter with black teeth, was a day out for an otherwise mundane existence. The chance to see someone that may have had a better life than themselves be ended gave sombre satisfaction to keep to their place and status.

He fought to suppress his panic and terror. He had been told that resignation and the need to get this done comes to a person when the inevitability of what is to take place is established. How he wished for that time to come that would bring the mental capacity to express his last words in a dignified manner. Of how he is about to leave this world with his loyalty to the king. For himself, he felt none of those thoughts. For it was the king himself that had brought him to this impasse. The hangman lifted the noose while one of the soldiers tied his wrists and legs together.

'Any last words Sir?' the hangman asked him.

He did not. Pulling the nightcap that he had worn in the cells roughly over his head, the hangman then slipped the noose around his neck, then tightening the knot looked to the prison governor for permission to continue with his duty.

After what seemed a lifetime the prison governor said that he will not bother with the outline of his crime, before thanking Goode himself for not wasting time as he needed an early lunch. This effrontery to Goode's status was too much for him. Loudly protesting that he and Timmins were carrying message from King George himself to Sir Richard Vyvyan demanding that he be released while proper inquiries could be carried out to substantiate that what he was saying was true.

There was a roar from the crowd.

The prison governor held his hand up to better hear what Goode was saying.

'Who is this King George and Sir Richard you speak of? the governor asking looking to the priest for an understanding that he might know.

The priest crossed himself saying, 'This man's treason is the work of the devil, it'll probably be as well that he is put out of his misery sooner rather than later, if only to save the embarrassment reaching the ears of King James.'

The prison governor agreed. He was about to give the signal for the executioner to carry out his duty when a woman jumped up onto the scaffold, approached the condemned man, grabbing him around the chest and protesting that he was right in what he was saying. The soldiers at first taken by surprise recovered their senses and tried to pull her off of him.

'Get your hands off me,' she shouted at them.

'Who's that woman? Take her down. What's she saying now?' the governor asked.

The hangman pulled the hood from Goode's face and repeated to the governor what it was she had said.

'Says she's looking for her husband, Governor. Wants to know what this man has done with him.'

'Probably murdered him as well. He'll swing for the sheep as well as the lamb. Get her away and resume your duty,' he said.

Soldiers stepped forward to remove her. Pulling her from the scaffold she began struggling and pleading that the condemned man had important information that was vital. Her pleas went unheeded.

'Do your duty,' the governor directed the hangman.

Immediately the wheeled platform that he stood was rolled away from from under him by the executioner's daughter. His neck took the whole weight of his body. Swinging as a pendulum, the kingspar holding the taut rope protested.

Jackie was pushed from the scaffold into the crowd where people jeering and laughing surrounded her. She had added to their day's entertainment. But it was soon forgotten. There came a loud crack. The kingspar that held the rope was splitting. The inevitability of it giving way under its gruesome weight was on the faces of those that were standing close to the front. It would hold, but not before threatening the life of the hangman's daughter should it collapse on her. Skipping off the scaffold unaware of the danger she faced, a collective sigh of relief went through the crowd as it held.

Struggling for a last breath that was never going to return to him; and with the sound of a blackbird singing somewhere in the distance to give him small comfort he quietly slipped into unconsciousness. Ten minutes later, John Goode Stannary officer for Devon was no more under James the First.

## Lovaton, Dartmoor 1716

The cart made its way down the rutted track to the farm. Its metal rimmed tyre jumping and sliding on the broken granite would – the officer from the Exeter Assize thought – at any moment break away from its rim tipping both driver and the body of John Goode into the stream that was running beside of them.

Jessie Goode hearing it first called out through an open window to attract the attention of her husband through the sound of his hammering. Hearing her calling he peered out from the doorway of the store shed that he was working thinking that the beam he had removed to affect the repair to the roof had allowed the struts to fall in, covering her in dried mud, moss, old straw, dead mice, spiders and laths. Wearing a leather apron with a large hammer that he had been using to beat a sheet of metal flat to use for the leaking roof watched as the cart approached.

Jonathan Goode thought it might be the Stannary parliamentary officer that had first approached John on king's business. Jessie his wife had not been taken with her son taking up such an appointment, not with the Jacobite uprising with danger for ordinary folk that had a mixture of supporters for both sides of the coin both Catholic and Protestant alike. With so much treachery, the result of changing allegiances, she feared for the life of her son, but not solely for those reasons. Jonathan had tried to reassure her, that as an officer of the Stannary he would be safe enough from harm. She knew better. She held a secret she had sworn to keep from both husband and son. Of course, John was not Jonathan natural son, he knew that. What he did not know was neither was he hers. A condition of her marriage to him was that he never ask the name of John's father. For his name would inevitably lead to that of the true mother to any with sense to work it out.

The cart stopped short of the cottage. The driver, with his assistant sitting in the back, had between them a body bag brought Jessie's worst fears with its appearance. Her instincts were that the secret she had carried for so long had not been affective.

Jonathan, fearing the worst, went to his wife's side and put his arm around her slender shoulders. She was already shaking uncontrollably. He tried to console her without words, words that if he had used them would have been hollow. That he would be putting off the inevitable for Jonathan recognised the man's uniform as he got down from the cart. The rough navy-blue serge of a prison officer was one he recognised, for he himself was no stranger to incarceration.

The officer nodded at him and his wife. His face grim, for though he was a hard man, the return of a dead son to his family was not a task that came easy to saint or sinner. The body of a hanged man brought for burial to his home, instead of a prison cemetery told him that the punished man was special.

Jonathan left his wife's side to accompany the officer to the rear of the cart. The officer's assistant pulled the body enclosed in its heavy cotton bag, opening its head end to reveal the deceased's face better to establish the remains were in the right place before going to the trouble of lifting him down only to lift him back up onto the cart again.

Jonathan looked at the face of their son and nodded.

The assistant covered it back up again.

'There's no room for a burial at Exeter. Governor Patterson considered as your son was a Stannary man, you'd like to see to those arrangements yourselves.'

Jessie Goode ran to the back of the cart and pulling the sacking from his face cradled the body of her adopted son in her arms. Her tears ran down her face and onto his. Her cries of grief pierced all men's souls there. The officer, strengthening his resolve to continue his duty forced himself to ignore the grieving woman and turned his attention to Jonathan Goode.

'He's still a hanged murderer . . .'

'*A murderer!* My son is no murderer Sir. A truer one you would not find. The good Lord will be hard pressed to show mercy and forgiveness to those responsible for this day's work.'

'Nevertheless madam, in cases such as these, the hanged body of a prisoner remains the property of State and as such, however unlikely the king's pleasure dictates otherwise, then a re-interment and a return to Exeter for cemetery burial in its prison grounds would need to be undertaken.'

Jonathan nodded. He would gain nothing arguing with messengers for he knew their duty.

Jessie looked up from her adoptive son. Her mind no longer on the view of Dartmoor that lay before her but on other thoughts. Further into England and a world as far removed from this desolation as it was possible to get. To London and the Kensington palace home to the Elector George the First.

You bastard! she cried out to the heavens. You bloody, murdering German *bastard*—!

# SEVENTEEN
## Tinners Hut, Nr. Crockern Tor, Dartmoor 2008

*JACKIE CAME AS CLOSE* to the site of the tinners hut as she dared. Having hired the Land Rover, she had no intention of sending it into a bog. The track from the road leading to the bottom of Crockern Tor went for two miles. A fence enclosing timber woodland was to one side and the moor proper on its other. The middle of the night was not the time of day to be engaged in this recklessness, but she had little choice if she were to go unseen.

Relying on nothing more than the vehicle's main beam she picked out the path she was to take. She called it a path, but if it was then it was a dangerous one. Strewn with rocks and boulders, that were damp to wet, the Land Rover struggled. She was continually fighting the steering wheel for control of its direction. The low mist was not helping the situation. More than once she lost direction wondering if at any second, she had gone off track and was about to lose the vehicle to a bog. She wondered how she would possibly explain to any emergency services that came out to recover her, what she was doing here with the remains of a three hundred-year-old body on the back seat that had been stolen from a Plymouth forensic laboratory.

Coming upon the site of the tent as close as she dares without dropping herself into the East Dart river, she stopped and got out. Opening the back, she manhandled the body in its green bag onto the ground and prayed that it would retain its grisly contents intact should it fall through the rent in the fabric caused by an exposed rib bone.

John Goode had told her where she was to leave the body, along with the scientific report regarding its demise. What Cluff was supposed to do with it for evidence, she could not imagine. As to why she was doing this – she had less of a notion. It was not every day that someone from the past would ask you to body snatch as if you were some latter-day resurrectionist; and then, to comply with their request as if it were an everyday event. Something to pass onto our grandchildren should I ever get the chance to meet their grandfather again – assuming I don't wring his neck first, she thought.

Leaving the remains of the body on the ground, she shone her torch into the distance. The tinners hut was away in the darkness. She shuddered. What condition the campsite was in she could only imagine. Looking to where their tent was still standing, she could just make it out. The police had been there. Crime scene tape surrounded it. She stared hard. She was looking for an air pattern. A change, that if one were not aware of such an abnormality, would go unnoticed. A refraction of air, that oscillated, was how John Goode described them; the manner of his description suggesting they were not unique, but naturally occurring. A wind picked up, blowing the site to pieces, their frying pan and other belongings flying into the air then sinking into the bogs hiding all trace that anyone had ever been there. The thought occurred to her that perhaps she and Phil had died. She shuddered. For sure no living entities could orchestrate events of what is happening to her now. The thought that the lives of children might be saved by a barrister of Phil's standing gave her some consolation that he was in fact still alive struggling to find her as much as she him.

She was not particularly cold, but the chill that crept into her bones at the sight of the apparition in the distance was of death and graveyards as old as time itself. She could not speak his name. It felt unnatural to her to address someone that had passed over. But then how does one address a ghost of three hundred years standing. The strange thing in all of this was that according to him he was not one. *Ghosts do not exist*; he had said to her over her bed in the hospital ward. *No one dies.*

'Our souls are frozen in time while our degenerative body falls into ruin and decay. And as such no longer be able to host its occupation. July the first 1726—'

'You were hanged—'

'Forget that . . .'

'How can I? It happened in front of my own eyes with a child looking on.'

'You are not listening to me,' he continued with no reference to the child. 'The life I occupied in that time ceased for me only then. I died of mature years in another. Time's door closed at my body's death reopening in another. An event that had occurred altered, to appear once again in another sequence of events. It failed then it cannot be allowed to a second time. It falls to me and the lawyer to put right the past.'

She pulled the hood of her kagool over her head. She should have brought a flask with her this could take some time. *Time, huh!* she said with a laugh. How can anyone arrange to turn up on time when according to Dr. Who here it does not exist?

Standing by the body bag, guarding it, she felt as a Lamassu from the Citadel of Sargon II might have. When her eyes accustomed to the dark she saw the haze of the time portal John Goode said she would. Where souls good solid or mist could pass through. If you didn't know where it was you could easily stumble through it. Standing by what remained of their tent he approached her. If approach was the operative word for it was more a glide closing as a lens will bring a subject closer. She had been up close and personal when he stood on the scaffold, the rope tight to his neck, and she felt sorrow for him. She would never forget the terror in his eyes as the bag was placed back over his head.

'Is that the remains of Joshua Timmins?' he asked pointing to the body bag at her feet.

'You tell me.'

He bent down and puzzled over the zip on the bag. 'What is this thing?'

She unzipped the length of the bag immediately turning away from its containment. He nodded. Then kneeling said a prayer. He then stood.

'Have you the papers, Mr. Cluff asked for?'

She handed him the folder.

He put it into a satchel he had over his shoulder.

'Thank you,' he said.

Picking up the body bag he slung it over his shoulder adjusting the load for balance. Then taking a final look back at her he was gone. The air that was translucent as a clear jelly returned to its natural state.

'Wait a minute,' she shouted after him. 'Where is Phil?'

Away from Forbes's view, in a woodland alongside the track she had taken, Noyon watched. He had seen her break into the mortuary in Plymouth, before following her out across the moor. Passing the prison, she had taken the road to Postbridge onto Crockern. In an effort to keep up with her stumbling over dead branches and left-over stumps in the darkness he decided to find his torch. He switched it on and pointed it down. The forest floor was a mass of broken timber. This was Forestry land and he had walked into a working area of tree felling where pine trees had been reduced to horizontal by cutting machinery that had dragged out trenches deep enough to bury a man. He was standing in one now its overlap edge of mud covering his expensive brown leather shoes matched the bottom of his brown corduroy trousers perfectly. *Bollocks! That's all I need*, he muttered to himself. *Oh well, in for a penny. . . .*

He continued more cautiously now worried that he may break ankle. Emerging onto the moor proper luck was on his side. He saw the brake lights of her Land Rover coming on, then going off. She had stopped and was getting out. He switched his torch off then using the moon to guide himself along a fence he came within fifty feet of her. He watched her as she removed what looked like a body bag from the back of the Land Rover placing it on the ground. Whatever she was doing, or waiting for, he had to admit she had bottle. For whom else would come out onto the moor in the dead of night with a body for company? It was bad enough being in the presence of someone that had. When he saw what she was waiting for he felt his skin creep. The ghost that he had first seen by her bedside was out there now. He was heading in the direction of a dishevelled tent. He had first thought the pair of them had organised an insurance scam and that she might be meeting him out here. Why they would need a dead body only added to the intrigue of the complexity for such fraud that had led him to investigate further. There was something else going on here now and it had nothing to do with Phileas Cluff who was by age, dress and general appearance according to the police's missing person's best description was not this man.

He hurriedly pulled his camera strap over his shoulder and unfastened the leather case protecting it. Looking through the lens, he focussed in on the scene. An Asahi Pentax with a focal plane shutter, an ASA 1600 film that would not need flash – that would photograph a black cat in a coal cellar – and he would have the first picture of someone from the past. Evidence of time travel. He kept looking through the camera lens. He could not see the person that was carrying the body bag putting it down to the lack of light. The film would capture the scene though. There would be no doubt of that. He lowered the camera to ascertain the man's position. He saw him. Then bringing the camera back into position said, *Got you!*

He fired off the first shot. Then rapidly pulling the film winding lever over and over changing aperture settings between each shot took six more. Then he was gone. He then concentrated on taking pictures of Jackie. She had walked back to the Land Rover. Reversing back up the track the way she had come. The rear spotlight shined a trail for her. With the occasional red brake light going on and off, she was out on the road and gone. He made his way back to his own car, then drove back to Plymouth. In the morning he would have the film processed to expose the mystery of the age.

## The Jurate Arms, Nr. Crockern, Dartmoor 1716

Despite assurances by Hilary Waite that it was possible to spirit a body from 2008 back to 1716 with assistance, Phil reiterated that Jackie could hardly be expected to rob a mortuary of one of its occupants and give it to the man that had frightened them witless out on the moor. At night!

'How would you even begin to persuade anyone to do that, let alone a person of Jackie Forbes' breeding?'

'The status quo for such time-shift is that the remains return. Whether that would be back to the site the body was first buried will not be certain. It has never been achieved before. Goode has to be the conduit. And in case you've forgotten, currently resides in prison. If officers from your time had not tampered with the burial site removing the body of Timmins in the first place, we would not have needed to go to all this trouble. Interfering with his last resting place was not Christian. As it stands, you will need to seek the man that saw the body fall. I have arranged for you to travel to Crockern.'

*Not Christian*, Cluff muttered to himself in the coach, *Rich coming from him.*

The driver shouted down the arrival destination to his passenger. Holding the brake against the horses' movements he continued, '*STAGING POST TWO! EXETER! BOY!*' Where's that *bloody* boy? *ANY PASSENGERS?*'

The ostler's son hurried across the courtyard, his only protection from the rain that was hammering down, a piece of sacking across his shoulders. Taking hold of the reins of the horses he managed to settle them down. They had been driven hard from Plymouth. The sweat steaming from the beasts testament to their exertions.

'No Sir. Only mail,' he said throwing the leather satchel up to the driver.

'Pretty penny in that,' he said catching it and spitting into the courtyard from his elevated position. He then banged the stub handle of his whip onto the coach roof and shouted down to Cluff, 'You getting out your fare will take you no further?'

Cluff turned the brass handle of the coach door and stepped down into a pool of water. God's sake, he said to himself shaking his right foot. Looking up he saw the inn's sign blowing in the wind. The Jurate Arms. The hostelry according to Waite being the watering hole of locals, more importantly tinners. A pub Cluff thought to himself. It had been a long time since he had last supped a beer.

He opened the door. A latched affair with glass panels that rattled as he entered, causing its occupants to turn around in unison looking to see who was causing the intrusion.

A smoky dingy dark and inhospitable atmosphere confronted Cluff. He was mindful of whether it was 1716 or 2008 bars the world over were the same, all capable of trouble if you looked for it. Peace and quiet if you weren't. He was in no mood to be intimidated.

A thin man behind the bar eyed him suspiciously. Calling to him he shouted out, 'Drinking stranger? Hasten up, I haven't all day.'

The man might be gaunt, Cluff thought, but judging from the scar down his cheek. His muscled upper body with its tight sinews running from his neck across his open shirt, he looked as if he was no need of waiting to earn any respect. Cluff did not immediately answer, instead, turning his back to him directed himself at the landlord's clientele. Farmers, land labourers. A scattering of rogues, soldiers, general scruffs and layabouts with scruffier dogs of the lurcher and mongrel variety tied to table legs occupied the sticky slate floor made up the rest. Cluff thought about how he would broach the subject he came here for. Hopefully among this cornucopia of humanity would be tinners. Speaking roughly and using an accent cross between London and Bristol in the hope they would understand he addressed them.

'Gentlemen,' he said as if lecturing a jury. 'There was an assault of a Cornishman by the name of Joshua Timmins recently resulting in that man being killed. A Stannary officer name of John Goode was hanged for his murder. I'm here—'

A man with a fat nose wearing a dirty red soldier's blouse under a bitten at the edges worn out tri-corn hat that matched his ears, interrupted stopped him. He lifted his head, coughed, then lowering it coughed once more before spitting a brown lung sweeping, the consequence from years of smoking rough shag from endless clay pipes, from his mouth. He missed the spittoon he was aiming landing the phlegm on a sleeping dog's tail sticking out from under a table. 'Body's hidden.'

*Heads!* Cluff said to himself putting his hand to his mouth to prevent himself gagging. 'Has it? *Ummh!* Well let me tell you I'm here representing the diseased. I'm seeking a body. Buried or otherwise.' He looked for any takers from the congregation one at a time before settling back on the only one to have answered so far. 'Where?' They muttered then looked into their tankards. 'Fair enough. If you're happy to let one of your own swing for the murder for another's advantage let it be on your consciences.' He turned to the landlord. 'I'll have a pint of cooking bitter if you please gov'nor.'

The landlord went to a three crossed barrel behind the bar. He opened the tap and filled a leather tankard to its brim coughing gently to himself. Then placing the filthy yellow slopped vessel of foaming ale on the counter in front of him said, 'What are you then? King's man? Jacobite? For you are strangely dressed.'

Standing over the spittoon with its contents looking the same as the drink in his hand his taste buds rebelled.

'No. I'm the man's attorney.'

He then placed the vessel to his lips and downed its contents in one draught. Turning back to the customers, he wiped his hand with the back of his shirt cuff, putting two sovereigns on the counter in front of him.

'Any man that can show me where there is a body come and see me. I'll be outside. There'll be two more waiting for any man that does.' He put his tongue to the roof of his mouth and poked it out, '*God's breath!*' he said bringing up the contents of his stomach into the spittoon. '*Ugh!* That's some way off being Wiper and True landlord.'

Opening the inn door he stepped outside into the fresh air and took a deep breath of fresh air. Leaning against the door frame he tried to bring up more of the foul liquid that was inside him. With no more forthcoming he satisfied himself that it could not have been all that bad as there must be a good half pint still there. Pulling a handkerchief from his pocket he wiped the sweat from his brow. Then the inn door opened.

'It's an acquired taste.'

Cluff looked up at the man. He wore clothes cross between a suit and a uniform. On his chest an embroidered crest, dirty and worn, but still recognisable. An emblem of an old man bent with arthritis, a spade in his hand. A token Waite had said that such a man wearing could be trusted.

'Not where I come from it isn't. You are?'

'Kenneth Mudge, mine captain. I fear you've had a wasted journey for I cannot tell you too much. You're right. There was a murder up here some time back. The mine captain at the time was Benjamin Aesop. He would have been the one to see, unfortunately he died from unnatural circumstances.'

'Dangerous job being a mine captain. Phileas Cluff, attorney at law.'

'Every tinner knew of John Goode. Not as popular a man as he should be. Some say he had the king's blood flowing through his veins. Others that of a German count. Others still that he was a conspirator. What do you know of such matters attorney?'

'Only that he was a king's messenger,' Cluff said in reply.

'Goode was hanged for murder. His body wouldn't be here. He would have been interned in Exeter prison. There is a rumour there's a body in a disused mine up at the Mires workings. But that's all it is. If there was it wouldn't be anyone important. Authorities were supposed to have come up and opened it during Goode's trial. It's blocked with rocks see. They didn't come. That's how interested they were in a rumour.'

'Can you show me. I need to see inside. And if there is. Who it is.'

'I'll show you. But it won't be Goode. Locals have heard noises coming from the mine. Ghosts. That's where a rumour of a body comes from. A load of rubbish. From where I stand that's all there is to it. As I said. . . . If there is. Who are you hoping for?'

'Joshua Timmins. The man Goode was supposed to have murdered.'

'*Timmins!* No, no. Don't take any notice of what that old fool in the Jurate Arms said about the body being hidden. Rumours abroad at the time were that he was thrown into the East Dart river were probably true. Or what was left of his remains after Goode finished with him. A meal for the eels.'

Cluff said nothing. Studied the mine captain.

'You want me to open that mine?'

## Whiteworks, Princetown, Dartmoor 1716

The wind was getting up on the open moorland at the workings of Fox Tor Mires. On the ground, two ravens were picking over the carcass of a sheep at the entrance to a disused mine blocked with boulders. Having fallen from the rocky outcrop over it had broken its neck.

'That's it. Wait here. I need a key,' Mudge said with a smile.

He watched as the mine captain went to an old store and removed a small barrel. He then went up to the entrance to the disused mine placing it down, rolling it underneath a ledge. He then removed a small wooden cork from a bung hole in it and inserted a fuse. Going into his pocket he took out a stone and flint and chopped them together. The end of the fuse took a flash from the sparks and began to flare. He then ran down to join him pushing him behind a rock pressing his head down. The explosion was colossal. Echoing across the valley below it showered them in debris. After a minute or two the dust cleared.

'Wait here,' the mine captain told Cluff.

With a still smoking open entrance Mudge went inside. A minute later he emerged pulling a body bag out after him. He waved him to come over.

'I'll be damned. There is a body,' he said crossing himself. 'Do you know who it is?'

The mine captain pulled the bag further down to reveal his upper body. The skin intact was tight to its skeleton. Dried out, the body was in a remarkable state of preservation. Looking at it Cluff thought it wouldn't weigh more than forty kilos. Jackie would have managed it quite well.

Mudge was puzzled. 'He was a fighting man. *A soldier?*'

He showed him his arm. A chainmail protector was lying loose on the skin. Around his neck, dirty, but still recognisable a black silk scarf was wrapped.

'Not a fighting man, although he may have put up a fight. For this is the Cornish Stannator, Joshua Timmins. The man I am seeking. Could you arrange for him to be removed to Bodmin?'

Mudge nodded. 'Five sovereigns.'

Λ

# EIGHTEEN
## Offices of Ellick & Waite,
## Plymouth 1716

ZAC ELLICK FELT THE SURFACES of the plastic bag. It held a strange fascination for him. Containing a dagger, he said:

'And you can get an acquittal – with this? Thought you said you'd do it with science, for that is what we had in mind when first we thought of you. How does this dagger help?'

He rubbed his fingers together as if he were trying to remove some unseen foreign substance from them before putting the bag to his nose and sniffing. He quickly removed it wrinkling his face.

Cluff knew that using science would not lead to an acquittal. But even though DNA and fingerprint evidence would clear Goode's name in 2008 none of that was going to be of any use here. If he were to convince Judge Skull of the man's innocence, he would need to give him a crash course in the science of whorls and genetics. The man was going to have to see what Cluff had seen. Evidence of torture carried out by third parties.

'Not in this case no,' Cluff replied.

'No.' Waite said. 'Then how were you to solve the case using fingerprints. We know the science exists don't we Mr. Ellick?'

'Indeed, we do Mr. Waite.'

'Well, they have known of its existence since ancient Babylon, but it wasn't until . . .'

'In point of fact,' Ellick interrupted, 'we spend a deal of money having them removed by the act of polishing them from the brass name plate outside of our office. Twice a week, at a pretty penny I might add.'

'Right. As to the subject of DNA . . .' Cluff added trying to move away from fingerprints.

Ellick interrupted him.

'I'm not conversant with that man's initials no. But I'm sure that when it comes to convincing Judge Skull. A man unlikely to want to show his ignorance given the opportunity.'

'And a man educated at the same school as Charles Darwin will one day be,' Waite interrupted.

'What?' Cluff asked getting more exasperated at these two men's ramblings.

'Quite so Mr. Waite. I'm sure that with a little explanation by this Denay fellow, it shouldn't be too hard for him to grasp.'

'An advocate of Mr. Cluff's standing shouldn't have too much of a hardship making himself understood anywhere I wouldn't have thought Mr. Ellick. Mr. Cluff, if Master Denay is a man of science what is it he discovered that Judge Skull would not be able to argue with?'

'It is God's key to identify the person standing before Him on the day of Atonement.'

Cluff wondered if these two speaking of the future with so much familiarity was more than coincidence. Did they know? Did they think that his mention of science was going to be the magic bullet? He barely understood conventional aspects of the subject himself. What chance was he going to have tried to convince someone in the year 1716 of its infallibility? A man that might have written the definitive guide to flogging and hanging. Whose judgmental decisions were borne from his own summing up rather than a jury of twelve men good and true often seemed to hang on whether his last bottle of port had turned to vinegar or not. He would have a better chance explaining television technology. Whether he had the technical expertise to understand it enough to convince a judge that was three-quarters drunk most of the time would be another matter.

'Forget DNA. It's going to have to be hard evidence that will win this case gentlemen,' Cluff concluded. 'Let me look at it again.'

Ellick passed the forensic report back to him. Evidence he would in other circumstances take for granted were going to be useless here. A pity, he thought, for those fingerprints belonging to another and not those of John Goode would have dismissed this case in minutes. He was going to have to take another path.

He took his handkerchief from his pocket and removed the knife from the polythene pouch. He examined it closely. There was blood down the blade and on its handle. Reading the report, he saw that it mentioned two blood types. The remains of the Scottish soldier they discovered in the East Dart made him the likely suspect. The report mentioned that the team of police officers had found four bodies in that same river. Stapled to it was a photograph with mud smears over it of the camp site. Three surely, he said to himself. Timmins, Goode, and a Scottish soldier. That's it!

He turned the page. It was signatured by a forensic pathologist the name of Mary Poltair. He guessed her qualifications would be more than adequate. He went back to the top. Here it read that the dead soldier would have probably been involved in the Jacobite Uprising in the southwest; and that this knife was likely the murder weapon. Its silver and ivory banded handle confirming it matched the slash wound to Timmins's throat. If this was Joshua Timmins, and he had no reason to think otherwise given his badge of office as that of the Cornish Stannary, then it was the same man as the photograph. Another problem, he thought. The photograph. Something else that would not be of any use. Although if he can get Skull to see the body then there was a good chance that he could at least establish the murder weapon and a chance to convince him that Goode could not have wielded the weapon. With the pathologist's findings that DNA from the blood matched the body sample being conclusive how did this Jacobite man die? Ah, heart attack he muttered seeing the relevant findings below:

> . . . he appears to have cut his own wrist and bled to death. The irregularity of the cut marks to the radiuses of both wrists pointed to the wounds being caused by a knife having jagged edges opposite to its cutting blade . . .

He opened the pouch and took out the knife. It certainly had a jagged edge. He looked closer. A piece of jag was missing. His thought for it being missing was metal degradation.

'Let me explain gentlemen. If this were a twenty-first century case, I'd have sufficient evidence here to acquit Anne Boleyn of Henry's charge that she had committed incest with her brother Lord Rochford. As it is, this one is going to need more than science. I need to examine the body of Timmins with Skull being present. Can you get him to do that?'

'And did she?' Zac queried.

# NINETEEN

## INTERPENETRATING DIMENSION DOME
### Bodnim Assize, Cornwall 1716

*I've often hear of Lydford law,*
*How in the morn they hang and draw,*
*And sit in judgement after*

*THE DOWN CHUTE BROKEN* from the roof of the assize building causing the rain to pour steadily down its wall cascaded over the stone relief below that bore the inscription James the Third over its entrance porch. To Cluff it was taking on a holographic image becoming George the First. He rubbed his eyes closing them tight, and then opened them praying for mastery of brain over vision. With the stone continuing to reflect James and George alternately he dismissed the phenomenon, making a conscious decision that he was not going mad. He climbed the wet granite steps and entered the court.

Inside Hilary Waite showed him into the chamber. By the commotion inside, he was on time. The case was well under way to the point of what sounded like an instruction for the jury. As for Judge Skull he was summing up and passing sentence all at the same time.

'What's going on? I've got Timmins's body outside in the cart,' Cluff whispered nervously. For this was eighteenth-century English law he was about to embark. All he knew of that was the 1715 Riot Act. Which ironically was invoked in the wake of the failed 1710 Jacobite Uprising. What he did know for sure was what Waite and Ellick had said about this case was that it was unusually being held in Bodmin. Lydford law practices were the normal order of the day for Stannary miscreants.

Waite held him in the aisle and waited for the Skull to recognise his presence before allowing him to take his place.

'Couldn't you have asked for an adjournment until I arrived?' Cluff whispered.

Skull irritatingly ceased his speech in mid-sentence. He then nodded at Waite with a wave of his hand signalling him to be seated into that part of the court reserved for legal argument before continuing to address the defendant. Directing his attention toward the defendant, Cluff recognised it to be John Goode. Dishevelled and ill, no doubt from a lack of food his incarceration in a bad place. Skull was continuing with his summing up.

'We can take it from written statements supplied by Lydford that you did indeed carry out the murder of Joshua Timmins,' Skull said addressing Goode before turning his attention to the jury. 'There being no body for he would have surely come forward had he been and as such it is my duty to pass sentence.' He placed a black cloth over his head. 'The sentence of this court using the Lydford guidelines, is that you be taken outside and hanged by the neck until you are dead, and may the Lord have mercy on your soul. And you can thank the Lord that drawing, and quartering has been abandoned. For the murder of a king's messenger is treason as would warrant such punishment. *Take him down!*'

Goode began shouting his innocence by saying that he was also acting as king's messenger alongside Timmins, but to no avail. Skull was pouring port wine from a decanter as sure a sign to the jury that he was finished with this case and would not need their verdict. He then became aware that a man he had not seen before was approaching his bench.

'*YOUR HONOUR!*'

The man was wearing strange clothes. Multi-buttoned waistcoat, cravat and black trousers he recognised might be common wear in the street. But it was his wig, along with his forthrightness in his addressing of him that put him off his guard that caused him to call for the man's arrest by Quince.

Waite immediately interrupted with an introduction of his lawyer. Skull stayed the shoulder of Quince, for if this was anything to do with Ellick & Waite Attorneys at Law then there might be something more to this intrusion.

'Phileas. Phileas Cluff. What kind of name is that for a barrister?' Skull remarked noticing his footwear with the word Adidas written along them. 'And what are those on your feet Sir?'

Unsure of himself Cluff looked first to Ellick and then Waite for guidance. They waved him to continue.

'I'm barrister for the defence Your Honour—'

Looking beyond the Judge Skull, Cluff became aware that the heraldic shield displayed on the wall behind the bench indicating the reign of King George the First, was morphing into that of King James the Third.

'*DEFENCE! DEFENCE!* What defence? There is no defence in this case Sir. This is murder. Lydford law is master in this court. There's no defence other than what I say it is. And all non-admissible. Certainly, none that would warrant an entitlement to a barrister. Reassume your place. *Quince!* Call for the bailiff!'

Cluff made his way back to his seat.

Ellick stood up as Cluff sat down.

'What is this, Bobbin the Bob?' Skull asked irritated. 'Quince. Didn't you hear me, I asked for the bailiff.'

'I did Your Honour. I fear the bailiff did not. He has an account of a hearing defect.'

Ellick stood his ground.

Skull sighed, 'Oh very well, have your say Mr. Ellick. Be quick about it for I've a chine of mutton growing cold in The Hole In The Wall hostelry.'

'I think where one is available and willing, that the accused is entitled to a proper lawyer to act for his defence,' Ellick said leaning slightly forward to emphasise his learning.

'Oh, you do, do you Sir?' Skull answered him. 'And who is going to pay for this defence pray? Not the King, you can most assuredly be certain of that, Sir.'

Judge Skull looked about the court concentrating his remarks toward the public gallery. The peoples' affirmation was his way of knowing his interpretation of legal points of order had their approval. The laughing at his assertion that the king might pay for a defence attorney persuaded him that he had their backing and that the culmination of the case by him and his subsequent summing up of a guilty verdict had met with their approval.

'John Goode is guilty of murdering his fellow officer from the Cornwall Stannary. I can find no other evidence for contradiction. My decision is final. John Goode will hang this very day. Take him down. He drained the last of his port wine.

'All rise in the name of the King. *God – Save – King James the Third!*' Quince shouted. Then hurrying called after the judge, 'Your Honour, Your Honour!'

Skull returned.

What in hell's name's going on? Cluff asked himself to have not had a proper response from anyone else.

Skull looked flustered and confused.

'Judge Skull. Edmund,' Ellick shouted at him. 'You have not the legal authority to conduct this case in this manner. You are a sham Sir. You must balance your judgement according to English law and fairness. For to do otherwise will condemn you in the sight of the Lord for sending an innocent soul to purgatory.'

Skull was taken aback at Ellick's contempt. He had never questioned him before, and the man's disrespect had raised his blood pressure. His top teeth ground hard down against his lower. He walked from the court to return to his chamber in a rage. Then he stopped. Something was amiss here, he thought. Listening closer now. A voice played in his head. Taking a deep breath, he turned demanding an explanation:

'*WHO SAID THAT?*'

Looking about the court his eyes settled on the line of prisoners awaiting their turn to be heard. Not for the first time, with nothing to lose, would one make a derisory remark toward him. The prisoners looked at each other to see who the guilty culprit might be. There was none.

'By the Lord Harry I'll take the blood ill of him when I find him and see the culprit astride a hurdle horse whipped around the county into the next world. I say again, who dares challenge my authority using the name of anarchy?'

'I do Sir. And you know me well enough. I challenge your authority, but not in the name of anarchy,' Ellick said.

Skull stared at him. Ellick, his finger waving furiously at him began his objection. 'Since when did you conduct law under James the Third? For he is most certainly not the king of England. You do not have his authority in this place and time. I repeat Sir. You do not have magistrature of Stuart here.'

'*QUINCE!* Did you not dismiss this court in the name of King James the Third or not?'

Quince looked at the judge for some sense of guidance.

'Only under your direction, Your Honour.'

'By God I'll have your practise struck from the books. You

cannot speak to me in that fashion. Bailiff arrest the barrister Zac Ellick. I'll see you transported for this day's work Ellick. When King James—'

Skull hesitated. His feeling that all was not well with this day when first he entered the court returned to him. He listened unable to move or further object. The bailiff looking on, for he had never had cause to arrest a lawyer before and knew not what to do next.

## INTERPENETRATING DIMENSION DOME
### Bodmin Assize, Cornwall 1716

'KING JAMES THE THIRD, SIR! How long have you been justiciar under such a man? No prince of that title is monarch in this land. Look if you've eyes for honesty. Behind you. Is that the royal coat-of-arms? Is it of a Stuart, Sir? For I beg it is not, Sir.'

Judge Skull turned around to look at the wall behind him. Moving closer to it, he ran his hand slowly down the crest. His mouth quivering. Ellick was right. He had given a judgement under the misapprehension that this was the court of a Stuart.

'No Sir. Your eyes do not deceive you. It is the armorial bearing of the Elector of Hanover, King George the First after the Act of Settlement. Touch the surface if you doubt me Sir. For its paint is as dry as summer's dust. You have condemned a man to hang without true king's authority. You will pay the price Sir. For the unlawful hanging of an innocent man and king's servant, with state papers for Sir Richard Vyvyan without proper legal defence befitting such a man is tantamount to treason Sir.'

'Sir Richard? The Jacobite sympathiser . . . isn't he . . . ?'

'In the Tower of London Sir. And not with the consent of a Stuart. And you may yet well join him,' Ellick stated.

Judge Skull was worried and questioning. What was happening to in this place? If King James the Third was on the throne what could

Ellick be suggesting? Sir Richard's in the Tower for being a Jacobite sympathiser. What was it? If the Catholic James Francis Edward Stuart, the Old Pretender, was on the English throne, why should Sir Richard Vyvyan be in the Tower? If Zac Ellick was to be believed why did the comptroller for James the Third, Hugh Boscawen, have Sir Richard arrested?

His heart began to race at the realisation of what he had done. Had Goode been a lesser mortal, his error would have gone unnoticed. Ellick might be right. Goode was Stannary Officer for Devon, of that there was no argument. Entrusted with the conveyance of state papers – by the king. Which one? For it was clear to him that it had been King James the Third when he came into court, and now King George the First at his departing. Had he gone out of his mind? A pain in the back of his throat followed by a tingling sensation caused him to panic. It was travelling from the top of his head down through his body reaching his feet.

'Water, Quince. For God's sake, bring me water. Adjourn the trial, my chambers. I'm having an attack to the heart . . . Bailiff! Hold fast the execution.'

The bailiff misunderstanding what Skull had said as, 'Execute the man fast', took him at his word immediately presented Goode to his executioner bound and bagged.

Ellick knocked on the door. Behind him, Cluff was standing nervously, for the evidence he had gathered that would assuredly bring an acquittal, would have to wait. The clerk opened the door.

'Judge Skull is seeing no one. He is ill and you've been his cause.'

'Let me enter you idiot,' Ellick said his voice threatening. He pushed the door from Quince's hands.

The clerk being heavier heaved the door back to within a foot of Ellick's face and no more. Ellick wedged his boot between the door frame and the frame.

'Did you not hear me, Sir? The judge will not see you. Remove your foot from the jam, Sir.'

'Let him in Quince if he must. They'll be no peace this day if you don't. Damn you Sir,' he said waving his hands at Ellick impatiently as he entered. Cluff reluctantly followed. Seconds later the judge's son, Ventonwyn.

'*Well?*' Skull asked of his son.

'Too late father . . . Your Honour. He swings as we speak.'

Skull leaned forward and putting both hands on his desk inadvertently scattering his ink-well, papers and quills across it. He then fell forward feigning despair.

'There's a point of law to be discussed here, Edmund. But I'm not sure I'm in the right office to argue it.'

Skull looked up from between his spread-eagled arms and said, 'Damned you are Sir, *SIT DOWN!*'

Ellick did as the judge directed. He then turned his attention toward Cluff.

'And you Sir. What'd you mean by coming into my court dressed in that manner? Out of your chambers, is he?' Skull said turning to Ellick. 'You didn't declare him as lawyer for the defence. Too late now for Goode has been dispatched to his Maker along with your point of law.' Skull peered more closely at Cluff. 'I fear you've missed your calling Mr. Cluff, for you'll make precious coins defending criminals and murderers. The Devon Stannary and their laws have no time for them. When they get them, they occasion them to Bodmin law. Saves their list of executions reaching too many pages when it comes to audit. Lydford lays the rules, leaving Cornwall to ask their questions, that's an end—'

'An end,' Ventonwyn Skull repeated.

Ellick looked at the boy expecting something more salient. No more was forthcoming. 'Seems to me Edmund, short of, *What is your name? How do you plead? I'm sentencing you to . . .* there doesn't seem to be anything else that constitutes proper justice in either county.'

'Why should I waste court time? I read Lydford's notes. I accept from them that after exhaustive enquiries the body of Joshua Timmins could not be found with the addition of Hugh Boscawen's sworn *affidavit* that he and people he could vouch for, saw Goode murder Timmins.'

'And how was he supposed to see the murder take place, he was in Helston arresting Sir Richard at the time? And if he was where he said he was, why didn't he arrest him instead of allowing him to wander off? He is after all Lord Warden of the Stannaries. He has that authority. Goode was supposed to be delivering a letter from King George. Sir Richard Vyvyan was to be pardoned for his part in the Jacobite cause. Where is that letter now?' Ellick said.'

'I know nothing of that. Either way, whether it's King Tut, or Titania Queen of the Faeries, a murder committed needs a guilty party condemned and exampled in this land. Who else did for Timmins if not Goode? And now the man's hanged, there's nothing more to be said that will bring him back.'

'*Hanged—!*' Ventonwyn echoed his father's words.

*Hanged. Nothing more to be said on the matter*, Judge Skull said to himself convinced of his rightful authority.

'Rope around the neck. Dropped. Finished with life,' Ventonwyn affirmed. 'No more to be said on the subject.'

'The king will, when he is confronted with the fact that his own blood had not received a proper hearing in a Cornish assize with you as presiding judge, Edmund.'

'Own blood Sir. What relation might exist between Sir Richard and the hanged man that would cause the king any consternation,' Skull asked nervously.

'Consternation Sir,' Ventonwyn mimicked.

'Not Sir Richard,' Cluff interrupted. 'The king himself. It is likely that Goode is his son and not who he believed was Count Königsmarck's, the queen's lover. The resemblance is uncannily that of the Hanoverian when a youth himself. And with this out in the open he's not going to want it known that he had murder planned for his own and his divorced wife Sophia Dorothea's son. To quote Shakespeare's Hamlet, *Where the offence is let, the great axe will fall.* And you can rest assured Edmund, the axe won't be falling Boscawen's neck.'

Skull's eyes rolled. He was in trouble and he knew it. He tried to stand, but his head went back at the thought, and he collapsed back across his desk.

Cluff wasted no time. On the floor with his legs astride each side of Skull's chest he pumped for all he was worth. He had never had to practise respiration on a man whose heart had stopped before, and he prayed that what he was doing would return this one into the land of the living. For if he wasn't convinced before of his importance in all of this he was now.

Already overweight, his fitness would not have gone unnoticed by a doctor in 1715 let alone 2008. With this man's fondness for port wine (he had not overlooked the amount of times that Quince had topped up his decanter during the trial), then standing up to confront Ellick, his face red, before falling across his desk rolling sideways onto the floor the way he had did not necessitate him being a medic to diagnose the man was having a heart attack. It was not science that would be in question should the man die, but knowledge of human physiology that would bring him back to life with his unorthodox approach in this world that should it fail, condemn him as his murderer that worried him now. Nevertheless, pressing with a rhythm, the heel of both hands, one on the other onto the chest he went all out to save the man's life. Then someone jumped on him and tried to drag him off. The man's son was pulling at his shoulders shouting at him to stop trying to murder his father.

'Get him off! Zac! Get him off me I'm trying to save the old fool's life. Get off me, you idiot.'

Ventonwyn was slapping Cluff's head in his attempt to rescue his father, only stopping when Zac and Quince managed to restrain him by getting him on the floor in an arm lock.

Cluff regained his position astride Skull and carried on with the resuscitation, praying it was not too late. Good a lawyer as he was, he would have the devil's own job explaining the mechanics behind external cardiac massage in an eighteenth-century court. Then to his relief, Skull started to breathe. Laboured at first. Then he coughed the cough of a Genesis giant. Cluff ceased his efforts then moved him into a coma position. The man's head moved slowly to one side, his face pallid, then slowly it returned to its normal port wine burgundy complexion.

'Water please Zac,' he said to the first face he saw.

Water was brought. Cluff put his hand inside his pocket pulled out a packet of aspirin. Popping the blisters on two of them he addressed Judge Skull.

'Here take these Your Honour, they'll help.'

'What happened?' he asked looking anxiously towards his clerk. 'And what's this fool done to me?'

Getting no response from the man, for the clerk had no idea what had just gone on, Skull took the tablets drinking the glass of water the clerk proffered. He seemed to know that Cluff had saved his life for he said, 'I don't know who you are, or from whence you came, but I am nonetheless indebted to you Sir. Thank you.' He then turned to his clerk saying, 'Quince I wish to speak with Ellick and Waite and their lawyer alone. You can go as well Ventonwyn.'

When they had gone Skull asked what was to be done now that it was too late.

'Fear not, for we have time on our side Edmund,' Ellick answered him.

Judge Edmund Skull's openness to what should have been nothing more than a foreign language impressed Cluff. Whether it was his offering of an explanation of how cardiac massage worked. Or a thirst for knowledge in the field of human anatomy that even with his own limited non-medical background he was able to explain he couldn't say. But forensic science was being given a chance. The fact that the man, with the body of Timmins laid out on a wooden table in front of them was willing to listen to evidence of a forensic nature would go some way to proving Goode innocent. With Dr. Poltair's evidence that the man responsible for Timmins's death was likely that of a soldier. He guessed they had found the man matching his DNA. The hand and thumb impressions, along with fingerprint profiles that were on Timmins's neck and throat were not quite enough to convince Skull. The blood on the knife not having Goode's DNA leading to an acquittal in 2008 was useless here. He was going to have to resort to evidence he himself would not find particularly palatable. To tie up this acquittal he was going to have to use surgery, and he was already gagging at the thought.

Without going into the details of where Ellick and Waite had obtained these notes or who Dr. Poltair was that provided them he didn't ask, neither did they offer any other than to say he was a medical surgeon from St. Bartholomew's Hospital (they were not going to risk Dr. Poltair's credibility saying she was a woman).

Cluff had puzzled how he was going to pass the medical findings from 2008 to 1716 for a forensic report in Times Roman printed out onto a sheet of 80-gram A4 from a computer. He need not have worried. Hilary Waite had copied it by quill and ink onto parchment.

Sniffing at it, he guessed that the faint trace of smouldering he was picking up from the newly written parchment came from a candle wick burned at both ends the evening before. These two lawyers had thought of everything. Or so he thought. The heavily stencilled words on the grey, heavy-duty plastic body bag, rang as an alarm clock in full pelt when he saw it:

**Please return:**

**Department for Forensic Medicine**

**PENINSULA MEDICAL SCHOOL,**

**DERRIFORD PL6 8BU.**

Discreetly kicking it under the table, he casually began in earnest as if nothing had just happened. Sighing a breath of relief he removed the gaffer tape from around Timmins' neck, while Skull and Ellick looked on.

The body having been returned to 1716 had a freshness that its 2008 version would not have had. The neck entry was crawling with blow-fly larvae. His mind went back to his days when he went to a primer lecture on the subject, Time of Death. One of many extraneous subjects the law school put forward from time to time they considered a useful addition to trainee lawyers. Although, why he had wanted to put himself through that particular one, he had no idea. It was something that he and a few of his fellow trainee lawyers having seen advertised on the notice board thinking it a laugh put themselves forward for. Until the surgeon lecturer having got as far as a corpse, the last but one resting place of a murder victim and the gut-full of bacteria that would leach from it. Where soil from around the body's drip zone, spilled out onto the ground, would tell a forensic scientist from the twenty-first century an exact time of death. The noxious fluids from such decay gave off an odour of disgust unmatched in nature. They had smelt a sample from a test tube, which put all of them off curry take-aways for some time after. And up until then, had also been the end of their forays into the world of forensic science.

He swallowed hard. Brushing the maggots from Timmins' neck, he began his explanation. Unmoved, Judge Skull shuffled his feet on the squidgy creatures that had fallen onto the floor, listening and taking notes with the aid of a stick of charcoal. A well-worn leather-bound notebook balanced in his right hand, Cluff guessed the man was not the Philistine he first assumed he was. The gruesome task, to get to the point that he had to demonstrate, lay deep within Timmins' throat. For that to be displayed it was necessary for him to pull his head back, open the neck and to look up into his Eustachian tube. Here where it connected to the back of his throat, he saw what he had been told to expect.

'What I am attempting to demonstrate is that Goode and Timmins were known and orchestrated at the highest level in their innocent ambitions. Politics resulted in the king going back on his promises to reform the Stannaries, while at the same time giving Cornwall rights to an autonomy for its own country, setting Goode and Timmins on a road to ruin.'

'According to evidence from the bailiff at Lydford for this trial, their man, one known as Sabine . . . I have it here,' Skull said pulling a reef of papers from a leather portfolio at his side. Thumbing through them he found the one he was looking for and began to read. 'I shall ignore its preamble,' he waved his hand over the pages in a sign of dismissal,

". . . I was called to Crockern to investigate what was reported as a violent exchange between two tinners by the mine captain, an honest fellow by the name of Benjamin Aesop, and one I can vouch. Fearing that one had killed the other, his body lying beside the East Dart river, he said he had cordoned off the area at great expense to the exchequer . . ."

he went on,

"an open and shut case"...

Oh yes,

"with the man from the Cornish Stannary dead from his injuries his murderer John Goode"... this other sheet reads that,

*"I believe arrangements were in place by the militia for John Goode to be arrested for treason at Okehampton. It was from there that he escaped"*...'

'And who else but Boscawen would have had the means to act so swiftly, and to orchestrate all of this after Goode's escape?' Waite interrupted.

'And if you need further evidence of Goode's innocence, then you need look no further than here,' Cluff said now having got used to this grisly business of destructive surgery.

Skull put down his notebook and leaned over the body. He stared into the chasm of rank flesh and looked down on blackened arteries, dried blood, semi-liquid fluids purulent and odorous. He sniffed and turned to Cluff.

'Good, God! Sir. I've handed down some verdicts in my time. And I might add, punishments, well deserved, for both example as well as retribution on behalf of the State, for I've a responsibility to uphold law, but I've never seen the like of this. Who in God's name has the authority to mete out punishment as this before us now in the name of justice, for it's clear to me, it's well thought out enough to be of a standard to induce fear—?'

'That'll be the Stannary Parliament, Edmund,' Ellick came in. 'And although no direct involvement can be shadowed at their door, nonetheless a blind eye for its fear to errant tinners on behalf of the duchy of Cornwall is well documented in people's minds.'

'And difficult, if not impossible for a right-handed man that had a nail driven through that same hand,' Cluff added. 'John Goode could not have committed that act himself. It would require the strength of someone with two good hands. His pain from such an ordeal would have made that impossible.'

'Goode could still have murdered Timmins. Nailing his own hand to the board after the deed,' Skull said reassuringly.

Cluff was ready for this. Taking the dagger from the paper bag he had replaced for the polythene it had arrived in he presented it.

'You see that part of the blade. The serrated edging. Now take another look at his injury while alive, then tell me Goode did that.'

Cluff pushed Timmins' head back fully to reveal the fullness of the cut open throat of the corpse. Skull sniffed then peered in.

'There! There man. What do you see?' Cluff said.

Skull looked into the sliced open human flesh. A lump of tin embedded perfectly in the man's throat shined. A sculptured fit.

'Is that metal?' Skull asked astonished.

'Tin Sir. Once molten. Poured into the gullet while a man still lives,' Ellick said. 'And you thought nailing a man's hand to a board bad enough. That's Stannary law for you. John Goode could not have done that to Timmins.'

Skull exposed his teeth while at the same time drawing a breath. 'Is that what I think it is?'

Cluff held up the knife for him to see.

'That Sir . . . is a jag of metal from this dagger. The strength required to break that off after hitting the tin globule would have required a man with more than a good hand. I suggest the dagger's owner wielded it. A soldier. A Scottish militia man by all account. And I fancy it was an act of mercy. The man cut Timmins' throat killing him to save him anymore suffering.'

Skull looked at him with a look of shock in his eyes. What had he done? A vacuum of blackness came over him erasing all time and memory.

## Bodmin Assize, Cornwall 1716

'I am indebted to you Sir,' Skull said rubbing his chest.

'Saved your life—' Ventonwyn added.

'Take these,' Cluff said passing him two aspirin tablets.

Judge Skull returned to the court and nodded at the standing assembly. Picking up the glass of water Quince had filled from the decanter; he emptied the two aspirin from his hand into his mouth. Swallowing them, he took a sip of water from the glass then resumed the trial of John Goode.

The clerk watched the judge drinking, wondering when he had last seen his honour drink that much water, when he became aware that he was drumming his fingers waiting for him.

'Ah, Your Honour. Sorry to keep you. All stand . . . ah . . . sit. The court is in session. Honourable Judge Skull presiding—'

'Never mind all that Quince. Will you go ahead with your submission Mr. Cluff? You are representing the accused I believe?'

Cluff stood, 'I am Sir if it pleases you.'

'And the corpse that is Joshua Timmins – the court has made its examinations and findings I believe?'

Cluff hesitated and looked toward Waite and Ellick, after noticing John Goode was not in the dock, mimed *Where is he?* They're making nothing of Goode's absence. God we're still in King James' the Third time.

'I am satisfied the defence has established cause of death?' Skull stated looking at Cluff. 'And have you anything further to add to these witness statements, Mr. Cluff?' Skull asked looking up.

'Only that they were possibly fabricated by Lydford's masters, maintaining the status quo, ensuring continuing wealth for the duchy.'

Skull was referring to notes without being aware they were not his. Hilary Waite had done yet another re-write. They were passing them off as being from a county medical expert. From that aspect, Waite did not see that he was misdirecting the judge. Merely bringing in evidence from the future.

Skull looked up and seemed satisfied.

'I am inclined to agree with you. Although, you did well to locate the body of Joshua Timmins. Perhaps a little too well, Mr. Cluff. . . .'

Ellick suddenly looked worried.

'That might imply some knowledge as to his demise. That you yourself might have been responsible for the man's death. Or if not you personally, complicit with others and knowing of them.' Skull studied him with seriousness on his face. 'Are you the murderer, constable and lawyer here, Mr. Cluff? Observations I am duty bound to bring before the court if for no other reason than to play the devil's advocate. Having said that for I am sure you are not.'

Cluff equally worried began to wonder if Skull knew what had happened to him and was now playing games with them for his own amusement.

Picking up the notes from Lydford moved the case forward when the lawyer for the prosecution stood up.

'I should make a point of order father, I mean, Your Honour.'

'Very well.'

'How are we to be sure that the body of Joshua Timmins is who they say he is? Further, how was the body discovered?'

Skull at first ignored him so much was he engrossed in Lydford notes. Cluff held his breath. He had overlooked such a fundamental submission. This idiot son of his had asked two salient questions. Observations though plucked willy-nilly from the air rare would not have been the first time in a court of law that such a question had been overlooked by the defence.

'I believe that you can identify the body as being that of Joshua Timmins, John Goode.'

Cluff was astounded. Goode was now standing in the dock.

'I can Your Honour. He will have a wound running from the middle of his hand that exits between his fore and middle finger appearing to make the finger twice the length it should be. As you can see, I have similar, the result of being nailed to a border post our hands together.'

Cluff added, 'The body of Joshua Timmins was discovered as the result of a lucky break Your Honour,' Cluff said hoping that that would be the end of any further inquiries on that tact. Then cursed himself for using those words.

Judge Skull turned towards Ellick and Waite asking, ' "*Lucky break*", break, Sir. What in the name of a king's whore standing in for the queen's intervals is one of those? Mr. Ellick would you kindly instruct your counsel to speak in mother tongue. I'll settle for Kernewek if he knows no other. Spare me German though, we've enough of that with one on the throne. *Mr. Clerk!* Decant me another bottle, for I am sure this case is going to run itself to St. Hilary.'

Ellick breathed a sigh of relief and looked to Waite whose job had been to act as recorder for the firm. This was the first time that Skull had mentioned King George. They had not won this case, but at least they were in the right place at last. Whether they remained would be another matter out of their hands.

The clerk removed the Judge's decanter and disappeared.

Cluff stood again. 'Apologies Your Honour, for I have been in the colonies these last few years. Please forgive my vernacular. I do not speak Cornish or German and shall continue in English.'

The clerk reappeared with a crusty bottle: its top broken off. Holding the glass decanter up to the light for any sign of water that might pollute the wine, satisfied that it had not, he poured the wine from the bottle into the decanter.

'The evidence I have is that both men were engaged on king's business. Though not friends, acquaintances, they had a vested interest in that they with Sir Richard Vyvyan's favour, were to forge an alliance of the two Parliaments of Cornwall and Devon's tin miners. The pardon from King George to Sir Richard for his part in the recent and ongoing Jacobite Uprising were to desist for that to take place. Obviously, there had been a change of heart on the king's part, no doubt under pressure from his court of Whigs, where instead of this alliance an arrest warrant was issued. Presented to Sir Richard at Trelowarren by Hugh Boscawen, the man was arrested for treason. The rest should speak for itself.'

Skull was worried. This was State politics that gave him little comfort. A look of annoyance was in his eyes. He waved for Ellick to approach the bench.

'Come to my chambers?' he whispered angrily.

He got to his feet, then bowing his head, the court was adjourned. Five minutes later both men returned, and the case resumed. Skull's disposition wasn't looking any better for the meeting. He addressed Cluff.

'I want an answer as to how you found the body of Timmins with the assistance of that "break" you spoke of earlier?' Skull asked.

'I was coming to that, Sir.'

Cluff sat back down when the Skull interrupted.

'Get to it quicker then Sir. And desist from your infernal sitting and standing up every time I seek guidance.'

Cluff stood up once more.

'I made my own investigation in the *Jurate Arms* at Crockern. Being the alternative meeting place of the Devon Stannary should the weather turn incle . . .'

'Yes yes, Mr. Cluff. I am well aware that good men of substance are reluctant to imbibe liquor in the open when the weather's inclement. Make your point.'

'He took me to Whitemoor where we discovered his body. I then planned for the body to be brought here for foren— . . . a proper scientific investigation to ascertain the cause of death. Those papers are here, with you now. I also believe that you were instrumental in that scientific examination of the body, for which we are grateful, m'Lud.'

Judge Skull acknowledged recognition of his credit, ignoring his reference to m'Lud, taking it for a complimentary title he would insist on the mentioning of in his court when addressed in future.

Ventonwyn interrupted.

'Of course, we've only his word that he found Timmins's body with help from local tinners. There is always the possibility that he knew where it was because he murdered Timmins himself.'

Cluff could see this question on the horizon. With prosecution procedures not yet up to the speed with those of the twenty-first century and given his legal training in the practice of dotting i's and crossing t's he automatically planned for its coming. Ventonwyn Skull was not as ignorant in these matters as he first thought and clearly it was not unknown for a lawyer to be involved with malpractice in the eighteenth-century, a fact he had overlooked.

'I'd like mine captain Kenneth Mudge brought to give witness to what I've stated, m'Lud.'

Ventonwyn Skull said he would have no objection.

The mine captain took the stand, acknowledging that Cluff was the man that had come to him.

'It hadn't been easy Sir,' the man said removing his bowler hat while putting his clay pipe into the top pocket of his long grey dress coat. 'I can vouch with what the lawyer gentlemen said. I did show him where Joshua Timmins was.' He coughed. The pipe was smoking in his pocket. Removing it he quickly stubbed his thumb into the bowl replacing it in his pocket.

Judge Skull nodded taking a moment to digest Mudge's submission.

'Thank you mine captain, you may stand down,' Skull said.

Cluff stood up. 'I should like charges against John Goode dismissed with no more to answer, m'*Lud.*'

There was silence. Then the court broke into wild cheering.

Skull banged his gavel.

'Order, order. I will have order in my court from the public gallery. The court considers the evidence before it as right and appropriate. John Goode's injury coincide with that of being pinned with a knife to his companion. For the murder of his fellow Stannary officer I can find no evidence. Further inquiries may have to be made to ascertain the murderer or murderers. As such my finding is that you are not guilty John Goode. You are free to go.'

Judge Skull left the Court with his decanter hanging from his hands. The clerk declared the court dismissed. Ellick and Waite came up to shake Cluff's hand, then stopped. Skull turned as a vacuum of blackness descended. A cracking sound like that of a spar snapping could be heard outside. A man hanging from the end of its rope along with his audience became another time no more. Skull shook his head and returned to his chambers as if nothing had happened.

## INTERPENETRATING DIMENSION DOME
### Exxeter 1716

John Goode, solicitor in the village of Heavitree, collapsed. He clutched at his chest. His heart had stopped. Falling face first against his desk he hit his chest. The blow accelerated his heart to resume its beat. Taking to his bed for a couple of days, he made a complete recovery. He couldn't explain the mark to his neck. But his wife and children did not care, for she still had her husband; her children, their father.

# TWENTY
## Truro Police Station,
## Cornwall 2008

*ALL THOSE ARRESTED* had been separated and taken to various police custody suites around the county to await questioning. The first of those two suspect inquiries were in Truro. DCI Kent Knapp from Thames Valley accompanied by Major Gerald Ford were about to question the first of those suspects. The decision, not to make mention of the organisation in questioning of the suspects had come from Ford. He felt they needed to eliminate other organisations. One being Mebyon Kernow, the political party representing the interests of the Cornwall, who over the years had unwittingly taken into membership those seeking more direct action before MK found them out expelling them. Clare Bray, an artist from Newlyn had come to their notice as being such a 'lapsed' member. She was sitting with her solicitor Henry Jelbert. The only other person present was a custody sergeant when the two officers came into the room.

'You wanted this, Sir?'

An officer passed him a list of members of MK taken from their offices. He was looking for the name of the man holding siege in Bristol. He wasn't expecting it to be in plain sight. For William Timmins would surely have used a false one. Wheal Brae appeared to be one that stuck out. Another was Philippe Charmolue. A foreigner? He showed them to Ford who nodded but made no comment.

Knapp came into the interview room. Introducing himself he sat down and switched on the tape. He stated the date, time, and person he was interviewing with that of the solicitor representing the interviewee. He immediately came under verbal assault by the solicitor Jelbert.

'You've not made it clear why my client is under arrest yet. Under the—'

Knapp interrupted him.

'Along with all others. Miss Bray wasn't cautioned. She was brought in under the United Kingdom Terrorism Act of 2007. Under that act, I am not obliged to go into details with you, only that she answers my questions, or not. She still has that right. Although, Miss Bray, you do not have to say anything, but it may harm your defence if you do not mention when questioned something you later rely on in court. Anything you say may be given in evidence. Do you understand?'

She nodded.

'And you are aware of that act and my powers under it are you Mr. Jelbert?'

'Of course, I am.'

Jelbert spoke quietly to her. She shrugged a laugh, crossed her arms, then turned her head sideways giving Knapp every indication she was not going to answer any of his questions. Ignoring her disregard for him he began his questioning deliberately belittling her craft.

'Your name is Clare Bray, painter from 14 Sithney Mews, St. Levan. Is that correct?'

'*Artist!* she snapped back at him. If you want a painter see Stephens, the undertaker and carpenter. I'm a landscape artist.'

'You were a member of Mebyon Kernow,' he said. 'Are you a member of any other political organisations?

Jelbert interrupted.

'Has my client been brought in for being a member of a cultural

236

and political party that may or may not be connected with Mebyon Kernow?' Jelbert turned to his client. 'You don't have to answer any questions regarding your membership of a political party.'

'Only if that organisation is intent on damaging people or property,' Knapp cut in. 'Are you Miss Bray?'

'What?'

'Involved yourself or with others with acts against people or property in the county?'

'No.'

'And why are you no longer a member of Mebyon Kernow? Were they not pro- active enough for you?'

'Couldn't afford the subscription any longer.'

'Are you married?'

'No.'

'Partner?'

'No.'

'Are you familiar with the names William Timmins or Wheal Brae?'

She turned and studied him seriously for a moment or two before answering.

'Would that be the cartwheel Bray, Chief Inspector? Though I do have a cousin in St. Austell. You might have heard of him. He makes pasties. Michael Bray. The only other Wheals I have heard of are those used for bequeathing.'

Knapp finished off his notes. Then said into the tape that the interview was over giving the date and time.

'Thank you, Miss Bray.'

'Is my client free to go Inspector?' Jelbert asked.

'Certainly not. She is to remain here under the Act until the rest of our inquiries have been carried out. We have several more interviews yet.'

'And how long will that be?'

'As long as it takes, Mr. Jelbert.'

'You have heard the name?'

Wright nodded saying in passing he had.

'And when did you first hear that name?'

'It's not an uncommon name in Cornwall. In fact, there's a large family of them in Helston. That's probably where I first heard it. Although only the surname. His first name. What did you say it was again, William Timmins? Only I would have thought there were more than enough Timmins' to couple with William in the Helston area let alone Cornwall.'

'Funny enough, there isn't,' Knapp replied. 'Eight actually. All of Cornwall. All of them excepting one, pillars of the community.'

Wright shrugged, 'What can I say?'

'According to computer files removed from the offices of Mebyon Kernow you were asked to leave MK because you were, to use their words, "over enthusiastic". Deleted files still on their hard drive show you had been writing articles attacking English holidaymakers owning properties in Cornwall. Were you "over enthusiastic" Mr. Wright?'

'It's a view.'

'And this *Democratic Republic of Cornwall*. Painting out English Heritage logos from road signs replacing them with flags of St. Piran. Scattering broken bottles on beaches was that not enough for you? If that's a view Mr. Wright, I wonder what you do consider direct action to be?'

Jelbert leaned forward.

'We've owned up to irregularities of accounting by Mr. Wright overfishing quotas that PC Trethewey earlier brought to your notice. Those we are not disputing. However, as to these other matters my client has no knowledge and refutes them.'

'*Mr. Wright!* Knapp snapped back ignoring Jelbert. 'They have been documented on MK's computers . . .'

'Anybody with malice against my client could have downloaded such information,' Jelbert said. 'The point is Mr. Wright has never been arrested or convicted for any such offences –'

'A bit of paint splashed on a few bridges over the A30 doesn't mean to say I've anything to do with terrorism. As for broken glass where children are playing, there's no way I would do such a thing. As Mr. Jelbert said, anyone with a grudge against me could say that about me. Apart from that what evidence have you that the organisation you are asking me about would place broken glass on a beach.'

'A Cornish terror organisation holding three hundred children hostage, threatening to blow them up, to my mind, is not an organisation that considers the welfare of children. So, if you'll excuse me, I will not apologise for asking such questions of people that might be members. However, for the moment I will not pursue it.'

Knapp switched the tape machine off.

'People don't crop up out of thin air,' Ford said. 'William Timmins must have connections in Cornwall. Someone knows who he is. The fact that a package was sent to the local BBC shows that. He has foot soldiers down here of that you can be sure. All we have to do is to keep digging. I've made arrangements to have these suspects removed to Nancekuke for further questioning.'

'What's Nancekuke? I know nothing of taking suspects in for further questioning to any place other than a police station. I'll have to let Rudyard know,' Knapp said.

'Out of the question, Chief Inspector. Events have overtaken us. CS Rudyard and Devon & Cornwall is no longer involved in this investigation.'

## Nancekuke, Cornwall 2008

It was two am when the minibus carrying the suspects arrived at the Remote Radar Head in Portreath. The former manufacturing factory for the nerve agent, sarin, it was now a supply depot for food distribution in the event of a national emergency.

Passing through armed service police and a civilian security company, the minibus was given a procedural inspection that included a disregard for the passengers chained into their seats. Inside: Clare Bray, Chris Wright, Allen Treffry. A man known locally as the 'Bard of Cornwall' was picked up on the road outside of Hayle. A placard around his neck daubed in red paint,

### ENGLAND OUT OF CORNWALL.
### DEMOCRATIC REPUBLIC FOR CORNWALL

'See they got the druid,' a G5S man was heard to say to his colleague as the vehicle went past.

The minibus drove up to a blockhouse of a building that looked as if it could sustain a direct hit from a 500lb bomb. The suspects climbed out and were taken inside by non-service personnel guards. Ford and his team of fellow officers were thorough for this place had been used for the interrogation of post-Cold War scientists from East Germany. Now used for suspected members of al Qa'ida and Britain's extraordinary rendition programme, where once again the old airfield had turned out useful for 'tourists' passing through.

The suspects were taken to individual cells, where they were immediately subjected to Ford's special kind of interrogation techniques.

Clare Bray broke down first. One look at the concrete floor covered in dry blood (spray painted in red for effect), was enough for her. She turned back to the iron door that had been slammed shut on her and began screaming. Her bladder opened then she collapsed onto the floor, hitting her head on the wall on her way down. Hearing the racket outside, the guard opened the peephole and looked in at her. She was moving. He let shutter drop before carrying on down the corridor.

If she had been conscious, she would have heard screams from Treffry. Tied to a wall, a hood over his head, his feet barely touching the cold concrete floor faced questioning.

'What'd you want of us? What have I done?' he asked through gasps of breath. 'I'm a doctor, well respected in the community.'

'A doctor that belongs to a terrorist organisation. And if not you, then I need names of those connected with Timmins and where they are. Make no mistake, doctor, we will get it out of you.'

The inflictor spoke in a soft voice that would send a chill through lesser mortals.

'Can't help you,' he casually said. 'Sorry.'

'Not sorry enough, doctor,' the inflictor said striking him a paralysing blow to his kidneys with his fist.

Treffry cried out sending an echo down the corridor, then drew in a deep breath, relaxed himself against the pain.

'Hang him up.'

Ford returned twenty minutes later and looked in on Treffry through the peephole. Hanging by his wrists to hooks attached to the concrete ceiling he hung silent. Ford nodded to the guard then walked away.

At five am the following morning a guard opened the door to Treffry's cell. Treffry, his feet on tiptoe, was conscious. Strung up for a couple of hours was usually enough for any man to break, this man had hung seven hours with not so much as a squeak out of him. He cut his bonds and lowered him to the ground.

Wright had suffered partial drowning falling from a fishing boat out of Newlyn when he was younger. A boom holding a winch rope swung across knocking him unconscious and into the sea. He had breathed in while under water which caused his epiglottis to lock. Had no one been able to get him to begin artificial respiration he would have drowned. He was experiencing that same nightmare now.

The sack placed over his head was soaked in water brought on his nightmare. Cold suffocating water going up his nose caused a burning sensation. His chest started pumping in an effort to breathe. The water filled his nasal cavities and chest. Only the angle he lay prevented it from going into his lungs. He struggled under the electrical tape restraints to his wrists and legs then ceased.

Bray was persuaded to come around with a tin of water thrown in her face. Dragged crying and screaming, a broken bottle held under her face threateningly by the guard wearing battle fatigues and an all-over black woollen face mask was all too much for her. Roughly pushed against the cell wall she awaited what Treffry, in his screams in the cell next to hers, had obviously gone through and screamed out her awaited fate.

'See this broken bottle. It's going right up your privates if you don't answer our questions,' he shouted at her full in the face.

The saliva from his lips splashed over her face. When she pissed herself uncontrollably feeling her warm urine running down the inside of her leg, she was taken to another level of helplessness.

'Where did Timmins operate from and who were the rest of his people? The right answer might just preserve your womanhood, assuming you've got one.'

She screamed at him her answer,

'*I'm not involved with this Timmins you speak of! I'm an artist, for God's sake!* Please. Don't hurt me. I'm not a terrorist.'

He pulled her legs roughly apart.

'Oh no. Why are you doing this to me? This is England we're not criminals. *No-o-o-oh!*'

'Okay. That'll do,' Ford said coming into the cell.

Her heart was racing now fit to burst from her chest. Sweat broke out and poured down her face onto her chest. The thought of what they might have done to her; what they still might do for this was clearly not over, overwhelmed her. Her head dropped forward onto her chest. For the time being she was going to be unconscious, she thought to herself, before succumbing.

'Get her cleaned up and taken outside,' Ford said. 'We're done here.'

'Has Treffry told you anything,' the guard asked.

'No. An angina attack. He's in the camp hospital wing,' Ford answered. 'I'll take care of him.'

'That druid we brought in; did he have anything to say for himself?' Ford inquired.

'We didn't bother,' the inquisitor answered. 'He was recognised by the RAF Police. Apparently, he's been walking the towns of Cornwall for years complaining of the English. They reckon he's off his head.'

'Aren't we all. What did you do with him?'

'Released him with a bottle of cider. We didn't get him as far as the cells. Anything out of the others?'

'Nothing. I've to call the Home Office. Apparently, they're calling us off,' Ford answered. 'Someone's not happy by all accounts.'

The two Land Rovers decaled Devon & Cornwall Police arrived at the security gate. They halted in front of the red and white open cantilevered barrier. The RAF guard on sentry duty was waving a Royal Mail van out. He then stepped forward, an S80 Assault rifle across the front of his body, demanded to know what they wanted.

'*The visitors book, Corporal!*' Knapp demanded.

'And who the hell are you? You don't have any jurisdiction here.

This is MOD property. I must ask you to turn around and leave. If you need an appointment you can phone the station commander. He's number's on that board over there.' He was smiling.

Then he wasn't. An armed police response officer stepped out of one of the vehicles with a weapon similar to his own. A man almost certain to outrank him had he still been in the RAF. Which he had been.

'Your visitor's book, Corporal.'

The corporal went into his station hut and past it to him.

'According to this entry,' Knapp said taking the book and going to the open page, 'the last vehicle was last evening. A minibus? Blacked out windows from the Ministry of the Environment? Warrant entry stamped Home Office. Is that right, Corporal?'

The corporal studied him hard.

'I shall need to speak to the Station Commander on that one Sir. Wait here please.'

'While you're doing that, corporal, raise the barrier please,' Knapp demanded.

Two more-armed response officers stepped out underlining his authority.

'Drive on. Did you say you know the way? You've been here before, Inspector?'

'Special Air Service before I joined you lot. It's not the first time that enemies of the State have been brought here. Been going on for years. Non-scheduled planes, landing and taking off all hours, expelling non-desirables. Rendition I think they used to call it. Turn right by that bunker.'


'Cornish terrorism. You've no concept of that as a statement have you, DI Knapp. We must deal with matters with what we know. Don't worry no one's been hurt, but I must insist—'

'You'll insist on nothing Ford. As to nobody being hurt. You a psychiatrist now. Police brutality is one thing I know about in Thames Valley. We have it in spades. I'm not excusing it; I understand the frustration some of our officers have. Dealing with real nasty bastards, with solicitors that could alibi Satan. Know what I'm saying. But what you're doing here to people that should be innocent until proven guilty is medieval. I take it the Home Office knows what's been going on. Of course, they do,' Knapp answered his own question.

'And I suppose terrorism in Bristol emanating from the west country doesn't count. Devon & Cornwall have been too soft when it comes to Cornish nationalism. Out of touch. In the backwoods. And should I remind you, you're Thames Valley. The reason you were brought in to help us sort this lot out in the first place,' Ford said.

'*God!* Is that what this is all about. A bit of Cornish nationalism that I think Chief Superintendent Rudyard is more than capable of dealing with. And the police authority reckoned Thames Valley were sometimes out of order. You people are all of that. I suggest you quietly exit stage left back to Whitehall Mr. Ford, or whatever your real name is leaving Devon & Cornwall to sort this mess out. In the meantime, I'll see if this officer from Thames Valley can keep the lid on what you've been up to when I attend the press conference we've been forced to make. *Follow?*'

*Devon & Cornwall Constabulary,*
*(Plymouth Central Sector),*
*Plymouth 2008*

Politics?' Cocksworth said in answer to his Chief Superintendent's analysis of the situation to date.

'Yes . . . politics . . . make an appearance, listen to what this Knapp fellow has to say about brown envelopes. Then back. Leave the rest for Thames Valley to sort. They made the original arrests. Have you got that Steven?' Rudyard said trying to make it sound more of a request than an order.

Cocksworth had never heard Rudyard as put out as he was now. He had said 'politics' and that is what he had clearly been subjected to from on high. Devon & Cornwall had clearly had pressure brought to bear down on them to turn a blind eye to what had been going on with MI5 at Nancekuke, and its representative was himself far from a being a happy bunny about it.

Cocksworth tried one more time.

'And if I bring in evidence of mainland torture against British nationals by MI5 and Thames Valley, what then, Sir?'

## Truro Police Station, Cornwall 2008

Threatening riot and disorder a crowd had gathered outside the police station. A disorderly gathering was something ordinarily the police took in their stride. Not this one though. The word was out. What made this worrying for Cocksworth was the banners being carried. Torture in dictatorships and pariah states around the world was an emotive subject that governments in the west can do nothing more than frown upon knowing politically their hands were tied. But England!

The media were going to be all over this like a rash, Cocksworth thought to himself. All Truro police could do now was contain an extremely ugly mood that was getting worse by the minute using no more than soft tactics. A pre-emptive press conference was being called, if for no other reason than the force making it clear that they were not part of any cover-up for being taciturn in their approach. And his boss, Chief Superintendent Irvin Rudyard, was 'politically' about to take the can for what had taken place at Nancekuke.

Cocksworth's arrival was supposed to go some way to alleviate

Rudyard's disquiet that MI5 and a unit from Thames Valley had been sent down onto his patch by the Deputy Chief Constable of the United Kingdom for their 'special operation' without any further need of their involvement for reasons of politics; and not for any reflection on their abilities to handle an operation that was: Bristol contained for the moment, SEVERE; Cornwall, MODERATE.

Announcing himself to the civilian desk clerk on his arrival Cocksworth was shown into Knapp's designated office. A police force of thugs known affectionately as Thames Valley soon paled into insignificance when he heard the full extent of what MI5 had been up to from Knapp. Their questioning methods would only add to police brutality if any of this was to come out proving they were complicit.

For the moment it had fallen to Cocksworth to distance Devon & Cornwall from the clandestine activities of MI5. Rudyard answered Cockworth's remarking question of knowing of torture against members of the public: ". . . what then Sir?" with, 'We've to police Devon and Cornwall long after this has blown over. What chance do we have of doing that when members of the public believe we have committed torture against them? If those above are turning a blind eye resorting to these methods, then I shall see to it, Chief Inspector, in no uncertain terms, that *I* know that *they* know.'

Young for a chief inspector, Knapp was lean and clean cut with brown hair and a well-trimmed moustache. He guessed the man was in his early thirties. Wearing an expensive hand-tailored three-piece suit of navy-blue wool was not how he expected a policeman from Thames Valley to dress. He was clearly on his way up. A man destined for great things. The fact that he had seen the 'arses' of MI5, persuading them that they were out of order was a credit to him. And it was certain he would not ask questions as to MI5s interrogation techniques. Mandarins from the Home Office would be appreciative of his obmutescence in the matter when they next head-hunted.

'I'm just finishing up, Chief Inspector. How can I help you?'

'I need to see a copy of statements extracted from those people MI5 tortured?' Cocksworth said.

Knapp was puzzled. Previously ordered to return all suspect statements to MI5 they were no longer in the south-west. He smiled. 'You want information gained by torture by MI5? The hullaballoo that's about to hit the fan, are you mad Chief Inspector?'

'On the contrary. An enveloped document sent to the BBC here in the south-west for forwarding to Avon and Somerset has information we would like to know about. The name of person or persons that passed it to the BBC for instance. Ford may be unaware that he has that information.' Knapp studied him. 'You see Chief Superintendent Rudyard's not as green as he's cabbage looking. Avon and Somerset have an officer with the name that the document was addressed to. DCI Grantley Goode. For the officer's safety they and he are anxious to know how Goode's name came to be on that envelope containing that ultimatum from Timmins' Democratic Republic for Cornwall.'

'So, it is Cornish nationalism,' Knapp said. 'Ford intimated as such. As to any envelope, I'm afraid all relevant information has left with Ford. I don't have it. What's more I don't have any reference to it.'

'Right, I believe you, but let me be plain. Whether what this is all about or not the fact is the south-west is part of the royal duchy estate. It wouldn't look good law and order breaking down, people being tortured with the Prince of Wales being the reason. And not just him. His descendants and the monarchy itself. This could go on for years. We have to police it.'

When Knapp gave his own version of events as he understood them, he spoke defensively at first, innocently, repeating a message he had been briefed. Information unsubstantiated to no one in particular. A seemingly ridiculous notion, rumoured, should they be accountable for the saying of it. At no time did we ever suggest textbook effectiveness. A practised piece of propaganda. Cocksworth couldn't be anymore wrong if he thought Devon & Cornwall were the only ones being kept out of the loop. Knapp was savvy enough to know the relaying message of their master's voice was designed for non-implication. Ford was gone leaving Knapp's presence in the south-west looking vulnerable with police brutality hanging in the air. He recollected from his own boss what Rudyard was rumoured saying about Thames Valley when his appointed transfer was about to take place as, *Officers I would as soon not have on my patch.* Having seen MI5 running alongside of them in this operation, Rudyard was partially right. All had been used as cannon-fodder up against professional high-ranking civil servants, politically motivated and unaccountable servants of the Crown. And Cocksworth was right. The damage done might take years to repair when it comes to public trust. And not just to Devon & Cornwall. It was his Thames Valley that had the reputation for bad practises.

'I think we can both be sure of one thing here, Chief Inspector Cocksworth. What I have seen here has opened my eyes. The British government would have no hesitation using violence to protect the interests of the Crown as long as there others to carry the can.'

'My sentiments exactly, Chief Inspector Knapp. Let's try and stay one step ahead of the game as long as we can, shall we?'

# TWENTY-ONE
## Devon & Cornwall Constabulary,
## (Plymouth Central Sector),
## Plymouth 2008

*RUDYARD WAS LISTENING* on the phone for the voice that would tell him to put a code in to take him further down the line. A voice crackled, then came through, a clue that the call was scrambled; or whatever they do to beef-up security these days, he thought to himself.

'You are connected to the priority coms line COBRA. If you wish to continue please identify yourself.'

A monotone voice came through that Rudyard could not make up his mind if it were an actual recording or some bored civil servant that had made the same announcement for the umpteenth time that day. All calls he made in connection with the siege from now on went through the same message monitoring station. Rudyard was not a fan of cloak-and-dagger operations that smacked of Sandbaggers. Leastways, not this side of the military. He was impressed they had his personal telephone number even though he had never divulged it to them. It made him feel part of the establishment. Not that he had time for such self-indulgences.

He removed the phone away from his ear that had become hot and sweaty, wiping it dry and cool with his handkerchief, then listening once more said, 'One moment, I have it here somewhere.'

He held the phone in the palm of his hand. Blackberry, he said to himself. What kind of fool name is that for a phone? What was wrong with proper phones that sat in cradles that rang? Look at this thing, he thought to himself. My father had a television set that had a smaller screen than this. If you touched the wrong place, you'd get a Chinese take-away wanting your order. He knew that from experience. He tapped out his identification password. And that had been more luck than judgement. He had had to look it up from the slip of paper in his wallet. A password he was supposed to commit to memory. E.*9g2? Fat chance of recalling that, he thought. Have enough trouble remembering my PIN in Tesco.

When a real voice came through it took him by surprise.

'Thank you, Chief Superintendent. I have security instructions for you. Please listen carefully. When you are satisfied that you understand tap the icon on the screen.'

He looked at the screen, *What bloody icon?* he said to himself before listening intently. When the security instructions had ended, the screen on the phone blinked up an icon. He tapped it.

'Go ahead with your message,' the voice continued.

He sighed. 'My name is Chief Superintendent Irvin Rudyard of the Devon & Cornwall Police. The time is . . .' he looked at his wristwatch. 'Eight am. This call is for the general manager of the Tamar Bridge Company in Plymouth. We have received a bomb threat involving that facility. I believe I have to inform you before I contact them. Well, I've done that, and now I shall use my own initiative in the matter and hang whoever objects.'

## Home Office, Marsham Street, London 2008

The offices of the home secretary in Westminster had the atmosphere of age. Years of civil service staff had given it an air of cups of tea, reams of paper typed on or otherwise. Even cigarette smoke, banned for the last four years, managed to hang on. More so through the door to the quadrangle every time someone came in or out. Inside the home secretary's office, a phone was ringing.

Blunt was outside drinking a cup of tea, eating a dough bun from the morning tea trolley when he heard it. He excused himself from the morning pleasantries he was having with Mrs Gladstone, the morning refreshments operative, Civil Service speak for her job. Walking quickly down the corridor he went into his office, sat down, and picked it up.

'Anthony Blunt . . . Sir Bernard! Thank you for getting back to me so promptly—'

'Your call to me yesterday, reference approaching the Prince of Wales. You asked if he had ever had any contact with an organisation known as the Democratic Republic of Cornwall,' Sir Bernard said.

'Yes. I realise it was a bit of a long shot, but it was imperative that we asked the question.'

'Well he has. And he's reluctantly asked me to mention it to you,' Sir Bernard hesitated to search for the right way to express himself on this delicate matter. 'We've a teensy-weenie bit of a problem. And not to put a too finer point on it, it's taken your hostage siege up another rung of the ladder.'

## Avon and Somerset Constabulary
## Mobile Units, Bristol 2008

'Yes, speaking!' Merriweather said listening at the same time taking the phone handed to him. His voice a whisper, anxious as to what the home secretary was to confirm or deny that would certainly bring more concerns for him and his team.

'Is that Acting Chief Superintendent Andrew Merriweather?' Blunt asked.

'Yes, Home Secretary,' he said impatient to hear what this was all about.

'Not good. I've taken a call from Sir Bernard, the Prince of Wales' Private Secretary. I'm afraid he does confirm what we spoke of earlier regarding Timmins. He not only managed to contact the man, but he did it on his mobile.'

'I trust he followed protocol and hung up.' There was a pause. *Not exactly*, Merriweather quietly said to himself knowing what the inevitable response would be.

'Timmins wants the English parliament to rescind the 1337 Act whereby the Princes of Wales along with the office of the dukes of Cornwall act in the spirit of Magna Carta as a precursor.'

'*A precursor!* To what pray?'

'That he disinherits his and his descendants' hold over the assets of Cornwall and what he considers to be the last royal dictatorship in Europe. In short, he wants to dissolve the duchy of Cornwall with all its assets after corporation and capital gains taxes have been paid with the remainder to be used to help finance the establishment of Cornwall as a country of self-governance in its own right. He is a modern man according to his personal secretary.'

'Yes, right. Your department there I think Sir. What concerns me are those children, and what he proposes on that front. As to how the man managed to get the prince's personal mobile number also worries me. That smacks of someone tucked away in the woodwork.'

'Wait, Merriweather. There's more.'

'Go on inspire me.'

'We've also had a call from MI5 to say they've received information that there's a bomb ticking under the Tamar Bridge in Cornwall. Timed to go off at 1500 tomorrow. Although it could be a hoax, we've to treat it seriously. Three hundred kids held ransom and he drops this on us for good measure. We knew he had someone down there to cause more trouble and now we know. Oh, and by-the-by, Timmins said he would call his Highness for a decision later today when he will then give the position of the explosive device. Obviously, he can't take such a call. You'll have to answer it. I've sent it over by government courier. You'll have it in the time it takes a motorcycle with clearance to break the speed limit getting to you from London.'

'Before you go, Sir . . .'

'Yes.'

'You mentioned hoax. Were you possibly thinking that an eighteen-hour advance notice was not the warning you'd expect from a terrorist?'

'With tongue in cheek. It was the nature of the call, or rather the person in question making it. According to Rudyard of Devon & Cornwall, someone using a code name, the Bard, made Rudyard think otherwise. He is treating the matter seriously enough to use his own initiative. He's out of order, but I'm inclined to his decision.'

Merriweather opened the door to the communications mobile. An engineer was lying on the floor with the front of a cabinet off. He had coloured wires in bunches, clipped and connected to hand-held system analysers. He was trying to read what appeared to Merriweather to be a working diagram with spectacles hanging off the end of his nose. Merriweather interrupted him with a gentle cough. The man looked up.

'I need all mobile phone networks cut off to the southwest of England. Not Bristol though. How soon can you manage that?'

'An hour. But why would you need to do that Sir?'

'We think our friends have planted a bomb on the bridge connecting Devon to Cornwall. A phone can activate such a device, so I thought—'

'You might consider taking down the United States' Global Positioning System as well then.'

'Why'd you say that?' Merriweather asked with a quizzical look on his face.

'I've heard SatNavs can be adapted for a similar purpose,' he replied with a smile with not a hint of humour.

## Dept. Anatomical Pathology, Plymouth Hospital 2008

Hugh McColl pulled open the cold chamber drawer that held the body of corpse label No. 3004. He needed to wrap it for removal. It was empty. He scratched his head. That's queer, he thought. He opened the other two drawers. The other bodies were still there. On top of that the Scottish soldier readied for a more intensive forensic investigation on behalf of English Heritage was now missing a dagger. McColl guessed they had picked up the wrong body by mistake. He rang University of Exeter Medical School that was to carry out the investigation, asking the secretary if they had collected the body.

'We haven't had chance; we're stuck for an ambulance. Should be able to collect it next week sometime. We'll call back to confirm.'

'Don't bother, someone's beaten you to it.'

He put the phone down. Dr. Poltair came in.

'Problem?' she asked.

'We've lost a body, the one that wasn't the soldier – the one from the sixties. It's not in the fridge.'

She pulled a face of incredulity. Going to the cold cabinet she pulled open the first drawer before doing the same with the second.

'Which one was he supposed to be in?'

'The empty one?'

'And English Heritage haven't got it?'

He shook his head no.

'That's strange. It was here. Have you checked the cadaver register see if someone else has removed it?' Poltair asked.

McColl opened the book running his finger down the list of bodies. Number 3004 was showing that he was still in residence.

Poltair walked around to the other side of the autopsy table and stepped on something hard. She bent down and picked up a dagger. 'Well someone's been in here.' Then looking up she noticed that the autopsy filing cabinet had been broken into. 'Know anything about this Hugh?'

He shook his head no.

'This has been forced.' She pulled open the distorted drawer and began thumbing through the indexes. The forensic report was missing. 'Not a chance you've mixed these numbers up Hugh?'

He turned around giving her an old-fashioned look. He was thorough if nothing else.

'Sorry,' she said. 'I would have liked you to have been wrong.'

'The Scottish solider is No. 2791. The body the police believe went missing in 1964, is 8303. That's the one Bristol police wanted to check his DNA with the barrister Phileas Cluff for. And No. 3004. Well he's gone walkabout. Lord it's a miracle!' McColl said.

She picked up the phone and called Devon & Cornwall police asking to speak with DCI Cocksworth. His sergeant answered and apologised that he wasn't there at the moment and that he had been called away to Truro. She asked the question if he was responsible for the removal of the missing body.

'Why would we do that? Where'd we put it? That's why we use you people. You *are* the mortuary,' Waverley said.

'Could you hold the line please, Sergeant. *Hugh!* The knife quickly . . . the dagger belonging to the soldier, bring it over here . . . yes Sergeant, security . . . *Hugh!* the dagger please.'

'*It's gone!*' McColl said looking at her. '*You had it!*'

'What'd you mean it's gone. It's on the autopsy table. I just put it there.'

'I'm going to have to call you back Sergeant.' She put down the phone. 'It was there,' she said pointing to where she had last seen it.

'Well it's not now,' McColl said his face flushed red that she would have thought him stupid mislaying it.

Turning the mortuary inside out they found nothing. The dagger that Forensic Pathologist Dr. Mary Poltair had personally handled not fifteen minutes before had vanished. She had never got her head around why anybody would want to steal the corrupted body of a man from the eighteenth century, then to wonder how, but that bloody dagger that she had in her hands . . . that had cut through an unfortunate's neck leaving a piece of metal embedded into a lump of tin at the back of his throat, was something else. Where in the *cutlery* drawer has it gone?

# TWENTY-TWO
## Devon & Cornwall Constabulary,
## (Plymouth Central Sector),
## Plymouth 2008

*RUDYARD MADE THE DECISION* that enough was enough. Somebody deciding they were going to set a bomb under the Tamar Bridge with those in their Whitehall ivory towers disapproval or not, he would sort it. To his way of thinking they had neither the wit nor wherewithal to deal with what amounted to a military matter. Sir Wellington had taken it on himself to take control, and he, Rudyard was having none of it. He would telephone him informing him of his discontent, and that he was the man to deal with this. Then, with the ball well placed in the Deputy Chief Constable's court, it would be for him to inform the Home Office, or whoever else wanted to make political gain out of trying to convince the prime minister that they had the tiller, and as far as he was concerned – for the record – he would not be steering this ship of catastrophe onto any rocks.

Eventually getting through to Sir Wellington after a deal of wrangling over who he was, what he was proposing, and how much was the price of bread, the voice at the over end said, I'll see if he's available, Chief Superintendent. Rudyard aware that this was the general put-off from over efficient secretarial staff designed for one thing – keeping the Deputy Chief Constable of the UK at arm's length from anyone that might want to interfere with his style of management was usually enough for the person asking to say they would call back some other time when it was more convenient. Naturally, the man himself, when he did finally get to the phone said he was glad to hear from him and was sorry he was kept waiting was all part of the game. There was already smears of blood on the carpet between him and Sir Wellington already, a little more was not going to make any career difference to him. People's lives were being put in jeopardy while they were talking. An operation that was clearly his responsibility could not be directed by amateurs looking for medals had to be made.

'I'm sorry, Sir Wellington,' Rudyard said, 'but I'm sitting a couple of miles away while your people are over two hundred. I've men and resources to deal with this. On top of which I have a close working relationship with the Navy and its bomb disposal team – experts and sound! It may be a hoax. We've a man in the frame that has a track record for such talk. But until I find him, I've got to take this threat serious.'

The previous spat with Rudyard was still very much on Sir Wellington's mind. The dealing with suspects on Rudyard's watch by MI5 and Thames Valley had caused him some embarrassment. He had lied to him already that he had any knowledge of such behaviour. Not wishing to embarrass himself further he listened intently to what Rudyard had to say. Then coming to a decision, he said,

'You make a case, Rudyard. I'll inform the Home Secretary,' Sir Wellington said.

*Bloody pompous arse* , Rudyard muttered to himself cutting off his phone. 'Ah Cocksworth,' he said as his DCI came into his office. 'I'm about to lose rank and I shall need your help to go down fighting.'

'Sir?'

'This bomb. On the Tamar Bridge. I'm taking control. Forget all this technology business from the Bristol experts of how these terrorists may detonate it. They know nothing. In this part of the world getting a decent television picture is hard enough without a metal coat-hanger to hand. The chances for someone getting a mobile telephone signal from the city end of Union Street to Stonehouse Bridge, then to bounce it across to Higher St Budeaux and the Tamar Bridge to set a bomb off, well, they'd have more luck using a fuse with a fast runner and a box of Swan matches.'

Cocksworth hoped his boss knew what he was doing in his assessment of technology.

'Steven, I want you to call up Drake Barracks and ask to speak with the commanding officer. Tell him that Rudyard needs Commander McPhail and his team urgently. If anyone knows bombs and technology, then Harry "Houdini's" the boy.'

Yes Sir,' Cocksworth answered. 'And your knighthood, Sir—?'

'Fast disappearing over Plymouth Sound, Cocksworth. About where the horizon dips away behind the Eddystone . . .'

Walking back across the Tamar Bridge with McPhail and not a word between them Cocksworth was utterly dejected. As for McPhail this jumped-up inspector asking if he was sure his team had carried out their inspections properly after having spent six hours using fifty naval personnel trained in such missions was enough for him to finally lose it.

'Listen, laddie. If there was so much as a sparkler under that structure, we would have found it. Now you want to shift the search. Since when was the Torpoint ferry a bridge. You've already got traffic backed up fifteen miles each side of the Tamar Bridge. Plymouth city centre has been reduced to a car park. And now. Now! That brothel-creeping boss of yours wants me to repeat the exercise scraping the arses off three ferries. Laddie, if I didn't have the respect for your boss that I have, I would say he should pack it in and retire.'

*Home Office, Marsham Street,*
*London 2008*

The Deputy Chief Constable of the UK was commanded into the Home Office for an update. As usual he had a lot to say with little progress to back it up. Not that he needed to be overly anxious. It was Sir Anthony needing to give answers. Sitting quietly around the large polished walnut table the interested parties waited the arrival of the prime minister. When he came, they got to their feet. He immediately signalled them to be seated. He then opened a file, took out his pen, and with no more of a preamble except for bidding everyone good morning asked Sir Anthony to update them the meeting he had with Sir Anthony earlier.

'Good morning everyone. Recent events – that the media has already guessed upon – are that the Prince of Wales is becoming exceedingly nervous about this situation. He has nobly suggested that he will do whatever it takes to get this siege brought to a safe and satisfactory conclusion. And this is where he and some of the less willing of the media indulge the public with their knowledge and divert. His suggestion is completely unacceptable,' Sir Anthony said. 'And quite frankly I'm only surprised he made it.'

'Would that be the story that's doing the rounds concerning dissolving the Crown's current business arrangements with the duchy?' Sir Wellington asked.

'Correct. Not with him or anyone else's power. He understandably worries what the country will think of him if he does nothing and the school is incinerated along with the children and staff. He's concerned over his conscience.'

'It'll be on all our *bloody* consciences,' Sir Wellington put in.

'Quite. Well, the Prime Minister agrees with me that there is no room for conscience. For any of us.'

'So, have you a solution?' Sir Wellington asked of Sir Anthony.

'Let's be honest. Despite mutterings from Cornish bards, and to an extent Mebyon Kernow, devolvement for Cornwall was never really on the cards to be taken seriously. But since statutory granting of powers from the Parliament of the United Kingdom to the National Assembly of Wales, the Northern Ireland Assembly, and now with Scotland's Act of 1998 giving their parliament power of primary legislation prior to them achieving devolvement, those mutterings have become more vocal –'

'Sir Anthony suggested to me earlier, that in light of the current situation the government bring forward a policy of devolution for Cornwall,' the Prime Minister said. 'And since I have considered that as a possibility, after seeking advice, it seems that they do not go far enough for this Timmins. As you are all aware there are certain conditions when it comes to devolvement. National security, taxation, international relations, defence, to mention but a few, all of which can be dealt with. It is these and more that are the problem for this Cornwall Democratic Republic. They do not want English monarchy or a duchy.'

The Prime Minister looked around the table allowing those attending the meeting time to let what he had just said sink in. All looked at each other. Sighs of breath could be heard. It was Sir Wellington that broke the silence.

'Under the British constitution can the duchy be abolished?' Sir Wellington asked.

'In a word . . . *NO!*' Sir Anthony came in quietly. 'If a king or queen were to sanction it, the monarchy would be up against more laws than enough.'

'What, laws of the land?' Sir Wellington asked.

Sir Anthony moved closer to Sir Wellington. He looked as if he were about to divulge State secrets that may be considered a thorn in the side to some. 'Have you heard of the Stannary Parliament?'

'I have, but I don't know where they come into the equation. Some out of date order from the past I assume.'

'You would think, so wouldn't you? Well let me tell you. All of you. The Stannary Parliament is the most powerful legal institution ever created in England and Wales. So powerful it can veto any Westminster legislation it chooses. And its job is to maintain continuity of the duchy of Cornwall.'

'You're not serious,' Sir Wellington said.

'Just because it was last convened in 1750 doesn't mean it cannot be recalled again. Any legislation for an abolishment of the duchy of Cornwall by a British Parliament would be stopped in its tracks.'

'Surely Parliament could overrule such an outdated system?' Sir Wellington said.

'An English Parliament, having sworn an allegiance to the monarch rather than to an unwritten constitution would be stumped up against the duchy. For the duchy of Cornwall read the monarchy. All allodial land rights of England and Wales belonging to the monarch cease at Cornwall's gate. From there they belong to the Duke of Cornwall,' Sir Anthony said.

'And if there is no Duke of Cornwall, what then becomes of the duchy?' Sir Wellington asked.

'The monarch would hold it until the next male heir came along. The duchy of Cornwall does not need a Prince of Wales for its continuity. It is, in perpetuity. Changes to the status quo would raise all manner of problems; not least being the current rents and taxes from duchy properties. On top of which no one has yet been able to decide what commercial organisation the duchy is. Hence the endless arguments over whether they should be paying corporation and capital gains taxes. Duchy properties currently owned by the duchy are administered for Princes of Wales. As you can see it's dissolution would be a mine field that would take lawyers acting for the duchy, and those that did not, hundreds of years to resolve. Years we do not have,' Sir Anthony said.

'The death of one child with the public knowing of this ultimatum Timmins has put to the Prince of Wales what then? Heads on blocks. The long-awaited revolution may not bother with the niceties of legal issues. I still want Rudyard involved,' Sir Wellington said.

'Nevertheless, that's the laws we have to live with. Let's hope it doesn't come to that. As for Rudyard's involvement, Prime Minister, Merriweather is more than capable of handling this situation. He is in Bristol. There's no need for anymore chief superintendent's getting involved. I'll go so far as to say that any decisions made in Devon and Cornwall and not going through Merriweather first may be counter to a successful outcome. Too many cooks,' Sir Anthony said.

'I think I'm inclined towards what the Home Secretary is saying Sir Wellington,' the Prime Minister added. 'Too many cooks . . .'

'I must object Prime Minister. Rudyard *is* involved. We believe this siege to be Cornwall inspired and Rudyard has a lot of experience that will be useful to Merriweather. If matters come up in the Chief Superintendent's backyard necessitating a decision, I can't see that an officer-in-charge will be in any position to orchestrate it from Bristol. Rudyard is a very capable man. One that is not likely to step on Merriweather's toes for want of seeing the whole picture.'

'Like this bomb threat I suppose,' Sir Anthony said.

'*Bomb threat!* Nobody told me about any bomb threat,' the Prime Minister said looking at Sir Wellington.

Sir Wellington explained that Rudyard had kept him informed of its progress.

'And have you informed Merriweather?' the Prime Minister asked.

'Not as yet Sir. Not really anything he should be concerned with as it's likely to be a hoax. Apparently, a man styling himself the Bard of Cornwall has threatened this sort of thing before. Nevertheless, until they've found the man and questioned him Rudyard is treating it as real. Wolf and all that. There is currently a man-hunt as we speak,' Sir Wellington said.

The Prime Minister thought carefully about what Sir Wellington had said. Caught in the politics between the Home Secretary and the Deputy Chief Constable of the United Kingdom was tantamount to being between a rock and a hard place. Sir Anthony was not the first home secretary he had dealt with. Unlike Sir Wellington his appointment fixed and permanent until retirement, Sir Anthony's position as cabinet minister was open to the vagaries of his government losing the next election. To say nothing of his own options for any re-shuffling of political appointments should fine tuning be necessary.

'This Rudyard you speak so highly. I don't think I've come across the name before. . . . Rudyard you say. Did you mention he was a service man in his former life?'

'Irvin Rudyard, Prime Minister. A one-time Royal Marine major.'

'*Rudyard*, Rudyard. Wasn't he the man . . . ? Yes, I remember now. He made the newspapers when he joined the police? Something on the lines of War Hero Becomes Peace Officer. Iran with Distinguished Service—'

'Your recall serves you well, Prime Minister. In my opinion, in Rudyard we have a very *sound* chief superintendent,' Sir Wellington said with a satisfactory look on his face.

The Prime Minister turned to Sir Anthony.

'On this occasion, Sir Anthony. With the kitchen being as large as it is, perhaps two cooks will serve better than one.'

## Torpoint Ferry, Devon 2008

A diver surfaced. Drifting to the ferry's hard ramp he stood up. Pulling his face mask off over his face he wiped the snot from his nose. He then shook his head no at the diving officer. A second diver came up seconds later signalling with his fingers a similar negative response.

Cocksworth standing close by was speaking on his mobile. It was Rudyard calling to inform him that the latest information they had was that the bomb was likely a hoax. Asking to speak to McPhail Cocksworth called across to him.

McPhail was busy loading air tanks and ancillary equipment into the back of a Navy Bomb Disposal Land Rover. Annoyed he declined the invitation. Instead he relayed the message to Cocksworth that perhaps his chief superintendent would like the Lion's Den searched while they were about it? Rudyard hearing McPhail's voice booming reacted in a puzzled way until Cocksworth informed him it was where MEN ONLY used to swim off Plymouth Hoe before equality of sexes forced the council to open it to all-comers.

'Right. Would you please inform the commander that I am appreciative of his further service to the country and that the latest information is that he can stand his divers down.'

Cocksworth feeling a fool in the middle passed the message on.

'Oh, I can stand my people down can I? Thank you very much. Well as a reminder to the major you can ask him from me . . .'

'What did he say Cocksworth?'

'Didn't quite catch it Sir. A tug steamed up the Hamoaze blowing its Siren.' McPhail repeated himself. 'He said something on the lines of . . . how did you managed to extricate yourself from that brothel in Singapore after the military police raided it?'

Rudyard studied the paragraph in question of the report sent to the BBC. He passed it to Cocksworth. '*Where?*'

He took it from him and studied the paragraph he had been

reading. 'You're right, Sir,' Cocksworth said ashamedly that he had not picked up on its specific detail. 'But it made no mention of the River Tamar. . . . We didn't really have the luxury of assuming it wasn't?'

Rudyard looked at his wristwatch. 'Fourteen-hundred,' he announced. 'Someone is taking us for fools Steven. Has that Bard been found yet? Never mind. Get McPhail on the phone again. It's a long shot, but with there being more than one bridge crossing the Tamar we may have picked the wrong one. Has Waverley returned yet?'

It fell to Cocksworth to call up McPhail once again. An exchange that improved Waverley's naval vocabulary immeasurably. The man's lack of amusement at his previous exercise was clearly apparent. With his team being called upon to repeat the outing he said:

'We've packed boats and stowed gear . . . and while we were still wet checked out the Cremyll ferry! What more does that man of yours want us to do?'

'Can you call him for a briefing?' Waverley asked.

A Royal Naval commander from the old school that would scrutinise his men's abilities, fitness, and care for their equipment when the mood took him. Catching them off guard didn't make him popular. But he earned their respect.

'Now Waverley I want a helicopter up and out over Milton Abbot, Gunnislake and Horse Bridge.' He turned to Cocksworth. 'Call Launceston and get them to close the road leading to Greystone where it crosses at Dunterton. Also, the bridge crossing Lydford and Launceston on the A30. Don't think there are any more unless you know of any.'

'Twenty-two, apparently. Mostly sticks across piddles. One on the river Wolf coming out of Launceston,' Waverley said adding, 'bottom of Lydford Down. We used to fish it when we were kids. Wouldn't have thought they could do much damage there though.'

'Check it out anyway.'

Cocksworth took another call on his mobile.

'It's Commander McPhail asking to speak with you Sir,' Cocksworth said handing him the phone.

Rudyard smiled. 'I'll give him *whore houses—*'

With overtures of cordiality done with Rudyard gave him details of what he had in mind. The briefing dealt with he then asked the Commander if it was too late to drag any of his team away from the Mess bar for such a protracted operation that might go on until midnight . . . *assuming any of them were still sober*.

He smiled through McPhail's tongue-in-cheek rant.

'And who's paying this time Major? Will it be the taxpayer or Irvin's personal budget I wonder? As for my men being drunk, having spent the best part of six hours undressing, kitting up, diving, un-kitting before moving on to whatever other muddy puddle of water the Chief Superintendent thinks we should search next, do I need to remind him that the Naval Diving Unit is more than suitably manned with personnel drinking shifts? Of course, I have another team ready to go.'

'I wouldn't expect any less of you Harry. As for those costs you mentioned, I suggest you take them from the navy contingency fund. You know the charity that paid for you to get the treatment needed for your pox that was doing the rounds in Singapore at the time. A disease a clean-living major as I avoided. Now, we wouldn't want that to get too far around Drake, would we? So . . . *Houdini!* Remove the chair you jammed behind the whorehouse door forcing me to take a window to avoid arrest, and I'll ignore your spots.'

\*    \*    \*

## Greystone Bridge,
## Cornwall–Devon 2008

Two horse riders approached Greystone bridge at Dunterton. One of three medieval bridges that separated Devon from Cornwall it was narrow, having six semi-circular arches, a tight kick on the Cornwall side, with passing places for pedestrians at three points across its centre. A lorry was moving off across the bridge on a green light at the same time as the riders were passing through red from the Devon side. Confronted by a situation, that had common sense prevailed, the horse riders would have stopped, dismounted and gone back. Instead they made the unanimous mental decision to continue.

The leviathan of a truck carrying stone from a local quarry, demanded a professional driver in full command of his faculties to navigate the narrowness of the bridge. The vehicle and its load passed by the two riders, who had reluctantly tightly positioned themselves each in their respected pedestrian passing places. The driver waved his acknowledgement that they had given way for him. One shouted at him giving him a hand gesture for his lack of manners. Dismissing his gratitude, they re-mounted and continued off the bridge onto the Devon side of the Tamar. It was at this point that a siren and a blue light from a police car a hundred yards or so back passed the lorry in the opposite direction coming onto the bridge. Determined they would stop for no one else, the riders, being two thirds of their way across ignored the approaching police car. With instructions to seal the bridge off from traffic as quickly as possible, it came down the hill towards the traffic lights at speed. The lights were red. Driving onto the bridge and seeing the horse riders, driver Constable Alan Peters from the Launceston Constabulary, with his passenger, trying to stop to avoid hitting them, changed his mind when deciding he could pass them safely. One of the horses rearing up on its hind quarters tipped its rider out of her saddle, over the parapet of the bridge into the river.

The other rider managing to control her horse, while Peters, fighting frantically with the steering wheel trying to avoid hitting part of the bridge slowed.

When the explosion came it blew the centre section of the bridge out and into the air, then landing on its bonnet stopped the car dead and hard. With its metal severing both high-tension cables and the car's fuel line it burst into flames.

Peters' co-passenger unbuckled their seatbelts and kicking at the driver's side door tried to push Peters clear. Overcome from heat and flames he was forced to see to himself, leaving Peters inside burning alive.

One of the riders was being helped out of the river by her friend while at the same time both horses, one badly injured, ran up the hill away from the scene.

A police helicopter flew overhead. It was two pm.


One of four wobbly wheels attached to the cart squeaked, squeaked, squeaked, at every revolution as it had done since before leaving Redruth 78,405 times on its journey to Dunterton. Attached by a metal bar to his old Hercules bicycle, the flag of St. Piran flying from the bamboo mast tied to it, the Bard of Cornwall was on his return, pedalling the A30 by-passing Bodmin, immune to the sound of the 43,090th grind of dried rust on the one-wheel bearing. Stopping in a lay-by he took out a brown paper bag from underneath the canvas sheet covering the cart and opened it. Pulling a half broken cold Cornish pasty out he began chewing on it impervious to the impregnation of vapours of ethylene glycol dinitrate emanating from it that only a canine sniffer can detect.

## Okehampton, Devon 2008
The sniffer came by way of a soldier at the 84,795th revolution of the

wheel of his cart when he entered the Regional Offices for the Government in the Southwest.

## Okehampton, Devon 1716

Coming out of the apothecary a ball discharged in a cloud of smoke from the militia's musket entered the Bard's jaw entering his brain addling it. The deflected ball from the militia's intended target of a horseman with his pillion galloping up the hill went no further.

## Okehampton, Devon 2008

The man known as the Bard of Cornwall lay dead in a pool of blood outside the Regional Offices for the Government in the Southwest. Over them were the administrative offices for the Duchy of Cornwall.

# TWENTY-THREE
## Avon and Somerset Constabulary, Portishead, Bristol 2008

*MERRIWEATHER* could not get out of his head the accent of the man he had spoken on the phone link to the school. Timmins had not been available to speak to him personally. A possible tactical reason, Merriweather thought. Timmins' Democratic Republic of Cornwall would be what was known in the trade as 'contingent terrorists'. That is hostage takers for publicity, ransom monies, or in this case a change of monarchical privilege. All of which were not to be underestimated when it came to violence of a kind that a suicide bomber, when the game was up, would take those around him/her with him/her. While that may be the doctrine of the organisation, it might not be that of its leader who would have made other plans. Horror of horrors would be an 'absolute terrorist' with a political agenda to make a point, sensing a betrayal of his *raison d'être* will adjust his suicide belt, taking them all out for the cause. As far as Merriweather knew the stand-in he had spoken although singing from the same hymn sheet would have an entirely different perspective when it came to his survival. When the man told him that Timmins would only talk to him and no other, Merriweather knew he was in trouble. Having to deal with terrorism on two levels would be hard enough for a trained negotiator. For him, with little training, would be doubly impossible. Timmins may well know that.

The assumption by the COBRA committee had been that the

leader would not be psycho-literate when it came to the game they were to engage. Terrorists with a super sense of superiority was a game-changer, making chances for the negotiating team to make them feel vulnerable using psychological suggestions in the search for a way out had, as far as he was concerned now, just gone tits-up.

'I cannot make that decision, but I'll put it to my people. Have you a name?' Merriweather removed the phone from his ear and turned to the team of negotiators listening on separate phones said, 'Well . . . worth an ask wasn't it. He was French though. Any thoughts Grant?'

'*Basque Separatist?*'

'The Deputy Chief Constable for you Sir,' the clerk police constable said passing him a phone.

He had difficulty hearing him with the background noise. Taking himself to a quiet corner of the office he listened. Such was the subject detail of the conversation he did not at first take it all in. Only when he was summing up did the realisation of what he had said hit him.

'And that's on a need to know. Understand that,' Sir Wellington warned him. 'If any of this goes beyond you or Goode then the consequence for all of us is dire. Need I say more?'

Sir Wellington did not. If Merriweather had any hopes that events might have got easier since this had started, then they had been dashed. The situation had got a whole lot worse.

'According to Sir Wellington she was a princess from the House of Königsmarck who at one time was muted to marry the Prince of Wales. Being a Catholic she was not considered a suitable match at that time for a potential English queen. It was the mid-sixties the hapless couple had to part. But not before she became pregnant. Are you with me so far?' Goode's expression nodded that he was. 'Subsequently marrying a Swiss count. He being a modern man for the time, accepted the baby as his own. Still with me? When the baby girl grew to be a woman, she married having two daughters of her own. The elder of the two is being educated in Switzerland. The younger, well guess where she's learning her twelve times table?'

Goode looked at Merriweather his face draining of all colour.

'*Yep!* His Royal Highness the Prince of Wales has a granddaughter out of wedlock over the road there at Stanners' and Haberdashers'.

Merriweather wondered what he was doing with this promotion turned poison chalice. Someone must have been aware of this situation. And Goode's remark to him that he could not wait for the film to come out had done nothing to make him feel any better over his situation. When the phone rang, he was hoping that it was Sir Wellington to tell him that it had all been a dreadful misunderstanding and that it wasn't Prince Cedric's granddaughter after all.

He signalled Goode to pick up. Listening quietly, he turned to Merriweather.

'There's been gun fire. Someone has just been thrown from a window out onto the quadrangle.'

Merriweather passed Goode a coffee. The handling of this situation moved up three gears without passing neutral. He now knew any advantage of time he might have enjoyed, with the death of that one teacher was no longer available to them.

A phone rang. Merriweather signalled for Goode to answer it. He was digesting the horror those children would now be going through seeing one of their teachers thrown to his death.

'You're joking,' Goode said. 'Please tell me you're joking. You're not Sir. Thank you. I'll pass your message on. Our condolences—'

'Not another body.' Merriweather said.

'That was Chief Superintendent Rudyard's office informing us

that a bomb went off over a small river crossing into Cornwall. A
constable has been killed.

# TWENTY-FOUR
## The Trafalgar Inn, Plymouth 2008

*IT WAS THE SACK CONTAINING* what Tony Noyon believed to be the missing body from the morgue dragged across the moor in the early hours of the morning by Jackie Forbes and her 'friend', prompted him to break his habit of speaking with the police. As a member of the free press this would normally be the last thing he would do but he needed a friend on the inside that might throw more light on a subject that, by his own admission, he had seen, his camera had not. He figured Waverley with youth on his side was more likely to listen to him than someone of a higher rank.

The occurrence he had to admit even to himself was beyond reality. The processed film in his camera showed nothing of what he had seen except one. Of Miss Forbes, a body bag, there was no image. The exception was one that was out of focus in the foreground that matched the man that was aiding Miss Forbes. He couldn't be exactly sure, but sure enough to say that it was the same person that he witnessed in Miss Forbes' hospital ward. He had taken the trouble to record the time he took the picture. It would not be conclusive. Either way they would have to listen to what he had to say, as it was not easy to fake a photograph from a camera that uses film as opposed to one that was digital. They may have the technology to enhance it.

Noyon was sat in the corner of the public bar when Waverley came in. He ordered an orange juice then joined him.

'You're going to want something stronger than that when you've heard what I've got to say,' Noyon said speaking with the seriousness of someone that did not suffer fools and their stories even though he was about to expose himself as one.

'I can hardly wait,' Waverley said taking a sip of the orange stuff.

'You've a missing body, haven't you?' Noyon said pulling his chair in speaking quietly.

Waverley stared at him. How could this man possibly know that? Unless someone from Poltair's office had been shooting his mouth off.

He shook his head. 'A missing body?'

'There's been one stolen from the morgue if I'm not mistaken.'

'Ah, that body. Well if one has gone walkabout, and I'm not saying one has, then it's possibly an identity mix-up. You know how things can happen. Paperwork goes missing. Someone not doing their job properly turns up and removes the wrong body. There might be all sorts of reasons. Hardly worth mentioning. Given time, it'll turn up.'

'Not anytime soon it won't. Can I get you that something stronger you're going to need it?'

'And you're sure it was a body you saw?' Waverley asked.

'It came away at the seam. It was a body all right,' Noyon replied. 'And I'm suggesting it's the same that's missing from the morgue

'We found three bodies out on the moor.' He had Noyon's attention. 'One was the body of a soldier. The other, a man. We believe murdered. His throat cut. What would she be doing with him?' he asked.

'And the other. You said there was three.'

'We believe him to be Cluff senior. He went missing out on the moors under similar circumstances to his son Phileas. That was in the sixties. We know it was him because their DNA matched.'

'So is the missing body Cluff senior?'

'No. The missing body is the one that had his throat opened up.'

'I keep asking myself, why would she be dragging a murdered man in a body-bag across the moor in the dead of night.'

'Assuming that what you saw, bearing in mind you don't have any photographic evidence to back up your claim aside from a black silhouette on a 35 mm negative frame, I guess to give him a proper burial. Perhaps she was related to him. I don't know.'

Noyon reached inside his jacket pocket taking out an envelope. 'Have a read of this.'

'What is it?'

'Jackie Forbes dropped it in the dining room of her hotel when she was having breakfast.'

Waverley picked it up and began reading while Tony continued the conversation.

'Do you think that those two lovers might be involved with that siege in Bristol. Working for MI5 perhaps.'

'Don't mention MI5 to me. No, I don't.'

Noyon was loath to mention his witnessing Forbes' dreams and wanderings of the mind when she was in the hospital ward. It was too preposterous for even him to admit it to himself let alone Waverley the existence of an apparition from the eighteenth-century.

'Spit it out, man. I can see it in your face. If you've information, then let's have it.'

Waverley was shaking his head in disbelief at what he was saying when Noyon reluctantly mentioned what he had seen. And although Waverley did agree with him that James the Third was a fifteenth-century Scottish king, and not 'The Old Pretender', he accepted the fact that James Francis Edward Stuart would have been known as James the Third but for being the side-lined Stuart.

'Ghosts are one thing, but this one, reaching across time and centuries professing to say what he did, persecuting Catholics, then I think his recording of history is stretching a point don't you?'

'Then perhaps you'd like to explain to me your version of what happened,' he said giving him the photograph that now had the image of the apparition previously unexposed carrying off the body bag with Forbes in the foreground.

## Greystone Bridge, Cornwall–Devon 2008

Looking across the bridge, Rudyard was sick to his stomach. But for his presence of rank he struggled to hold himself together. It was not for the carnage of body parts and blood sprayed everywhere, for he had been in war zones where it was common place, no, it was the fact that it was serving police officer that should not end his days in such a manner that made him feel the way he did. Watching paramedics trying to put into a body bag the remains of Constable Peters was not sound. They were having difficulties. The one doing the deed calling across to his assistant for a second bag with additional smaller ones was finally too much for Rudyard who, turning away, could be seen by other officers wiping tears from his eyes with his handkerchief.

'I want those Democratic— . . . or whatever those murdering bastards are calling themselves, brought to justice. I want them taken apart Steven. I want every damned one of those druid scums brought in and questioned until they bleed. I want what they know, what they're involved in, and who they are, without fear of rank, privilege, profession or background. And Steven . . . . I don't want MI5, Thames Valley, or any other glory seeking bastards interfering, is that clearly understood? We'll do this our way. If I learned nothing else from my time in the marines . . . well.'

'Harry? Couldn't be worse,' Rudyard answered his mobile phone. 'Yes! ... No. Worse than that. It's bloody awful. What shrink-wrapped head case does that? ... Eh. ... Oh, you haven't heard have you. This is not bloody sound, Harry. Not sound at all ... Eh ... Well, that's something at least. ... Thank your team for their messages of condolences, much appreciated, I'll pass them on. ... No, no, no, none of what happened is your fault. Don't run away with that idea. It's the bravery of men under our command that make these sacrifices. I'll let you get on, goodbye.' Rudyard waved Cocksworth over. 'Constable Peters. Alan—'

'Dan Sir.'

'God! Damn me! Of course. How could I be so out of touch? D-A-N Peters,' he said chastising himself for being a bloody moron before continuing. 'Penzance Pirate lock, wasn't he? Look can you deal with his family for me Steven. I wouldn't ordinarily ask but—'

'Of course, Sir. Not a problem.'

'Thank you, Steven.' He shook his head unsure that passing the responsibility to his Chief Inspector was the right thing to do, but he was needed back in Plymouth for what would inevitably amount to an inquiry. He would have to attend to that first. 'That was Harry McPhail, by the way. His men found another device under the A30. Where the bridge crosses into Cornwall. They disarmed it. Apparently, a dog walker saw someone acting suspiciously climbing down one of the buttresses on that Greystone bridge last evening. Pity he didn't call us straight away. Still you can't win them all. Have you carried out a search of this area?'

'Not thoroughly, but we have found evidence of bicycle tracks down on the bank. Someone's been sleeping rough out here.'

There was no textbook for dealing with the death of a fellow officer, and it weighed heavy on Rudyard to the point that he was having difficulty thinking.

'Not as rough as Peters is now—'

'No Sir.' Cocksworth replied. Rudyard's face was blank.

\* \* \*

## Cornwall 2008

An armed response unit of police officers arriving in Cornwall under Rudyard's orders would be sure to annoy MI5. He knew that. Trying to put a restraining order on Rudyard's interference over their methods using Sir Wellington for leverage, Rudyard had finally got his way. Forced to agree with Sir Wellington, the home secretary now turned a blind eye. His view being that Rudyard was a sound officer deserving of all their support whether they could show it or not. His general, admittedly old-fashioned view being, If Rudyard was prepared to put his career on the line to protect the integrity of law and order, then it was his duty to give him slack. Having lost the verbal battle of argument, MI5 reluctantly offered up all the information they had on Cornish nationalism, with the proviso that one of their officers was to liaise with them. Rudyard argued that the man was too over the top for comfort that had caused them a deal of embarrassment by his methods in the first place.

'Well if it's any consolation,' Sir Wellington said, 'he was one of yours . . .'

'One of mine, Sir. I don't think so.'

'Major Gerald Ford was a former SAS officer. He lectures on Security Studies in Terror, Insurgents and Domestic Extremism at universities not just in Britain, but also Europe and the United States. He specialises in terror groups, insurgents, and domestic extremism. He helped set up SO13 and Special Branch's Counter Terrorism Command along with Dr. Treffry. Recently the pair of them set about digging out every scrap of anti-English feeling by the Cornish since the rebellion of 1497. Obviously, they glossed over any they could do nothing about they instead concentrated on the 1970s on.

'Unemployment in Cornwall at that time was dire. Second homes were being bought up by people from outside the region. Celebrity chefs opened restaurants to feed this new rich influx. That was the start of the troubles. Following the example of the Welsh Meibion Glyndwr, who having had similar problems with housing and unemployment as their Celtic brothers, the Cornish nationalists as they came to be known formed small groups to fight this inequality. The Cornish National Liberation Army founded in 2006 was a direct-action organisation likening itself to the historical An Gof. They set about launching a campaign of arson and vandalism on English properties going so far as even opposing the flying of the English flag over Cornwall. That was when William Timmins changing its name to the Democratic Republic for Cornwall, which is where we are at now.'

'That does not make him one of mine.'

'Does it not Irwin. Well let me tell you that Major Gerald Ford, RM, DSO was an IRA infiltrator along with another by the name of Charmolue during the Irish troubles. And I believe he was close to your unit in Iraq during the 2003 war. You were one of those SAS officers helping to secure the Al Faw Peninsula allowing humanitarian aid in, weren't you? So was he. You are the same rank as the Major. Have a listen to the man before you form an opinion that might be considered bias.'


Rudyard listened to what Ford had to say on Cornish nationalism at the same time taking in the official government report of their later activities. He had understood his 'constabulatory constituency' from an aspect of crime, but he had no idea the extent of discontent and hatred that existed among this inner core that seemed to have emanated from the Cornish Rebellion of 1497 under Michael Joseph.

A blacksmith, Joseph went under the colloquial name of An Gof. In response to Henry the Seventh raising taxes from the Cornish for English campaigns against Scotland, the Cornish firebrand still commanded a following five hundred years after.

'Read on Irvin,' Ford said, 'it gets closer to home.'

It indicted An Gof for being responsible for bombings against non-Cornish businesses with connections in England. Rudyard turned to him and said, 'This all happened in the eighties. Surely we would have heard more from them since then?'

'We did. Rather we did. Although, I doubt they were the same people. Acts of aggression against restaurants and hotels belonging to celebrity chefs threatened only a year ago. Where were you then?' Ford asked.

Rudyard had only been with the Devon and Cornwall police since 2005 and what with his secondments and training it would have been before his time.

'Courses.'

'It's as well someone's got a handle on things then isn't it?' Ford said. 'For the Democratic Republic for Cornwall read William Timmins, the same that's holding those children hostage in Bristol. Though where he's been all these years is open to conjecture.'

'When you said, "Of whom were you speaking", in what context were you talking?'

'Dr. Allen Treffry . . .'

'*TREFFRY!* One of the people you tortured. Running a medical practise in Polgarrow. That one?'

'An intelligence officer working with MI5. He'd been involved with *An Gof* and *Mebyon Kernow* for quite some time. As well as that he was a good doctor for the local community.'

Rudyard was having trouble taking all of this in, before it dawned on him that there was a bigger game being played out here. Did the government have a section of MI5 working on behalf of the interests and security of the duchy for the Prince of Wales? For fear of making himself look foolish, he would keep such thoughts to himself.

'Why Bristol though? Is there some significance to that place?' Rudyard asked.

'We think that it's because of it being an easy target while still being of a significantly high profile in a city that is technically Westcountry.

Rudyard was smiling when he said, 'If there is information that might be of use to me during this investigation that is related to those children being held hostage, then now's the time to tell me, because if this mad man manages to carry out his threat and those children are killed whom might otherwise have been saved, the result of information being withheld by you, and which I subsequently find out about preventing it, then I will track you down and wring your neck with my bare hands. Is that clear?'

Ford's dealings with Rudyard, of what he had heard of him, to an outsider gave little indication that the man was anything other than a bumbler that had secured his position with Devon and Cornwall police to finish off a service career before retirement. That clearly was not the case. The man made promises not threats, and he would have to impart to him information of a highly secretive nature if he were to retain his own credibility.

'Fair enough. You've been straight with me. Your question as to Bristol being the modus operandi has foundations. We hope we're wrong in our assessments of that place, but the chances are Timmins' has done his homework. The Prince of Wales has a granddaughter. A relationship with an Austrian princess when he was twenty-two and she was nineteen. He had wanted to marry her, but what with her being Catholic, well . . . protocol and all that the powers that be could not allow it.'

'Don't tell me,' Rudyard interrupted. 'She attends the school. And there was me thinking that it might have had something to do with Bristol hammering Penzance Pirates 47–2 at rugby last year.'

'Well tell me this then Chief Superintendent. What do you think you can do, that the Sir Wellington has such confidence in you that MI5 has been side-lined?'

Rudyard smiled, 'At the risk of ridicule from you . . .' he called across to Waverley. 'Fill our friend in on the information given you by Noyon, there's a dear fellow. *Cocksworth!*'

'*Sir!*'

'When Waverley's finished with Major Ford, be so kind as to escort him out of the county. His work is finished here.' Turning back to Ford he said, 'Before you do go though, tell my people who murdered Dan Peters.'

Rudyard considered the facts. A body had been removed from Poltair's workplace. Forbes was missing along with the forensic report that suggested DNA evidence of the companion bodies matched Phileas Cluff. While blood samples taken from the blade of a Scottish soldier's knife, also gone, had DNA on it matching the missing man from the morgue. The irrefutable evidence before him that would need picking over with a crab pin was that a man from 1716 had somehow murdered another from the 1960s before slaying himself back in 1716.

## Devon & Cornwall Constabulary (Plymouth Central Sector), Plymouth 2008

The last time that Cocksworth had the time to sit in front of a police station's television was September 11, 2001. Other police headquarters, another time, another career. Then it was a case of compulsive viewing. This time he was sitting in the office of CS Irvin Rudyard. Then it was people from another country, underlining their faith exampling their resolve that politics of the western world should poke their noses out of theirs by flying four hijacked planes into the twin towers in Manhattan killing three thousand people injuring six thousand others. This hijacking of a school in Bristol, with three hundred hostages, and not yet dead – to some – might pale into insignificance. Such was the public's indifference when it came to violence thrust into their faces with their morning paper.

In answer to Rudyard's question. The same question repeated first to Cocksworth and then Waverley over what had taken place in Truro his one response was:

'There was nothing we could do Sir. MI5 were onto us straightaway. They knew what they were doing,' Waverley said. 'Torturing—'

Rudyard incensed over the hearing of this at the time had his own doubts as to what he might have done with people suspected of the murder of Dan Peters had he been in that same position. He tried not to think too much about the morality of torture concentrating on the things he should have done to prevent the blowing of the bridge in the first instance. Like locking down every crossing point on the Tamar as soon as they had the first warning. Although the reason for his apathy was not all down to him. Sir Wellington offered the opinion of the Home Office that they considered it was a hoax perpetrated by Timmins. They had reasoned, after listening to radio traffic conversations from inside the school, that they would not have had the means to conduct such an operation from Bristol. There was a splinter group here. For the moment though he had a funeral to attend, and it would not be the man specialising in sabotage, whoever he was working on the behalf of, that would share his mourn.

# TWENTY-FIVE
## St. Maddern's Church, Madron,
## Cornwall 2008

*THE FUNERAL FOR DAN PETERS* was a sombre affair.

Rudyard had been to funerals of brother officers that had fallen in the Falklands, or Iraq; they were soldiers at war, not police officers. It was to be expected. Peters was a policeman. Nothing special. Certainly not one armed to kick someone's front door in screaming, POLICE! Neither was he up there with the heavy brigades of Manchester or London; that had to deal with career criminals in no-go areas, where shootings and stabbings was an everyday occurrence that necessitated the wearing of body armour. Violence had now travelled. And Peters, as Rudyard, had not seen the coming of it.

A former lock-head for Penzance Pirates he had as many friends here as his own officers from the Devon and Cornwall police force. Rudyard looked down at the two lines of his own men, then at the line of Peters' former teammates, wearing shirts of their team. Their armbands were emblazoned with the flag of St. Piran. In front of them, Peters' mother and his two sisters were huddled together for support. They stood at the blackened and rusted gate of Madron churchyard awaiting the hearse. None of the family could bring them self to accompany their loved one in the car, preferring instead to let him have his last day on earth in peace.

Rudyard was to discover that Peters' father was killed serving in Iraq. His were a family that had known grief in the service of others.

The sound of the motorcade coming through the village of Madron instinctively drew him to attention. The hearse came into view slowly, having had to reduce its speed to get though the throng of people that lined the narrow street at the top of the hill before negotiating the narrow-walled lanes to the church. As soon as it came into view mourners began showering the car with flowers. Setting the pace for the grievers, wearing a top hat and full mourning suit, the lead undertaker, a female manoeuvring a silver-tipped walking cane shoulder high before bringing it back onto the road. Her appearance giving Rudyard the thought that not all needed a career in the armed forces to take on a military bearing. Her marching step reminiscent to the French Foreign Legion's eighty-eight steps a minute gave grandeur and respect to the man she would accompany as close to the other side of the veil as was possible for a living person to go. Her over length cane expertly handled in time to her march was mesmerising.

Halting at the church's lych-gate a bearer opened the tailgate of the hearse. Three men from the Devon and Cornwall constabulary, with an equal number from the Pirates slid, lifted, then shouldered high this precious Son of Cornwall from the vehicle. The assistant undertaker alighting from the hearse stood alongside the vicar in readiness to enter the church. A march beat from a drummer, unseen, gave time.

Inside the church a cool dryness. A scent of flowers and incense pervaded a sweetness that no other place could ever compare. The organist playing Verdi's Requiem brought voices to a whisper and the memorial for an end of a life to a beginning. Standing, after a short prayer from the vicar the mourners sang Rock of Ages. Dan's youngest daughter, Mathilda, read the lesson taken from Chronicles I chapter 29 verse 15 brought a stream of tears from the congregation. Rudyard judged her no more than eleven allowed his own emotion to unashamedly wash down his cheeks. His own officers as well as rugby players wept like children. Wives and loved ones clung to each other.

Outside the church, looking past the rough gravel driveway; and over the churchyard wall, local people waited patiently to glimpse the burial into the ground of the coffined man. Damp moss covered granite stone memorials, some inscribed from the sixteenth century, gave those that remained a sense of their own immortality for the briefest of moments. Amongst so many monoliths standing unseen ghosts waited for the living to let him go and for their chance to welcome him into a better life and a world where death had a permanence against life's fleeting moment.

The soldier Rudyard could not remember how many times he had heard the words earth to earth, ashes to ash, dust to dust in his career. Words that summed up human worth, to not only men like Peters but also every one of his worth, to Rudyard said it all time and time again. Born into a world our utmost endeavours for the betterment of it in spite of its obstacles, as so many others, had been his goal. And as so many others of his kind, words of adoration and love for duty were scarce on the ground, only heard at death. He held his head high feeling as a man grateful for his own life gave a resolve to face his own death with dignity and fortitude.

He whispered the lines of a poem he had once heard,

*And death, who had the soldier singled*
*has done the lover mortal hurt*

knowing not from whom, or even where he had heard them.

*Devon & Cornwall Constabulary*
*(Plymouth Central Sector),*
*Plymouth 2008*

Sir Wellington was informed by Rudyard that the person answering the description of the man they wanted to interview in connection with the Greystone bomb incident had recently been seen going into an office in Okehampton later being found shot dead outside. As the building shared office space with the duchy of Cornwall and a regional Government office for the Southwest, they had questioned those inside as to who he was and what he was doing there. As such they had drawn a blank. Rudyard was not satisfied. Convinced that somebody knew what was going on he pleaded an explanation.

'I cannot. I'm sorry.'

'*Or will not?*'

'Let me make myself clear Irvin,' Sir Wellington answered. 'You seem to have it in your mind that there is a conspiracy of silence. Firstly, attributed to MI5, then the Home Secretary, and now me. Well there isn't. Now you suspect the duchy of Cornwall of fogging . . .'

'Not at all Sir. But someone knows something.'

Rudyard heard the man sigh.

'I see little value in continuing this conversation Irvin. Your mourning for one of your officers is obviously clouding your mind. Might I suggest you take some time out, then come back to me when you're in a more rational state.'

Despite what Sir Wellington had said Rudyard could see nothing but conspiracy. Perhaps he had gone too far accusing Sir Wellington. The Home Secretary, well he would be a different kettle of fish. Someone with knowledge to build and plant a bomb capable of blowing two central sections of a bridge built like the proverbial brick shithouse clean out of the water had to be from the military. And there was that second bomb found under the road bridge at Dunheved on the A30. That, had it had not been discovered and defused, could have been equally as catastrophic as the first. And that, according to McPhail, would have been.

'Someone knowing his trade had put that together. The man

that's holding court in that school in Bristol would not have had the background. If he had then we would have known about him. No Irvin, this man would have learned his tradecraft in another theatre of belligerence. Fortunately for us he was a professionally trained saboteur. For that bastard built the thing too well to be otherwise. Fortunately, we knew how to take it apart.'

When he mentioned what Sir Wellington had to say on the matter, McPhail *hmmphed*, going on to say that in his opinion, Rudyard might well be dealing with a conspiracy and to be careful.

'You can bet your life they know who this man was. Taking him out quietly will have tied up any loose ends. Why they would use a musket ball to do it though is a mystery. Still, it wouldn't be the first time waters mudded by the good to denigrate the bad was employed in the world of the cloak and dagger. You can't fight these people you know Irvin. Take my advice. Take Sir Wellington's. Let it go. I know you've just buried one of your own, but they won't have any qualms about burying you alongside of him if you get in their way.'

What McPhail spoke made sense. He knew that. But for the look of those people silently crying out for justice at the burial of their loved one from that hole in ground for the husband and father then he might have let sleeping dogs lie. Sir Wellington intimated that he leaves it. Perhaps he was right. Words that between the lines amounted to a catastrophic downfall for the man known and respected in the Devon and Cornwall force as the Chief Superintendent that was Sound, would be to use one of his own phrases to overzealous constables that to this day no one never really understood, *Duck shovelled into oblivion*. He could not do that. Instead, resolving to himself to get to the bottom of who had employed that bomber, for he was sure it was not Cornish nationalism; and no matter their status or importance he would go down with his ship to find out if he had to.

McPhail did not wait for any argument from him, for he could see it in his face.

'If there's anything I can do for you Irvin, for I can see you'll not bow. For what it's worth, you'll have my support.'

Rudyard sat at his desk smiling grimly to himself. He stared at the framed photograph of a boy. Killed by a blue-on-blue missile attack by an American helicopter gunship that had mistaken him and his group of marines for Iranian soldiers escaping back into Iran from Kuwait, his son would have been forty now. No one was responsible. Rudyard's wife never forgave him for encouraging their son into the Royal Marines. She had divorced him shortly after. He gently coughed and picking up his phone speed dialled the desk sergeant.

'Can you ask DCI Cocksworth and DS Waverley to come and see me straight away?'

Rudyard decided that if he was going down in an investigation that might implicate others, then he had a duty to those involved of his intentions removing them from the case. His intention of removing Cocksworth and Waverley from the case was interrupted by the desk sergeant knocking on his door mentioning that the press was eager for a statement from him. When it came it mentioned that a number of arrests had been made in various locations around the county following the death of local police constable and rugby player, Dan Peters.

Cocksworth shook his head. 'Have we arrested anyone? And what's that all about?'

The newsreader continued.

'The authorities believed the man responsible was the same one at the centre of the hostage siege in Bristol. William Timmins, known as Wheal Brae of the Democratic Republic for Cornwall, a breakaway group from Mebyon Kernow, who are believed to be seeking a Cornish Assembly with powers in line with the Scottish and Welsh

Assemblies. They are also demanding the disbandment of the duchy of Cornwall. Further news. A source close to the police has said that a team of scientists have closed off an area of Dartmoor, the site of the missing lawyer Phileas Cluff was camped with his fiancée, Jackie Forbes with a three-mile exclusion zone. Strong bursts of radioactivity have been reported and the public have been asked to keep away.

'Switch it off Waverley this is getting all too much for me,' Rudyard said. 'In fact, close the door on your way out. I need to think.'

'*CRICKET* . . . The start of the three-day test in Adelaide . . .'

Cocksworth and Waverley left Rudyard's office quietly closing the door.

'They made no mention of the man we suspected as having been responsible found murdered in Okehampton,' Waverley said to Cocksworth. 'Did somebody make this all up? This has all gone *bloody* weird. What the hell's he going to do now?'

No sooner had Waverley said the words than a voice boomed out from his office.

'*CHIEF INSPECTOR!*'

Cocksworth turned around at the sound of Rudyard's voice and opened the door. '*Sir!*'

'Call the Deputy Chief Constable's office will you. I haven't the time to go through all their office preambles. Tell them that Irvin Rudyard would like to speak to Sir Wellington Beaufort as a matter of urgency. You have my permission to add whatever expletives you feel are necessary to get to the man.'

Cocksworth hesitated – his face questioning. He was about to say something on the lines of 'are you wise to do that, Sir', but Rudyard came back at him before he had the chance.

'*Go to it then man!* It's an order, not a request.'

To Cocksworth, Rudyard had gone from a man crushed to one

having been suddenly dumped upon by Divine inspiration. His words – first demanding, then half whisper – took Cocksworth off guard.

'*Sir!*' he answered closing the door behind him once more. He turned to Waverley, 'Does that answer your question Detective Sergeant?'

## Dept. Anatomical Pathology, Plymouth Hospital 2008

'I'm afraid I've to ask you for a second time, Dr. Poltair. The body is to be released into my custody immediately,' the smartly suited man said.

Poltair studied him. She did not intend to do any such thing. The silver-grey Volkswagen private ambulance outside with an assistant unloading a body trolley was already preparing to push it to the side entrance of her department. He gave all impressions of authority and confidence that he would get what he came for. Nevertheless, as far as she was concerned there were procedures to be followed and she stated them:

'For me to do that requires a piece of paper from the Coroner's office. Have you such slip?'

She detected a, *Why?* in his facial expression, that a mere 'country' pathologist should challenge him in this way.

'It's a green form if you've never seen one before. If you're not in possession, then you can leave me to continue in my lawful duty. Who did you say you were again?'

'Dr. Harvey Brigstock, Chief Forensic Pathologist for the Home Office.'

'Are you now? And am I supposed to be impressed by such a title? I think not. I am the Director of Forensic Pathology for Devon, and as such, you have no authority over me or my work. As for the removal of any bodies, before I have completed my examinations you are going to need a lot more than a Home Office title. Now, if you'll excuse me . . . *Hugh!'*

'With no disrespect to your office Doctor, but my title does give me the authority to do that. I shall also require all reports. *ALL* reports of your findings as to the cause of death. Can I take it I have your co-operation?'

'No, you cannot. Green form from a coroner is the minimum requirement. And she will ring to ask me if I have completed my examination before she signs it off. Good day Dr. Brigstock. *HUGH!'*

McColl asked by Poltair to leave them when Brigstock first arrived was close by. He had heard it all. When he opened the glass door to the examination room, he was prepared to escort the man from their offices.

'This way Sir,' he said.

Brigstock was not going to make a fuss. His kind did not resort to such practises. Instead, he would seek advice.

'I have authority and when I return, I shall expect the body to be ready for transport. With everything I requested. Good day to you Doctor.'

When he had gone Poltair got to work. She discovered a bullet embedded in the deceased's brain. Skilfully removing it she passed it to McColl for his assessment.

'Nine millimetres,' he said aligning the Vernier gauge across its width, then placing it in a see-through plastic bag wrote the measurement, date, time, and Poltair's name on the tag.

'Don't go away,' she said looking at the wound seeing a glint of something else where she had removed the bullet. 'Pass me the forceps, Hugh.'

Digging them in, she clamped the forceps, but they slid off. It was bigger than she first thought. Pushing them in deeper she opened the forceps fully clamped it on what she could see looked to be a ball and removed it. She dropped the bloody object into a dish.

'*God!* Where did that come from?' McColl said picking it up and with the Vernier jaws carefully measuring it. 'Diameter thirteen millimetres. Man, that's some conker Doctor.'

'The question is, how did a musket ball come to be in a man's brain; with a twentieth century bullet from a handgun lodged behind?' Poltair answered.

### The Diplomatic Service for the Crown.
### Offices for the duchy of Cornwall.
### Okehampton, Devon 2008

'He was under directives from our overlords, as I am. We answer only to them, not you or yours,' the diplomat answered.

'Was he? *Are you now?* Well, humour me on a couple of points, you owe me that much at least. I take it he wasn't the druid he appeared to be, why should you kill him before the police had the chance to question him? Surely you owed serving officers that much, or at least the family bereft of a loved one. Have you no sense of shame?' The Secretary Chancellor's face showed none. If Ford found himself in any other operation, he would take this excuse for a man out. Even though the arrogant bastard had the advantage of a gun over him. As it was, he would keep his professional cool, for the moment at least. This operation was too important. If it were to be fucked-up he would leave that for others to do. 'I'll tell you what I think shall I?'

'If you need to get it off your chest Major, be my guest, I can't stop you.'

'These overlords you speak of. Are they working for Timmins, or is it the other way around?'

'I said, I don't answer to you and I will not. Different department, different agendas. You know the game Major Ford.'

'This is supposed to be an MI5 operation, and as such, comes through me.'

'Everything but—'

The diplomat hesitated.

'What? You were about to say. *Who?* Who are these overlords of yours that have immunity from law when it comes to life and death?'

The Secretary Chancellor laughed.

'I'll tell you this much and no more Major. They are powerful and savvy. Savvy enough to set you up. They have had control of England, and up until the latter part of the twentieth century – Europe – for nine hundred years. Now, as for you, and as far as the Home Office is concerned, you *were* informed of what has happened here; sanctioned the *execution* even. Fortunately, your job does have a degree of immunity built in. But a word of advice. Perhaps you need to have a word with Charmolue and get your story straight.'

'*CHARMOLUE!* What do you know of Phillipe Charmolue?'

'I know he infiltrated Timmins' operation. That is him in that school isn't it? Did you think we were not aware you had a mole? And now it's your operation that will be held to account for the killing of an innocent druid. For my slate is clean. There's nothing to implicate me for that man's death. I am returning to London. It's for you to explain how you came to be here. I've already let the police know there is someone here that might help with their inquiries.'

'You think I'm just going to let you walk?'

'Don't think you have a choice Major. Am I not holding a gun against you? Have a look at some of the duchy leaflets while you're here. You might find something that will interest you. We've some beautiful properties in the westcountry.'

'That the gun you murdered him with?'

'That was one of the guns he was shot with, yes.'

'*One!* Explain?' Ford asked.

'There was another entry in his skull when the deed was done.'

'So, you . . . shot him a second time just to make sure he wouldn't talk.'

'As you said, his actions killed a police officer. The good people of the duchy when they discover that will come out in sympathy for a police officer killed in the line of duty. As will His Royal Highness Prince Cedric. The duke of Cornwall's reputation and lineage brought to a rightful conclusion intact. My work is finished here. Now will you stand aside for I need to be gone.' He smiled. 'Nice to have met you, Major.'

He held his hand out to shake his, but Ford was in no move to reciprocate.

Shrugging his shoulders that he wasn't bothered the man picked up his briefcase and walked out of the offices.

Ford looked out of the office window after him. A diplomatic-type limousine was waiting outside the building. A maroon Daimler if he was not mistaken. The chauffeur was opening the door for him when he heard shouting. An armed response unit had arrived. Surrounding the car, they demanded chauffeur and passenger get out and to lie face down on the ground. When Ford got out into the street, a cordon of police had already had it closed off.

'You've got the wrong person. He's the one responsible,' the Secretary Chancellor called out.

'*YOU!*' Cocksworth shouted. 'You can join them.'

Ford did as he was told. He was not flavour of the month with Devon and Cornwall as it was, he was not about to make any false moves that might give them an excuse to shoot him for resisting arrest.

'*CHECK HIS RIGHT HAND!*' Ford shouted at Waverley as he was being handcuffed.

'His right hand. Why? What am I looking for?' Waverley asked.

'I'm a servant of the Crown,' the man shouted. 'I have immunity.'

Waverley went over asking him to show him his hand. He saw nothing.

'Get them up on their feet,' Waverley shouted. 'What mark? What are you talking about Ford?'

'Between his thumb and forefinger. You can see it. I noticed it earlier.'

'I still don't understand. Again, Sir, and spread your fingers.'

'This is an outrage; I have already told you who I am, and you will soon see the folly of your actions.'

'Concentrate on his fingers,' Ford called out.

He did. Seeing the marks that Ford was on about he didn't understand the significance.

'Now look in his briefcase. You will find the Browning that did that. The same weapon that was used to murder their own assassin; killing your police officer. If you know anything of the peculiarities of the Browning, then you'll know that when it's discharged it tends to catch the skin of the hand between the hammer shank and the grip leaving a mark. *Sore is it?*' he said directing himself to the Secretary Chancellor. 'And you'll probably find cartridge discharge residue on his clothes and hands. You won't on mine.'

'Your paperwork Sir. Everything is in order as you said it was. I'm only sorry you've been put to any inconvenience. You are of course free to leave the county.'

Waverley's face was red with rage against what he saw as this travesty of justice. Cocksworth's was not without a similar pallor. Forced to witness their boss cow-towing to the man implicated by Ford for passing the order that inadvertently led to the death of Dan Peters, then killing the man responsible, both looked hesitantly at Rudyard pleading a change of heart. There was none to be seen.

'Steven, see that the Secretary Chancellor for the Crown has a motorcycle escort organised out of the county for his safe return to London will you, there's a good fellow,' Rudyard said handing the man back the brown envelope.

The Secretary Chancellor satisfied, nodded. He then placed the credentials of his office into his leather satchel. And with the embossed gold and red lettering below a State port cullis with the words:

**THE DIPLOMATIC**

**SERVICE**

**FOR THE CROWN**

he departed Rudyard's office accompanied by the custody sergeant to the vehicle bays.

Cocksworth holding his breath for the duration of the meeting, let out a gasp of air and was about to protest when—

'Give me five minutes, Steven.'

Cocksworth was taken aback at being asked to leave.

'*Five!* Please, Chief Inspector.'

For the first time in his life Rudyard had been used to set free a person of the Crown that had aided, abetted, and carried out the murder of a man on homeland territory to which he, Rudyard, was caretaker. The killing of Dan Peters murderer raised questions of who had sanctioned it and why. There was conspiracy likened to that of Lee Harvey Oswald's death by Jack Ruby for the murder of the US President John F. Kennedy here he thought. As to the method. A modern day 9mm bullet close to a round lump of lead (God alone knew where that came from); with marks from the shank of the pistol along with the discharged residue on the skin of his hand was enough to reasonably convict any man. Something had been taken from Rudyard with that call to release the man by the Home Secretary and he felt it. The King's Shilling, that had been his life's backbone for both careers had now become a tarnished eleven-penny fake.

With his jaw set square, he picked up his telephone.

The Daimler pulled over onto a lay-by off the A30. A picturesque and much preferred road into London by the man suited to the finer things in life. Flowers, countryside, England, '*O, to be in England now that April's there . . .*'

He had a patriotism for the continuation of kings that he would die and kill for and was not alone in. Switching on the communicator to the chauffeur he queried as to why they had stopped.

A motorcycle outrider dismounted and came back to speak with them. His Triumph motorcycle up on its stand. The other rider alongside of it was speaking on his telephone.

'What is it inspector?'

'Cattle on the road Sir. Perhaps you would like to take the opportunity to stretch your legs.' He smiled.

'Very well, but we haven't all day, see what you can do to move things along will you officer?'

The chauffeur came around to open the door for him. He stepped out, and in the briefest of a moment he watched as his chauffeur was shot dead before the gun was turned on him. Tight-lipped, wrongly guessing that a directive had been passed down by his overlord, he pulled his shoulders back and held his head high. With stature and dignity, he tore open the front of his shirt to reveal the heraldic shield of William the Conqueror. With his shout of, *God save the King*, a single shot rang out and he fell to the ground.

In less than half an hour both bodies had been cremated with only the briefest of ceremonies. The Daimler Super Eight was returned to an address in Whitehall on a low-loader transporter to be signed for.

# TWENTY-SIX
## Crockern, Dartmoor 2008

*CLUFF STEPPED OUT* of the offices of Ellick & Waite and was immediately hit by darkness. Stark and frightening he wondered if the state he now found himself was for an eternity. It wasn't. Dumped unceremoniously back into the light by forces experience told him existed he was back on familiar ground. The freshly animal manured wet ground of Dartmoor. Time–transference at least had had the good grace to bring him home to somewhere familiar. This bloody! moor.

The only consolation a swinging inn sign above his head that read, *The Jurate Arms at Crockern*. The true meaning of *déjà vu* came over him. He had been here in another time. Getting to his feet he pushed open the door and went inside. He would at least get a decent drink this time.

Unconsciously brushing the rain and animal surplus from himself he became aware he was as dry as a bone. Pushing his wig into his jacket pocket that was showing he gathered his rationale together and muttered to himself, Must be New Year's Eve, there's four of us in here if I count the dog.

'What can I get you?' the landlord asked.

'A taxi if you'd be so kind.' He pointed to one of the hand pumps. *Mm, Jail ale*, he muttered to himself once again. 'I'll have one of those while I'm waiting.'

'*MILDRED!*' the landlord shouted into the draught curtain covering the entrance to the backroom. 'Call a cab for the gentleman?

Seems to be too rowdy for him in here,' he said smiling looking at his two regulars. 'That a straight glass or handle?'

'Whatever's to hand.'

The barman took down a pint glass from a hook suspended from the shelf behind him, took it to the tap, turned it on and began pouring. Cluff subconsciously watched the man closely. Whether it was because he had suffered a bad pint when he was last here, or his standing in this verse was to remain, for the moment at least constant, he could not say. As to the liquor emanating from the tap it was of a consistent enough colour likely wholesome to satisfy both his hunger and thirst.

The landlord seeing him watching said, 'I charge extra for entertainment. You got cash, only the bank machine's on the blink?'

Cluff put his hand in his pocket was relieved to find he had a twenty-pound note. He also had two sovereigns, one of which fell rolling across the floor towards one of the other customers. He quickly dived on it. He did not want to have to explain why he had coins from the eighteenth century on his person. He dropped it back into his pocket.

'And a large whisky . . . and some cigarettes, seem to have run out.'

The landlord took the twenty-pound note saying, 'Whisky! Not a problem. *Cigarettes!* Don't do them anymore.'

'Here boss have one of mine.'

The voice came from a heavy-set individual, Cluff guessed to be in his fifties. He looked like he might be a farmer. Next to him, at the same table, a younger man, slimmer. An auctioneer perhaps, that dealt in livestock if he was any judge. *Or old coins.* He hoped he was not the latter that might have seen the sovereign.

'You'll have to go outside if you're going to smoke,' the landlord said to him.

'Why?'

'Have you been in prison? Smoking in public places is banned.'

Cluff took the cigarette from the stranger and stuck it between his lips. Then picking up his two drinks said to the landlord, 'I'll wait for the cab outside. Thanks for the cigarette, mate,' he said turning to his version of what an auctioneer might look like.

No sooner had he gone than the auctioneer called across to the landlord.

'That's him isn't it? The one half the county's been looking for.'

'Who you talking about?'

'That Cluff fellow. Unless I'm very much mistaken.'

'What the barrister? No. He didn't look much like a barrister to me.'

The farmer asked, 'Who we are talking about?'

'You know, the guy that went missing. Down by the East Dart. Where the police had that old tinners hut cordoned off and where all those scientists are wearing those weird suits. You know with his girlfriend.'

The farmer nodded.

'I remember now.'

'And did you see?' the auctioneer joined in. 'That was a sovereign he dropped on the floor. Wouldn't mind a couple of those. And he had a wig hanging out of his jacket pocket. Got to be him.'

The landlord went to his telephone.

'Well if it was him. ... Hello, I'd like to cancel the taxi I ordered, the fellow's decided to stay.' He hung the phone up and took a business card down from the cork board that was hanging behind the bar. He picked the phone up again and rang another number. Then waited.

'Hello, hello? Yes. You the guy from *The Sun* that was in my pub yesterday asking if I had seen that missing lawyer on my travels ...

Well, if you get a shift on, he's outside ... Yes, and he has a lawyer's wig in his pocket ... Yes, that's right. You mentioned information leading to his whereabouts would be worth two hundred quid?'

'Don't worry old son. I know where your fiancée is. Jackie Forbes isn't it? She's staying at the Plymouth Travel Lodge. What I'd like to know Mr. Cluff is . . . have you been lost all this time?' Noyon asked.

'Time! Now's there's a concept Mr. Noyon. *Lost!* I don't think so, for I know where I've been.'

'And where might that be Mr. Cluff?'

Cluff was in no frame of mind to expose his soul to this or any other man. From whatever newspaper. He was not seeking an offer for a story. What had happened to him and what was going on in Bristol superseded any thoughts of telling a tale that not one sane person on earth was ever going to believe. But, on reflection he thought, this man could be useful.

'One of those bodies they found,' Noyon continued without prologue, 'was he your father? You were looking for him?' He continued digging as discretely as was practical but Cluff was in thought. 'Two of them eighteenth-century. Would that be right?' Mr. Cluff. *Phileas!* Can I call you that? One a Scottish soldier.'

'You seem to know a lot of this business. Been breaking into official buildings, have we?' Phileas asked with a smile.

'What makes you say that. No, no, of course not. It's just that . . .well let me be frank. I've been keeping an eye out for your girlfriend while you've been . . . away. She has been appreciative of my help,' Noyon said genuinely.

Phileas looked at him suspiciously. As things stood it probably seemed he had abandoned her. If Noyon had looked out for her he looked as if he would have been more than capable despite his age. He looked like a man that could handle himself. His broken nose suggesting he may have been a boxer in a former life. An ally such as Noyon might well have been useful. How much help he had given her would have put him in a position of trust. He would have known some of what had been going on. With his ability to contact her across the centuries using what might be considered a spirit guide he would have had some inkling. If she had confided in anyone then she could have done worse than choose the man from *The Sun*.

Zac Ellick and Hilary Waite had laid the foundations for his help in saving the lives of many hundreds of children. If at any time they had got their timing wrong their deaths would be an inevitability. Not to mention his own place in time. He could end his days as his father. Locked into 1716 with no chance of returning. Was he prepared to see this through? The gamble that Ellick and Waite had asked him to take. The one that he had been unable to refuse.

'And I thank for that Mr. Noyon. Now I have to return to Bristol,' Cluff said. 'With or without Jackie. It appears I'm an important cog in a hostage siege wheel. What that is, I've no way of knowing. But I do need to get away without having to explain myself to the police. Can you help me do that Mr. Noyon?'

'Let's get you to Jackie first, shall we? She deserves that much. As to the rest, you can trust me. For unlike most of the world I have faith in you two bordering on gullibility, so help me God.'

## Travel Lodge,
## Plymouth 2008

She was in his arms. Sobbing her heart out. Saying that she thought she would never see him again. Then she backed away from him and hit him full hard across the face.

'They found him. Did you know that? Your father,' she screamed at him. She regained her composure. She studied the man comforting the red mark down his face. He had tears of sorrow in his eyes. With the ability to return through time as John Goode had shown himself capable, she wondered what magic he was going to contrive to resurrect Phileas. Now he was standing before her whatever it was that returned him to her the magic had worked. 'Tell me honestly Phil, was it your intention to find your father when you first suggested going on this . . . *adventure*?'

'Just needed to be close to him. That's all. The rest, well that was something else. My mother never did get over not knowing where he was. I can at least get him back to London and give him a decent burial away from this accursed place.'

'Did you see him alive?'

The vacant expression on his face was enough for her not to pursue the question. He opened the satchel. Old leather black with age and handed a parchment that was inside to Noyon.

'Read this. Should something happen to me it's all there.' Then turning to Jackie, he said, 'It's for your security as well. You are after all part of this *adventure*. The body of Joshua Timmins you secured from the morgue with the forensic report was enough for me to acquit John Goode.'

'I saw him hang,' she said.

'I know you did, Jackie. And I wish you hadn't.'

You remember the night we first saw him, moaning asking for our help?' She nodded. 'He had only recently then been hanged for the murder of his Cornish counterpart. And now, with what was done to him back then we have arrived at a madman that wants independence for Cornwall, the destruction of the duchy, the means of its achievement his ancestor would never have sunk to.'

'Who did you say was king in 1716? Oddly, this reads, James the Third,' Noyon interrupted.

'Look again, you've read it for the first time, as I did. You have misread it.'

Noyon skipped the preamble, taking in the last paragraph once more he read out:

*That the Cornish Stannary Parliaments of Devon and Cornwall are never to be allowed to amalgamate. Such an arrangement would affect the constitutional and semi-autonomous region. The last rights of the monarch to endow upon his son, the Prince of Wales, after the act created in 1337 by Edward III to provide an income from its assets and for future first son of a monarch and male heir to the throne and shall be the last remaining means of taxation by rent from all places including foreshores rivers estuaries mines and all mineral rights.*

'And it's signed, King James the Third. Here.'

He passed it back to Cluff.

'Cluff took a cursory glance before passing it back, '*George the First!* Have you a problem with that?'

'*Piss off!* I know what I just read,' Noyon said turning the parchment over to look at the over side, wetting his fingers to try and separate them as if there were more than the one sheet. 'That was definitely signed King James the Third. That would have been the Old Pretender. James the Seventh of Scotland. Son of the deposed James the Second. Where's the other sheet, lawyer?'

'And that . . . concludes the case for the prosecution, m'Lud. God bless him – for this royal throne of kings never did allow him to become monarch on this sceptred isle.'

Noyon studied the signature once more, at the same time shaking his head.

'Not least in this singularity,' Cluff added.

'Well, I'm off to Bristol,' an exasperated Jackie said to Cluff. 'And I've no intention of crossing Dartmoor. I'll go from Plymouth. And you can carry on and do what you have to . . . alone, or with Mr.

Noyon, if he's mad enough. *ME!* I've had it up to here . . . with the pair of you.'

Noyon was settling Jackie Forbes' bill. Behind him, seated at a foyer lounge table finishing up the last of their coffees, DS Waverley and DCI Cocksworth came in.

'Are you Phileas Cluff?' Waverley asked.

'You know he is,' Jackie said, 'and you're welcome to him.'

'It may be in your interest to accompany us, Mr. Cluff,' Cocksworth said. 'Our chief super wishes words with you.' He called across to Noyon, 'and you, Sir. You can come to.'

# TWENTY-SEVEN
## Home Office, London 2008

*AS IF THE INFORMATION* reaching him that the Prince of Wales had an illegitimate child from an Austrian liaise when a young man wasn't bad enough; but then to find she was a hostage among so many others at Stanners' and Haberdashers' was downright depressing. His plans to bring this situation to a swift ending had been thrown into turmoil with this latest revelation. In all his political life the chalice cup of poison was never fuller than it was now.

'Better send for Major Ford?' Sir Anthony said to his personal secretary.

Ford turning his attention to Sir Wellington and Sir James said: 'We have one of our own with him.'

'A Spaniard, isn't he?' Sir James queried.

Sir Wellington turned to Blunt.

'Haven't we got any of our own people capable of carrying out such an undercover operation?'

'We have. But not with this man's expertise and pedigree. We needed someone convincing. A British undercover man would not have cut the mustard with a Cornish Timmins. He knows his reputation,' Ford answered.

'Can we trust him? I mean he's not capable of being turned, is he?' Sir Wellington asked Blunt ignoring Ford once more.

'Ask the man. He recruited him.'

'*Major Ford.*'

'With an English accent there was a good chance that Timmins would become suspicious. It was Treffry that passed the word out that Charmolue was in Cornwall on the run from the Spanish authorities. And it didn't take long for that information to reach the ear of Timmins.'

'I repeat. With the situation we now find ourselves can we trust such a man?' Sir Anthony asked.

'Philippe Charmolue is Franco–Spaniard. I first came across him when we were both recruited by the British army to infiltrate the IRA. Before that he worked for the Direction Générale de la Sécurité a division of Spain's Centro Nacional de Inteligencia. That's the anti-terrorism unit of the General Commisariat of Intelligence specially formed to combat Euskadi Ta Askatasuna. I take it you've heard of ETA?'

'A breakaway group of the Basque Nationalist Party, weren't they?' Sir Wellington came in.

'You are informed Sir. As you know they used violence to establish an independent socialist Basque state. Not dissimilar to the Cornish problem we find ourselves in now with this Timmins. Charmolue, like many undercover infiltrators, can find it difficult to get information back. He seemed to have gone to ground, or as many thoughts been turned. He hadn't. The bombing in 1987 of a supermarket in Barcelona causing the death of twenty-four innocent people was the start of ETA's problems. Public support for them waned. Later in the same year when five children were killed after they bombed the family quarters of the Civil Guard at Zaragoza public support for them was about done. Along with their funding. With money drying up they set up training camps for rogue organisations. Getting drawn further in the man found himself training the Libyans and the Taliban. People you would not want as friends. They trusted no one persuading ETA that they needed proof that the people they were being trained by were kosher. Charmolue came under their spotlight. He was taken in, questioned and subjected to torture to prove himself. They failed to crack him. His skin watertight. His hands and fingers were not. That was when the General Commisariat of Intelligence asked the British government if they knew a man that could get him out. The point is Basque Separatism is not a million miles away from Timmins' ideals. Charmolue knows Timmins' mind.'

'And you got him out?'

'I did.'

'I just trust,' Sir Anthony came back, 'that his lack of communication skills with ETA has not been compromised in this theatre.'

Sir Wellington looked hard at the photograph of William Timmins that was in front of them.

'Is that a tattoo of a bird on his arm?'

'The chough. The national bird of Cornwall.'

'So that's it gentlemen,' Sir Anthony summed up. 'Major Ford will be guided by Charmolue whenever and wherever that is possible. Should the situation breakdown, then we will have to work on instinct and psychology. If you're in agreement.' Sir Bernard nodded that he was. 'Very good then. Thank you all for your support. I've to see the prime minister and inform him of the situation.

The front desk secretary quietly opened the door and mentioned that the Sir James had a call. He was not sure who it was. The home secretary said that he could take it here.

Sir James picked up one of the desk phones.

'Sir James Kirkby. Who am I speaking to please? … *Irvin?* … Chief Superintendent how can I help you? … And he's a barrister by the name of Phileas Cluff? … Right yes … *Right!* Thank you. I'll pass your message on. Goodbye. Well, that's interesting. That was Devon and Cornwall. According to Rudyard we have a fellow by the name of Cluff that has important information for DCI Goode that is likely to be of use in the Bristol siege. If you didn't already know, Goode's name was the addressee on a letter sent to BBC Southwest. Is it in order for Goode to speak with him?'

He looked around seeking confirmation.

'That was the barrister that went missing on Dartmoor causing the police a deal of trouble looking for him,' Sir Wellington added to any that didn't know. 'If we don't like what he has to say, I'll get Goode to arrest him on behalf of Devon and Cornwall.'

Hearing no objections Sir Wellington took it as agreed.

## Avon and Somerset Constabulary, Portishead, Bristol 2008

If this man were supposed to be a barrister then he sure could do with a shower and shave Goode thought to himself wrinkling his nose.

'At last the infamous barrister Phileas Cluff and Miss Jackie Forbes. You've given us a right merry chase I can tell you. I know where you've been Miss Forbes but where in the name of God have you been Mr. Cluff? Didn't you know there's been a nationwide search out for you. Have you any idea how much that has cost the tax-payer?'

'A pretty penny I shouldn't wonder.'

'*A penny!* And I'm not in the mood for flippancy Mr. Cluff. I'm a chief inspector. I am also the acting deputy in charge of one of the biggest siege's this country has been involved. If I had my way Mr. Barrister I would have had you arrested. That is what Devon and Cornwall wanted until somebody who shall remain nameless suggested otherwise.'

'No real case against me then.'

'Unfortunately, apart from wasting police time no. At the very least the Law Society could be informed of your conduct. If nothing else, they might be persuaded to take proceedings against you for being a *bloody* nuisance. Anyway, I have been informed you can help us. Can you do that Mr. Cluff because from where I'm standing, I think we could do a whole better on our own?'

Cluff studied the man whose ancestor he fought so hard to acquit; and who now was giving him such a hard time and wondered. How many other descendants of ancestors gave their passed distant relatives in life a hard time without knowing it? How many owed their very existence to an ancestor they could be turning on without knowing?

'Our going missing is intrinsically linked to this siege not something we were looking for. And in that matter neither myself nor Miss Forbes will add anything further. When this is all over a report will be sent to Avon and Somerset *and* the Devon and Cornwall constabularies. It will be then up to the Home Office to take up with me anything they feel could be in the public interest. In the meantime, I will be obliged if you will show me the back of your right hand.'

'*My right hand!*' What's my right hand got to do with anything, eh? You are unbelievable—'

Cluff while understanding Chief Inspector Goode's attitude towards him did not have the luxury of time to stand on ceremony. He would wrestle the man to floor if he had to.

'*Show it me! Damn you!*'

Goode's eyes glazed over with rage. He stared into the face of this barrister that had more than pushed his luck seeming to have authority on his side. Seeing something suggesting that this was no piss-take, and that what he was seeking to be showed would be commiserate with the way a barrister might conduct business in getting to a truth at the Old Bailey he did as asked.

'The back of my hand. *Satisfied! Advocate!*'

Goode studied the mark on his wrist with a fresh eye. The faint white scar running the length of the back of his hand, seemingly having been there forever, was beginning to feel sore.

'Well, Mr. Cluff, your verdict?'

'You are going to have to brace yourself, Mr. Goode. For what I am about to tell you is beyond reality. Without going into detail at the moment, I need you to accept what I am telling you is a truth. You and I both know that there are three hundred children in that school. All unwittingly dependent on you for their survival.'

Cluff suggested the scar he bore was the result of his ancestor having been nailed to a border post alongside Joshua Timmins. At that point Goode thought that he should throw this barrister – clearly on something illegal – out of his office. It was only remembering the document addressed to him by name from the same man now holding hostages did he decide not to. William Timmins had sent them to him with reason for what he was doing. That document, along with what Cluff was now telling him appeared that a twentieth century Timmins would somehow gain sympathy from the twentieth century Goode for an alliance they were both complicit in the sixteenth century.

The puzzlement for Cluff was how the result of this ancestor of Grantley Goode's being saved from the gallows was going to change history as it stood now. Ellick and Waite hadn't got that far into the story. Perhaps the reasons were that they didn't know. They did mention that the future doesn't move on with death to be able to see into the future. On that then, they were right. Which didn't help him now. What he did know was that he had to tell his story, or part of it as soon as he could. He was a messenger in time, and he did not much like it.

### Bishopston, Bristol 2008

'Scar. What scar?' Eileen Goode asked her son.

He showed her his hand.

'That's not hereditary. You did that falling off a hayrick stacker on a farm. Aunt Violet, your dad's sister, put us up for a fortnight's holiday. And if my memory serves, you were a right little sod. Seven I think you were, climbed up the thing, slipped, and went down the length of it missing every spike without impaling yourself. It could have been nasty. I had nightmares for the rest of the holiday. You did badly gash the back of your hand though. Doesn't bother you does it? We took you to hospital. They gave you a tetanus injection so you shouldn't have any problems now, if that's what you're worried about.'

'Well, not really—'

'Why bring it up then?'

'Where did we come from? Not just you and dad. I mean, our ancestors.'

Grant had a troubled look on his face. Nothing unusual in that his mother thought. He was a policeman after all. This was a different though. It was as if he was watching a disaster unfold unable to avert it.

'What's this all about?'

'You did a family tree some time ago didn't you?'

'Yes . . . *and*?'

'Did we come from the westcountry? Were any of them Stannary officers?'

'*Stannary officers!* What are they?'

She stared at him. Something serious was troubling him.

'No. Not as far as I know. Traced your father's family back to 1680. They came from London. My lot, well I got as far as 1600 with them. Norfolk. Brewers, farmers . . . one was a blacksmith. Your father's side . . . one was a tanner, most appeared to have worked in print, apart from one that was in the merchant navy.' She smiled at him. 'Anything else while you're here?'

'You're absolutely sure?'

She changed the subject.

'You having lunch?' she asked in a manner that she would not demean herself by reaffirming what she knew to be true.

*Avon and Somerset*
*Constabulary Ops. Units,*
*Bristol 2008*

Merriweather took out an architect drawing from a desk that had been jammed into the corner of the ops room. Written in the corner, the drawing's title, handwritten in black ink in neat sans serif was its title:

STANNERS' AND HABERDASHERS'

SCHOOL FOR THE POOR

He placed it on the desktop and nodded at Charmolue to fill in the details they needed. He was about to ask him how he managed to get away to get them this information when the building was surrounded by police marksmen.

Ford knowing that the next question as to how he managed to persuade Timmins that he was AWOL shook his head at him as if to say, *Leave it!*

Charmolue pushed it to one side. Taking a sheet of paper from the printer in the corner of the cabin he put it on the desk in front of him. Then with a stub of a pencil started drawing a detailed map of the inside of the school. It was clear that walls that had been on the original drawing had been knocked down and others put up in other places throwing the drawing out of date.

'Put the alterations on there,' Merriweather said pointing to the architects drawing.

He carried on drawing. He was detailed and thorough putting arrows in and writing what they indicated. When he got to the bombs hanging from the ceiling of the main hall wired across the parquet flooring, Merriweather knew then what a kind of man he was dealing with that could put children through such trauma.

'Exits. All covered with mobile alarms. No one can get in or out,' Charmolue said.

Goode who up until now had remained quiet asked how he had managed it.

'Cigares. I put it in his head that we could do with some cigars to celebrate. He challenged me that I couldn't get out and back getting them.' He then looked out of the window. It had a direct view of the side elevation of the school. Studying it he then made a note on the plan. 'More paper.'

Merriweather fumbled at the printer to pull another sheet. He was taking too long.

'Come on this'll do,' Charmolue said grabbing a green operations folder held by a police officer. 'It doesn't take this long to get cigars. The man's going to smell a rat.' He emptied it out then began sketching more detail of the types of explosives being used on the inside cover. He pulled a crushed pack of Gitanes from his camouflaged combat trousers, took one out and stuck it in his mouth. Fumbling around the pockets he pulled out an old petrol lighter and lit it. Drawing in a deep breath of the smoke he exhaled and carried on.

'Give me some room here,' he said unrolling the original plan, turning it first one way, then the other for comparison. His head down he was sketching for all he was worth. 'See here. *Here! Look!* Those explosives are rigged to two computers. Two. If one goes down, then there's a back-up.'

Merriweather leaned closer over Charmolue's shoulder to get a better understanding of what he was explaining on paper that was going to help them when it came to defuse the explosive devices. Should they be so lucky. As far as Charmolue was concerned this was a lost cause with nothing left but an exercise in damage limitation. Merriweather gave instructions to the officer to get the listening lines re-allocated according to this new information.

'Wire me Major,' Charmolue said removing his navy-blue t-shirt to reveal a muscular physique. Across his chest, a tattoo with the legend of the Democratic Republic of Cornwall in green overprinted with a black chough. Merriweather was not sure if it were one of those water tattoos that could be removed but having met the man decided that he would have gone all the way with electronic ink.

Charmolue nodded to the Ford. He then put his shirt back on.

Handing Charmolue a packet of Gitanes Ford said, 'That's the radio controller linked to our weapon of mass destruction. He can have as many back-up computers as he wants. This is one device that will turn them off.'

'Let me make one thing clear,' Charmolue said to both officers. 'Timmins is not interested in the lives of those children. Count on it. They're hungry, thirsty, pissing, shitting and generally crying out for their mothers. Some are no more than three. It makes no difference to him whether they live or die to get what he wants. His orders to his men are to simply ignore all pleas. This is no consolation; I will likely be killed trying to protect them when the time comes. An act that is not in my training manual. A sacrifice that won't save them if you get any of this wrong.'

He smiled. Then he was gone.

## Stanners' and Haberdashers' School, Bristol 2008

Slipping unseen through an iron grating outside the school building once used as a coke intake chute for the now defunct boiler. With a pack of Castella Panatellas in his combat trousers thigh pocket, he landed on what remained of a pile of old burned fuel. An obnoxious smell of sulphur from its dust went down into his lungs from its disturbance. He coughed. A set of stairs, the caretaker's access to the heating furnace took him to the back of the performance stage, then into the hall. The familiar depressing sight waited for him.

The children and staff. A smell of confinement from so many unable to control bowels and bladders pervaded. Here was proactive Cornish nationalism sunk to depths. Not quite ETA, but fast heading in its direction. Would these people ever run their own affairs, he thought. Idealists that would follow any man with a penny whistle, prepared to send children to their deaths, to dilute the estates of future kings and queens of England, he didn't think so. In this regard, it was the Prince of Wales having treason working against him; not the monarchy in particular.

Charmolue had done his homework when first he had allowed himself to be conscripted by Timmins. As an historian in a previous life he had seen both cause and effect of this insurrection. And the duchy of Cornwall was not without sin. A state within a state was an anachronism no longer fit for purpose. Ignoring the genuine needs of the indigenous population, allowing outsiders that had money to buy up property and call the shots, looking on those in need as dole scroungers where no other choices were available in a county where work, poorly paid, was asking for revolution. A long way from London they were being rained on by both English government and duchy. He was not political, but history taught you cannot keep people down forever. In the case of Timmins though, when he looked into his eyes, he could not decide if the man had genuine Cornish interest or seeking something else. For he had the look and actions of man ravaged with revenge.

He opened the door to the head teacher's office where the computers linked to the explosives were streaming their data. Timmins smiled.

'Not long now,' Charmolue said. *'Cigare!'*

# TWENTY-EIGHT

## Stanners' and Haberdashers' School, Bristol 2008

*WILLIAM TIMMINS* sat at the head teacher's desk. A large nineteenth century Victorian oak affair having an antique pen holder at its front with an old-fashioned dialling telephone at its side. He had a fountain pen in one hand and a cigar in the other. The ash close to its tipping point was precariously balanced over an upturned cocoa tin lid. He was writing up notes in a large desk journal. Open files listed members of his organisation that would become administrators in his new Assembly for Cornwall. Titles included a First Minister, a Lord Advocate and a Solicitor General. Appointments generally only sanctioned by a monarch of England he, as the self-proclaimed Protector of Cornwall would now assume. Others were made up from the present lieutenancies, sheriffs, and those holding high office from the present duchy having their eyes on the new ball. English Heritage and land-owning trusts all eager to maintain patronage from another source if the duchy of Cornwall was disbanded were all secretly keen for representation. If William Flamank Timmins was aware of nothing else in this world, he knew that there were always people and organisations willing to trade allegiances to progress their causes. With treason in mind, for that is what it was, should the duchy fall repressive acts against him by the monarchy would be imposed on Cornwall as an act of retribution. Without interference by an English parliament becoming involved the monarchy already had the power to veto against any Assembly of the United Kingdom – Cornwall or otherwise – where the duchy had a hand in accordance with its charter. In that respect he needed all Cornish nationalists and those sympathetic from across the United Kingdom to counter what appeared to be dictatorship by the monarchy and the power behind their thrones that kept them there. The Cornish Revolt of 1497 was his model now. A Revolt that saw his own ancestor Thomas Flamank along with Michael An Gof being hung, drawn and quartered at Tyburn for standing against Henry the Seventh for raising taxes from the Cornish for his war with James the Fourth of Scotland.

### Clarence House, London 2008

The door was answered by a footman. The Home Secretary waited the few moments it took Sir Bernard Naismith to come down the stairs to greet him before making mention of these new comings to light. His face said it all. For anyone's telephone number to have been hacked into was one thing. For it to be the Prince of Wales' was a security breach too far. He felt both personally responsible and annoyed.

'How did His Royal Highness react when you told him?' Blunt asked trying to put as much concern as was possible in his voice. The man being heir to the throne did not give him the right to act the bloody fool, he thought.

Sir Bernard touched his arm to indicate for him to go in front of him into an office. He quietly shut the door and offered him a drink. Blunt sat down and nodded that a gin and tonic would do fine. In answer to the Blunt's question as to the emotional state of His Royal Highness since Sir Bernard stated:

'He's shaken. As you can imagine. You know Anthony, I cannot begin to understand how they carried this out with all the electronic gadgetry we have at our disposal.' He sighed. 'However, it has, and there's nothing we can do about it now. The point is . . . where do we go from here?'

'Have you the transcript?'

Sir Bernard opened a drawer in his desk. Taking out a small compact cassette he passed it to him.

'I've had words with Sir James Kirkby, and he's agreed with me. We cannot allow this man the demands his Royal Highness has agreed to,' Blunt said.

'Well no. I think that goes without saying,' Sir Bernard said.

'Have you spoken with His Majesty the King on this matter? I realise it would have been a conversation of some delicacy.'

'Not him personally. His private secretary Lord Bellowes. What came back was that His Majesty is not best pleased.'

'Would that be royalty-speak?' He shrugged his shoulders. 'Did he make any suggestions as to what he thought we should do? I take it he will be putting the onus on others to sort his family's mess out?'

'Only that his son's capitulation to Timmins was out of the question. He mentioned to Lord Bellowes to remind those overseeing this attack on the monarchy of the Royal Great Charter of 1337.'

'*The Royal Great Charter?* Go on then, remind me,' Blunt asked.

'A charter applying to the Dukes of Cornwall laid down by King Edward the Third. That is. A legal document for the enrichment of Dukes and the Monarchy of this land. With the creation of a duchy next to legally watertight wording on the lines of:

*Therefore we have given and granted for us and our heirs and by this our present Charter confirmed to our same son under the name honour of the Duke of the said places.*

'It then goes into all the assets, lands, fisheries, and mineral rights etc of the duchy of Cornwall. All of which extends beyond that county into others. Devon, Surrey, Wales to mention but a few.'

'And it can't be repealed?' Blunt asked.

'Anything can be repealed given time. In the case of this document it would take lawyers a millennium to untangle.'

'*Or a revolution!*'

'*Ooooh!* Heads on blocks, Home Secretary. What are you suggesting? No, I don't think that is likely in this twentieth-first century sceptred isle do you? The point is that now the present incumbent has made promises to Timmins, his retracting them now is likely to lead to a backlash of blood,' Sir Bernard said.

'Well we cannot be seen to make compromises with a terrorist?' Blunt said.

'So, what does your government suggest you handle this situation?' Sir Bernard asked.

'Well, silly as I found this the first time, I heard it, but some young bright spark of a civil servant came up with the idea of using an impersonator as a placement to His Royal Highness. You know. A dialogue with Timmins that would make him think he was actually speaking to the man.'

'*A what?*' Sir Bernard asked.

'As I said my initial thoughts exactly. Thoughts I originally dismissed. Then I thought about it once more. If we were to use an impersonator, locking the Prince out his negotiations with the man, then breaking promises would no longer be of his making,' Blunt said.

'I see. And how exactly are you proposing to carry out such an operation without His Royal Highness being rumbled?' Sir Anthony asked. 'Then there's the matter of discretion over His Royal Highness having a granddaughter out of wedlock in the school entering into the equation,' Sir Bernard said.

'Some technical wizardry. Obviously care in the man we select will need consideration. We wouldn't want the maintenance of His Royal Highness's credibility to be compromised, would we? He will of course be subject to the Official Secrets Act,' Blunt said.

Sir Bernard shook. His whole life job seemed to be concerned with nothing else.

'You can always behead the mimic for treason should it reach the Sunday newspapers Anthony. After all, he wouldn't be the first to have bothered with any Act spilling beans over the royal family and its indiscretions when it comes to making a few bob,' Sir Bernard remarked.

'Beheading for treason was abolished in 1973. You might have to think about method again Sir Bernard.'

## Avon and Somerset Constabulary Mobile Units, Bristol 2008

Acton-Vean was computing figures and co-ordinates alongside a technician from the missiles manufacturers to test out an electromagnetic pulse device over a corridor of Bristol in line with the school. Those that saw it agreed that its sleek white aerodynamic shape with the manufacturer's logo, BOEING in blue running its length was reminiscent of a piece of art. As to the missile codenamed Crossbow it was under canvas in a side street known as Brunel Villas overlooking Stanners' and Haberdashers' and was secured by military police officers from the USAF section base at RAF Lakenheath. It had been explained to Merriweather and Goode that although this 'piece of kit' was still in its experimental stage the idea was that it would deliver high-power microwave bursts down onto the school disabling Timmins' computers. The computer, according to Charmolue, was connected through wiring running through the building to the explosive devices taped to half of the older children. Only Charmolue would be able to tell Acton-Vean when it would be detonated. A narrow width of time in which by then he would have been exposed as an infiltrator likely shot dead. The radio transmitter strapped to his chest automatically signalling assuming he was not alive to do it himself – Acton-Vean game over: final option.

Merriweather was nervous. The thought of a missile even without an explosive warhead taking off under their noses from ground level, exiting through a tent flap, searing everything in its path was worrying. If its guidance system were affected causing it to waver from its programmed and predetermined journey randomly landing in a built-up area of Bristol, well it would be catastrophic. And that was before the computing systems of half the manufacturing and service industries of Bristol had been put out of operation as it passed over.

He and his team had done their bit. Electronic surveillance cameras and sounding devices had been inserted into the walls of the school had been difficult. The thickness of its walls, reflecting its age had seen to that. Television cameras in one of the other mobile units had not recorded a pleasant image to work. And not for the first time had Beslan been mentioned. A word that he had bent over backwards to avoid. Synonymous with the deaths of six hundred people, of whom three hundred were children, made him shudder. He was not in a good place as team leader, neither did he wish it on any other serving officer.

He stared at the blue light emitting electronic timer. '1350.45,' he read. Not that Acton-Vean needed reminding seeing him noticing it. He smiled at her as she looked up at him. She twisted her lip then instinctively returned his smile. An emotional expression that gave away small assurance to him. Pressing the fire button was not something Acton-Vean was happy about.

The Home Office had not wanted the military involved. At least not in this aspect part of the operation. This was to be between the police and the perpetrators of this crime unfolding. Acton-Vean had been the natural choice since she had been involved with armaments when serving as an officer in the army. In that regard the Home Office was happy with the arrangement. Nevertheless, the timing would be critical. That, they were not happy with. Should it fail there would be no second chance. Charmolue had closed the door on that as an idea. He had calculated that $x$-number of explosives would be more than sufficient. Timmins' demand for $3x$ was to be more appropriate. He was looking at not only taking the school and its inmates out, but a good proportion of the city of Bristol as well. When the prime minister, faced by cabinet ministers and the top brass from the military after arguing among themselves at the last meeting of COBRA as to whether Charmolue – a double agent for *Chrissake* – was the right man to liaise with over the timing, Merriweather had answered: *Who do you think's better placed? If anyone of you thinks he can do a better job, I'll take volunteers!*

There were none.

The last conference before the event and it was Merriweather that recalled his own doubts now. That COBRA question. Did he have faith in a man indoctrinated with so many different ideas and beliefs in his varied theatres as Charmolue?

'Goode backed him saying, 'You're right, we have no choice. A Franco–Spaniard with past involvements with Basque Separatists, Taliban and al Qa'ida he may be; and he would not have been the first to fool handlers; but it was Gerald Ford from SO13 that put him there. That's got to be good enough for us.

'Even he was unable to give a definitive character reference of the man with such a curriculum vitae.'

Putting the question to Acton-Vean, Merriweather asked if she was comfortable with the arrangements as they stood.

'If my daughter were in that school, I would clutch at any opportunity to save her using the arrangements we have. Far as I can see, we don't have a choice *but* to trust Charmolue.'

He agreed their options were limited. And while all hostage sieges were different, manuals writing the importance for nut and bolt detail were common to all when it came to negotiation. In that regard Merriweather went into 'Plan A' hoping any success in that one would negate using 'Crossbow'. The conversation that was about to take place between Timmins and 'His Royal Impersonator', being his salvation.

The critical need to assimilate emotions allowing the person to speak while listening yourself, building trust, not being aggressive while at the same time gaining a rapport were all very fine if the man speaking was psychologically trained in these techniques. For the lowly desk sergeant that was Ian Duffy he would have his work cut out not least because of the latest revelations.

'The *damn* clock has moved its big hand to the metaphorical minute to twelve,' Merriweather said to Goode. 'I trust to God that Duffy is up for this.'

'We're good to go,' the engineer said to Merriweather on the phone. '*Two signals!* ... Yes, I've secured help from some geek from British Telecom they poached from Ribbit. Would you believe Graham Bell? ... All done. Don't ask how. Something to do with equalisers and filters. As soon as your man's good to go, timed exactly with His Royal Highness' mobile being answered with his first syllables, we'll synchronise ... That's the idea ... Yes it will cut him out of the conversation completely. The voice output will override his Highness replacing it with that of your man's. All His Royal Highness will be able to do is listen ... Yes, of course, but mark me well Chief Superintendent Merriweather, the timing is critical. Timmins may not be following the graphic equaliser all the way, but initially he will confirm the voice of His Royal Highness. After that, well, you know the score ... Follow you ... *Good luck*, yes, thanks for that, we're going to need it. Will call again when we're ready to go Chief Superintendent.'

## Stanners' and Haberdashers' School, Bristol 2008

Charmolue was standing alongside Timmins.

For someone with revolution in mind in a twentieth-first century world punctuated at both ends of the proverbial cradle to grave by civil service departments adept and well organised, knowing who was where and when, would be difficult – nigh impossible – for anyone to aspire with or without parents' registering and acknowledging their birth. More so when the issue in question, given life by an unmarried living alone young woman in a run-down granite barn green with damp from the persistent rain and salt air from the Atlantic Ocean; on an equally run-down farm back of beyond of Zennor with the hastily given name Wheal Brae, born December 1, 1963; and with scarce a breath drawn departing this world before sunset of that same day: William Flamank Timmins appeared from a mist of one time into another possessed of a handful of Stannary gold coins impressed with the name of Sir Richard Vyvyan, gave to the inconsolable mother such poor recompense for her loss: he now had an identity in another.

His black leather jacket removed and hanging on the back of the headmaster's office chair, the man bare armed except for what Charmolue took at first glance to be a fashion accessory, changing his mind when it came to closer scrutiny. A chain mail armlet with no refinement was clearly an example of a metal forger's skills. Handcrafted from a time past, if he were any judge – a swordsman's accessory to carry his fight forward that would otherwise disable a man were it not for the wearing.

With sunglasses on his head and his rugged good looks he would have passed as protagonist character from an action movie. In the role he had carved out for himself now, to Charmolue at least, he was every bit that character's alter ego, for the preservation of his life and the furtherance of his cause he was unremitting and ruthless.

When the telephone rang Timmins turned to him and smiled. Then moving the lap-top computer displaying a screen with a voice recognition program installed, he looked at its flat line. Picking up the phone he politely answered (which came as a surprise to Charmolue):

'Your Royal Highness, thank you for returning my call so promptly . . .'

## Avon and Somerset Constabulary
## Mobile Units, Bristol 2008

The engineer listened for the thin pip that was his signal to override the Prince's voice. At the same time Merriweather, holding his finger aloft waited. Ian Duffy, with the phone in his hand was shaking. Everything was riding on him getting this right and he was suffering a serious case of the stage fright.

'*Now!*' the engineer shouted using whisper voice.

Duffy took a deep breath. A script in front of him for guidance had answers to possible questions.

All those listening agreed Duffy's impersonated voice of the Prince of Wales had it all. The I's and the One's that were particularly specific to the man's vocabulary being spot on. Even down to his mannerisms of mouth movement. His lips drawn back revealing his teeth when he hesitated another trait Duffy mimicked.

Desk Sergeant Ian Duffy had a professional background in acting and voice impersonation. Often doing voice overs in the media industry of famous names, where costs to employ the actual person were prohibitive, he excelled. The script, in light of the already agreed arrangement the Prince of Wales had given his word had to be carefully arranged in such a manner as to suggest that his surrender of the duchy of Cornwall to its people might have been premature; that they would be counter to parliament and the people of the United Kingdom. In short, he did not have the authority. Having said that he was scripted to say other concessions would be available to Timmins when he surrendered up the souls, he held captive.

When Timmins' answer came. An answer that was listened to from the Home Secretary down all froze in terror. The game had moved up another level, with the Home Secretary Anthony Blunt having to consider informing a public that saw three hundred children about to be cremated with bombs, demanding a republic option to save their lives, the impossibility of such a request.

## Stanners' and Haberdashers' School, Bristol 2008

'If that is your answer, Cedric, I suggest you continue wasting more of your breath speaking to the real powers of the land. Only then will you discover they are not who you thought them to be, namely the ancestral institution you represent. For assuredly they are not. There is another between Kings and God your institution knows little of, and who you all unwittingly answer too. In that we are equals. Your royal protection extends only so far. For you will now find that you will be dealt with in a similar vein as your ancient ancestors so treated and meted out justice to the proletariat since the reign of Edward the Third. For the contempt shown to your people by your institution is not one-way. Did you think it otherwise? Did you further believe that

I would not have found your Achilles heel that they are all too aware? Your granddaughter is with me now. And you can go ahead and plead royal protocol to those powers until the end of time for her consideration. They will not hear you for the din that is your institution's preservation.'

Timmins replaced the receiver. A flat line re-appeared on his lap top screen.

He looked at the small girl playing a computer game with her friend and smiled to himself. So that was what the granddaughter meant to the Prince of Wales. The file record of who she was had been coded. An Austrian princess being educated in this country with the right name; and the vanity of a headmaster scribbling in green ink in the margin of a foolscap diary to remind him, hinting to parents that their 'little darling' would be playing hockey with a European princess had given the game away. Charmolue was not surprised at the Prince of Wales's quiet denial. Royalty were hardened survivors where relatives were concerned. Especially in the saving of their own skins. He was reminded of Tsar Nicholas the Second and his plea for asylum in the United Kingdom. While the British Government agreed, his cousin King George the Fifth declined any invitation fearing similar revolution in his realm.

The school hall stank of urine and excrement. Children as young as three were expected to fend for themselves by their captors. All male members of staff had been incarcerated in the school music laboratory; their female counterparts in the dining room with only a handful being allowed out to settle the children down at night seeing to their more urgent needs like washing stained clothes and drying them on the radiators. The only contact the children had with staff for these necessities of hygiene was half-an-hour in the evening when their captors expected them to sleep. Crying for their mother's between occasional shouts of, *Shut the fuck up!* from their captors on the edge of their nerves. The unbearable heat from their confinement was overpowering causing children to strip down to knickers and vests. Food was running out from the kitchen stores and was now rationed. And although water was plentiful guards were restricting the children's intake of it to keep their bladders empty. Timmins had so far refused all requests for outside help, only allowing a doctor to attend to a boy that had an attack of what appeared to be acute appendicitis, where he allowed an ambulance to come close to the school to take him out. Merriweather refused such a chance for an assault, seeing Timmins's 'humanitarian weakness', as some suggested as a strength that he may be able to work on for an eventual release of at least some of the children later.

The incendiary devices strapped to a selected group of some of the older children was something Charmolue never imagined Timmins would carry out. None of which had been put in place by the Cornish nationalists with them, that would not have had the skills or experience for such an operation. He had a team of professionals, some Charmolue personally knew from his training in Spain. Libyans, Taliban, and al Qa'ida, all factions he would not have wished on the world serving such apprenticeships.

If he hadn't been able to convince anybody else of what he saw as a last resort, having the firing pin to a weapon that would bring this siege to an end through the window of the headmaster's study, following a full frontal assault by a police Task Force, then he was glad that Merriweather had the sense to listen to him when he was mapping corrections. There would be bloodshed, of that he had little doubt. Neither did he discount himself a victim. For he had his doubts for the technology that said it could burn out computer wiring systems. To his mind, it would only take a minute electrical discharge to break through setting off the devices like so many party poppers incinerating everyone in the building. The control boxes that these were attached were in the headmaster's study controlled by the bomb-makers, so that if things were to go against them, they could set them off manually. If that were not going to be possible, the suicide strapping around their bodies would be their second option. All were prepared to die for the man that had instigated this attack. Cornwall and its democratic freedom were not the issue for them, merely an excuse, for some had a separate mandate: an attack on the West in the name of Allah on the children of one of England's most elite schools.

Charmolue felt for his pistol and then the radio device for Acton-Vean to launch the rocket. The point he would have to shoot it out to the death with Timmins's two al Qa'ida bodyguards. Looking at him, trusting no one, not even the man that had trained them, they hardened their stance towards him. Seeing their attitude, without thinking, he did the same back. Ill trust was in its ascendancy in this place for enlightenment.

### Forbes' Apartment,
### Royal Court Crescent,
### Bristol 2008

Forbes left Cluff on his own to what seemed to her to have become an obsession. Alright, news was not good, and no one wanted this to end badly, but was he any further forward in knowing who John Goode's descendant was to prevent any of that happening.

'You don't even have the right man. After all we went through. Me. Dragging a dead body across the moor in the middle of the night. Conversing with a ghost. What was it that psychiatrist said I was suffering from?'

'Spiritual possession,' Cluff replied.

She laughed to herself at the answer she gave to him. The point was neither of them was happy continuing their relationship and it would be better giving each other some space until rational decisions could be made as to their future with each other.

When they had first arrived on Dartmoor it was the 24th of May. Today was the 27th of May. Considering they had spent most of yesterday with the police. The whole episode had lasted seventy-two hours. He reckoned it was closer to a week.

'It must have been,' he had told her. 'Getting the case together had taken the best part of three days. Then there was my investigation at Crockern Tor. Getting the body back from there to Bodmin for a postmortem with the judge. Then finally an acquittal and John Goode's release. You work it out.'

She did. She was right. And so was he. Or rather his watch was. A time shift of at least eight days showing on its calendar. His watch displaying 4th of June.

The both of them were exhausted from treading sands of time. She is blaming him for taking her on an expedition in the footsteps of his father. He had denied any such intent. She had followed up by saying that he must have had something in the back of his mind that sent him on such a mission. A subliminal thought playing in his head until he had to act upon it perhaps.

'You saw. You got involved. You teleported it. You organised a forensic report transfer. Explain that to me if you can?'

Then she walked out on him.

'What of the children?' he called after her.

She turned on him. '*Fuck 'em!* I've been traumatised enough as it is, to say nothing of what they've done to you. You might look and feel okay, but you're not. We will live with this for the rest of our days whether those children come out of this in one piece or not. And you can bet your life their parents will not give a flying fig for our well-being when we're both banged up for wasting police time and God alone knows what else when it's all over. My life has been turned inside out to the point I no longer recognise reality from truth. I'm sorry, I can't take this anymore,' she said standing up. 'You know where to find me when you come to your senses. Assuming you ever do. *Goodbye!*'

Then she was gone. Out of his life? He couldn't say for sure if it was permanent. He knew she was right though; and that there was nothing he might have said that would make any difference to her or the immediacy of the situation she found herself. Perhaps time would heal, but not if she were with him. Perhaps it was as well. He would return to Ellick & Waite's. He needed to drag the information out of them as to who John Goode's descendant is. Though what he was supposed to do with it when he found them was another question. He would take Tony Noyon with him as witness.

The day after Forbes had given Cluff his marching orders she was preparing for the office. Though what reception she would get after her and Phil had had their names splashed all over the newspapers she couldn't say. Applying lip stick in front of her bathroom mirror the telephone rang.

'Hello, Jackie Forbes.'

It was Cyril Timson wanting to know if she was back in the land of the living and was, she coming in today. He had clients to see and needed her input, adding that things had been a bit hectic back here without her.

She went quiet. There was something wrong with the bathroom mirror.

'Jackie. You still there? *Jackie!*'

Something's going on here. This is not right.

'Sorry Cyril. I'll call you back. Minor emergency.'

She dropped her phone. The mirror had a haze over its surface. Thinking at first it was condensation she took up her face cloth quickly wiping it off. Then moving closer to the point where she thought her soul was about to be swallowed, the image of a woman came into focus. And it wasn't of her.

She was shaking when her phone rang once again. Her partner, she thought. What does he want now? Picking it up she said, 'Sorry Cyril, spilt a bottle of hand lotion on the floor.'

'*Jackie Forbes?*'

'Ye-es. Who is this please?'

'Not sure if you've heard of me. I came to your offices when you were missing. I'm Grantley Goode involved with the Bristol siege.'

'I've heard of you through Phileas. Thought he had already eliminated you from his inquiries. What do you want, I've got an important meeting and I'm already late?'

Although he was answering the reason, he was calling she wasn't actually listening. Her mind, torn between who the image was that was fast fading in her mirror, and the possibility of DCI Goode calling her to warn her of imminent arrest for any number of misdemeanours she had incurred while in Devon she focussed her mind to listen closer.

'Did you hear me Miss Forbes, I said don't take this the wrong way, I was asking how sane did you think your fiancé is? I don't mean generally, more. Did he, for instance, experience anything that would have impaired his judgement when you were with him on the moors?'

Annoyed and defensive of the man she loved she answered, 'Without knowing *your* present mental state, Chief Inspector, my barrister Phileas Cluff is as sane as you and I, which at this moment in time may not count for much.'

*Offices of Ellick & Waite,*
*Lincoln's Inn Fields,*
*London 2008*

Cluff stood on the pavement outside his office. He was nervous and despairing. All he had done seemed to have been for nothing. All he had lost had been for nothing. The greatest of these was Jackie. Not that he blamed her after the way he had treated her. She had been as much a part of this as he had been. More so in fact. She had done blindly what she had been asked and for what. The ancestor he had – they had – brought evidence for an acquittal. For what? For the answer to the question as to who Jonathan Goode's descendant was in the twenty-first century still unresolved. For DCI Goode, the man that had taken much joy in ringing him up to tell him so, finished by saying he should think seriously about getting himself sectioned under the Mental Health Act. He would be right there. For what he might try to explain would mean being sectioned for the remainder of his days.

He had to admit to himself that 2008 was not 1716, and with no one to resolve the question, the very pursuit of it may well lead him into obscurity. *No, no, no*, he said to himself, *there's got to be more to this*.

All that had happened and Noyon had a foot in both camps. A single-minded journalist prepared to see this story through to a conclusion was now asking him to end it. One that would finish his career at Canary Wharf for the telling of it was not sure what he wanted for himself now.

'Arm-in-arm with a barrister leading their daughter into middle earth. Not something I'd wish for mine. Assuming I had one,' Noyon said. 'Even now you continue in the forlorn hope that you might achieve a séance of sorts with the founding fathers of the law firm you

work today. Dead in this time. What are you looking for barrister?'
Cluff stared at him. A face that had more questions than answers.
'Yes. Of course. Your father. That's what this has all come down too.
You think . . .'

'You think too much, *Sun*.'

'I'm a newspaper man. I can find the whereabouts of anyone,
anywhere, and anytime. Except your middle earth. Your father is
gone. The story will be written without any conclusion that will satisfy
you.'

'And where are you going to file it? In an archive. For sure it can
never be read by the public. A story purportedly bound up with the
deaths of three hundred children will make you the press pariah of
the decade.'

Noyon turned on him.

'Give you a hard time your detective friend of yours? Well there's
a surprise. You approach a police officer involved in the Bristol siege
telling him he is also personally involved . . .'

Noyon was right. The realness of what had happened to him and
Jackie along with his enthusiasm had created an assumption in him
that an explanation of how Goode had got the scar on his hand
believing he would be convinced he was indeed the man's descendant
and that he could bring about a successful conclusion to the Bristol
siege. What was he thinking of?

'Listen to this Cluff for I'm not going to repeat myself. That scar
is not some mediaeval throwback passed down by way of my genes as
if it was some hereditary disease. Neither did I get it the result of
horseplay at school. We didn't go in for nailing each other to fences at
the school I attended. What went on in yours would no doubt make
interesting reading in the Sunday newspapers. I'll tell you how it
happened shall I? According to my mother I did it when I was a small
child. When I was acting the *Cunt!* Not her words I hasten to add.

Mine. Language not entirely alien to you I shouldn't wonder. I fell down a hay-stacker catching it on a tine. They gave me fifteen stitches and a jab up my arse for my trouble. All of which was so far distant in my childhood I could not recall. Now don't bother me again, not unless you want to turn yourself in for being a *bloody* nuisance for wasting police time in Bristol as well as Devon.'

The call ended abruptly with not so much as a good-day.

'You've made your point, Mr. Noyon. Now come and meet my head of chambers.'

Noyon held the door to the Chambers of Ellick & Waite Est. 1690 for him. He hesitated.

'*Well!* . . . we going in or not? This is your juris consultancy after all isn't it?'

Obviously, the man from *The Sun* had more faith in him than he had in himself. Cluff knew the answer was in this place somewhere, something had come over him, and it was not 2008. He looked in at the open door. There was another between it and the reception area. With its all-glass and plastic façade fronting the old woodwork with its shelves of legal books, all locked, he barely had time to consider that he would make a fool of himself when the secretary would ask him if he had had a good holiday. He moved forward.

'Here,' he said to an astonished Noyon. 'Hold my hand.'

In an instant a dark curtain descended taking the two men with it. He had returned to Plymouth.

'Are you ready to encounter the supernatural made whole Mr. Noyon? Ghosts. Up close. Neither finite nor infinite. Spirits from the past ordinarily only seen from beyond the stars where time is relative, and nobody is really dead.'

'You may, Sir. We may. An excellent explanation by the young barrister don't you think, Mr. Waite?'

'Indeed, I do Mr. Ellick.'

Cluff and Noyon stepped from the veil into the light. The plastic and glass now gone, the ancient furniture and books were as they once were. A girl picking up a toy dolly from the desk skipping out of the unmanned reception area left Noyon to wonder who the hell she was and what place Cluff had brought him too.

'Who's replaced the electric light with candles?' Noyon asked.

Staring at each other Cluff shouted out in the vain hope it would bring someone into the reception area to attend him, but the voices in his head overwhelmed him.

'For Christ's sake, *NO!* Not again, I want answers not a re-run.'

He shook his head. Voices were coming from all directions sending his head into a spinning confusion. He should not have come. Too late now it was done. He was going to have to follow Alice if he were to get at the truth.

'You'd better wait here.'

'You are joking, aren't you? I've seen your ghosts. If it's all the same to you, this is a rare opportunity for a mere mortal to get to the bottom of a mystery that has baffled man since time beginning. That we have life after.'

'If that's what you want but there's still no story for you whether you get to a truth or not. Fear of the unknown is a state of mind most live with. Fear of a known brought out from a dark age obsession, given the light of modern-day physics that anything is possible, will put us back among ancestral myths and legends. We like to watch films comfortably knowing it's all a hypothesis. But you now know different.'

'None of which would make me want to draw back to want more,' Noyon replied.

'Very well. This way then. There was a conference room at the end of this passage the last time I was here. On your head be it.'

Without electric lights to guide them they came across some stairs. Risers and treads moved dangerously under their weight and movement. Noyon found a rope hand hold. At the bottom, a wooden table storage unit greeted them. A lighted candle set on top of it flickered across the face of Alice standing by a door. She was talking to her doll. The door opened.

Cluff could not speak for Noyon, but for himself, he feared they would be caught in time. If he was expected, then the want of an answer gave him a degree of comfort to enter. He smiled at Alice, but the only emotion returned was that of the feeling of a hangman's rope about his neck and his waiting for the drop. Putting the emotion to the back of his mind he drew a deep breath and entered this place of doom.

Looking back for his fellow traveller he noticed Noyon was no longer with him. Whether it was because the door had closed before allowing him to pass through, he could not say. All he knew for sure was that he was alone. He stared into the darkness. There was nothing, except. *What is that?* he asked himself. An odour of old books with a hint of the scent of vitulinum vellum and one he was familiar. A legal document written onto a skin would last a thousand years or more. An odour that at the very least signalled to him that perhaps he was not about to enter an abyss of a pre-dawn universe but was in the offices belonging to 1716 Plymouth.

'Mr. Cluff. Are you returned so soon?'

'Not in less than ten minutes of the sand clock,' another answered. '*Eh!*'

The voice echoed before the owner's face came into view.

'Please sit yourself down. What can we do for you now, for we both of us wished business to have fulfilled to completion?'

A familiar voice of Zac Ellick came to him. Fully formed now his face was illuminated by candles. Alongside of him at the double desk sat Hilary Waite. He wasted no time, for there was none to spare.

'A Detective Chief Inspector Grantley Goode of my time,' Cluff said as affirmatively as he could. 'With the scar on his right hand running between his fingers, the result according to you of being nailed to a fence post . . .'

'Did we mention a name Mr. Ellick?' Waite interrupted looking toward his partner. 'For such assumptions are a legal quagmire are they not.'

'They are indeed Mr. Waite.'

Cluff sighed. He did not have time for all of this.

'Apparently, for I have it on best of authority, the man is not of *Mebyon Curnow* stock. Not now. Not ever. His ancestral past goes no further from London than Norwich. No further back in time than the seventeenth century, that is, according to his mother who researched their family ancestry. How do you propose I can get back on track to prevent the deaths of so many children now?'

'Track!' Ellick said confused. 'Ah, an analogy Mr. Cluff. I understand. As to your question. We were not remiss in the mention of the descendant of John Goode's name as we do not know it. An officer we said. A descendant of John Goode—'

'Yes, that's right. Grantley Goode of the Avon and Somerset Constabulary. One of those officers overseeing the siege. Who else has the scar? I have seen it.'

'I repeat an officer,' Waite said.

'*For God's sake!*' He drew a deep breath before continuing. ' *Who?*'

Ellick was taken aback by this outburst of anger. He spoke disapprovingly at Cluff tone of voice.

'We cannot see into the future. We've both told you that.'

'*Yes! Yes!* When natural life ended for you, so did the future. You did mention it. Laws of physics, paradoxes and all that. But you got me into this as you did with my father before. It cannot be solved without a name, don't you understand?'

He watched as Waite tapped Ellick on the arm in a consolidatory manner.

'Look I'm sorry I went off on one. But you must see the problem I've got is. Who in *hell* am I looking for if not Grantley Goode, that can prevent this terrible disaster from occurring?'

He stared in the direction of the two men, but the downstairs office from 1715 was no more. A feeling of despair came over him bringing on tears. He took out a handkerchief and wiped them dry. He was going to have to come to terms with the fact that Ellick and Waite were no more able to reach out to him from where they were in 1716 than he to them from 2008. It had all been a pointless exercise. One he fully expected to wake up to find himself on Dartmoor cooking eggs and bacon over a stove for him and Jackie. *Oh, Jackie!* He opened his eyes. All the furnishings were still here as was the smell of must. The office deep in the bowels of Lincoln Inn was no more than a time capsule; kept that way by the chambers for posterity. All that was different was that the founders of these good offices were no longer present to help, and he felt anger with himself for having driven them away. With nothing more to be done he got up to leave.

Outside Noyon waited. Passing his time, he was trying to converse with what he now knew was a ghost. She looked at him as the door opened then skipped three steps to disappear into a mist that was rolling down the rickety staircase. The doll that had been in her hand fell to the floor. Noyon smiled. At last, he thought to himself, he had something to back up his story. A momentum from the past that could be tested. Carbon dated perhaps. Something that might reveal its age. The material it was made would show that. Proof conclusive that ghosts of people from the past did exist in time capable of being recalled as Barrister Cluff had said they were. He crouched and picking it up pondered the implication of what he now had in his hand. He felt an excitement flow through him. He was about to stand when a tiny hand and arm appeared from nowhere. He quietly gasped. Before he had time to recover his composure, the hand smacked the back of his wrist causing him to drop the doll. Her hand then came forward, picked it up, then vapourised back into the time mist it had come.

Cluff laughed.

*Damn!* Noyon muttered to himself. *Damn!*

## Offices of Craske-Forbes, Bristol 2008

Forbes was standing alongside the water dispenser. She did not want a drink, she wanted time to decide where she went from here after her experience in front of her bathroom mirror that morning. Excusing herself from the meeting, asking Cyril to continue reading her notes, she smiled pleasantly and left the room. With no immediate thought as to where to go she settled on the water cooler. It seemed as good a place as any.

She had subconsciously decided earlier what she needed to do. But the operative word here was needed. Did she really have to need to call him? After all, she had washed her hands of his obsession, why go back and involve herself now on what was no more than a freak light reflection in a mirror. She took a cup and filled it with water. She then went into her office and sat down at her desk and took her mobile from her handbag. She made the call.

'You are looking for a man by the name of Goode with a scar on his hand, right, *yes*?'

'Oh, and good morning to you.'

'Morning Phil. Sorry. How are you?'

'Well enough, you?'

'Yeh . . . yes. Listen, don't take this the wrong way I've had a thought about your man.'

'Yes.'

'Have you found him?'

'No. Have you?'

'What if he's a woman? One that is not called Goode, but with another name. Perhaps blessed with a married name. Sorry, didn't mean to put it like that. Freudian slip. You know. Descended from John Goode's maternal line.'

He was silent.

'*God!* You could have something there. I never saw that as a possibility. You're right. Jackie! Will you marry me? Soon.'

'I'll give you until next month to do the deed.'

She rang off. She was breathless. That was a woman. That was *the* woman.

# TWENTY-NINE
## Avon and Somerset Constabulary
## Ops. Units, Bristol 2008

*MERRIWEATHER CLOSED HIS EYES.* The blue light was inked into his frontal lobe. Wormed into his head. On every occasion he came close to the rocket and its launcher he could not stop himself from staring at it. Emitting blue light with the regularity of a clock, which of course was its function, it burned into his brain. He looked at the timer display below it. It showed 1405.50 before jumping to 1405.29.

'I can't help noticing,' Merriweather remarked to Acton-Vean. 'Not every time; occasionally, that digital timer skips twenty-four seconds. Is there a reason for it doing that?'

'We're waiting for the manufacturer's system analyst to check it out. It's not essential for launching the device if that's what you're thinking?'

'I wondered if it was Charmolue playing around with his transmitter causing it to malfunction.' His phone rang. 'Who? ... What the barrister? Right (he lowered the tone of his voice) ... But I doubt Grant will have any more to do with him ... Well if it's that important you'd better put him in my office. Tell him I'll be down shortly – and Duffy, if he asks, DCI Goode is not available ... See you. Sorry about that Delia. You will let me know when it's been sorted. Only I'm suspicious of ghosts in machines. Especially where they haunt things that can go bang.'

'So, you're the famous Dartmoor legend that has been causing the police to waste their valuable time and resources to search for Mr. Cluff,' Merriweather said. 'Now you've come to Avon and Somerset and want us to waste more of our time on you. DCI Goode has already filled me in on what you had to say about him and his family. Quite frankly it has to stop otherwise this barrister is going to find himself the wrong side of the dock. Now before you interrupt, there's more. I've agreed to meeting you for two reasons. One is that I am curious to know what sort of man we have been dealing that seems to know more than he's letting on, and . . . will you let me finish please . . . and two, to warn you not to involve any other police officers in your quest to find this one-handed man of yours.'

'*Scarred!*' Cluff interrupted. 'I said the man has a scarred hand. And on reflection, I am now of the belief that the man may be a woman.'

'Whatever. Listen Cluff you've already made a fool of yourself with these wild accusations of yours. I've heard all the stories coming from the Devon and Cornwall constabulary regarding you and your girlfriend. Of how she mysteriously disappeared on the road to *Damascus—*'

'Yelverton.'

'*Whatever!*'

'The officers involved say Jackie disappeared after they apparently run into her with their Land Rover between Princetown and Yelverton.'

'Don't split hairs with me Cluff. Whatever road it was those officers were on they were obviously up to no good. Probably been on the piss needing an excuse for being late for duty. The point is—'

'The point is Mr. Merriweather, you've three hundred children about to be cremated and I don't know how you intend to prevent that from happening – assuming you have a plan and can. What I do know is that someone with a scar on his or her hand is the key to prevent it occurring. That's why I need to speak with DCI Goode once more.'

'Well he's not here. For my part I don't know anyone with a scar, and I shouldn't think he does. And not to put too fine a point on it, I treat you with suspicion. As a barrister if you don't like that as a character reference of you, think, that would probably be your reaction for treating you.' Merriweather nodded his headed at him as if to underline the statement. He began to raise his voice. 'For all I know you're part of this hostage siege. A Cornish nationalist. Are you? Have you such a dark past that is forever Cornwall Barrister Cluff. Have you aspirations to be Cornwall's First Minister as our friend over the road has? Well, have you?'

Merriweather was beginning to lose it when the door opened.

'*DCI Goode!*' Cluff said by way of recognition welcoming the interruption.

'*Stay where you are!* Cluff got to his feet. '*No, I said stay right there*. A word Andy. *Ian!* You about?'

'Here, Sir,' Duffy said on his way down the corridor.

'Get this man a coffee, or whatever he wants. And detain him.'

'*Sir!*'

Goode followed Merriweather into his office. Indicating to him to take a seat Merriweather back kicked the door closed behind them. *Allah! Help me*, he said to himself. Taking out a bottle of whisky and two glasses from a Tesco carrier under his desk he poured.

'Thought you were a practising Muslim, Andy,' Goode said taking the proffered glass.

'That man's a *bloody* idiot. Didn't you say it yourself? I am,' he continued taking a mouthful of whisky. 'Only on my mother's side though. The drinking habit comes from my Canadian father, also of the faith – *lapsed!* He was the Crown Royal whisky fanatic in our family. And the way this is all going I've caught it. Now what was it you wanted to say that you couldn't in front of that *idiot* barrister?'

'Only that—' He hesitated. 'Have you confidence in that pulse device that's supposed to take out computer systems from a great height. Or is it their sales bumph we're swallowing?'

'Right, now tell me what's really on your mind.'

'*Ah!* If you insist. Well, as you probably already know both me and DS Hymer were involved in the disappearance of Jackie Forbes and Phileas Cluff from the outset. That was before what happened over the road. As time has gone on things have changed. Whether they are conspirators or innocent bystanders the jury's still out, however, and the point I am making is stories that have come out from Devon and Cornwall since . . . you made mention of the two policemen that ran into Jackie Forbes out on Dartmoor,' Merriweather nodded. 'The inquiry found both officers to be of good character and were duly exonerated. Not because there was any cover-up on the part of the Devon and Cornwall police down there. The chief super wouldn't have anything like that on his patch, no it's because there was one other witness to what happened on that road and the subsequent disappearance of Jackie Forbes. A journalist.'

'Not the man from the *Sun*?

'No not him, another journalist. One from the local rag. He swears blind Jackie Forbes disappeared in front of his eyes. That's not all. There have been stories of other strange occurrences coming from that neck of the woods of late.'

'Other occurrences. What for instance?'

'A body missing from the morgue. Still not recovered. Another, that has the same DNA as Cluff, likely the man's missing father. There were others recovered close to the site that Cluff and his girlfriend were camping. Not part of any police inquiry being of more interest to historians at the local university. *And*, on top of that, the man suspected of bombing that bridge over the Tamar, killing that policeman, was found shot dead outside the Okehampton offices occupied by both the Government for the Southwest and the duchy of Cornwall. Everybody working there when questioned by Devon and Cornwall said they had heard and seen nothing of the incident. The conclusion by Devon and Cornwall is that inquiries have faltered for want of further evidence. When last I spoke to DCI Cocksworth, my counterpart in Devon and Cornwall, he jokingly suggested it smacked of MI5 involvement, going onto to say, after I asked him what made him make jokes like that, he mentioned two bullets. One 9mm from a handgun and the other a musket ball from a matchlock. The forensic report was that the musket ball in his brain was in front of the 9mm bullet.'

'Implying.'

'That the musket ball was fired into his head after the 9mm bullet. Which would put the firing of both projectiles . . .'

'A couple of hundred years apart. I hear you. Where is the body now?'

'It was in the same morgue as the others.'

'*Was!*'

'Person or persons unknown had it removed in a private ambulance to some other destination. One they have not as yet been able to ascertain. According to Cocksworth, when he asked the NHS Trust responsible for the removal of bodies said they knew nothing about it. Neither does the team that work there, *umm* what's her name, Dr. Poltair. One of her assistants managed to get the number plate.'

'Great.'

'It was false. Now if it's not MI5 that had the body removed, then my view is that some equally sinister operation is involved. Cocksworth said to me, and he pointed out that it was only his view, although his boss knew – conspiracy.'

'Why? For what reason? Did he make an opinion?'

Goode shrugged. 'He didn't. All I can say is that . . . you know that paperwork concerning the activities of the Democratic Republic for Cornwall with their aims was addressed to me, don't you?'

'Do you think that was conspired by Cluff then?'

'He wouldn't have known anything about it. The only people that did are Devon and Cornwall, you, and the BBC down there,' Goode said.

'Not unless it was, he that sent it. Just thinking that may have been the reason that Cluff came to you with this scarred hand nonsense,' Merriweather said. 'Did he say where he got it from? More importantly, why he would be seeking him out?'

'He said that as, yet he didn't know, but if he found him he might be closer to ending the siege. But it's not important, I wasn't the man he was after. What I do know is that something has occurred on Dartmoor involving this siege, and it's being covered up by someone, or some government department buried in its fabric.'

'Question him, humour him. Do all you can with that barrister friend of yours, we need to keep him close. Did you know Helen Moyles has a scar on her hand?'

## Crowlas, Nr. Penzance, Cornwall 2008

The Curnow Star Inn was packed to the eaves with the news that the Prince of Wales was to make a statement that would affect the lives of the people of Cornwall. Such statements rarely made, drew in more punters than the Cornish Pirates game against Bristol the week before. Extra quantities of good Cornish ale were brought in from St. Austell and Roche being served as fast as the landlord and his staff could manage. Outside in the street, men and women that had been denied a traditional smoke at the bar – another English law one was heard to remark – were leaning up against the wall outside indulging in what they perceived would be the last time they might have to stand outside in all weathers to enjoy their favourite pastime.

With working mines unable to cope with cheap imports of tin, the duchy had closed shop on them putting them on the dole. Not just miners, but farmers that leased duchy farms already coping with the effects of a foot and mouth outbreak had seen rents rise year on year. The coming of wind farms on land and sea. Again, the duchy holding those rights, were turning their attention to resources the Cornish had no management over, making more profit for an organisation to financially succour one man was to many an anachronism, to others, out and out robbery. With rumours rife that the monarchy was to finally favour the Cornish by giving back concessions stolen by Edward the Third in 1337 made many sceptical; would none the less make interesting television. Attached to the wall of the bar, over the fireplace, was a large flat screen. Normally showing football, it was showing a picture with nothing much happening of Buckingham Palace the only movement being the royal standard flying in the breeze.

The cameras slowly came away from view. In the studio political pundits were being asked as to what the royal household was to announce. Coming up with everything from the king's abdication to the birth of a royal baby not one of them was going to involve themselves with the siege in Bristol and the rumours surrounding it.

When a newscaster appeared on the screen, a cheer went up.

'Good evening. This is the BBC from London. I'm George Harriet with a special bulletin from His Royal Highness Cedric, the Prince of Wales from Clarence House . . .'

At that point, the screen went blank. To what to many seemed like hours, but was closer to half a minute, the service was resumed with the appearance of George Harriet. He was looking nervous as he apologised for the break in the BBC's regular service for having to switch to News 24 for technical reasons.

There was another brief break in transmission then the Prince of Wales appeared. His face ashen, he looked old. Was he going to make an announcement that the King had died.

The Prince coughed gently then began to read from the statement in front of him, then, for a third time the screen went off. When the picture returned George Harriet was on the phone. Underneath him, a rolling banner announced that the Prince of Wales had suffered a heart attack.

George Harriet read the teleprompt.

'As we've heard . . .'

Cheering was drowning out his words. Fighting began breaking out with patrons supporting the monarchy blaming republicans for treating the monarchy with such disrespect.

'*Come along now!*' The landlord shouted standing on a stool in front of the bar better. '*Ladies and gentlemen, let's have some order!*'

The staff recovered glasses that might be used as weapons in the ensuing melee.

'*Cornwall is not going to get its freedom bringing down a duchy prince! There's always a spare in the wings!*'

## Avon and Somerset Constabulary, Portishead, Bristol 2008

Timmins and Charmolue were watching News 24. He had spoken with the Prince of Wales and he was now making his televised promised statement. Lands and possessions under the estates of the duchy of Cornwall were to be disestablished with Cornwall being given its own Assembly. A monumental change of heart by the monarchy and the English Government that at times, Timmins doubted would take place without bloodshed. He looked sideways at Charmolue, who seeing him, smiled and nodded back. Pushing his lips forward and frowning, Timmins' mind was working overtime. Surely it could not have been this easy. Something was wrong.

The Prince was reading his statement while at the same time the rolling banner at the bottom was showing that he had suffered a heart attack forty-five minutes before; the same time that he was having his conversation with him.

He was speaking to an impostor.

'There must be an explanation,' Charmolue said. 'We'll have to give them more time. The news could be wrong.'

It was obvious now to Charmolue that Timmins had not been speaking with the Prince. They had set something up. He went to the computer and switched on the voice recognition application. Examining it closely, he could see that it configured exactly to the earlier one they had taken of the Prince when first Timmins had spoken with him. Then seeing the deviation wave patterns of another voice he quickly switched it off.

'It checks out, William. You definitely spoke with Cedric.'

Timmins was not convinced. Someone had done something. He gestured to one of his men. An al Qa'ida terrorist stepped up to him. Whispering into his ear, the man nodded, then beckoning his compatriot both men left the Head Teacher's office taking automatic weapons out from their shoulder holsters as they went.

'What are you doing, William?' Charmolue asked.

'Obviously one teacher being thrown out into the street is not enough for Merriweather. He needs lessons in modern terrorism he should have sought from his masters.'

'When we are so close. There's got to be a reason for that news item. It must be wrong. God you spoke to the Prince not half an hour ago. *You want to give them another teacher?*'

'*No!* I've given my orders. *I'm giving them five children!*'

Charmolue, accustomed to blowing up trains and shooting enemies dead for the Basque cause had not the stomach to shoot children in cold blood, or any other temperature for that matter protested. His disapproval went down badly.

Tony Noyon had found where Cluff was being held. Not for one minute did he think those in authority in this siege were going to let him wander around with information on him of a person with a scar on their hand, when there was a chance that they could bring it to a safe conclusion by finding the reason why then acting on it themselves. The problem for Noyon was with Cluff not knowing the reason he needed to find such a man, how was he supposed to convince commanders of the operation of his sincerity without exposing himself to ridicule and arrest.

Subjected to intensive questioning by DCI Goode and ACS Merriweather, Cluff was exhausted and washed out. The Deputy Chief Constable of the UK, Sir Wellington Beaufort, watching proceedings from behind tinted one-way glass in a room over had pressed them, short of torture, to get the information out of him at all costs. And desperate for sleep and an answer to what he had been seeking himself they would have got there by now. But, as he knew from the court room, you cannot get a statement of a truth from someone that's ignorant of it. Stone will not weep blood however crushed. When the next interval in questioning came, he dropped his head onto the table and closed his eyes.

Noyon gate-crashed the interview room to find Cluff collapsed across a desk. He was looking unconscious. Before he had chance to go to his assistance he was restrained by two burly police officers. To he's relief Cluff looked up.

Sir Wellington shouted through earpieces demanding to know what was going on, who this man was, then get him out.

'He says his from *The Sun* and was with Forbes in Plymouth when Cluff went missing Sir,' Merriweather said.

His voice went from earpieces to speaker.

'The *Sun* newspaper. God this is turning into a farce,' Sir Wellington said. 'Get him out.'

Noyon broke free from the officers holding him. Then looking straight at the tinted glass shouted back at who was behind it.

'Whoever you are, I don't care what you think of me or my newspaper, my concern is what's going on in that school over there, and this man you're holding. You've just *fucked up* haven't you. I've seen the television. He's going to start murdering soon. Cluff is nothing to do with what's going on over there. I know that because I know what I saw, and science will one day prove me right. You need to get him on board, for the people he has been with have also been trying to save the lives of those children. Believe me. They have. This luckless couple have been torn apart by . . . and I use the word loosely for want of another, *Ghosts!* Apparitions that have the power to reason then cajole. God alone knows how this man and his girlfriend are going to cope mentally when they come back from this and the realisation sets in. For what *I* saw was enough to give me the heebie jeebies. Shall I tell you where Barrister Phileas Cluff and CEO Jackie Forbes have been this last week.'

'Go on. Tell me,' Sir Wellington called down.

'He took me to his office in Lincoln's Inn. He needed more information of an identity. That very information you are trying to get out of him now. The problem is, he didn't get it. Those he spoke with are from the past. The long past. 1715 to be precise. He fought a court case to save the life of a man from hanging whose descendant would be instrumental in the saving of those three hundred children. That man has a scar on his hand. If it isn't you,' Noyon said turning to Goode, 'There is someone else. He needs to find him. And quick.'

Cluff looked up and drank the remains of the water he had in a plastic cup beside of him.

'There are those able to come and go at will across frontiers of life and death to put right wrongs goes against the grain, I know,' Cluff said. 'We've been told by scientists that should we ever find a way to go back, change a situation by murdering our ancestral fathers as an example would be tantamount to putting us in another time. William Timmins is a tortured soul from that past. His genes, mentally scarred from the torture inflicted on his ancestor the Cornish Stannator Joshua Timmins, who along with his Devonshire counterpart, John Goode, fell foul to rough law practices of 1715.' Cluff looked at DCI Goode. 'Now you know. And now I know you are not the man. I have failed as my own father did.'

'Well, Mr. Noyon . . . Mr. Cluff. Fairy tales aside, we don't need any more information,' Sir Wellington said coming into the interview room. 'We thank you for your help, but we already have the solution. We need neither man or woman with scarred hand or not to sort this out when a rocket up the bastard's arse will adequately suffice.'

# THIRTY
## Diplomatic Service for the Crown
## (Old Sarum Rooms),
## Whitehall, London 2008–1956

*WITH THE VEIL OF MIST* clearing, leaving no more than a room with the air of cigarette smoke to replace it, Charles Hagan, chairman of the Diplomatic Service for the Crown hurried down between rows of typists, ushering from 2008 to 1956; and with a heart racing too long from the experience of his trans-time, it finally began to normalise.

Engrossed in their fingering of keys on their Underwood typewriters, the typist pool of lady employees giving him no more than a cursory glance despite his modern dress continued in their duties. Old Sarum Rooms was at the end of the corridor. He knocked, then opening the door went inside. The man he had come to see had his back to him. Lord Richard fitz Gilbert hearing him close the door turned to face him. Behind him on the back wall was an heraldic shield significant to that of William the First; the man also known as: William the Conqueror, William the Bastard, Duke of Normandy and the first Norman king of England. Below that was a flat screen television. A 24-hour news programme was showing. On it the continuing and escalating events at Stanners' and Haberdashers' School in which five children were being exhibited on a balcony, with five hooded gunmen behind each, was approaching a climax. Hagan stopped in his tracks and stared. Were they too late?

'Nothing happens suddenly in these situations Charles.'

He asked him to take a seat and to update him.

Hagan went over the details of what he knew of the events leading up to the death of the society's Secretary Chancellor in Somerset.

'Nothing else,' fitz Gilbert queried somberly.

'*God save the King*, were his last words. Followed by two gunshots. There was also a mention of some cattle, but it was garbled. Fortunately, he had the presence of mind to speed-dial the office answerphone. Not that we know who delivered the deed, but at least it was something. He must have felt something was not right my lord.'

'So, he was either in company or being apprehended. Have you made inquiries of the police? Silly question, of course you have.'

'They know nothing about any shooting or killing involving our Daimler. Only that they had reports of a limousine having broken down waiting for the Royal Automobile Club. All we got out of the motoring organisation was that they were asked to recover the vehicle in a layby without affecting its repair. When we made inquiries as to who asked for its retrieval, they informed us it was a . . . Mr. Horace Drinkwater, the transport manager.'

'And do you have a Horace Drinkwater?'

'We do my lord. When I furthered it with Mr. Drinkwater he denied making any such arrangement. In fact, he said that the first he heard of any car waiting to be picked up was when the Daimler turned up on the low-loader the day before yesterday. I think it's safe to assume, he's as mystified as we are. It's in the underground car park being investigated by our forensic people as we speak. You do know, my lord, whoever murdered the Secretary Chancellor, took out his chauffeur as well. An innocent employee. In my opinion, this was an execution by an unknown group that had no intention of leaving their spoils or witnesses for their monstrous attack on the Crown.'

'Excepting those that carried it out. And I have my suspicions as to who they might be.'

He was not about to go into that now. With the collateral death of a police officer in Devon, coupled with their lack of activity in their attempts to discover who was responsible for the slaying of his brother, led him to believe they knew more than they were admitting. Bodies going missing from a car with government registration numbers – unheard of in his experience – without an investigation needing looking into by the Independent Police Complaints Commission from the sheer dereliction of duty aspect alone. Their silence spoke volumes confirming their guilt; or some military force allied to them. But there were more important issues to be considered first.

'Timmins' bomber. Our man. Currently residing in a Plymouth mortuary, I believe. I want his remains brought to London before anyone investigates further.'

'Already taken care of my lord. My immediate concern was that they may have had him down for carbon dating, what with the musket ball. Having said that, the mortuary was not exactly co-operative with our arrangement to remove him. Their forensic officer informed the coroner asking for a restriction order. I had to steal the body away before he could get involved.'

'Good.'

'Only fly in the ointment my lord, the forensic surgeon has removed the Secretary Chancellor's bullet from his brain. We don't think she got as far as discovering the musket ball though. There's also the matter of the missing Secretary Chancellor himself. We cannot answer what's happened to his gun, only that it's likely in police possession. If that is the case, it won't take them long to discover the weapon's government issue registered to the Crown. I'm expecting a visit anytime soon.'

Fitz Gilbert shook his head. 'You said it yourself Charles. Crown issue. They'll not be able to connect it with us. Nine hundred-year-old secret societies are scant too few if any even in this green and pleasant land; and certainly not easily discovered when they are sewn into the hem of this government department for the Crown. Apart from which, even if they had discovered the musket shot, they would not have been able to conclude which around saw our bomber's demise. As for any carbon dating, no expert is going to risk their reputation suggesting he came from 1716 having a musket ball in his head that would have killed him then; merely, that he must have died now the result of some historical re-enactment that went wrong. He was, after all, a touch eccentric with his wearing clothes from that period. A member of an historical group would be no surprise to anyone. And of course, there is a record that he was a member of the British armed force's bomb disposal team for quite some years before he worked on our and Timmins' behalf. You worry too much Charles. Speaking of which, has that particular . . . channel . . . been secured?'

'The tinners hut is about to be concreted over, with the monument to Cedric Prince of Wales planted firmly over as we speak. Another is being erected on Goss moor reinforcing the Prince's commitment to ensuring the future of both counties. There's no way back for Timmins through that particular hole in the ground.'

'Good. Let's hope there are no more.'

'Scientific evidence suggests they are impossible. They would be the size of a pin head if they were. They would burn up entering our atmosphere. They cannot exist.'

'Apart from the other one here—'

'A similar singularity then, *my lord?*'

'Quite so. Then we will give grateful thanks to what will be the late anti-royalist, Jacobite and Stannary officer for Cornwall 1716, William Joshua Timmins; our unwitting participant in returning the national spirit away from republicanism and onto the path of righteousness that is the monarchy and the duchy of Cornwall.' He stumbled over his thoughts, before continuing. 'The inevitable death of the Prince of Wales' granddaughter and her friends, though unfortunate, are necessary in this endeavour. The nation's sympathies to Cedric and his bungling attempt to surrender the crown to succour them, will now secure him and the monarchy into the next millennium.'

'*Amen* to that my lord.'

## Diplomatic Service for the Crown, Whitehall, London 2008

Ford's latest information received from Charmolue via Merriweather was that Timmins was going through mental turmoil. Seemingly fighting inner demons and fast losing it. He had five youngsters hooded and bound. Crying in terror for want of their parents to save them. On the balcony waiting to be executed for all the world to see. Merriweather and his team were resolute for hanging fire, but a fully armed police task force, with their officer-in-command demanding the ear of Sir Wellington was not helping. Everyone, including them, knew they would not be able to move six inches before those children were shot. From Sir Wellington's point of view – much to the officer-in-command's relief – sacrificing five children against those remaining was not a strategy.

Ford's suspicious of conspiracy after his conversations with the missing and presumed dead man known as the Secretary Chancellor in that Okehampton office had lighted another torch for him. No such officer working for the government, the Crown offices, or the duchy of Cornwall has such a title. The man was simply *non esse*. Fortunately, Rudyard handed back to him the Secretary Chancellor's gun with the words that he might need it for evidence. He found that a strange action at the time. It was as if Rudyard had not wanted this Secretary Chancellor being found with it in his possession. The Chief Super knew more than he was letting, on he was sure. The weapon's registration led him back to London, the offices for the Crown, and the chairman of their board, Charles Hagan.

Confronting Hagan regarding the ownership of the weapon with him answering, *I do not*, before going on to ask if he knew the man was wanted in connection with the bombing of a bridge over the river Tamar that resulted in the consequence of death for a serving police officer on the Devon–Cornwall border; who has now been misappropriated from a Plymouth mortuary, Hagan answered, *Ford, I cannot help you. For I know nothing of any bard, any bombing, or who was responsible for any police officer being killed. And why should I?*

Ford took him by the scruff of his jacket lapel and said:

'Because whoever that person is, going under that title Secretary Chancellor, likely the same I conversed with, was too *cocky* by half; and too *inflated* with his own self-importance. His mere mention of the good of the monarchy and his precious Crown office; with his consideration that they are above the law left me cold. As to this British intelligence counter terrorism officer, as in, me, he goes under the title . . . *Major!* . . . Please use it when addressing me.'

Ford released him.

'And where is your evidence Major Ford?' a red-faced Hagan asked brushing himself down. 'For I see no bodies or know of any Secretary Chancellor to corroborate your accusations.'

'Do you not? Well, we have a private ambulance in our possession that has fingerprints all over it. We can prove it was recently driven from Plymouth by the data tracker installed from the company you hired it from. As to the body of the bard, well, that's only a matter of time before we find what you've done with him. And before you tell me you didn't murder anyone, you possibly didn't. But what I do know, is that you were complicit with that Secretary Chancellor of yours in the man's murder. And of course, there will be other charges brought.'

'*Other charges!* What other charges?'

'*Treason?* I wonder if the King knows what you and your cronies have been up to in his name. You may like to mention names when the time comes. For instance, who the Secretary Chancellor is, for we have no record of any such title? For the moment though, an officer all the way from the Devon and Cornwall constabulary is here to arrest you.'

'Would you come with me please, Sir?' DS Able Waverley said entering the room.


Ford's phone rang as the arresting officer and his suspect left. At first mystified, for there was no pretence of what the call was about. It seemed to begin at a point the caller assumed the person he was speaking was up to speed with him. His mind went into concentrated overdrive until he cottoned on. The caller, informing him of events that had already occurred involving the school, with no details added; that he ought to be aware of required explanation and input. He had been expecting some interdepartmental pressure being brought to bear on him from his superiors over Hagan's arrest. No doubt instigated by the Crown office. God alone knew what powers in high places these people could wield; that could get their man released with no charges to answer. But it wasn't that. When he asked for the caller's name, he would not answer. Anonymous calls in his line of business were to be treated seriously. Unheeded threats from nameless individuals could end your days with a pointy umbrella end tipped with polonium stuck up your arse on a dark night. In his experience you take the initiative and deal with them at the first opportunity. As a humorous aside guaranteed to get a laugh, given to his students at his spy master lectures, breaking their necks or shoving them off a platform under a train usually did the trick for such characters. His first thoughts on such occasions (on which there were many), were not always a million miles away from such jocularity. In this instance though, there was something about it that told him that it would not involve umbrellas. And in any case, what could anyone do to him in a barrister's office in broad daylight?

'Hang on then, let me find a pen and paper; but you'd better not be pissing me about. . . . Okay, fire away.'

He jotted down the address of a legal partnership in Lincoln's Inn Fields asking what time they should expect him. The voice informed him, *In the matter of that school, time is no longer relevant*. With that phrase ringing in his ears, he took a taxi to the offices of Ellick & Waite.

## Offices of Ellick & Waite, Lincoln's Inn Fields, London 2008-1716

Entering the reception area, the receptionist got up and immediately pointed him to a flight of stairs. Pushing past him, she led him down into the gloom.

'I'm Major Ford,' he said.

'We know who you are.'

It was at that statement he panicked. His earlier thoughts regarding his safety in broad daylight paled. The thought that, that Crown office had set him up after all worried him. He was armed but knowing who he was they would be expecting that. He shouted for her to slow down, but she ignored him continuing to run down ahead of him until she came to a door. Having come this far his choices were somewhat limited now. She opened it beckoning him to follow. He was having none of it. Picking up a chair by the side of the open door, and with its legs facing forward he lowered his head and followed her in. Whether the solid oak seat would stop a spray from an automatic weapon, brought him doubt, but it was better than nothing.

What he came across shook him rigid. Events had overtaken him, and he was no longer in control. He appeared to be in some Dickensian lawyer's office with people he did not know or like the look of. A shit brown and dark green floral pattern wall flickered in the half light of a dozen candles placed strategically around the office. Seated at a large desk were two bewigged lawyers.

'Please. Put that down and sit on it,' one of them said.

Ford slowly lowered the chair relieved that he hadn't needed it, for all the use it would have been. Plucking up the courage he asked, 'And who might you be?'

'My name is Zac Ellick, and this is my partner Hilary Waite. Next to him, Mr. Philleas Cluff.'

'*What! Cluff!* I've heard that name before. Aren't you? What's he doing here?'

'We'll come to that, for too much time has been lost,' Waite said.

'Twenty-four seconds to be precise,' Ellick interrupted.

'Quite. Now I have to inform you Major Ford that at 3.33 pm and seventeen seconds, five children from Stanners' and Haberdashers' school . . . were unfortunately shot dead along with your agent. Philippe Charmolue. I believe he was yours,' he said looking at him. 'Not, I emphasise being any of his fault. In fact he tried to shield the children with his own body.'

Waite continued his account. Ford was no longer listening. This was not how it was supposed to end. He had been drafted in from the first to stop Timmins and his Democratic Republic in their tracks only to be thwarted for his heavy handed approach with those Cornish suspects. If only they had given him more rope and time.

'Why have I heard this only now? I've driven half across London. The taxi I came in had the news booming in the passenger half. There was no mention . . .'

'Likely you would not have done. It's all matter of time you see Major. However, what I am telling you has happened with a force of your militia going in as soon as the children were executed. I'm afraid to tell you they fared no better. There were several massive explosions. Indications are that few survived the maelstrom.'

Ford looked down the long desk in Cluff's direction. 'What's going on Cluff?' he asked collapsing back down into the chair after attempting to stand.

Cluff came over to him and put his hand on his shoulder. 'You are in, what is known in this world, as the year of our Lord 1716. Please don't be afraid, accept what is being said to you, for I can assure you we will be back in our own time sooner than you think.'

Ford looked at him.

'*Fuck-off Cluff! Fuck-off all of you!* I don't know what game you think you're all playing, but I'm not part of it.'

He stood. Opening the door he came in, he stepped out into the corridor. At one end was what appeared to be a servant. He was standing by a steaming water boiler.

'Sugar for you Sir?' the man asked him. 'I'm Eadhild the scrivener. Shall I bring it in?'

'You are joking?'

'No Sir.'

Seeing a door at the end he opened it and walked out. He was expecting to see a view of Lincoln's Inn Fields. What he was not expecting was another place. Old, for there were no cars. Only carriages. Horse carriages. People were dressed weirdly. Shouting back from the doorway down the corridor to . . . what did that man call himself?

'Ead!'

'Eadhild, Sir. The scrivener.'

'Whatever. What is this place Eadhild? Where am I?'

'God bless you Sir, you're in Plymouth.'

'*PLYMOUTH!* Are you mad. What year is this then, eh?'

'Why, 'tis 1716 Sir.'

'1716. Yeh right. You're all as mad as March hares.'

He looked back out of the front door. The scene was at it was before, except, a carriage drawn by six horses was fast approaching along the road. Inside, the passengers were shouting drunkenly for the carriage driver to whip the horses up to run a man down that was crossing the road. The man they were referring was in their path and he hadn't seen them. It looked like Cluff.'

'*GET OUT OF THE ROAD YOU FOOL!*' Ford shouted, but his warning came too late. The luckless man disappearing first under the horse's trotting feet, then under the wheels of the carriage; his broken body tumbling out from the rear wheels was left lying in the road as the carriage, with no thought for the man's well-being continued on its journey. *God!* he said to himself. Am I in a place where life's so cheap. Those people couldn't have cared less. *And* it's carrying a royal coat-of-arms—

'Come back inside Sir,' Eadhild said taking him gently by the shoulder. 'I'll bring you some tea. Four sugars?'

He nodded.

'That *was* me being run down Major Ford.'

'*You!* That man that brought the tea said this was Plymouth 1716. What kind of a mad house am I in?'

'He is right. 1716 inside, 1788 out. And you've just seen me being run down and killed by, William Henry the Fourth, George the Fourth, along with their brother, Frederick Duke of York. And as you can see, I'm still in one piece. Another time; another place. Take it from me Major, if you are going to be run down and killed, you'd be hard pressed to find a better class to do it. Or, to put it another way, royal *bastards* from an age where there was no thought given for the life and safety of their regal subjects. Now drink your tea, and listen to what's being told to you, for I can assure you as a member of the bar, it's all true. You are in Plymouth 1716, get used to it. Now that man sitting at the end of the desk, do you recognise him?'

Having taken in what Cluff had told him stared into the darkness. He had not noticed anyone there before. It was as if he had appeared to order. He studied the man's face. This was impossible. The country's number one most wanted terrorist was sitting there opposite him. This was all too much. Casually getting to his feet, for on this occasion he was not about to take no for what he intended. Reaching across the desk he grabbed at the man's throat, then squeezed with all his strength. His action convinced his brain that what he had between his hands was solid matter to choke the life from. The reality was somewhat different, for he was grasping at air. He stood back, then reached into his shoulder holster.

Cluff saw what he was about to do and reached across taking him hard by the wrist.

'Put the gun away Major Ford. It has no place here. As for the man you attempted to throttle the life out of, you are right. For that apparition is that of Joshua Flamank Timmins, Stannary officer for Cornwall 1716. And the same that was brutally murdered by soldiers of George the First. For this is the time–shifted man that is holding those children hostage. Or put another way, what his multi-versed copy has become in 2008; the result of his ancestral self being tortured beyond endurance determining a descendant of hatred. A rare condition, and an even rarer likelihood for him to have transcended time; and but for another time–portal, on Dartmoor, was brought here to wreak havoc on the duchy of Cornwall. He is the product mix of metempsychosis and physics. And, like the apparition you saw of me being run down: as every human being on the planet plays out, the nature of physics duplicates us a multi-verse with every decision being open to alternative lives creating an infinite number of ourselves. You think you know who you are Major, but you can never be sure. You cannot touch him anymore than you can touch the two lawyers opposite. And as for firing that gun, don't even think about it. It's likely to blow in your face, sending you spiralling off anywhere.'

'But why was *I* brought here to see this?' Ford asked.

'Can we continue please Mr. Cluff,' Waite interrupted. 'Time for explanations later. Now, Mr. Cluff, we assumed that John Goode's descendant was your police inspector. That is clearly not the case now, and we have ruled him out.'

'Goode's descendant?' Ford interrupted. 'Who's he, and what's he to do with that school?' Ford interrupted.

'It's a lady,' Ellick added.

'*A lady!*' Cluff said. 'And is she anyone I might know – my mother for instance? You have given the impression all along that John Goode's descendant was a police officer closely involved with the siege. That should have been DCI Grantley Goode. At least it was until I questioned him over the marks to his hand, and his ancestral place of birth. None of it ties in with it being him. Is that what you brought me back here for, to tell me something I already know? I thought it was to tell me who it was. And now, it appears it's too late anyway. Far as I know there are no ladies. Let alone any police officers carrying that surname. Do you know any Major?'

'Not off hand, no. But then I haven't been that closely involved at the front end. I would need to speak with Andy Merriweather. But then, as you say, it's too late anyway.'

'Come on Major,' Cluff said getting up to leave. 'For we are in the company of dead men that are slow off the mark.'

'*We are not dead!* Well, we are. But we are not,' Ellick said his voice full of disappointment and emotion.

'Major. Welcome to 1716. For they are correct. We are their future. They our past. They are not dead, for they haven't arrived at that happy state of bliss yet. They were the cause of my own father's demise and know more now than they did then.'

'Twenty-four seconds, two hundred and 82 years to be precise,' Waite said. 'I have been there to see. Fixed in time. Time you still have Barrister Cluff. She goes under the name of . . . her name is Delia Acton-Vean. And she is a descendant of John Goode twelve times removed.'

'*How did they do that?*' Ford asked Cluff.

### Stanners' and Haberdashers' School, Bristol 2008

Philippe Charmolue stood over five children crying for their mothers. Kneeling on the balcony of the school. What parents and teachers remained, shouted, and screamed at Timmins of his inhumanity asking for humanity, then screaming once again. He shrugged off their efforts Five men, each with a gun to the back of the head of each was awaiting his order. The children with hoods over their faces were thankfully spared seeing. A sixth man held a gun to Charmolue's head, his arms tightly bound behind his back he could do nothing

### Avon and Somerset Constabulary, Mobile Weapons Unit Control Centre, Bristol 2008

Andy Merriweather's face was ashen. His hands were shaking. For all Acton-Vean's protestations over the timing devices he was forced to relieve her. Not that she would have made any difference. The systems analyst had said as much. Having trouble with the timing device, Merriweather thought, was hardly her fault. A glitch was a glitch was a glitch, and down to software programmers. Knowing it was now a pointless exercise; and with no other choice, he gave the order to fire the missile by her assistant.

Screaming off its launcher at 15.32.51. With the situation as it was there was no other way. Acton-Vean was not prepared to take the responsibility for so many deaths.

## T minus 24 seconds: Apocalypse
The timer on the pulse rocket launcher was showing 15.32.51 when Merriweather was given the order to fire from the task force officer directing him. The pulse was left idle on its launcher when all hell came out of the ground the school occupied. The shooting had begun, then the bombs went off. In half a minute a pile of dust and smoke was shadowing the earth from the sun over Bristol. All Merriweather could do was look on. He had failed, and three hundred and forty-eight people had perished in the fire ball he was watching.

Merriweather put his feeling like shit down to too many sleepless nights. Major Ford's insistence that he was here in the forlorn hope he would be able to contact Charmolue. As for Cluff, and without going into any details of what the conversation would be, Ford said he was going to try and get him to speak with Timmins through Charmolue. Merriweather had laughed. Goode, in principal, was more amenable, saying considering the situation they had nothing to lose now. Though what he thought Cluff could say to a man that would make him give up his ambitions with his clearly state of mental health he could not imagine.

Timmins had made the last of his demands to the Prince of Wales. One that Prince Cedric was in no position to make. Overtures by him to the Crown's Diplomatic service that they make one last appeal to the King that his son's granddaughter out of wed lock was one of the children in the school fell on deaf ears. The King had already made his decision. She was not to be a consideration. The Prince was bereft.

When Ford pulled a gun on Merriweather, he didn't know whether to be relieved that he was about to be taken from any decision involving so many deaths or not. Whatever his thoughts, he could not accept being ordered by an officer from the Counter Terrorism Unit to relinquish his command. He made a move on him. All he got for his trouble was a pistol whip to the back of the head knocking him to the ground.

'Sorry about that Chief Superintendent.'

Merriweather, still conscious but disabled, took a handkerchief from his pocket holding it to the back of his head.

'You got someone here by the name of Acton-Vean?' Cluff asked him in an impatient tone.

'And what's she got to do with you two? *GRANT!*'

'Stay where you are,' Ford said as Goode came out of the portacabin.

'What's going on? You all right Sir?' he asked seeing Merriweather on the ground.

'Take note of what's taking place here. These two men are working with Timmins.'

'I think you know we're not Chief Superintendent. Delia Acton-Vean was my question,' Cluff said. 'Get her?'

'Do as they ask Grant,' Merriweather said. 'Use my phone. God's sake, am I the only one concerned with the welfare of those children? You know she absented her from the responsibility.'

Delia Acton-Vean came off the phone. She was fuming. Despite her earlier refusal with the weapons malfunction, she was now being ordered to fire it away by someone she did not come under the jurisdiction of.

'And who the hell are you that you give me orders?' she demanded of Ford. She turned her attention to Merriweather. 'So what's changed, have they fixed the timing?'

'Far as I know, they have.'

'And when it goes pear shaped, and that missile malfunctions, what then? You bastards will put me to the rack for gross misconduct of duty. You're looking for a scapegoat, well you'll not have me for one.'

'Well there you are Ford. You've had your answer. She's the weapons expert and she'll not do it.'

'She has to do it,' Cluff came in.

'And up speaks another. And who are you? This another of your experts, Chief Superintendent?' she said looking at Cluff. 'Come on handsome, explain yourself.'

Like that was going to happen, Cluff thought to himself. His priority was in convincing Acton-Vean without explaining everything that it was her that was the key was going to be hard enough. Merriweather was a long way down the list when it came to his wanting an explanation. The best he could come up with was telling Merriweather that the timing would be critical and that nobody else was up to the mark and qualified more than Acton-Vean.

'You don't look to me the kind of man that's qualified to judge my qualities in the field. So don't. I'm not launching that rocket, and that's my last word on the subject. Chief Superintendent Merriweather, do what you like with me, you going to have to fire it.'

'Well, whatever you people decide, might I remind you that five children are about to be slaughtered by that malcontent over there; and it has to be done *now!* Decisions and choices are no longer on the table,' Goode said.

'Will you show me what I'm to do then?' Merriweather said to Acton-Vean.

'Wait a minute,' Ford said. 'She has to do it.'

'She can tell me when to push the button. That way we got the expert overseeing the event without taking responsibility should anything go wrong. That's it, live with it.'

They moved out to the containment area the rocket was set up. Ford's mouth dropped at what he saw.

'It's not ready. *Merriweather!* The missile's not set,' Ford said.

'That's Chief Superintendent to you Ford,' Goode said.

'Delia,' Merriweather said.

'*OUT OF MY WAY!* Let the professionals do their job,' Acton-Vean said to the systems analyst lying on his back a screwdriver in his hand, tinkering with the timer.

'I've told your people already, you're artillery; not qualified.'

'I can read a clock and push a button, that's all the qualification I need. I did it in Iraq, for sure I can do it here. Now *fuck off!* before I punch your lights out *Yank!*'

The man angrily put his tools in his case closing the lid.

'I'm not taking any responsibility for whatever goes wrong here now. You can tell Sir Wellington that my embassy will be informed.'

'That makes three of us,' she said picking up her binoculars training them on the school. 'Here have a look Chief Superintendent, see if your psychological face profiling can tell you how much time you have before Timmins gives his orders.'

'Right, I think that's it,' Acton-Vean said to Merriweather re-setting the timing on its computer against her Breitling Navitimer chronometer. She then set the elapse timer. 'Now it's your turn Chief Superintendent.'

Merriweather moved into position. She passed him the electronic trigger device. He was nervous. He was white. He felt sick.

He nodded to Acton-Vean that he, although ready, and taking stock that should the faulty timer fail, the lives of so many rested on his shoulders.

On the ground, watching intently, a task force officer held his breath. He was to give the signal to Merriweather the moment the glint of a safety catch came off the first of the executioner's gun. For Merriweather's part he was to calculate the time it would take for the sound to travel to his ears. He looked at his watch. It was 15.33.17. He froze rigid with fear.

'I implore you Delia. Please take control,' Cluff said.

She studied the man not knowing who he was or what right he had being here. But his voice. Quiet and soft. It was almost as if it came from her past. There was a power in it that told her she should do what he was asking. An emotional power came over her that it was her, and only her that could do this thing. Without knowing, she took the controller from Merriweather.

Her finger hovering over the control trigger cover, she got herself into position and lifted it. She nodded, then smiled at Merriweather. It was 15.33.16 when Merriweather, taking instructions from the task force officer called quietly, *now!* He tensed expecting the missile to go away, but it remained on the ground. The timer had malfunctioned once more.

She heard his order to let go, then hesitated. She was somewhere else. In a place she neither recognised nor knew. All she did know was that hanging in this country was ended sometime in the sixties, which was of no help to the person before her now. Not that was any reference to a point of time she found herself. For these people were wearing clothes from the eighteenth-century. Clearly she had arrived on a film set. The scene being acted out was of a hanging. When the stool the actor was standing was pulled from under him her body went into shock. He had been hanged for real, in real time. Her skin was becoming translucent and she was losing strength. She did not even have the strength to expand her lungs to take in breath. She was dying from the inside out and did not know why or care any longer. When the kingspar holding the rope on the gallows snapped from the strain of the man's weight her own body weight was lifted. The man landing back on his feet; the rope having gone slack, there was a yell from someone to, *Cut John Goode down, for the Stannary Officer for Devon has been found not guilty!*

Her malaise began slowly to return. When she looked at the man being helped off the scaffold, with people cheering and slapping his back, if she had not known otherwise she would have sworn blind it was her own father.

She looked at the timer in a panic for people were shouting to launch the pulse device. Now showing 15.32.51, the second counter blinked blue, then it displayed 15.32.49. She had clearly missed her cue. As if to reinforce her failure to take out the computer systems in the school, the explosions from Timmins devices had already ignited sending the building's roof high into the air over Bristol. She wished she had allowed the systems analyst to do his job. He was right, she was clearly not up to the playing around with computer timers. For now the timer was going backwards.

Merriweather put his head in his hands in despair.

Cluff could not understand what had gone wrong. He or she was supposed to be the one that could save these children. The descendants of John Goode having the chance of life going into the future. All he had been through to get to this stage had been for nothing. Now he was wondering if this was a re-run of his father's watch, where a different set of circumstances leading to this catastrophic failure, led to him going out and committing suicide; not having a heart attack as those two lawyers had said after all.

Shaking her head she was mesmerised by the blasted thing, unable to put it down. Now showing 15.32.39 she heard a tiny voice in her head saying, 'Not like that Delia.'

It was a child. 'Who are you?'

'I'm Alice and this is my brother. We're playing toys. Press the coloured button when I say, then all the little dolls will be safe.'

She was on the floor trying to balance a spinning top that kept falling over. Her hands were too small. Alice snatched it from her saying, 'Not like that. Like this.'

Taking it back, and with a determination that she would make the top spin this time, she took a firm hold of it, and pushed. The top began to spin, then stood upright on its own. She smiled and Alice clapped.

The timer was showing 15.08.51. The missile went away with a roar in the direction of the building. Going through the head teacher's office window of Stanners' and Haberdashers' School for the Poor, it exited the window opposite, burning out the circuits on the computers as it went. It then carried on – seemingly to those watching its progress with a mind of its own – in the direction of the Severn river. Returning to earth on a bank on the Welsh side of the British isles, it stuck itself firmly upright in two feet of muddy sand and water rapidly cooling down in a cloud of hiss and a dying roar from its engine.

Acton-Vean looking at the computer timing controller noted it was showing 15.30.51. When she looked at the elapsed timer on her chronometer, it was displaying 15.31.39.

Charmolue saw the plastic ties round his wrists dissolve. He rubbed his wrists. The executioners about to shoot their charges, froze, then disappeared. Only then did he realise that they were not wearing modern clothes. Something he had not noticed about them before. He called to a teacher to take care of the children. He was going after Timmins.

Timmins was heading back into the the head teacher's office as he was about to catch up with him. The young princess was sitting at the table playing with bricks. Timmins took her up in his arms. With the girl in one arm and his gun in the other, he ran out of the office straight into Charmolue. Using the girl as a human shield, he pushed Charmolue over. Struggling to maintain his balance losing it he fell down a flight of steps. At the same time, the princess, struggling to break free from Timmins' arms caused him to stagger at the top of the steps before the two of them followed Charmolue.

An assault team came in with stun grenades from three different directions fired at him. Timmins, seeing the game was up, passed back into time the twenty-four seconds he was in front, leaving Charmolue and the princess at the bottom of the steps.

Charmolue seeing masks and black suits bursting through the lower corridor door carrying assault rifles realised his own fate if they mistook him for one of the terrorists. He put his hands in the air shouting who he was. Stepping away from the princess as he was asked; but either unheard, unbelieved, or his body armour mistaken for a suicide vest, the machine-gun fired off short bursts into his spinning body.

*MAN DOWN!*

# THIRTY-ONE
## The Sun HQ, London Bridge Street, London 2008

'I'M SORRY, MR. NOYON, I've no idea where Mr. Cluff is. All I can say is that when you do find him, we would be interested in speaking to him,' DCI Goode said. 'There are loose ends that need tidying.' Tony replaced the receiver.

His memory of events over the past two weeks were slowly fading, but not so, that he did not remember relevant incidents. That he had been back in time was not in question, and certainly not the least of them, but how? Whilst DCI Goode acknowledged that Jackie Forbes had returned to Bristol, neither she nor anyone else seemed to know what had become of the man himself. He had gone right off the radar. He did ring her. She had been polite enough, wishing him well and all of that, going onto say that when Phileas ceased turning his head he might be pointing in the right direction enough for them to get married and settle down; but that as things stood, she would not be holding her breath. As for the Lincoln Inn Fields office of Ellick and Waite, well, that was plain and simply a barrister's office, if one could ever be described as one. They were keen to know when he was returning to work.

Information relevant to the siege, that should have been in the official police report for the media was scant to non-existent. He could understand there was a need for security details to be kept stum, but why was the people involved not even given a mention; or a hearing for that matter. For apart from Cluff, others that were not so much missing, more redeployed, as out of reach. Delia Acton-Vean as an example. A serving police officer who had also been a major in the marines was supposedly the officer responsible for the launch of a rocket that took the school out, even though there were denials of one being used. He knew otherwise. You just can't go dig out of the remains of a missile from mud in the hours of darkness under a cloak of security, then for it to be driven away to RAF Lakenheath without someone local knowing about it. Not in Wales you can't. When he mentioned what he had heard to Merriweather asking for any comments he refused saying he would be in breach of the Official Secrets Act.

*Official Secrets Act!* Now there's a thing. Why should he say that?

Then there were the reports of members of the public coming forward to say they were suffering strange flashbacks for events that had not taken place. With clocks going awry to the tune of twenty-four seconds. *What was that all about?* he asked himself. Some forward, some backward. Although, there's always some sad bastards that like to keep their clocks accurate to the time signal saying not twenty-four but twenty-five. What was important was that the children escaped unharmed. But not the traumas that would almost certainly follow. Then, yes, he thought. What happened to the man that had instigated the siege in the first place? The leader of the nationalists in Cornwall. His body was not found at the scene. The police said he had been burned alive from an inflammable accelerant he had been playing around with. Hard to believe there would not have been *any* remains. *And* very few of his men were captured. Four he heard, none of them particularly important, except Timmins' number one. A Frenchman supposedly working for a Major Ford. Shot dead during the assault, his body never recovered. All mysterious spirited away. Both Merriweather and Goode confirmed all had either escaped or been killed. *Order restored. Case closed.*

*Goodbye Mr. Noyon, there's nothing for you here .*

Bollocks, there wasn't. He had been back in time. Seen things. This was one massive cover-up and if he was going to get to the bottom of it, he needed to find Cluff.

He remembered Cluff saying that his father had disappeared on Dartmoor, perhaps there might be some item of news to that affect in the archives, he thought.

Checking out the newspaper's microfiche film documents, back in the day when it was the *Daily Herald,* he came across the story of a London barrister who had got lost on Dartmoor while hiking. Dated March 22, 1960. Nothing new in that, Cluff had already told him his father had gone missing then. It was when he leaned back from the screen, page five with its heading and sub-head the words emblazoned took his mind by storm:

### EQUERRY TRIAL:
### DEFENCE COUNSEL
### BARRISTER MISSING.
### IS HE ON DARTMOOR?

An all-out search by police, army, and Tavistock Dartmoor rescue failed after five days of intensive activity to find the missing London barrister, Mr. Phileas Cluff. Last seen leaving Okehampton with a ruck sac on his back along with his fiancée Jackie Forbes. Was he taking a brief holiday? Mr. Cluff QC, a defence lawyer from the Lincoln's Inn Fields offices of Ellick & Waite, lawyers acting in the high profile case at the Old Bailey trial of the man accused of the attempted murder of William Pleydell-Bouverie, Seventh Earl of Radnor, and Lord Warden of the Ancient Stannaries of Devon and Cornwall since 1933 has

absented himself. John Goode, former equerry to His
Royal Highness, the Prince of Wales, Duke of Cornwall—

What! he said to himself, same story, different circumstances then seeing the name he recognised said, Not another Goode! He then skim read on to the last paragraph.

The case has been adjourned due to the unexpected
death of Mr. Justice Edmund Skull, after a mysterious
illness, and is not expected to be resumed until his
replacement can be found.

The phone on his desk rang and he picked it up. It was the front desk.

'Tony! Got someone by the name of... Colonel John Maclean? He's in reception. He would like a word.'

## Offices of Ellick & Waite, Lincoln's Inn Fields, London 2008-1716

'How on *earth* did you come to know such an eminent man?' Cluff asked.

'Night-cap the candles before you leave, Mr. Waite. I bid you a good evening Mr. Cluff, I'm to retire. Don't forget lawyer fees,' Ellick said with a confirmed smile.

'Mr. Newton came to see us in London . . . yes, goodnight Zac.' Waite continued, 'In science, eminent indeed Sir; not so in law. He needed our advice regarding Charles the Second's edict that all academics be ordained Church of England ministers regardless of their scientific persuasion if they were to continue at Trinity College. I believe that was 1672. Or it might have been 1673. It's of no consequence. As it turned out there was no need to represent him in the end, the king capitulated. Later again, 1685, Mr. Newton encountered the vagaries of yet another monarch. This time it was over politics, religion and education. King James the Second demanded Trinity College award unearned degrees to those whose religious beliefs agreed with his own. Because they would not, Mr. Newton with eight other teachers from Trinity were brought before the High Court to answer for their dissent. Rightly their lordships dismissed the charges at little cost to the appellants. When the universe opened its door to us; when events played out before our eyes of grief and destruction from our time overlapping with yours, we despaired. For reasons obvious to us now, not then, I needed to seek his opinions on time past, present and future. In particular, the difference between 1716 and 2008. Coincidentally a date no more than eight years distant from his earth's predicted end of time yet to come in your time. With the mathematics still in his head, he went into the structure of equations comparable to absolute and relative time coming up with a figure equating to the length of a day in comparison to the next. That he calculated was 2.24 milliseconds. Now coming back to the twenty-four seconds that John Goode's descendant seems to have locked into her head. Divide that into 24 seconds then you have 106,945 days elapsing. That will take you back to the place of John Goode's hanging, while at the same time being found not guilty. Ten am, two hundred and ninety-three years and twenty-four seconds ago. The only way he could be stopped was for Goode's descendant to go back while at the same time maintain her alternative self in 2008 time.'

'And what of Goode's descendant? Why did we get that so wrong? After all, Timmins sent a letter to Grantley Goode outlining his proposals for a Cornwall to become independent. He must have been under the same misapprehension.'

'Timmins was throwing you off the scent. I don't know. Anyway Mr. Cluff, with your help, it's all turned out for the best in the end. Ah, before I forget. Your fee. A little more than we anticipated, never mind. £24. 7s. 4d,' he said taking an envelope from his desk drawer.

Cluff went to take the envelope, then hesitated.

'Problem Mr. Cluff. More than you expected?'

'No Sir,' Cluff said. It's Mr. Newton's theory.'

'And calculated exactly using universal mathematics.'

'It's not the mathematics that concerns me Mr. Waite, it's his theory. If it's correct, then three hundred children have just perished in another time.'

Hilary Waite studied him.

'Did we have the right to do that Mr. Waite?'

# BIBLIOGRAPHY

While this novel is a work of fiction, it could not have been written
without relevant, as well as historical facts being made available.
The author is therefore indebted to the following people and
publications in the furnishing of these.

*The Kings and Queens of Britain,*
JOHN CANNON and ANNE HARGREAVES
Oxford University Press, 2001

DR. JOHN KIRKHOPE,
Visiting Research Fellow, Plymouth University
Notary Public

*Civil War – The Wars of the Three Kingdoms 1638–1660,*
TREVOR ROYLE, Little, Brown, 2004

*Breaking the Chains,*
JOHN ANGARRACK,
Cornish Stannary Publications, 1999

*Terrorism,*
International Institute for
Applied Systems Analysis

# BIOGRAPHY

Mr. Jackson was born in Wandsworth, south London. He left school at sixteen to begin a career in the old Covent Garden district of London. As an apprentice compositor he composed in London's burgeoning advertising industry.

Attending what is now the London College of Communication he studied hand composition, graphic art and typography. The typography gave him an interest in ancient writing and the City College at Aldersgate and Barbican – along the old London Wall – taught him that cuneiform was not a way forward in his career.

With his love of the sea – sub-aqua diving in particular – he moved to Plymouth with his then girlfriend, Rita. At a local branch of the British Sub-Aqua Club, he became their training officer.

In his professional life he worked as an origination manager for several print companies. From there he set up his own typesetting business originating books and magazines. He now runs a graphics and print business using his know-how to produce e-books and paperbacks.

With her permission, he married his girlfriend, Rita. A Surrey rose – they have three children and two grandchildren.

# A WORD FROM THE AUTHOR

Most indie authors don't benefit from the massive promotions afforded by publishing houses or book shops, their only promotional ability is by social media or word of mouth, and while those limitations may suit the conventional book trade (agents and publishers), for indie authors it's their only book shop window. The fact that you use the facilities of Amazon, Barnes & Noble, and many other e-publishing outlets, tells me that you are in favour of seeking out books that would otherwise not see the light of day. For myself, I do not pay for reviews; neither am I on social media, trusting instead to my readers for any accolades or criticisms they may have to review on the source of purchase.

Good Luck, and Peace to you All,

Gil Jackson

# THE TINNERS HUT

Has been adapted for television in Three One-Hour Episodes. If you are an agent, or in the business of producing dramas, then I would love to hear from you.

Email: **gilvjackson@hotmail.co.uk**

for details

# OTHER BOOKS BY THE AUTHOR

Available on most Indie publishing platforms

9 781838 232689